CARMEN *and* GRACE

CARMEN *and* GRACE

A NOVEL

Melissa Coss Aquino

𝓌𝓂
WILLIAM MORROW
An Imprint of HarperCollins*Publishers*

FIRST EDITION

Designed by Elina Cohen
Illustrations courtesy of Shutterstock / magic_creator and Essl

Library of Congress Cataloging-in-Publication Data has been applied for.

ISBN 978-0-06-315906-8

23 24 25 26 27 LBC 5 4 3 2 1

THIS BOOK IS DEDICATED TO TWO PUERTO RICAN KIDS FROM THE BRONX WHO TRIED TO MAKE A WAY FROM NO WAY: MY MOTHER, EDELMIRA ALERS, AND MY FATHER, WILLIAM COSS. MAY THEY REST IN PEACE AND POWER.

I want to love the story of my life,
the stories. Then I shall seem
not so much a creature in an index
of adventures or of dreams,

as an interactive force that fed itself
on love, a force that did not atrophy.
And if it was reckless,
what will it matter?

—Chase Twichell, "Worldliness"

WALKING THE SPIRAL

Carmen, Summer of 2014

The small cement room was not built for the woman wearing a long black skirt, with a lot of initials and titles after her name, who passed through the steel threshold of the doorframe radiating light like the full moon hanging low. She was coming through, like so many before her, to do a workshop for those of us getting ready to get out. There would be hoops to jump for sure, so we jumped. Out was something that kept us awake at night. It kept us dreaming. She walked in, set a big stack of books down on the table, and smiled at us. She wrote on the board: *Walking the Spiral*, then drew a big spiral underneath it. On the other side of the board, she wrote: *Instinct Injured*. We were a captive audience for a lot of bullshit. I was ready for her stuff to be more of the same.

Her flow, for a second, reminded me of Grace. How she might have looked in her sixties. You could tell this woman wasn't scared of us by how she went up and down the aisles between us with her handouts instead of standing in front of the room and passing them back. When she bumped my shoulder by accident, she turned her hips to fit through sideways. She placed her hand on my arm and winked as she said, "Sorry, mija. I take up a lot of space." Her body language was singing loud and clear: I am free as fuck and would like to show you the way. I liked how her gray and black bun was tied back with one of those rubber bands that has a big fake red flower attached. The beads around her neck surely meant something; I respected that, even if I didn't know what they meant to her. She introduced herself in Spanish: "Hola, soy la Dr. Guerrera. When was the last time someone read you a bedtime story? Pues, get comfortable, but don't fall asleep. I'm going to read you one now." People carry energy into a room. She snuck a quiet magic in while no one was looking. I wasn't expecting it. I liked the surprise. I hadn't been enchanted in a long time, even if I still remembered the long slow-motion ride down a dark tunnel that made magic and danger feel the same. She read us her version of the fairy tale "The Red Shoes" and ended by saying, "Sometimes you have to cut off your own feet to stop the crazy dance you've been doing. Don't worry. They grow back."

We were there in our same khaki suits of armor acting like we cared, or like we didn't, depending on how we rolled and how close to getting out we felt. How close we felt, I had learned, had nothing to do with the date that we were given. There were girls leaving tomorrow who felt like they were going home to something worse than what they had in here. The very guy who beat their ass and got them thrown into jail would be picking them up. It was crazy, but true. The feeling of "close to getting out" had a lot to do with already feeling free. It was about cultivating abandoned gardens by planting seeds where nothing had grown in a long time, if ever. It wasn't easy to do or feel in here, but people did it and showed others how to find it for themselves. I felt close and ready. I had been a Goody Two-shoes once. It was a long time ago, but my body still remembered, so I leaned forward, put on my listening face, and folded my hands on the desk. Just like third grade.

The teeth suckers and groaners were sitting in the back row, just like high school. They were about to start their shit when she took a deep breath in and opened her arms out to us. "I am so grateful you invited me here. Thank you." A few laughed because of course none of us had invited her and she knew it. Instead of responding, she turned and underlined "Instinct Injured" with a bunch of wiggly lines on the board behind her. She looked around the room, then said, "You are all here because of something you did, in addition to a lot of things you had nothing to do with. The question is what will you do with the time you have left when you get out." She caught us off guard by saying there were things we had nothing to do with. It hit a nerve. We all felt that way but didn't think anyone else believed it or cared. Walking around the tiny room as if it was the great outdoors, stretching her arms and taking big, deep breaths like the air was the cleanest she had ever taken in, she looked genuinely happy to be there. She had our attention.

"At some point you confused raw survival instincts with self-protective instincts. They are not the same. You stayed overlong in habits that had not served you since you were little girls. The worst one being clinging to the strongest force in your environment instead of focusing on becoming that force for yourselves."

She gave us silence to take it in, then added, "When the little voice inside told you to run the other way, you ran fast in the direction of the very trouble waiting for you. We all think we are rebelling when we dig ourselves into holes too deep to even let us breathe, but we are just reacting, and usually, with little self-awareness on every front." Her switch to the *we* did not go unnoticed. She was one of us somehow, and not afraid to say it, except she would leave today. We were not there yet, but she was here to tell us we were close.

There are levels to listening. She pulled us in deeper, one layer at a time.

"Remember, there was a little girl who used all those things to survive when she had nothing else at hand. It is possible she had no other choice. It is possible she is the only reason you are even alive. Forgive her for going too far in trying to save your life. Let all of it go. Accept responsibility for being here, then accept your own freedom as real and possible. More real than all the bars and gates that surround you."

We all exhaled with her. She was teaching us how to breathe again. It was a skill I once had; she made me realize I had been holding my breath since the day they'd locked the gates behind me.

The worksheet was full of circles, arrows, lines, and a spiral at the center. Her arms opened out wide as she explained, "I want you to know that there are people out there who won't let you forget where you've been or what you did. I'm here to tell you that they are your new trouble. They will pretend to be very serious and very smart and very important. They will pretend to know you very well. They are not important. They are not smart. They have no idea who you are. They don't know any more about turning a life around than they understand the weight of an eighteen-wheeler making a U-turn. I know both and so do you. Let them talk, but inside your head just keep saying, 'Fuck that.'" We all laughed in a huge wave of relief that led some of us to tears. She would be Dr. Fuck That from there on. She pointed us in the direction of the paper in our hands. She held hers up and said, "You see all those arrows and lines going every which way all around the paper? I call that the land of good advice gone bad, or the best advice is the one I ask for, or the well-meaning are often full of shit. You pick." There was more laughing. She was serious, though. We had to pick what we wanted to call it, then circle all of it and label it. I picked "the well-meaning are often full of shit." I liked that it didn't say always. I'm an optimist like that.

"Okay, mujeres, now I want you to go to that spiral in the center of the page. You have walked it many, many times in your life. You see it has a center and an entrance far away. But the entrance is also the exit. Many of you have never quite made it to the exit yet, but some of you have been close, and turned right back around and used it as the entrance again. Don't feel bad about that. It is what we do. We will all walk it many times before it's over. The trick is to get out at least once, so you know what freedom feels like and you can really decide what it might be worth to you." Standing close to my desk again, she smelled like lavender, a scent that filled me with thoughts of Sugar and all the letters she had sent me over the years. Sugar had made it to the exit in time and taken Destiny with her. That meant I knew at least one person, really two, who had made it out. That had to mean something.

She continued, "I'm sure you have heard this before, we all have, it goes: The only way out is in, etc. It is not a joke or a cliché. It is far more serious than that. I need you to listen carefully: The only way out for you is through. Through. So put a little arrow in the center and write: *I am here.* Then draw a little stick figure of yourself. Make her cute. Give her earrings or a chain, a hairstyle, and an outfit that suits you. Don't be cheap with yourself. Then, along the first line out of that center write the name of the person you associate with why you are here. There is always someone. Don't argue with me. Write it down."

It was déjà vu. I had been clinging to it all these years. My third-grade teacher, Sally Sunshine, used to say that shit all the time. Especially when we were working on those puzzles to learn the multiplication tables. We would complain when we got to the sevens and eights because they were too hard, to which she would say, "Quit the complaining. The only way out of that maze is through. Work your brains, little ones. Work them. Go on through." In third grade we bent our heads, got to work, protected our papers with our hands from cheaters on all sides, and sometimes a few of us burst into tears. We did the exact same things in that room with Dr. Fuck That. Grown women, who mostly liked to play the badass, bent over their papers drawing stick figures and writing secret names with hands covering what would only have meaning to them anyway. A few of us burst into tears. I won't say if it was me, but Grace would say, "Of course it was, crybaby, of course it was." It got heavy fast. I wrote *GRACE* in big, beautiful letters all along that first line, but it was interesting to see myself at the center. I wrote *CARMEN* in script and gave myself a long skirt—though I hadn't worn one since Pete—big hoop earrings, and my old long, curly hair, even though I had cropped it short years ago. Then Dr. Fuck That said, "Now at the exit write the name of the two people you most want to make proud. Only two, and one of them has to be you. If you have children, and you are using them, then write all their names. I don't want to fan the flames of sibling rivalry." I laughed and cried because all I could think of was Grace close to the center and Artemis at the exit.

"So, you will all have to get through what you did with and for, or because of, that first name, and what you felt or feel about how that affected that second name at the exit. I said through, not over. You are never getting over what has happened to you. None of us do. However, you can, will, and must get through. I believe in you. So should you."

· · ·

Later that night, I fell asleep and into a dream of all of us getting through. Grace was standing under a doorway hugging each of us as we passed. I wrote it down in my little book of dreams in as much detail as I could remember. The very way the dream lady years ago had taught me. Dr. Guerrera had left us with a question: "What will you do with what is left of your one precious life?" She gave us a poem that asked that same question, then left the room clearer than it had been when she walked in. I tried to imagine myself as a force that could change the energy in a room. Grace had been that. I would now have to become that for myself.

The Mother of
Wild Things According
to Carmen

Summer of 2002

1
❧

ARRIVALS AND DEPARTURES

Where I'm from, there's a million ways to fall out of grace and into trouble; but once in, there is no way out but through. No turning back. No do-overs. No starting fresh. No new beginnings. No clean slates. We carry all the shit we've done, even some shit we haven't done, like turtles carry home on their backs. Knowing that never kept me from wanting what James Bond always had. I wanted the little button I could press to just like that escape from the car about to explode, no matter what I had done to get myself into it in the first place. What I had instead was the Virgin Mary hanging from the rearview mirror on a pink and green string. She looked neither pleased nor worried. Her eternal calm was irritating.

Grace had sent me to pick up Red from the airport in a Honda Civic hooptie with no air-conditioning, during rush-hour traffic on a summer Friday in June on the Grand Central Parkway. Alongside the ice-cold Beemers and Benzes all headed to the Hamptons, I had to rock my open windows and dented door. It was a car that had "no escape" written all over it. The only cassette she'd left in it for me was Biggie's *Ready to Die*. I'm sure she was laughing the whole time just thinking about it. She was also throwing code by leaving Biggie and sending me in one of our very first cars. *Remember where we started. Hold your ground. Loyalty above all else. Don't punk out.* She could feel me slipping, even if she didn't know why. Had she known I was pregnant, she might have enjoyed my suffering even more. I threw the cassette on the floor out of spite. I dreamed of escape the way you dream about having expensive cars before you ever learn to drive. The way you dream of falling in love without ever having felt it. I believed in it hard but would not have known what the hell to do with it if someone just said, "Here, take it." Doña Durka being dead felt like a "here, take it" kind of situation. I was already fumbling the pass by going to the airport.

Red could have taken a taxi. Grace could have sent a limo, any of the other girls in any of our cars, or even one of the young bucks who clearly needed something to do. Doña Durka's boys had spent the last few days circling the house making noise and stirring dust like elephants do when one of their own dies. They couldn't cry, so they chewed Skittles, Starburst, and sunflower seeds, spitting empty shells and dropping wrappers all over the front porch where they gathered in constantly shifting herds. Things they would never have done when Doña Durka was alive. When they got tired of spitting and chewing, they drank forties and smoked blunts rimming their eyes in red to hide the terror and the tears. They knew what Doña Durka had offered was not easily found or replaced. It had a price, though none of them came from lives that didn't. That someone had dared to shoot her in the parking lot at Orchard Beach, in broad daylight, meant none of them were safe. I say them and mean us. None of us were safe. But it was hard to feel danger when you had never really felt safe.

Grace sent me alone to the airport to put the fire to my feet. What she didn't know was that I wasn't riding alone anymore. I had a ride or die she couldn't see coming growing inside, and it all scared the shit out of me. Somehow, it also made me brave. My belly was no bump, but more like a spread, not round enough to rub yet, just thick and hanging over the sides of everything. I rubbed my palm across the rolls of fat like a Buddha belly for good luck. I was already making the mistake of trying to use my baby to save me when it was supposed to be the other way around.

. . .

I arrived at JFK baggage claim just in time to throw up in the bathroom. First-trimester drama, according to the book Pete was reading out loud to me, but it was still not over for me. Seventeen weeks in, and I was counting the days till it might end. It was like holding a secret that kept trying to get out one way or the other.

I did not have to look hard to find Red. She towered over the tired, sunburned tourists coming home, who didn't seem nearly as happy to be there as she did. Covered in sweat stains, she pulled me into her massive wingspan for a hug. My head ended up stuffed somewhere near her armpit. She hugged me like she had missed me. I hadn't missed her and wasn't willing to pretend. My arms hung at my sides till she let go. I was tempted to whisper, "Redrum," hoping it might still piss her off. *The Shining* was Grace's favorite movie, and Teca had started calling Red *Redrum* at some point, and we'd all followed, because the pale, terrifying twins in the hallway looked how we all imagined her as a kid. Grace tried to make us stop, but we snuck it in every chance we could. It was hard to get to Red. It was an easy cheap shot that always worked. Red standing over me now, grinning from ear to ear with her "Here's Johnny" look made it obvious it was too late for kiddie shit like name-calling.

Red was in her mother's sleeveless Janis Joplin T-shirt that she had been wearing since high school. It was so old and faded you could see her bra right through it. With her cutoff denim shorts and giant gold bamboo door-knocker earrings with "Red" in script in the middle of each one, she was in what she liked to call her white girl from the hood uniform. She was still rocking her thick, fake, bright red braids, one on each side and one down the middle. She had sent us a picture from Jamaica when she got them done. There was snickering and comments made, but Sugar shut it down with, "Girl out there doing things, I say she can wear what the fuck she wants on her head. We all know she has that dirty mousy blond hair under all them years of hair dye and now she got some *Run, Lola, Run* red extensions. You all take her shit too serious. Which is what she loves, attention!" Sugar said her truth plain and mostly we listened, because mostly she was right. Only Teca ever argued, "Nah, bitch can't be wearing no braids from Jamaica. I say no."

Red's snake tattoos were peeking over the high-top rims on her black-and-gold Air Jordans, and wrapped for all to see around her muscular, freckled arms. She had gone head to toe on it. The blue-black snake that circled her torso was hidden, but you could see it through that old-ass T-shirt if you knew to look. Doña Durka had made a big show of making Red leave New York because of those tattoos. She had called us all to the house where she'd packed a bag for Red, which was at her feet, then held a ticket out in her hand and said to her, "Those tattoos are a show for your father. You know that I am not interested in performances. Now you are a walking target so easy to identify, you put us all at risk. If you leave today, and do as I say, I won't have to kill you. I'm not offering this again."

Red took the bag and the ticket and left us with a smile. Her parting words had been, "This job even comes with paid vacations. You can't beat that." We knew, even then, it was the violence, specifically the dead body of a dude who had crossed Red, and not the tattoos that made us vulnerable. Doña Durka covered Red to cover us all, though she kept her close, even as she sent her far away. With Durka gone, Red was coming back free. It came off her body like heat. I never understood how anyone thought Red was inconspicuous to begin with, except the way being a white girl gave her a quiet pass to be less afraid.

When I turned to walk out, she slapped me below the belt from behind and said, "I don't remember you having such a nice ass. I only remember your shitty attitude. It's nice to see some things haven't changed."

. . .

She laughed when she saw the parked car. "Grace is still fucking with you, huh?" Ignoring her was supposed to make her shut up, but it didn't work. She was pressing me from all sides. As soon as we got in the car, she reached over and grabbed my belly, which popped out over my pants more when I sat. "What's this? Suddenly you have an ass, tits, chichos, and a belly. La flaca got curves? You're not pregnant, are you?" It was hot. Ours was a drama so old that all I could think to do was turn and slap her. I was slow and soggy. She hollered as she grabbed my hand in midair, "Holy shit! You are pregnant. Ooohh wee. Maybe that baby is finally gonna give you some balls. Does Grace know?" Even though she still had her sunglasses on, I could see her green eyes burning with joy behind them. She knew Grace didn't know because Grace would've told her. She hadn't been back in New York for an hour yet, and Red already had me by the balls she claimed I didn't have.

"Looks like I got back just in time."

I didn't have to look at her stupid face to know. This was the kind of shit she lived for. Petty. She picked up the cassette off the floor and looked at the baby picture of Biggie on the cover.

"Who's the daddy? Are you gonna have one of these cute brown babies or a little blanquito like me? Hope it ain't Chad's cuz that shit would suck. Or is it Painter Pete? Ohh, that would be good."

We both knew I wasn't going to answer that question. I did know one thing that might finally shut her up. "So, does your dad know you're in town?"

She ignored me, pressed play, and rapped along with Biggie the whole way home.

. . .

By the time we pulled up in front of the house on Grand Avenue it was dark. Grace was waiting for Red on the porch. They hugged, laughed, cried, and yelped like baby wolves. They didn't even turn around to look at me as they went inside. Grace was already leaning deep into Red as they walked. I sat in the car watching them as Biggie told a story about remembering where you came from. He was also foretelling his own death. I wasn't in the mood for that. Even more than I was craving the salt and vinegar chips I was eating for breakfast every day, which I had to sneak after Pete made me eat oatmeal covered in blueberries and cinnamon, I wanted a clean slate. I even liked the word: *slate*. It sounded like a slide where things could slip off without a trace. Red coming back was Grace writing more and bigger in permanent ink across the wall. There would be no wiping it clean.

I'd been thinking about Ms. Sunshine's words of advice from third grade a lot lately. *The only way out is through.* They appeared like a smooth stone I could rub with my mind. If I couldn't get a clean slate, at least I could get through. *Through, through, through.* I was tired and I wanted out, but I had no idea what it would take. That was a good enough reason to not even try.

• • •

The next morning when I arrived at the house, our usual security stood on the porch looking hot and awkward in their black suits and ties. They nodded me toward the back kitchen entrance. Doña Durka's house on Grand Avenue had always been quiet unless there was a party, and those had been rare. It was dark in the center hallway where there were no windows. I could hear voices from behind closed doors farther down the hall. Her office was open and overflowing with candles, flowers, and incense. Dolores and Maria, the women who had been with Durka since even before me and Grace, were bent over the altar they were building on her desk. I could not remember the last time I had seen them. The silver streaks in their hair felt new. They tended Durka's altar like they had tended her life, with love and reverence. They had been good to us when she was good to us, and would shut us down if she did. Their loyalty was only ever to her. If you asked them questions about themselves, they answered without answering. "How long have you worked for Doña Durka?" "Mucho tiempo. Longer than you. From the beginning." Their responses changed depending on mood or moment, but nothing was ever actually revealed. They didn't even look up as I walked past.

Each creaky step I took on the old wooden staircase announced my presence, even if no one was listening. I tried to take two at a time, and it was one more thing my body laughed at me for trying to do. Pregnancy was turning out to be a total betrayal. My body had decided that a tiny intruder was more important than me and my business as usual. I was scared. Had I ever not been? It was too hard to tell if any of the fear was new, so I blamed it all on being pregnant.

I found Grace on the second floor getting dressed in her old room. It was still covered in the fading pink and purple satin of her and Durka's mother-daughter dreams. Durka had decorated it ten years ago for the teen girl version of Grace that she had never really been. It was a fantasy they'd both enjoyed for a little while even as they'd destroyed it. We had been doing most of our work out of the apartment for the last few years, so I hadn't been in that room in a long time. It hadn't changed much except for how what had seemed huge and perfect to us when Grace first moved in just seemed old and faded now.

Grace was calm for the first time in days. She looked like she had finally worn herself out fighting, crying, and breaking shit. Her first words to me didn't really acknowledge me.

"Pass me that." She pointed her head in the direction of her gun. It looked out of place, like we did, on the purple satin quilt.

I was so hot and nauseous all I wanted to do was press the cold metal to my forehead like a bag of ice. I hoped it looked enough like mourning and my usual nerves to go unnoticed.

"You really think you're gonna need that today?"

She looked at me with her "what the fuck do you know about what I need?" face, so I passed her the gun. Grace was walking a closed circle of grief that looped in on itself. All we could do was stand around and hold her when she cried, or take her punches when she needed to throw them. She'd send me to sweep the porch clean of the sunflower seed shells and candy wrappers the boys left behind. Then she'd yell at me for doing bullshit busywork when I had real work to do. Sometimes I had to look away. If Grace was lost, who were we following? Even worse, where the hell were we going? Questions like that were not good for business, but even worse for the kind of fake-ass brave-face frontin' we did night and day.

There were pictures of Grace and Doña Durka all along the walls. Photos I had seen a thousand times: Orchard Beach, the Puerto Rican Day Parade, La Fiesta on 116th, La Fiesta Folclórica in Central Park, their first trip to Brazil, and their last one to India. Grace would come up with exotic destinations and Doña Durka would turn them into opportunities. I stared at the blurry images to keep from crying or throwing up. Her pictures, books, and music collection were all covered in dust, but they were the solid things Grace had always wanted, which brought her to this house in the first place. Her collections filled every wall of the floor-to-ceiling shelves I remembered Toro building for her over those first few years, when he had still wanted to make her happy and she still believed he could. The old Puerto Rican flag she had kept from our grandmother's house hung behind the canopy bed. It had always felt wrong here, and now it felt abandoned.

Hormones had my original crybaby status turnt all the way up. Grace was acting like she didn't even know I was in the room again. Running hot and cold was her way through, so I tried to focus on not crying, picked up my favorite picture of the whole crew in Van Cortlandt Park that she kept on her desk. Even though we were all seventeen or older by then, she'd bought us bikes and pimped them out with whatever it was we'd wanted when we were kids but had never been given by anyone before her. We looked like overgrown ten-year-olds, riding through the woods with our baskets, bells, and whatever else little girls love on their first set of wheels. She had even gotten Santa a puppy for her basket because Santa had mentioned always wanting one that she could ride with through the woods. We had been watching too many movies and reading too many books about places that had nothing to do with us, but those dreams were sticky, and Grace was all about making them come true.

The ones who knew how to ride taught the ones who didn't. Red's bike had a giant horn in the front. You could see she must have been fire even as a little kid cuz she kept creeping up on us, blowing the horn, then laughing like crazy when we jumped or fell off our bike. The picture was memory perfect with our big smiles and Santa's puppy hanging two paws over her basket as the sun was starting to set behind us. The story it couldn't tell, that you had to be there to know, was the ride Grace made us take after. She took us through the wooded dirt trail on the Van Cortlandt side all the way up to Yonkers, where the path turned to asphalt and grew wide and spacious. It was a long way for the ones who had only just learned to ride, and for the rest of us that were mostly out of shape. But she made us go till we reached Tibbetts Park, where a tiny wooden bridge crossed over a stream. You could only ride one at a time. It was short, tight, and dangerous, as it ended abruptly, with water on either side just a wide turn away. Grace waited for us at the other end. Once we'd all made it across, we realized we'd have to ride back on that same path in the dark.

"You all asked for a lot of shit for those bikes, but not one of you asked for lights."

She gave each one of us a handlebar light and a back light. We snapped them on as she said, "We ride in the dark, but we have light when we need it. Keep them off till I turn mine on."

We rode back over the bridge with only the sound of water and the feel of trees on either side to guide us. Santa was worried about her dog and passed him to Sugar, who had been riding a bike since she was ten years old. Sugar shook her head as she took the puppy and muttered, "Fucking Grace." The half-moon peeking over the treetops sent us into hollers and cheers. We did some singing till someone came out on their porch and threatened to call the cops. We were quiet after that as we rode to the border of the Bronx where the asphalt gave way to a dark wooded dirt trail. That was when it all got horror-movie scary.

Grace called out in the dark, "As long as we stay together and don't leave anybody behind, we good." We rode on, with Red tearing up the path in front and Sugar holding us all in sight from the back. Grace had been weaving through till she finally took the lead and turned on her light. Our lights went on one by one, and we lit up the trail to the lake where we had taken the picture. We were sweating and breathing heavy by the time it was over. Destiny was shaking with fear as we walked our bikes to the cars parked in the lot near the golf course. I still remembered how good it felt to be so scared and do it anyway.

Grace was looking in the mirror, so it was hard to know if she was talking to herself or me when she said, "Hold it together, ma. No pendeja moves. No checking out. Today's a hard day, but we seen harder." She cracked her neck on both sides. A bright, concentrated beam of sunlight through the bedroom window lit up her many shades of brown from behind. Everything from her tight, dark curls to the scarred skin on her chest shimmered in the light. Grace slipped her gun into the waist of her pants, then looked at me through the mirror. The last thing she snapped in place was Doña Durka's chain with the silver-dollar-sized gold medallion of La Virgen on one side and Maa Durga on the other. Grace had it custom made for Durka. I couldn't remember when it had gone from her neck to Grace's.

I should have been comforting her. Instead, she gave me a hug and kissed me on the head. "We gonna be aight. We always are. We always been. We always gonna be. And remember, we still got our teeth."

A crazy line that made us laugh as it always did. We used it as a reminder that we had watched both of our mothers lose their teeth before they turned thirty. Grace walked out with her shoulders bent forward as if already protecting herself from the blows to come. She kissed a picture of Durka on the wall before going down the stairs.

I hadn't seen Toro yet, but I could see Jimmy, Doña Durka's younger son, through the window. He was standing in front of the house in full uniform. There was a picture of him in his Marine whites on the wall. We had all seen it, commented on how fine he was, taken turns talking about how all we needed was one night to make him come home for good. The truth was that we had no idea who he was, or how someone could stay gone so long from the only place we called home. Doña Durka had sent him away to military school when he was about ten years old. He had never spent much time in the house. She used to visit him regularly, went with him to see family in Puerto Rico for the holidays, took him on vacations, but she kept him and Toro mostly apart. Standing by the front gate, he seemed rigid and out of place, like the stranger he was, especially surrounded by the slowly gathering army of young men in giant T-shirts and baggy pants who felt more like sons of Doña Durka than he probably did.

We found Toro, dressed in a suit that made him look his age, drinking a forty in the kitchen. He was visibly drunk. Grace walked right by him and went out to the car that was waiting to drive them to the funeral home. Toro and Jimmy followed her into the limo without even making eye contact, on their way to bury the only tie that bound them.

The streets around the house must have filled while I was inside. Grand Avenue was lined on both sides with women dressed in black holding orange marigolds—Doña Durka's favorite flower. Their crying was hushed and strong like wings in a crowded flock. There were hundreds of them too far back to even see where they ended. With police cars in front and behind, the women created a living, writhing snake that filled the streets. It looked like the Good Friday processions Grace and Durka had walked through the Bronx together every year and marked an underworld journey just the same.

These were the women Doña Durka had helped, quietly and without fanfare, with money, abusive husbands, landlords, and even their own children lost to drugs or gangs or jail. Doña Durka saw no irony or absurdity in helping to supply the drugs, creating the gangs, and helping someone's daughter go to rehab. If one kid got killed or clipped on the street, Doña Durka made it her business, and a promise to the mother, to make sure the remaining kids went to school or got their shit together somehow. It was all an enormous pulsing circle of need and want; she simply answered the call no matter what. She had many names for and ways of talking about how some of what she did on one end of that circle made what she did on the other end possible, and also necessary. "It is, mis hijas, an imperfect system. I never found one that served me better. If you find a better one, let me know. That is your job, find a better one."

Someone had built an impromptu altar in front of the house. Like all true street altars, as many hands had built it as had been touched by the life lost, creating a memorial that was not orderly or controlled, but communal. Doña Durka's grandmother's statue of Yemaya, our Great Mother of the Sea, stood among blue candles and blue and white flowers covered by a white veil. The figure of Durga with her ten arms extended in a fan of weapons and tools sat on a tiger in the center back, placed on a tall ceramic stand within a large gold-painted box, as if she might ride away. This was not her hood, but it was her universe. She seemed at home, even familiar, if you knew how to look. There was a string of marigolds around her neck, and a cleaned Café Bustelo can that held a candle and incense burning at her feet. It must have been Grace that brought her outside from Doña Durka's office. Ma Durga, as we had come to call her out of love, wasn't from around these parts, and yet she had found us, or we had found each other. Ma Durga had both lifted us up and plunged us deeper within. We were still working out what it meant to discover that we weren't trash; that in fact, in some parts of the world, a thick Mother Goddess with a nose ring, who was known for her fighting skills, was worshiped as the Supreme Mother of us all.

If anything was true, it was that Durga had given us things we weren't ready to receive. Things we had to grow into. Bringing her outside, if only for today, was Grace's way of paying respect to the mystery she still was, and the unyielding hope and love she offered the most hopeless daughters of the world. We were those for sure. Now that we didn't have Doña Durka, we needed the impenetrable and unassailable sanctuary of protection Ma Durga offered, words we had not known before her, more than ever. Smaller altars to La Virgen and various saints surrounded Yemaya and Ma Durga. There was a golden laughing Buddha encircled by small candles, coins, and flowers on the table under the tree where Doña Durka had loved to sit. I bowed my head to each one, paying respect to the blend of fierce and gentle that had allowed Doña Durka to hold so many worlds in one. My eyes lingered on the conch shell Ma Durga held in one hand. I was trying to listen, even as everything true felt very far away.

The mourners on foot would follow the cars, a pilgrimage to where Doña Durka had lived as a child and along the blocks where people knew her best. I wanted to be waiting at the entrance to the funeral home when Grace got there. I also couldn't bring myself to pay respects to Doña Durka herself. I had only ever really been here for Grace. There was no use pretending otherwise anymore.

...

Pete was waiting for me on the next block over. I had asked him to drive me because I knew I would eventually end up riding with one of the girls or in several cars together. I also knew it was a mistake to keep including him. We were taking turns testing each other and failing. He didn't even look at me as I climbed in the car. He just went straight in.

"So, is it possible for you to go to this funeral and not feel the danger you and our baby are in? Like are you seriously capable of that?" His voice always grew pitched and irritated when we argued about this. Today, it was wet with real fear. He looked like he might have been crying.

"Look, I can't do this now. I'm here for Grace and I'm here for my crew. Just drop me off at the pawnshop on Tremont. We're closing early and going to the burial. That's it."

I had sold him a story he wanted to buy about pawnshops and strip clubs being an easy way to go clean because few people asked questions and they moved a lot of cash. The restaurants were next. I explained that we were only a few steps away from being in the clear. We had all of that, of course, plus a lot more, but he didn't believe any of it. He knew that Grace had not released me. I hadn't really been showing any signs of letting her go either. If he was giving me a temporary break from the fight, it was because we were both tired of it. Every argument since we found out I was pregnant was him trying not to stress me out because of the baby, but also wanting to curse me out for not seeing things exactly as he did.

In almost a whisper, he said, "Right, okay, please be careful. Just come home." He reached over and kissed me on the forehead and then on the shoulder and then on my hand, which he held the whole time he was driving. He kissed my hand again as I climbed out of the car. "Wait, I got you this little book. It's like your dream notebook, but for the baby. You know, like a dream we can share. It goes with the book we are reading about what to expect." I took it without looking at him and threw it in my bag.

Fucking Pete. He made everything complicated. Sometimes I hated his good as much as he hated my bad.

BURYING THE DEAD

Pete sped off like an angry teenager in his parents' four-door Camry. He refused to use any of my cars, though he would ride in one if I was driving it. Strange contradictory rules had become his own language of rage. I was just as bad. Grateful he had been here; happier still that he was gone. Tremont Avenue offered the familiar blend of home that allowed me to drop my shoulders for a minute. The cuchifritos, clothing and sneaker stores, dollar stores, and pawnshops sharing sidewalk space with McDonald's, Payless shoes, and Rite Aid. The heat-trapped smell of bacalaítos in the air made me relax immediately. On our little chunk of the block there was the music store Red had forced Grace into buying, the pawnshop that had been Durka's, and the women's clothing store Destiny dreamed of expanding. Under Red's guidance we had started offering lessons and selling instruments in addition to records, cassettes, and CDs. Red had named it Love Alive Music. She was the one who'd found a bunch of old congueros, jazz musicians, and salseros from the neighborhood who played everything from percussion, flutes, and trumpets to piano and guitar. She connected them with teachers from Harlem School of the Arts and created a place where kids and adults practiced scales with salsa classics and Mozart. It was small but impressive, and like all that we built, it took on a life of its own. It was the way of money to make things that looked hard so much easier. It was impossible to unsee that kind of power.

Love Alive Music had back rooms that were connected to our pawnshop next door. This allowed us to move things, without going in and out of the same storefront, with access to hidden storage spaces and back exits. We had relationships with the supers that gave us creative ways to maneuver through alleys and basements as needed. The clothing store was three doors down from Love Alive. It was a place where big boxes full of "dresses" or "shoes" could easily move in and out. This was one of many blocks like it that Doña Durka had built with Toro, but this one was ours. Grace had asked me to keep my eyes open. To be on high alert. I wasn't sure what I was looking for other than odd behavior or unexpected packages or requests. We would all be on edge until we found out who'd killed Durka, but more important, until it became clear that we weren't next.

Teca was reading her favorite newspaper, the *New York Post*, at the front register by the pawnshop's window. When she saw me, she smiled, buzzed me in, and came out from behind the bulletproof glass to give me a hug. Teca had been around for years, but still looked very West Coast with her long, straight, dark hair, thin eyebrows, and thick eye makeup. She had adjusted her wardrobe and slang, but you could tell she was far from home.

"Check it. Look who went down today, Dapper Don, everybody's favorite gangster. They got twelve pages of pictures in all his best outfits and at his daughter's wedding. Spooky coincidence, no? Plus, it was cancer." She wrinkled her nose at me like she didn't like it. I looked at the cover.

"Weird." I gave her back the paper. I knew she was also noting that Doña Durka would never receive coverage like that. None of us would.

Red was strumming her favorite solos on a black electric guitar in the back room. She kept the amp low as she watched Destiny and Remy packing the drugs they'd deliver across the city as soon as Doña Durka was buried. It was as if Red had never left. Everyone gave her the respect she had always been given. It was one thing we gave each other that we had never felt anywhere else. This was probably what Red had missed most, other than Grace, while she was away. It was what I was most afraid of losing. Filled with fear, surrounded by random piles of shit people once loved, but also left behind in a pinch, we had the discipline to do what had to be done even under fire. It made me stupidly proud of us, even Red.

I wiped my finger along an empty shelf. "It's fucking dusty back here. Does anybody ever clean this place?"

Teca looked at me as she pulled down the gate and locked the door. "Does it look like we have cleaning ladies here? Which one of us would you have do the dusting?"

Sugar came around and hugged me from behind. Her thick arms, always smelling like her favorite lavender cream, folded me into her chest like giant raven feathers. She glanced over at Teca. "Don't mess with my girl right now. We all got the feels and shit, and rightly so, you got to be crazy not to feel when shit like this happens. We all have our ways." She kept one arm over my shoulder and pulled Destiny in with the other. "This one here cries like tears are some kind of magic potion that will protect her. I don't cry like that, but that don't mean she's wrong." Destiny, beautiful and paper thin, rolled her eyes and teared up at the same time, which only made Sugar laugh.

Red spoke over the soft sound of her guitar. "Yes, well, what we feel doesn't really matter."

Remy ran her long, red nails along her skintight black pants and added, "I'm with Red, no one gives a shit how we feel. Everybody out here just lookin' out pa' lo suyo, entiendes." Sugar nodded her head as if she couldn't really argue.

Santa never even looked up as she asked, "So what do you bitches want for dinner tonight?"

• • •

The work of packing and planning drop-offs went along as it always did. We all knew we weren't just burying a body today. Making sure we worked was Grace's way to guarantee we were all on board when everyone had questions about what next.

Sugar called out from the door she was opening to the back, "How's Pete the painter? I saw he dropped you off. That is not a bird we often see around these parts."

Red answered before I could, "How would she know? She sees more of you than him from what I can tell."

Sugar held out her hand and said, "Easy there, ma, you just got back, so don't start your know-it-all shit. There is shit you know and shit you don't. So slow down, cuz we don't have beef till you start talkin' when I ain't talkin' to you."

There we were. Teca's arm looping behind Remy, to pass Santa a bag, as Destiny weighed each one and zipped double liners. Sugar holding Red in check. What we did was both secret and obvious. If everyone is getting high, someone is supplying, and each group that did created a language only they spoke. Grace had taught us to live, breathe, and speak as a single body. This sense of never alone/never separate was one of the things I couldn't explain to Pete about how this had come to feel safer than anything I had ever found anywhere else. Even with him. I took Sugar's cue to let her handle Red, and answered as if nothing had been said, "He's the same, you know. The less he knows the better, but Doña Durka getting killed has him spooked like all of us."

Sugar answered, "He ain't wrong, mama, this shit is real."

Destiny whispered loud enough to be heard, "Ain't nothing like a dead body that you know and love to make it real as hell."

Sugar moved us along toward the exit. She closed the metal gate with a blessing: "May the Great Mother protect us when the ones closest to us can protect us no more." Santa was already behind the wheel of the first minivan. I saw her make the sign of the cross before turning the key in the ignition.

• • •

The funeral home was across the street from Poe Park on 192nd Street and the Grand Concourse. It was a corner connecting old and new terrors in the night, even if the little kids running around the park didn't know who Edgar Allan Poe was or what dark worlds, imagined and real, he and the funeral home represented side by side. The place was filled to capacity, overflowing onto the street. Without the funeral sign as a backdrop, it could easily be confused for the summer flood of people hanging out on the block. The boys were wearing oversized white T-shirts with a picture of Doña Durka on the front, and on the back, the words: *Doña Durka, La Madre de Todos, RIP 6/9/02.* Grace pulled up in her limo with the long line of women walking behind it. She had timed it all so we'd arrive right as the pilgrimage around the Bronx ended in front of the funeral home. It was a joining of two worlds that had coexisted for a long time, but never came together in public: the boys and the women of Doña Durka's world. To the boys she was a general. To the women she was a mother and a protector. She was all of it, none of it, and mostly a mystery no one understood, but everyone feared and respected. When Toro got out of the car, he was immediately surrounded by Nene and his closest crew. Jimmy was alone. His only connections to the neighborhood were the two cops standing together at the entrance, guys he had met in the Marines, by chance.

When Grace climbed out, we formed a half circle around her. She turned to hug each one of us tight to her chest, then kissed us. Even in her grief she held us in her gaze long enough to let us know she knew we were scared, that she had our backs and she loved us. I don't doubt she was also looking into our eyes to see what was up, and if there was anyone that for any reason could not hold her gaze. I was the last one to go up to her. She let herself go soft in my arms like when we were young. I was grateful not to have to look at her face too long. She called Santa's and Sugar's kids to her and squeezed them tight. She gave them lollipops from her always well-stocked candy stash pocket. Grace popped M&M'S like some people popped pills. Seeing her surrounded by kids gave me a second of false hope that she'd embrace my pregnancy, though I wasn't stupid enough to believe it. Santa and Sugar had arrived with their kids in hand. My body was becoming vulnerable on her watch. I had defied the very rules that were supposed to protect us.

The crowd opened to let Grace through. The boys backed up but looked away, having never been taught to respect her as more than Toro's girl. The rest of the crowd knew her in relation to Doña Durka. Women kissed her or grabbed her hand as she passed. They were clear about who they would turn to next. The suits in the crowd, men and women, young and old, cheap and expensive, moved quietly toward and away from Grace in whispers and nods. Some left quickly, having come only to pay respects and get on good terms with whoever would feed them next, while others stood back waiting for instructions. It was only a few feet of sidewalk between the curb and the entrance, but it was packed with shifting loyalties trying to attach themselves to whoever would come to fill the hole Doña Durka had left. Where Toro was the clear and obvious choice to some, Grace was the force holding those who knew Durka well. The ice-cream truck across the street by the park was oddly silent. I watched as the man who owned it closed the windows and made his way to Grace. He offered her a picture of him and Doña Durka in front of his truck when he had first bought it. He was young and skinny. Durka had a vanilla cone with sprinkles in her hand. He had tears in his eyes as he said, "People don't know how los atrevidos help the people no one even sees." Grace hugged him and slipped the picture into her pocket.

We followed Grace in through the double doors. The rush of ice-cold air in the funeral home was a relief until I remembered that the AC was kept on blast to keep the bodies from rotting faster. Grace called those my intrusive thoughts. I liked to think of them as my reality check. There were so many flowers they had started setting them up in the hallway. Durka was in the largest viewing room. It had folding walls covered in beige and olive-green-striped wallpaper that had to be opened out twice into other rooms because of the overflow of people. Octavio, the owner, had expected this, and not accepted any other families after he found out Doña Durka had been killed.

From the entrance to the room, I could see Durka's body in a white casket with gold trim under dim lights. She was surrounded by marigolds in every imaginable funeral arrangement shape and combination, covered in red and yellow sashes with messages of love and devotion written in gold glitter. The words *gracias y amor* appeared on almost every single one. Doña Durka was literally buried in gratitude and love. Only Jimmy had ordered roses. His flowers stuck out as much as he did, but they were also placed on the casket closest to her heart. Her casket was set farther back from the seats than was normal to accommodate the number of people moving through.

I sat right behind the front row where Grace, Jimmy, and Toro were sitting or standing, depending on who came to them, to receive condolences. Everyone moved toward Grace first: politicians, cops, old women, young girls, mothers with babies. Only the young boys went to Toro as they started to reorganize their sense of who they would follow. A congresswoman from the Bronx, who was taking a risk just by showing up, approached and spoke directly to Grace.

"I'm so sorry for your loss. It was a loss for a whole community. Your mother did amazing things for people. She was so proud of you."

"Thank you."

Toro interrupted drunkenly, "She wasn't talking to you. That wasn't your mother. That was my mother."

Ignoring Toro, the congresswoman leaned in closer to Grace. "She never asked me for anything, and she gave everything. I know she did the same for you."

She shook Toro's hand, then Jimmy's, adding recognition of his uniform by saying, "Thank you for your service."

She slipped her card with a handwritten number on the back to Grace and said, "Don't hesitate to call."

Toro reacted by throwing his hands out like he was ready to go off.

Jimmy moved toward him, put his hand on Toro's arm, and tried to whisper in his ear, but it was loud enough for all of us to hear, "Listen, bro, keep it cool, you know that's how Mami would've wanted it."

Toro pulled his arm away and started yelling, "Get the fuck off me. How the fuck would you know what Mami wanted? ¿Dime? ¿Cómo? You been gone for fifteen years. You think you big in that uniform. That monkey suit don't mean shit out here."

Toro pulled his gun out halfway, and his boys closed in around him. A few pulled their guns, but Nene, who was never far from Toro, came forward to cool everybody down. His was the deep baritone voice of reason, and he was also twice the size of almost all of them. We'd all had a crush on Nene at one point or another, but his was a loyalty the streets made into legends—he was Toro's boy, and that is who he would always protect.

"Chill, man, let's show some respect for Doña Durka. Just chill." He led with his arms gently sweeping guys along in different directions.

Grace signaled us back with one hand and put the other on her gun behind her. Jimmy's two cop friends started moving in our direction. Everyone settled down and put their guns away.

The skinny, tall cop asked, "Yo, Jimmy, should we step in? Do you need backup here?"

There wasn't anything Jimmy's friends could do if captains and detectives that went from Doña Durka's payroll to Toro's weren't giving the orders. They had to put up a good show though, even if they knew better.

"Nah, nah, leave it alone. It's good. It'll be over soon." Jimmy's face gave away what his uniform was meant to hide. His Adam's apple bobbed up and down as he struggled to swallow back tears. His resemblance to Durka became obvious to me for the first time. We had only ever really seen him in pictures, but the crooked lines of grief mixed with rage across his face, revealed Durka's full lips, dark eyes, and wide cheeks beneath the stubble already forming on his clean-shaven jaw. You could tell from his fist clenching that he also had the same quick temper as Toro, he had just redirected it somewhere else.

As the crowd thinned out, Grace finally made her way to the front of the room. She stood over Durka's body, sobbing into her own chest. Toro stood as if he might go to her, then turned his back on her instead, so he was facing the other side of the room, making it clear he would not be offering her any support. Red moved toward Grace as soon as she saw Toro turn away. Sugar and Destiny had taken up a post by the front door, while Remy and Teca held the back exit. Santa had the kids in the hallway playing quietly in a circle on the floor. When they saw Red moving toward Grace, they all followed. Red tried to wipe Grace's face with a Durka T-shirt she found on a chair. Grace hugged the shirt to her face and kissed the picture of Durka as she hung in Red's arms. I stood there waiting till she needed me again. I would be lying if I said I wasn't a little bit happy Doña Durka was dead though. She had never been to me what she was to Grace. Being pregnant in Doña Durka's world made my life feel shrunk down to the smallness of stereotype, but Grace stood in that shrunken world with a love so fierce it fed everyone around her. All along what we were doing had felt like something accidental, some loca shit we fell into. I was always saving a little piece of the before Doña Durka dream life of Carmen and Grace. When Doña Durka died, it rose to claim me again, even if only for the first few days. Watching Grace cling to Red now, I knew for sure none of that was ever coming back.

. . .

At St. Raymond's Cemetery there was a long line of cars, and a woman dressed in white stood over the coffin with incense and water. June already felt like summer in New York burning high and hot, even nearing the late afternoon. I was worried I might faint. Grace walked through the crowd with all of us at her back. Her face twisted in pain. She put on her sunglasses and rubbed her chest as she made her way to the front and spoke. "My mother, Durka Rodriguez, was an amazing woman. She may not have given birth to me, but she gave birth to who I am. There are many of us here who know we would be nothing without her. She always said she didn't want crying at her funeral. She wanted us to play music and celebrate her life. As we say goodbye, let's remember how much she loved life. How much she loved us. How hard she fought. How much she gave. ¡Que viva Doña Durka!"

The crowd sang back, "¡Que viva!"

A group of congueros and eight women dressed in white joined the woman who had been there from the start. They set up behind the coffin and began to play a slow bomba version of "Nadie llore." The women moved from slow to fast, leading the beat with their bodies in an act of mourning that was a reminder that we were alive. They danced as a long, undulating line of people crying and swaying and saying goodbye moved past the coffin. Toro then played the salsa version of the same song by Willie Colón and Héctor Lavoe on a loudspeaker. Toro and Nene spilled beer on the ground in Doña Durka's honor and others danced. It was a scene that could have just as easily been at Orchard Beach if you ignored the tombstones and the open grave. Grace stood there hugging hundreds of people. She held each one as long as they needed holding.

We all waited till the end, after the last of the crowd had headed back to their cars or walked off in groups, to step up to the grave and throw a flower and a final prayer. We stood behind Grace waiting for the moment when she'd say goodbye. She waved me and Red over. We each held her by an arm. As soon as I felt her body go limp in my hand, I signaled the girls to shield her in a tight formation to protect her from anyone who might be watching for signs of weakness, especially Toro, who was leaning against a tree, unwilling to let Grace be the last to leave.

Grace fell to her knees in the dirt and stretched her arms across the coffin as her head came to rest against it. Her body groaned from the pressure until it finally gave way to sobs and moans that left her gasping for air.

Red's veins were pulsing in her temples and stretched hard across her neck. I could feel the seeds of revenge taking root in her. She was not one for tears and suffering. That Doña Durka was dying from cancer anyway didn't matter to her. I also knew that Grace was crying not only for Durka, but for herself. I knew because I was doing it too. My only prayer over her grave was, "May this pain be the one that makes us walk away." My dream of escape, when we were twelve, and now at twenty-four, always had Grace leaving with me. It wouldn't even feel like out if she wasn't there with me on the other side.

Propping her between us, we pulled Grace away from the grave. We crossed the cemetery path back to the car, a line of grown women holding hands as we navigated the tombstones. The only cars left, other than our limo, was Nene parked in the distance waiting for Toro, and Jimmy's friends' unmarked cop car. Jimmy had been watching us from the back seat the whole time. They only drove off when we started in that direction. It scared me to see him pull away with his two cop friends. Red looked over at me as if to acknowledge that she didn't like it much either. Did he think Grace had his mother killed so she could take over? There was no room for that thought in any of us, but there was no way for him to know that Durka was just as much Grace's mother as his.

. . .

Doña Durka's house was dark with strangers, music, and food she would never have allowed to pass through her doors. Grace was trying to pay the caterer Durka always used, but he refused, while pizza and Chinese food deliveries started showing up along with cases of beer and Hennessey for Toro. Everyone was paying their respects in the way that made sense to them. Grace made her rounds with those in the house that she knew, but it was clear there weren't many left. Her people had been the first to come and go, if they had come near the house at all. Seeing Toro and Grace together in that crowd made it seem impossible that they had ever been in love or partners of any kind.

Slowly, as night fell, girls no one knew started coming in. It looked like a strip club. Old-school Nas played in the background . . . "Street dreams are made of these" . . . Toro raised his forty in the air and motioned to Nene to lower the music. Looking directly at Grace, he toasted Doña Durka: "To my moms. There will never be another like her. She knew what the real world was all about. She never backed down and her memory will live forever." He took off his shirt to show a second tattoo on his arm next to the one with his father's name and date of death. The new one was a picture of Durka and his father on their wedding day, the date of her death right below it.

Toro added, "Now they are finally together for eternity where they belong." Nene and his boys all raised their bottles and slapped him on the back. Grace was eyeing Toro as he sat down and motioned for a girl, who looked only a little older than Grace had been when she first arrived, to sit on his lap. Grace went upstairs. Jimmy had slipped back into the house after the cemetery. I watched as he followed her. I stayed only a few steps behind.

I went down the hall and stood outside of the bathroom door, trying to let them hear me before I went to Grace's old bedroom where they were. He moved closer to the wall to look at the pictures of Durka with Grace. He wiped his face several times before saying, "My mother talked a lot about you."

"Well, she never stopped talking about you." I couldn't see his reaction, but he moved closer to Grace.

"What's your plan? You leaving? I heard you were in college. You're still young."

Facing the pictures, Grace answered him, "I wanted to be a teacher, but she wanted me to do something bigger. Something involving money. So, I'm probably going to work on an MBA, lots of school left for me. I would've become an astronaut if she wanted me to. There was nothing I wouldn't have done for her."

"Including staying with my brother?"

Grace turned to face him like she was jumping in a fight. "What? Look, you don't know me and you don't know my life, and from what I hear, you don't even know your brother. It's cool. So, let's just leave it at that." I could tell she was holding back tears by the tremble in her words. She turned back to the window to keep it all in check. Jimmy shook his head and squeezed his fists like he knew he had taken the wrong turn too fast and was skidding, then he went for the full spin.

"You're right. I had no right to say that. I knew about the cancer. I also know she didn't want to go down like that. Sick. Weak. Bald." He let it hang in the air before gathering enough swagger to continue, "That is not the Doña Durka way, right. Maybe she reached out to you for help with that?"

Grace didn't even turn to look at him. "Whatever you're trying to imply with your bullshit detective work is guilt talking. You know your mother gave you the world and you gave her nothing in return. You didn't even invite her to your wedding even though she paid for it, or let her meet her grandchildren. Don't be surprised if in the end you killed her, asshole. You can fucking leave now."

I pushed the door wide open before he could answer. "Hey, I was looking for you. What are you doing in here?"

"Nothing. Jimmy's just getting ready to leave."

Flatly, he added, "Yeah, I better go. Here's my number in case you need me for anything."

"Your mother's lawyer will be contacting you about the inheritance. He has your contact information." She didn't take his number.

He stood there with no choice but to leave with the card in his hand. He tried one last time. "Right. Okay. Well, it was nice finally meeting you. We'll be in touch."

"Probably not."

We looked out the window and watched him leave with his cop friends who had been waiting outside. I turned to Grace to try to lighten the mood. "He's even better looking in person. But he seems like an asshole. Should we be worried about him?"

"Not really. No more than we should be worried about anyone else. He just doesn't get how we live."

"Yeah, well I can't say I blame him. He would get along great with Pete."

Half smiling and half squinting her eyes at me, she said, "Speaking of assholes, I noticed he didn't even come today."

"Yeah, you know how he feels about all this and me being here and . . ." I paused long. I tried to make the words come out. I wanted to get it over with and be like: now that I'm pregnant. I couldn't. I didn't. The space between us grew, in secret and in the dark, bigger every day.

Grace filled in for my nervous silence. "Toro's buggin' down there. I guess we could see that coming. I need to clean up and get out."

I grabbed her hand and asked, "What about you? How are you? Really?" I wanted to hug her and let her cry, but this was not that Grace. There was no room for contact. The door had been shut.

"I'm fucked up. I'm pissed off. I should've been there. Something about it is all wrong. Like whoever did it knew we sometimes went to the beach and sat in the car so she could smell the ocean, even if she was too tired after the treatments to get out. So, she wouldn't have even found it weird to head over there." She pulled away and started moving around the room, pulling down shades.

"What do you think Toro is going to do?"

"What he always does. Nothing. At least nothing that matters."

She struggled as she pulled a heavy metal box out from under her bed. Grace's comfort in handling it made me think she knew all along how far this would go. She had jumped in headfirst because she'd never felt there was anything to lose. My stomach twitched. I instinctively put my hand over it. She watched me do it, lifted her chin as if to ask a question, but then turned back to the guns. It made sense, now that Doña Durka was gone. We had to have our own backs. It was obvious. It was natural. We each already had a gun and some of us more than one, but the message here was that we needed more.

"What the fuck is all that?"

"Haven't you learned to stop asking questions you don't really want the answers to?"

I wanted to say so many things right then, but there was no space.

"Get Red to come help you pack these and take them out. If Toro's idiots ask any questions, tell them you're moving me out. I'll deal with him. Come back into the house through the kitchen in case some shit goes down. Let Red drive away with those bags."

· · ·

Red came up to pack the guns in her guitar case and duffel bags. The bags were heavy, so we had to make two trips. To get outside we had to walk through the house that was full of smoke, alcohol, and random girls. Toro was letting Grace know this was his house now. If she wanted to stay, there would be new rules. He sat on the couch with a girl on each knee. I avoided eye contact, though I could feel him staring. I could also see Nene standing off to the side, near the window, looking from me to the car outside. Once I was out the door, all I wanted to do was run. Instead, I came in the back way and went up to Durka's room where Grace had asked me to meet her. Red drove off with the guns. I felt like I was breaking in using the tiny back stairs. Heart racing, blood pumping fear. Whatever this was turning into, it did not yet have the strength to stop me from acting on my training.

Durka's bedroom was a sea of orange, red, and gold with candles and flowers in every corner. It looked like her office, but it was more intimate; it smelled like she did, of cinnamon and wood. I could see why Grace had loved her so much, even if I did not share that love. Durka had carved herself out from places few ever escape. Grace went into Durka's walk-in closet and took a few pantsuits, a white linen shirt, a red silk bathrobe, a wig Durka had worn during chemo, her signature Panama straw hat from Ole's in El Viejo San Juan, her favorite red shoes, and her makeup bag. Then she went into a safe and took Durka's gun, the knife she always carried, and a folder full of papers. She left a large stack of cash as if she hadn't even seen it. Grace was already wearing Doña Durka's jewelry, some of which Durka had given her long before she died. She put all of what she gathered into a carry-on Louis Vuitton suitcase. I walked through a wall of fur coats, leather jackets, and shearlings. There must have been at least a hundred coats along one wall. I was distracted petting one and feeling sorry for the animal that lost its life to hang in a closet when Toro surprised us both. He burst into the room and yelled out, "What the fuck you think you're doing?" I crouched at the edge of the closet waiting to see how Grace would react.

She stepped right up to him and said, "Just go back to chillin' out there. I ain't gonna mess with you tonight."

Toro moved in close, pressing her, "She ain't even cold yet and you think you're running something. I know you ain't trying to take her shit."

"You're drunk. Back off. I'm not trying to tell you what to do. Just chill. I'm not taking anything you would want."

"What the fuck do you know about what I want? I don't take orders from basura. You in my house now, so drop the bag. We ain't got no kids, so we ain't got no ties. That was your big mistake. If you leave here, you leave like you came. Sin na'. That's how it goes for girls like you."

"That's funny. I haven't been a girl for a long time. I'm also your legal wife. Remember that? Durka knew exactly what you would try to pull on me if anything happened to her. I don't want no problems with you. Go play with your girls outside. That's about all you can handle."

"I'm your legal wife" landed like a slap across the face. I had no idea they were legally married or even when they had done it. How had she kept that a secret from me for so long? I felt like I might throw up, so I eyed some boxes in the corner where I could go if that happened. Grace told everyone that she wore the ring he gave her at sixteen as decoration. It was all for show. It made me think of how many times Pete had asked me to marry him. I kept putting him off because I couldn't figure out how to tell Grace. Toro grabbed her arm and squeezed it till she dropped the bag. He kissed her hard, pressed her up against the wall, and started crying into her hair.

"So start acting like my wife. Console me. Give a shit. We had some good times, mami. Let's keep it simple. You give me what I need, and I'll keep taking care of you. But you gotta stop acting like you run the place. My mother ain't here to protect you no more." He leaned in for another kiss, shedding drunk tears.

When he looked in her stone-still face, she just said, "Don't get it twisted cuz you never took care of me."

He grabbed her crotch. Grace slapped his face and kneed him between the legs. He bent a little and punched her in the stomach. Still unstable, he lunged to grab her by the hair and pulled her down with him. They both fell against the dresser, sending small glass bottles smashing all around them on the floor.

Nene heard the commotion out in the hallway. He came into the room right as I turned to throw up in a shoebox. Nene stood there looking at them, then back at me at the edge of the closet and shouted, "What the fuck is going on in here?"

Grace yelled at Toro as if Nene wasn't even there, "Yeah, motherfucker, she ain't here to protect you either. I think we both know who needed her protection more." She struggled under his body weight, but freed one arm and kept at him. "I know what's mine and what's yours better than you do, bitch."

She pulled out her gun. Toro rolled slightly to the side and pulled his too. Nene jumped in, dragged Toro off Grace, then took Toro's gun out of his hand. "What the fuck you doing? Get off her, man. You want this place crawling with cops? Don't give Jimmy the pleasure of walking in here with badges, yo. Come on." Nene was shaking his head. He looked at Grace with disgust as he dragged Toro from the room.

Nene turned back while he was still holding Toro with one arm and spoke directly to Grace, "Just make sure you don't take more than you can protect."

Once Toro and Nene left, Grace picked up the bag she'd packed and walked out without even looking behind her to see if I was following. I leaned against the soft fur coats as the hype and exhaustion fought it out in my bloodstream. I wanted to punch her in the face for leaving me like that. I wanted to lie down and fall asleep. I was tired of Grace, I was tired of Pete, I was tired of me. By then I was just tired all the time and kept forgetting the who and the why. My head was a cage with no bars and no locks spinning in circles like the rims on Toro's ride that spun even when the car wasn't moving. I heard Grace come back down the hall.

"What the fuck is wrong with you? Get up! Why you throwing up so much? That can't just be nerves." She extended her hand to me and pulled me up.

"The stomach flu. I think I have the stomach flu."

"Disgusting. That shit is contagious. Stay your ass home if you so sick."

She shook her head, dragged me along, looking back only once like she knew I was lying, but also she didn't have time for my shit. All I could hear over the music as we slipped out the back door was Pete telling me to make sure I came home that night. The strength of Grace's hand around mine made it feel like there was no way that could happen.

3
❧

HOME

When Grace and I got back to the apartment that night, we found the crew all huddled up on the giant purple couches talking shit and making noise. Laughter over a low sax playing on Sugar's favorite light jazz radio station mixed with the smell of onions and garlic frying in olive oil coming from the kitchen, which meant Santa was cooking. Lately, I had started counting us every time we were in the same room together like toes on a baby's foot. This time there were nine, one more than the usual. I had to scan the room again to make sure. China, Nene's ex, was sitting in the hall by the door on a little bench we used to take off our street shoes and put on clean sneakers that never left the apartment. We couldn't be barefoot or rock fuzzy slippers in case we ever had to run. The whole thing was a nod to how much we'd loved Mr. Rogers when we were little. China had been around the house on Grand from time to time doing small stuff after Durka was diagnosed with cancer, but she had never been in the apartment. I looked at Grace to see if she had been expecting her. She looked as surprised as I was.

Grace spoke out loud, not making eye contact with China, "So who sent you?"

China answered quietly, "Doña Durka told me to come here if

anything happened to her. She said you would look out for me and my kids." She handed Grace a piece of paper with the address written in Durka's unmistakable script. We also knew that just because Doña Durka had written it didn't mean she had given it to China.

Grace still hadn't even looked at her. She took the paper and was busy moving things around in the hallway as if she might be making space for a fight. "What did Doña Durka think you could do around here? Or better yet, what do you think you can do?"

"I'm not sure what you have going on. I just know the little bit Doña Durka had me doing. I'm good with numbers and you already know I can kick ass."

This got everyone's attention on two fronts. It was an open dis, reminding Grace of that time China kicked her ass in front of Doña Durka's house because she'd seen her with Nene and gotten the wrong idea. It was a long time ago, but it had not been forgotten. Still, "good with numbers" is what really had our focus. For all we could do, and all that Grace was trying to make us learn how to do, we were, as a whole, math limited. Grace had dragged everyone who needed it, except me, through a GED program or made us finish high school. As a group, we could do the basics. A few of us were even in and out of community college. But none of us would ever have claimed to be good with numbers. When we ate out together, we'd throw money at each other because no one wanted to figure out how to split the bill or the tip. Grace and Sugar could do it, but they'd never loved it, and Grace had come to rely on her boy Chad far more than she liked. China claiming to be good with numbers gave her a clear purpose.

Grace asked, "Good how?"

"Good like good. Like I don't know. I always did good in math at school, did the books for my uncle's gym, took some accounting classes before dropping out of college. I'm good. I know what to do with them. Unlike most shit, numbers make sense, and they don't lie. Or when they do lie, you can force them to tell the truth if you know how. I like that." She was sweating in her tight khaki-colored Levi's with her Timberland boots. Only her sleeveless Yankees T-shirt showed she had any idea it was summer. Her premature gray streak was thick and wide across her pale forehead. She nervously pushed it back behind her ear.

"You think you can help us clean money and grow it?"

China shrugged her shoulders. "Doña Durka had to have people a lot better than me doing that kind of work. I mean I can do basic stuff, but I'd have to go back to school to do heavy shit like investing. If not school, then some kind of training or coaching. I don't doubt I can learn it, but I don't know it." It wasn't clear if China knew to hit that "I can learn it" button or had stumbled upon it by accident. Either way, it worked.

"Would you be willing to go back to school? To learn?" There was both caution and growing interest in Grace's tone. Grace saw potential whenever she heard anyone talk about learning something new or going back to school.

"I guess so. I mean, if you think it's worth it and that's part of my job. The thing is I gotta make some money. I got myself and two kids to look out for, and I try to help my little brother out. He's trying to go to college, trying to box too. I mean he's doing good, but I don't want him getting distracted by not having change in his pocket. Boys fall off easy like that."

"Nene looks out for his kids, doesn't he?"

China blushed, then jumped to her own defense, "Yeah, but that baby mama shit is not for me. He makes it seem like he's doing us a favor every time he gives me money, and he only looks out for them. I need to look out for my own damn self." China had trained since she was twelve in her uncle's gym. She was taut muscle from end to end. She had gone from boxing to MMA when that became a thing in the small underground gyms. She was still and calm except for the way she pulled her shoulders up and back like she had wings to spread. When Grace just stared at her, China jumped back in with, "I came because Doña Durka told me that if anything ever happened, I could turn to you. I always did low-key stuff for her, but Nene didn't like it, so I never tried to get in. He wasn't having it. You never seemed that interested either, so it's cool. If you want me to leave, I will."

China had a line of sweat running down the side of her face, but she didn't wipe it away. She also didn't leave. If she had done the books at her uncle's gym, she could do books elsewhere. Why would a girl with real-world skills, two little kids, and a man in this life already come looking for it herself? Most of us had gotten here feeling like we had nothing the world wanted. That didn't seem to be her case though. We had all come from a funeral for one of the strongest forces any of us had ever known and something about this didn't feel right, but then again nothing felt right.

I knew I wouldn't be making this decision anyway, so I stepped back a few inches to signal to Grace that if she had this in mind, then it would be what it had to be, but all on her. I played games like that all the time once I started nursing my dreams of escape. Standing a few inches away, turning my back when she was talking to us as a group, ignoring a phone call or a beep, answering on the second or third try. It pissed her off when she noticed, but it made me feel like I was preparing for something. Baby steps.

Grace spoke quietly to China, "Let's go to the back to finish this conversation," and then announced to everyone, "For the record, China is down with us, so make sure she knows how we operate. Carmen, help me show her the counting room." Only Sugar and Red had been paying enough attention to look at me as if to ask, *Did you know about this?*

We went into the back room, which was supposed to be a bed-room. We had turned it into an office and storage space. It was full of boxes, bags, scales, a desk, a chair, a bunch of calculators with printing paper, and a big boxy computer that college boy Chad had thrown into the mix. When we had shipments, mostly weed and coke, but increasingly huge amounts of pills, we'd bring them into the back room and divide it into our signature packaging. We never handled crack. Toro and his boys covered that. We didn't store large amounts of anything, and we kept everything moving as quickly as we got it. The back room had three closets. My clothes hung in two of them like placeholders for a life I did not know how to leave.

The third closet had reinforced locks that a locksmith had installed. Grace was the only one with the keys. Once we were all inside the room,

Grace locked the door behind us and punched China in the stomach as hard as she could. China went down on her knees more from surprise than from the hit. That girl was made of bricks, and it was not the first time Grace had taken a chance by hitting her. The last time hadn't turned out so great from all we'd heard. Grace grabbed China by the hair before she could get on her feet. "I don't trust you and I don't like that you came here without my permission. We both know that little piece of paper don't mean shit. You did say some things that made me like you some. But I want you to understand that liking you doesn't mean the same thing as trusting you. If you're here to spy on me, forget it. I have nothing to hide. But if you're here to really break free and make something of your own, then stop chasing Nene and start paying attention. It won't bother me to kill you if it comes to that. Nene will always look after his kids. Doña Durka looked out for me. You have no special position here, no protection, unless you earn it."

China looked to be thinking about a lot of things in that moment. She had to want to fight back, and could have, but she was showing the sort of discipline most of us didn't possess.

"Doña Durka didn't mention getting fucked up as part of my job. Is this some gang initiation bullshit? Cuz whatever, I can tolerate pain, but I ain't gonna put up with this kind of shit all the time."

Grace tugged harder on her hair, and said, "Doña Durka didn't give you a job. She sent you to me. You should understand that. And this won't need to happen again unless you create that need."

Grace pulled China up off her knees and opened the closet. On the top shelf sat the little yellow suitcase and the first scale Durka had given her in high school. Just below that, the custom-built safes. She opened all three to reveal stacks on stacks of hundreds and fifties in neat little rows. Even I didn't know about this, and it was being handed over to China like she had been here all along, and that felt downright stupid.

"I know what I got in there. I want you to run it through those counters, attach amounts to specific small groups, and figure out how to get it into bank accounts. Do nothing until you check with me, tell no one what you do for me, and soon Nene's money will look like a joke to you."

Just like that, we walked out and left her in there with all that cash. Before Grace locked her in from the outside, she offered a last bit of advice: "Knock if you need food or to go to the bathroom. We will come get you for dinner. Also, dye your fucking hair. You look like a ghost." Outside the door, I pulled Grace into the bathroom.

"You got anything you want to tell me?"

"Not at this time. Nope. Remember what I said about you and the questions."

"I hope you weren't stealing from Durka. Toro will kill you no matter how much you think he or she loved or loves you. Him and Nene will figure it out."

"I would never steal from the one who was feeding us, stupid. I'm not even stealing. I'm just reallocating resources from the clowns who don't know any better." She went on, "Don't go all 'I need the truth' on me now. Looking at me like I owe you something. You got your own shitty lies to deal with." She pulled away and looked me over from head to toe, resting her eyes on my belly a second too long. She gave me her back and added, "You turned out to be a real weak link and a super fake bitch. You lucky we go so way back."

· · ·

I sat at the edge of the tub in our midnight-blue sun, moon, and stars themed bathroom, lovingly painted and decorated by Teca, feeling kicked to the curb. Even though out was something I supposedly wanted, it came with an emptiness my baby was not yet real enough to fill. I locked the door and ran a bath. We had air conditioners in every major room, but the bathroom still had that sweaty New York humid that made a cool bath with an open window a familiar pleasure. I could see a corner of the real moon hanging low over the building next door, where Cheo, who looked out for us sometimes, lived stuck in 1977. Some deep wounds had left him stranded there. Today, he was playing his slow jams and Lavoe was singing about the woman he missed and waited for: "No importa tu ausencia, te sigo esperando, no importa tu ausencia, te sigo esperando." Lavoe was the voice of a people who long deep and wait long. I looked at my phone knowing what I'd find. Five missed calls from Pete. I didn't bother calling him back. The only thing he wanted to hear was that I was coming home. He loved this song too, but for now it was just me and Héctor Lavoe through the bathroom window, waiting and longing for everything at once.

I took off my clothes and stared down at my belly. It would soon be impossible to hide. It probably already was. It felt real and unreal, not yet solid. I had never dreamt of babies or loved dolls like some girls, so it was more like a "what the fuck" than an "oh my God" when I found out I was pregnant. Which didn't mean the baby wasn't already pulling me toward her like the moon pulls tides millions of miles away. I slipped under the water, body first and then my head. I tried to imagine my baby swimming inside of me. Pete had all the details. He knew how much it grew every week, and what it was doing. He was the one who wanted to know if it was a boy or a girl. I could wait. I would listen if they told us, but it was not what I needed. I referred to her as a girl out of respect since girls were mostly still received with dismay, people saying things like, "Pues, por ahí viene otra chancleta." Old slippers that could take a beating and give one too. I would be just as excited to have a son. A man in the making from my own body was its own miracle. I also didn't know when the whole boy/girl divide even began in there. I'm sure Pete knew though. He would read it to me eventually. I didn't need facts. I needed to connect with my baby alone. I needed to feel her knowing me. Looking for me. Wanting me. Needing me.

The tightness of the tub surrounded me like a womb while my thoughts drifted from my baby into memories of my mother, our mothers. For me and Grace they had always existed as a unit. We were the only two daughters of two sisters. We belonged to both and were claimed and abandoned in tandem, or by turns, depending on the year. I remembered my aunt, on the rare occasions when she wasn't high or furious, making fun of my mother, saying, "I couldn't even get pregnant by my-self. The minute you saw my baby you had to have one too. You were always following me around." I turned from side to side, held in place by the smooth, cool porcelain of the tub, and tried to imagine what it had been like when all we knew of our mothers was the quiet, watery inside. The home of their bodies before their words could wound us; before they could drag us through the wreckage of their lives like cans tied to a newlywed car. They had been hopeful mothers too, once, hadn't they? Grace would say no, but I felt like maybe.

A loud banging on the door scared the shit out of me. I popped up on instinct to grab a towel and look for my gun. Red laughed when she heard all the splashing and said, "I hope I didn't interrupt before you hit your high note, I would hate it if you did that to me. Anyway, no time for horny bitches, dinner is served, and the queen is making us wait for you, so hurry the fuck up."

· · ·

We sat down to steak with onions, maduros, white rice, and red beans. This time there was a salad with fresh avocado slices served on the real ceramic plates that Santa had insisted we buy even though no one ever wanted to do dishes. She claimed her food deserved more than paper plates. She was not wrong. It deserved plates of gold. We couldn't have the ritual of a meal after a burial at Doña Durka's house because of the chaos. There had been food, but none of us ate it. I was starving, but there was a whole thing we always did before we ate together in the apartment, so I sat there impatient.

China looked surprised. It was clear this was not what she expected. The desk chair had to be brought out for her. We had reached capacity at eight and now we were nine. She didn't say much. Grace waited as usual to see who might start the conversation, even if she sensed the introduction of a new face was going to keep people quiet. We of course "knew" China, just not like that. We didn't know China's backstory, and in a crew like ours, that shit mattered. It wasn't so much a rule as it was the magnet that had drawn us all together. We were a tribe of lost daughters born to mothers who had somehow refused or been unable to enact the good or even good enough mother; women who broke out, acted out, even at the expense of their kids, but mostly at the expense of themselves. Rebels and fuckups. Whatever you called them, they were all different, but the impact had been the same: each gave what she could, but it had not been enough. If China was going to belong, she'd need to share something good, and we were going to need to get it out of her.

Grace started talking about an article she had read in the newspaper. She pulled it out and passed it around so we could each read it and comment. That was our cue to start passing the plates. China looked up confused and asked, "God, I hate reading. Do you do this every time you eat?"

"So, the girl who loves numbers hates to read. You are in the wrong place, girl." Sugar laughed as she said it, then added, "Sometimes it feels like fourth grade, and we supposed to be keeping reading logs and shit. I been waiting for Grace to put one of those posters with our names on the wall with a little gold star sticker for everything we read. You know, to put some competition in it."

Grace laughed and said, "You know I can't believe I didn't think of that one myself."

Teca had the article in her hand as I read over her shoulder, chewing loudly. She looked at me and said, "Girl, move back. I don't need to hear you eat." It was about some study on teen pregnancy and sexually transmitted diseases. I wasn't a teenager anymore, but it caught my attention. Although we were all embodiments of the poor and statistical, there was an order of extremity and intensity. There were degrees of suffering even in a room that had hot as hell as a baseline. Santa, our chef and patron saint of all kind words and deeds, was the textbook case study. No known father, mother died of AIDS, foster home bouncer, sexually abused, high school dropout, teen mother, the list went on and on. She was also an amazing chef and had a gorgeous voice she would use to sing while she was cooking. But there were no statistics on that. Santa had no shame and would tell you all about it if you asked, sometimes even if you didn't. She wasn't like the rest of us with our secrets and our fake hard. She wore her life with pride.

"What happened to me ain't me, so why should I be ashamed?" Her favorite line after telling some horror story she had lived through: "I'm a work in progress. Don't give up on me though. Cuz I ain't done." She was the first to jump on the article.

"I don't know about all those statistics. Of course, they gonna find more STDs in pregnant teens. Like obviously we are having sex, then we go to the doctors more because we're pregnant. Them other girls just sitting there with their chochas on fire not telling nobody and spreading it around. What the fuck is the point of this study other than to say pregnant teens are a bunch of sucias? Why don't they do a study on the boys?"

"Cuz those pendejos won't go to the doctor till the shit is falling off," Teca threw in.

We were all laughing and splitting off into side conversations. But really, we wanted to hear Santa say it again. That we were not who they said we were, even if we had not yet figured out who we were; it was enough to hear one of us say it out loud. Teca changed the tone of the conversation. "My compliments as always to the chef, Santa. You always bring it. My aunt loves to watch all those corny-ass cooking shows. She likes to try new things like a spinach quiche, which sounds and looks nasty, but tasted kind of good. She makes the best tamales I have ever eaten. Ain't nobody doing no studies on her coming home from teaching her little runny-nosed kindergarten kids to make me tamales."

Santa faked shy and grateful before she answered, "Thank you. Praise is a nice change of pace in this group of ingratas. Get the recipe from her and I'll try it out. I've never made tamales, but I ate them once at a school party. But be prepared for my own twist, I don't exactly follow instructions well."

And just like that we were off talking about elementary school parties, the most positive memories many of us had of school, and favorite foods and recipes. Even Red threw in a story about her mother's corn beef and cabbage on St. Patrick's Day and how her first Puerto Rican neighbors had complained about the smell, but then always invited her and her sisters to dinner after her mother had died. She added in a quiet tone that was unlike her, "I don't know how that lady did it. Mrs. Nuñez. There were four of us, she had three of her own, and she would just bang on the pipes to let me know when dinner was ready. There was always a huge pot of food, enough for all of us."

"That is the Puerto Rican way, girl. Where one eats, ten can eat, and the pot is always on the stove in case somebody drops by. My abuela was like that, and my mom too, when she could." Santa came into focus slowly each time she spoke. Just when you thought you had her figured out, she opened some other dimension with a sentence or loving look or a hand on your back. It was like she fed us from her own severed head and broken heart. Sugar talked about her great-grandmother's tea from natural leaves in the garden and her lemonade. I spoke last. I could feel Grace watching me. She was careful not to reveal that she was uncomfortable with how much of what she had lived since moving in with Doña Durka I didn't really know or understand, or how much it had all meant to her. "I prefer to eat alone, but I remember liking school breakfast. You know early in the morning the cafeteria wasn't that crowded. The lunch ladies could pay more attention to you and ask about your hair or your homework. The cereal and the bananas always tasted good there." I was trying to think of a way to pull China in to see what we could get, but Grace jumped in first.

"I never ate a meal at a table other than in school until I got to Doña Durka's house. When I turned fifteen, she had a birthday dinner for me with cake and candles and my favorite food. It was so weird because it felt like I was watching a movie, you know, like who does that shit? I said something like that to her. She looked at me and said, 'A lot of people do it, mamita. You don't need a lot of money to make tostones, chuletas, and bake a cake. You just need to be paying attention.'"

Neglect was the hallmark of our existence, and even a little light shed into those corners felt like scalding heat. Red broke the tension by announcing, "I'm not having one of these corny-ass spill-your-heart-out dinners every day now cuz we sad and shit. What about you, Storm?"

Staring straight at China, she asked what we all wanted to know, "What's with the white hair? They got colors now, you know. I ain't even a real redhead." We all turned to look at her, surprised at her sudden honesty. "I mean I have that reddish-brown, ashy-blond, every color no color kind of hair that my father has, but my mother was a redhead. The real deal. I started going red after she died. Sometimes you gotta pick who you gonna be and you start with your colors." Without waiting for China to answer, Red started clearing the table.

Santa was quick to uphold our rituals and called out to Red, "You know, I'm not cooking for you ungrateful bitches if you just gonna act out."

China answered defensively, "My mother went gray at twenty-eight, and as soon as she started dyeing her hair, she left us. I went gray at twenty. I ain't leaving my kids and I ain't dyeing my hair."

Teca stood and gave her a high five. "I respect that. Don't let them mess with you and your hair. They be talkin' about how I'm destroying the ozone layer with hairspray. Haters, every last one of them. Like they even know what the ozone layer is cuz they read one damn article about it. Pay them no mind, so they will learn to mind their own business."

We all bumped and pushed as we helped with cleanup. It felt like we were outgrowing the apartment. China volunteered to dry and put away the dishes. It was past one in the morning by the time we finished. I knew I should have called Pete. I wasn't even sure who would stay in the apartment tonight. We couldn't all stay. I was waiting for Grace to ask me or make some sign that she was leaving for the safe house. There was still no TV in the living room, just piles of books and a sound system with speakers. Then there was Grace, the mother of wild things, sitting on the eggplant-purple couch looking lost and exhausted. The circles under her eyes, and the candy wrappers peeking out of her pockets, giving her away despite all the strong she was trying to front.

Sugar went into the living room and leaned into the doorway. "I don't know about y'all," she said, "but I'm hoping we can get some answers as to what happened to Doña Durka and what we doing next. Grace, you got words for us?"

Grace turned away to look out the window. "Not today, Sugar. I promise by tomorrow I will have some for you. We got a light load tonight, so just do your drops and come back in the morning. I'll have some words for you then." I waited for the indication that she wanted me to stay with her. Then she said, "Red, lock the door after everyone leaves."

. . .

I took a convertible from the dozen or so cars we kept in the garage on Jerome Avenue. I slipped into the soft leather front seat, put the top down and the AC on high, and exhaled. This was the freedom we had fought so hard for; I was going to feel it before I gave it all up.

I had no love for Brooklyn yet, but I had love for the Brooklyn Bridge and how crossing it in either direction made me feel somehow out of reach. I wasn't, but I liked to pretend Grace couldn't find me when I went there even though she was the one who'd brought me in the first place, or that Pete couldn't find me in the Bronx even if he knew every corner I covered there, other than the apartment, which no man that I knew of had any idea how to find. The shortest route from the Bronx to Brooklyn is the Triborough Bridge and the BQE. I used it sometimes for business purposes, but the long way offered the magic of the Hudson River along the West Side Highway, giving way to the majesty of the Brooklyn Bridge crossing the East River. I needed that ride to clear my head. If Grace was setting me loose, then it would go both ways. This is how I spent my days: flipping around like a fish gasping for air on dry land. I wanted out, but I didn't want to get left out. I wanted out, but it felt so much easier to breathe when I was in. I was ashamed of myself for not knowing how to do it better on my own.

. . .

When I came into the apartment, Pete was working on the mural he was painting for the baby in the farthest corner of the loft that he'd turned into our bedroom. He had designed a whole wall as the ocean with beautiful colored fish, mermaids, sea horses, and a coral reef. There were two little fish in the bottom corner that had shades of us: his little fish with a cleft on its chin and short, tight, curly hair with black-rimmed glasses; my little fish with a big pouty mouth, long, loose, curly hair, and a squinty look he put there to make fun of me for not wearing my glasses.

"I like the two fish at the bottom. They're kind of cute."

"Yep, I was going to paint a giant shark trying to eat them, but I didn't want to scare the baby."

"Again? Is there going to be even one day we don't talk about this? Can I put my bag down before we start?"

"I don't really see how there can be. Can you at least answer your fucking phone? Do you know what it feels like to sit here and wonder if you are even alive? Then you show up at two in the morning freshly showered wearing different clothes. Like what am I supposed to do with all this?"

He stood and stretched his arms over his head the way he had been doing since I met him, probably way before me even. Pete stretched his long wiry frame like some people shake their leg, wring their hands, or crack their knuckles. It always made me want to stand close to him because as soon as I did, he would bring his arms down and pull me in. I couldn't decide if he was doing it to keep from hitting me or crying or packing his bags. I knew he'd never hit me, even if he was way past frustrated with me. He looked like he was twisting himself inside out trying to save us. I started taking off my clothes. If he ignored me, it would hurt every soft spot I had, but I wanted to try. I stood as close to him as I could, without tripping over the paint cans, pretending I was looking for a T-shirt. He pulled me in. I burst into tears, and he took off his T-shirt to wipe my face. I pressed it to my nose, inhaled deep. He smelled like vetiver and cedar. It was an oil his grandmother had made for him. She taught him to use it instead of cologne. He also just smelled like Pete— paint, sweat, and Ivory soap. His body was warm and hard and covered in a thick layer of soft body hair everywhere. My head only reached the top of his chest. I buried myself in hope every time my forehead came to rest on the small patch of chest hair that was already turning gray. It was only a few hairs, but I loved them more than all the others. They made me believe in the future.

"You act like you didn't know me before I got pregnant. Like I just sprang out of the closet or something and yelled surprise and by the way this is how I make all my money!"

He put his head on top of mine and whispered, "Shhh, we don't need to do it again right now. Let's just be here, alone. Together."

I threw myself back on the pile of pillows in every shade of blue and stared at the ceiling he had covered in glow-in-the-dark stars because I'd once said I always wanted them as a kid. Pete never pulled any kind of shit, except what I could not deal with, especially trying to take care of me and be that guy. The harder he tried, the more I hated him. I could not explain why.

I whispered to him and to the baby, "It'll be over soon. Doña Durka's gone. You have to believe me."

"I wish I could. But right now, it doesn't matter. You came home. I'm still here. That is what we have."

Pete was gentle everywhere except in bed and on the canvas. He lost himself in those two places. He watched my body for cues, especially my face, and never held back unless I seemed uncomfortable. If I did, he'd always ask, "Is this okay?" He grabbed me in chunks now that there was so much to grab, and held himself on one arm as he turned me over and bit me softly from my neck all the way down my legs. He turned me over and buried himself in dreams of who I might be someday. For a little while at least, I was sure I could live without ever seeing anyone other than him and our baby again for the rest of my life.

. . .

I had only slept a few hours but stayed in bed watching the light start to come in through the window, listening for the sound of birds. Pete lived in a world where the birds had names, sounds, and migration patterns; before him they had all been just birds to me, or pigeons, if I noticed them at all. We grew up in the same New York, but you would not know it by how we talked about birds. Pete loved to test himself. He would listen to their song before looking out the window. He had been teaching me their names and sounds like his grandmother had taught him about the birds of Brooklyn, and those she'd loved in the mountains of Puerto Rico. I strained to hear something I might ask him about, or that would make him see I was learning the difference between a crow and a blue jay. He was in a deep sleep no light or birdsong would be interrupting, so I got out of bed.

I sat on the couch and opened my purse. There were two calls from Grace on the new Motorola. She'd also sent a backup code on the beepers we hadn't let go of yet. I walked to the bathroom to call her without waking Pete. She picked up on the first ring.

"Pack your bags cuz we going on a road trip."

"Road trip?"

"No time for questions. Get your fat ass over here. Bring a sun hat and a bathing suit. We going to Disney World." She laughed and hung up the phone.

. . .

Pete was following me back and forth from the closet to the suitcase, getting in my face. "This is a trip you were supposed to make with me and our baby. How can you not see that? Have you even looked at the little book I gave you? It's all about making memories, sharing stories. This is too much."

"It's not that kind of trip. It's not like we're going to Disney World to go to Disney World. She wants us to look at some land investments in Florida. They are cash only and it might help us clean up and get out. But also, I think she just really needs a break. She wants her girls with her, so taking the kids to Disney is a way to do that. That's not a bad thing."

"Why don't you take a break from what you're doing instead? Doesn't your organization offer maternity leave?"

"I can't have this argument again. I just can't."

"Well, I'm getting pretty tired of it too. To be honest, if you go on this wild ride across state lines with all this, I can't promise I'll be here when you get back." He had never threatened to leave me. His face was drawn down into his chest with sadness as he said it, but when he looked up his eyes burned with rage.

I could not explain why I felt relieved, but I did. Finally, he was showing some self-respect. I looked him dead in the eye, closed my bag, and answered, "Do what you need to do to get right with yourself. That's what I'm doing. Hopefully, we will both be right by the time this baby gets here."

4

THE MAGIC KINGDOM

The trip to Miami as a crew was a requirement so the suppliers could meet Grace. The game had been changing fast, but some transactions still required direct introductions. Doña Durka had left instructions about when to go and who to speak to first. It was a way to make clear we were our own thing even without her around. Grace's desire to regroup happened to coincide with some problems the suppliers were having of their own.

It was Santa's idea, not Grace's, to take advantage of the trip and bring the kids. Key crew members did this kind of shit all the time with Toro and Nene. For them, a trip to Vegas or the Dominican Republic was like a corporate business retreat. Grace took to the idea because she wanted Toro to see it only as a trip to Disney for the kids. She needed to keep him guessing because, as far as he knew, we were out of the game now that Durka was gone. He didn't believe it, but he didn't know enough to prove we weren't. We operated in completely different settings, so it wouldn't be hard to keep working off his radar. A trip to Disney felt like a good way to send a signal that her death had been an ending, and now we'd go off and be something else. I also knew that if the timing was manic, it was a sure sign that Grace was under fire.

Since we were kids, the more cornered she felt, the more dramatic and consequential her actions. Where I was trying to survive, Grace was always daring life to try her. Maybe the trip to Disney was also me daring Pete to try me. Our plan involved taking the minivans we usually used to look like soccer moms on our suburban drop-offs and moving along I-95 south undetected. We pretended this was bold and not reckless.

. . .

When I reached the block where the apartment was located, Grace was waiting for me on the corner. She jumped in my car all nervous energy and strapped on her seat belt.

"Toro and Nene want to meet before we leave for Miami. I said no. But Nene said some shit that got under my skin, so I said yes, but that you were coming with me."

"What did he say?"

"Never mind. Just drive to the house. Red is going to be with Sugar at the diner. That way they're a few blocks away in case anything weird goes down. Let's go."

The drive was quiet. She didn't want to talk. She lowered the volume on WBLS and stared out the window as I crossed Fordham in heavy morning traffic. I turned left onto Davidson Avenue and went around on Kingsbridge to turn left on Grand from a long enough distance to see what was going on around the house. We had been there less than twenty-four hours ago, and already it felt smaller, like every time we went back it was shrinking. I parked in the driveway.

A young kid was guarding the front door from the porch instead of the inside window. My mind started running a list of things that never would have gone down while Durka was alive as we went in through the side entrance and found a group of guys playing cards in the kitchen. They just nodded as we walked past. We didn't even know half of them, and all of them had their guns visible. Durka had rules about who was allowed to come inside the house with weapons. The order she brought to the chaos was made obvious by her absence. I knew Grace was feeling it too, even if she seemed distracted and out of place.

Durka's office door was open when we passed, but there were no fresh flowers or incense burning. Grace walked ahead into the dining room with its heavy, dark wooden table and high-backed chairs. The thick, forest-green, velvet curtains were closed, and the room was dark. It felt like a waiting area in a funeral home. Toro was sitting in Durka's usual seat at the head of the table. Nene to his left where Grace usually sat. I stayed by the door because I didn't know where to sit. Grace sat herself at the opposite head of the table, leaving four empty chairs between them. Toro laughed.

"No kiss, no hug. Nothing. Just like that." His face was soft as he said it. His mouth turned down under a new goatee that had a sprinkle of gray hairs. Toro had always been clean-shaven. The lines around his eyes and across his forehead were deep. It was as if the glamour of him had faded overnight, revealing the raw unsteady power of a wounded bull.

Grace answered quietly, "I'm not in the habit of kissing people who treat me like shit anymore. You were here last time I was here, right? That was you?"

"Why you sitting so far? I mean. I know why you sitting there. But we don't need to play these games. We family. I know what that means. Probably better than you."

Toro leaned in, rested his forearms on the table, and focused all his energy on Grace. He was pulling hard on old tricks that hadn't worked in years. She sat with her back straight. Steady. Calm. Nene shifted uncomfortably in his chair, scanning the room. His eyes moved from me to Grace before looking back at Toro and shaking his head. Grace stared straight ahead at Toro. She acted like she didn't even know Nene was in the room.

I stared at the wall-to-wall wooden cabinet bursting with all the things Grace had helped Durka collect. Waterford Crystal sat next to Williams Sonoma serving dishes shaped like turkeys and pumpkins—a mismatch of money and dreams that showed no commitment to any one way of being rich; it was more like a museum honoring the freedom of having money and no one around to tell you what having it was supposed to look like. Grace could tell you where everything came from. I could tell you how old she had been when that brand or store came into her awareness. Her teen dreams were written in that china cabinet the same way Red's were in her basketball trophies and rock concert ticket stubs. Toro's dreams had been carved into Grace. He looked to be trying to get some of them back.

Toro cleared his throat and let out a long sigh. "Okay, so I didn't call you here to—"

Grace interrupted him, "You didn't call me here. You don't call me anywhere. You invited me and I decided to come. So just tell me exactly what it is you want to talk about."

Nene, frustrated from the start, ran his hands across his face. Toro smiled. He got up from his seat, put his gun on the table, and gently raised his hands in the air.

"Not everything has to be a fight, Grace. We don't need to fight. We just need to come to some agreements, you know, we need to clear some shit up."

"Like what? I feel clear."

Toro moved to our side of the table and sat in the chair to her right. Grace leaned back when he pushed his chair closer to hers. He drew the circle tight around them by inserting his knee slightly between her legs. Her eyes grew wide, but she held his without looking away. They weren't touching. But any release of tension on either side would bring their legs into contact.

"I know you ran some small-time shit for my mom in the suburbs. She had dreams of taking the drugs out the hood and turning them loose out there, but those places have rules just like we do, and plenty of drugs. I'm sure you've learned all that. I'm willing to let you keep a cut for running it, but I need to be brought in on what exactly it is. My mother liked to keep secrets. But secrets are not good for business. She has all these locked drawers and cabinets, and nobody knows where she hid the keys."

Nene called out from the other end, "I'm sure you know where those keys are, Grace. So turn them over. It's not like we won't open them one way or the other."

Toro shot him a look to shut him down. "I told you I would handle this, bro. Don't. Just don't. You ain't here to talk. Not today."

Toro leaned in on Grace till they were close enough to kiss. He kept moving his hands like he might touch her face or hair, but he didn't. Grace relaxed her shoulders like she was somewhere familiar. They shared small space in a way that revealed a history of tenderness. He closed his eyes as he spoke her name only inches from her ear.

"Grace, Grace, Grace. Beautiful little Grace."

I didn't like how close he was sitting or how deep he was leaning. I remembered when she was falling for Toro's version of love and how it had, for a short while, eased her suffering. It made me even like him a little to have seen Grace so happy, but I had never trusted him. Grace leaned back in her chair as if she had only now noticed his closeness. Toro did not miss a beat. He followed her smallest body movements. They moved in slow motion like tigers that might sit there and smell each other, or just as easily bite at the neck.

"We both miss her, Grace. To be honest, I miss you too. We had a unique thing here. We both done shit to fuck it up. I know that. But only you and me really know what went on. This is between us. We both in danger too. Right? Like who the fuck knows what's going on out there and who they coming for next? Maybe you know something that can protect us? Maybe I do? We are safer together than we are apart. You know that."

Grace surprised us both by putting her hand over his, tenderly patting it, then yanking away fast. Toro folded in at the waist like her touch had burned. She turned from Toro to Nene and back to Toro before answering.

"Right, so you want me to tell you shit that your own mother didn't trust you with while she was alive? You also want to make me believe that what only I know, and I built, somehow belongs to you? This is your peace offering? Fuck you and you too, Nene. It's not my problem if you don't pay enough attention to what is going on right under your fucking noses. You got what you got and that's it. Funny enough, on paper, half that shit you got is mine as your legal wife, but I'm happy to earn my own out there. I'll get a job. I'll figure it out."

Nene couldn't resist. "You don't sound like nobody applying for a job. You sound like you got one."

She pushed herself back from the table. The chair made a loud screeching sound, then a bang as it tipped back and hit the wall. Looking straight at Toro, she said, "I'm not fucking with you. If you really want to talk, then call me. We talk alone. We have always been separate, and whatever you think you'll find in those cabinets and drawers you won't understand anyway. So just leave that shit alone. Ain't none of you even close to who she was. You lucky she gave you what she did. Just make it work with what you have and what you know. That's what I'm gonna do."

Nene stood and banged on the table so hard it made the cabinet shake. He looked about to lose it. "I told you she thinks we're stupid. I told you that shit! She's playing you like a little bitch."

Toro yelled at Nene, "I told you to shut the fuck up. This is my fucking wife. I will handle her. Go see what you can do about yours." Nene wiped his hand across his mouth, trying to hold in what was spilling out from every pore.

Toro pulled out his chair as if to make space for Grace to walk through, then pushed it back hard to cage her between the chair and the table. I moved closer, but Nene was already at my right blocking me. Toro's eyes looked watery, the veins in his hands visible across the grip he had on the chair. His face was red and raw.

"If this is how you want it to go down, just know that when you leave here today you just become one more player out there. I ain't never gonna protect you."

Grace practically spit in his face when she said, "You never did."

Toro was trembling when he responded, "For the record, my mother never gave me shit my father hadn't built."

Toro pulled the chair back to release her, and then threw it after her as she walked out. By then a few of the guys from the kitchen had rushed in to see what was going on.

Nene stepped aside so I could leave and said, "Be careful who you follow. Shit is real. Your man is right. You might end up dead." Just his mention of Pete's fears brought new terror. What exactly did they know and how?

When I got outside, Grace was already walking fast in the direction of Fordham Road. I got in the car and pulled up alongside her at the light.

"Get in."

"Nah, I need to walk. Meet me by the garage."

My heart was racing. I had pressure points from head to toe and they all felt pressed. I was tired of holding back, so I called out the window, "You really think what just happened in there had nothing to do with China showing up as soon as Durka died? Nene's ride or die shows up out of the blue at our door and you lock her in with the cash you stole. Why you making this easy for them?"

Grace was looking straight ahead as she banged hard on the hood of the car and made me jump. "I didn't steal anything! You let me know when you ready to run this shit. Till then, stay in your motherfucking lane."

I leaned on the horn hard. I knew she hated that shit. I also didn't know what else to do. She gave me the finger without looking back. I saw Red pull up on her motorcycle at the next corner. I need to walk, my ass. She already had Red on standby.

I turned left on Fordham and again on Jerome. I was driving in circles. I couldn't catch my breath. I thought of the baby and slowed my breathing by going deep and counting to ten. I pulled over by the church that looked like an old haunted graveyard, across from the municipal parking lot. We had walked past this church so many times, on our way to or from St. James Park, without ever reading the plaque right there in front of me: *St. James Episcopal Church, built in 1865.* Behind the chipped black paint of the iron gates there was a tree full of crows making a racket. A black cloud of crows. A murder of crows, Pete would correct me. A murder of crows on Jerome Avenue. There had probably been more in 1865. That is how the vulnerable survive. We stick together. This was the story I told myself, the reason I had to stay.

I drove to the garage closest to the apartment. Everyone was there preparing for the trip to Miami. Toro was right about one thing, any one of us alone was a fucking disaster. But all of us together had the air of good and right and safe. We were safer together. It was impossible not to get high off the fumes of that kind of love.

. . .

Our caravan included three minivans and the nine of us, along with Sugar's kids, Serena, Victoria, and Michael; and China's, Josué and Damaris; and Santa's, Anthony and Julissa. We packed almost nothing. The plan was to hit a mall in New Jersey for a shopping spree as our first rest stop. The road trip itself was supposed to be a joyride with speed limits and video players showing Disney movies nonstop. The kids all had headphones, so we played our music loud and had our own fun. We were doing our "Money Ain't a Thang" trip and ready to spend it fast and free. Not one of us had ever had the carefree youth you hear so much about, and so we lived it all in one shot. It could be argued it was all we had been looking for from the start.

Our first sleepover stop was in North Carolina. Even though we could all afford a room of our own, we did the old-school four of us get a room, and everyone else wait in the car and then pile in. The truth was we were a lot to take in if you saw us all together. A stray lone wolf is scary, but a pack of wolves surrounding you is terrifying. We knew that. We had not invented it, but once we understood it, we cultivated everything from hairstyles, to jewelry, to the volume and tone of our voices to shift the energy we gave off. All nine of us together did not mean we posed any danger, even if it felt like a flood to the unprotected; it just meant we did not mean to be the ones who felt endangered.

The next day we took a little detour to visit Sugar's great-grandmother in Georgia. She was ninety-five years old and had never met any of Sugar's kids. Sugar hadn't been back that often. She'd been sending her great-grandmother money, but was careful to never send too much. Sugar explained that we only had one chance with Granma Helen. "Granma not about that life at all. So, we gotta go in real humble. Leave all your chains and rings and shit in the car. She don't care for nothing that glitters if it ain't the sun."

I landed on Granma Helen's porch seeking relief from the southern midday heat; even the short walk from the car had been too long. We spent an afternoon drinking fresh-squeezed lemonade on a bench right under the tree where she had picked the lemons. Sugar walked the garden with Granma, who was pointing out herbs for her to take home, and from behind, other than the white hair, they looked exactly the same. It was her great-grandmother's body, thick and strong, tall and wide, that made Sugar and Destiny appear so different. Sugar carried weight in the world and filled spaces. It wasn't till I saw her bending, pulling weeds and herbs, alongside Granma Helen, that I realized a body was something that came to you from somewhere else. That it wasn't just you making it up as you went along eating cheeseburgers or rice and beans. Sugar even laughed like her granma holding herself to one side, waving at whatever it was she found so amusing as if to make it go away. It made me think about my baby and if she would look anything like my mother, and how that might make me feel. Destiny, according to Sugar, looked like their mother.

Granma Helen stood by the door to the house and waved us all in. "Come on now before the food gets cold." Sugar was already moving around the kitchen and signaled Santa to join her.

There was a picture of Sugar and Destiny's mom, Happy, in the living room. Granma Helen saw me eyeing it and picked it up. She said, "She was pregnant with Sugar there. Tall and skinny even eight months along. You could easily mistake Destiny for her. But that there is Sugar in her belly. Sweetest baby. That's how she got her name. Beautiful mama, beautiful baby girl. Too bad beauty ain't all you need."

The way Sugar and Destiny told it, they were born to a stripper named Happy (they claimed to not even know her real name); raised by her best friend, Loretta; and then spent summers in Georgia with their great-grandmother. According to Sugar they'd cramped Happy's style.

Granma Helen added to the story as if she knew it was only half told, "Ain't one of us born broken, and cracks along the way ain't signs of it either, and neither is dancing on a pole the worst a woman could do." She put the picture down.

After lunch, Granma Helen went out on the porch with Victoria and Serena. Santa called us in to help with cleanup in the kitchen.

Teca broke the flow, sucking her teeth and saying, "Why everywhere we go, even on vacation, got dishes? Why?"

Santa wasted no time to answer, "Cuz you eat, bitch. That's why. It ain't magic."

I watched Michael from the window over the sink playing on a swing with the other kids. You could see them all laughing. I wondered how we could want so much for our kids and still not know how to get it or give it or even have it ourselves.

• • •

Granma Helen cried as we left and held each of Sugar's kids to her chest as she called out to Sugar, "Don't be getting into no fool trouble like your mama now. That child was always too Happy for her own good. Watch out for your baby sister. She got that Happy blood in her. You can tell. Come visit sooner. Don't wait till I die."

Destiny teared up and called out, "Don't talk like that, Granma. You ain't gonna die no time soon."

Granma Helen shook her head and insisted, "It will be sooner than later, so just be sure you get back here before I go."

I was the last one to leave. Something about the long history of family and name and love made me think of Pete. I went to say goodbye.

Granma Helen held me tight. She looked me straight in the eye as if she knew I might be the worst trouble her great-granddaughters would ever find, but also that we mostly get into a mess to get out of the ones we're already in. "You be careful out there and pay attention to your driving. You got half my bloodline in those cars. You also have yours." She said it with affection and a deep sense of blessing as she looked at my belly, which I kept thinking was well hidden, but obviously wasn't. She laughed before she added, "I ain't a witch or nothing, but my mother was a midwife and me and my sister were too. Not hard to see if you know what to look for. Take good care of yourself. Just cuz your body knows what to do, don't mean you do. It also don't make it easy. Nature ain't never been easy. Ask a hurricane."

Once we were in the car, I asked Sugar, "What about your grandmother? I mean you call her Granma, but she's your great, right?"

"Oh, she died giving birth to my mother, so this grandma acted like my mother's mother, and then her and Loretta shared raising me and Destiny."

Destiny chimed in, "It's funny how Mom's name was Emilia, but according to Granma she was such a happy baby they nicknamed her Happy, and it stuck. I don't think she ever was that. She felt like a fake happy to me. Who knows?" She closed her eyes as she rubbed her long fingers down her neck, touching parts of her mother she didn't even realize she had, and trying to know her just the same. Motherlessness was also something that got passed on. Weird as it was, it came from our mothers.

• • •

We pulled up to Disney and everyone lost it. The kids started banging on the car doors, screaming as soon as they saw that damn castle glittering in the sunlight as if the magic fairy dust they used in the commercials was real. Not one of us had ever been, one more thing to add to the growing list of places we had seen because of Grace. She looked overwhelmed, but happy as hell as the kids jumped out of all three cars and she tried to pull them in around her. At the gates where they took our tickets, we crossed a border into make-believe. The underpass in the castle reminded me of the one near the fountain in Central Park, but what stood out to me the most was how clean everything was despite the thousands of people moving around, eating and drinking. On the other side of the castle, we split up. Grace arranged shifts for taking Michael, Josué, Anthony, and Julissa on the kiddie rides then went off to get on the bigger rides with Serena, Victoria, and Damaris. It was a way to make sure we all got a little time with the kids and some to ourselves, a gift to the moms in the group that I did not yet fully appreciate. Teca and Remy soon became obsessed with that stupid ride "It's a Small World After All." They made us get back on line eight times and sang the song all day long. It felt fake to me, all the cultures, languages, and races in one place, happy and singing along.

We bought every single thing anyone asked for—we were the Magic Kingdom's ideal visitors even if they didn't know it. Destiny, who looked like a real princess every day of her life, ran around wearing a pointy princess hat with the little veil hanging off and like ten beaded neck-laces. After lunch in the German Beer Hall, Grace seemed restless and tired. I knew there was more than Disney on her mind, but she wouldn't speak or even stand next to me. There was nothing I could do but watch till she opened the door for contact.

After a trip through the castle, we stopped at another gift shop. Grace looked over at Destiny and said, "You know, there is more to want than a prince and a crown." Destiny rolled her eyes and bought another plastic necklace with a Pocahontas medallion on the end of it.

Grace moved on to Remy and said, "With all the real bling you got, why you buying fake shit?"

Remy snapped back, "Mija, lighten up, we're in fucking Disney World. Why'd your ass bring us here if you didn't want us to have any fun?"

Grace rolled her eyes and then went for China, who still didn't really belong. I had started to notice how she met Grace at her same level of intensity, which made me think Doña Durka had maybe sent her to look out for Grace. Loud enough for the cashier to hear, Grace said to her, "You can knock dudes out in a single punch. Why are you buying that shit for your daughter? You really got any Prince Charming stories for her?"

China was calm and sure, rocking her gray streak under a purple velvet crown her daughter had put on her head. "Yeah, I know there's more to life than that. I also kinda feel like everybody is always going after what girls like. Like nobody talking about don't let boys wear blue or play with cars or make them play with dolls. I know the shit is fake, but it makes little girls feel sacred and powerful to pick their own stuff. It's like they remember we were queens and shit. I'm down with that. My daughter can like glitter and kick ass. She don't need to choose. She can have both."

Everybody who heard it felt it. Grace looked away and said nothing more. Destiny gave China two thumbs up and did a little victory dance.

By the end of the night even Grace had a crown and a wand. We were watching the fireworks, high on cotton candy, when Serena went up to her and said, "You the real queen, so you have to wear one."

Grace had no choice but to bend her head and let Serena joyfully crown her queen. It was scary what Serena had put together without being told. Grace was game faced as she waved the wand around like it was magic that gave her the power to buy us whatever we wanted or needed. It was June in Orlando hot. Our clothes were sweat-stained rags sticking to every inch of skin. I kept self-consciously pulling my T-shirt off my belly, and caught Red smiling at me like the evil witch in *Snow White*.

Once the kids got tired of asking for things, it felt like time to go. While we were sitting on benches near the entrance, bags spilling out all around us, Santa came up with the idea of buying all the kids an oversized stuffed animal.

Sugar pressed her, "Even the kids are tired, Santa. Let's go."

"Nah, these are going to make for a great group picture. You'll see."

I didn't understand what a giant Minnie Mouse, Mickey, Goofy, Donald Duck was about, but figured Santa was feeding her childhood dreams like the rest of us. I passed my giant Minnie Mouse to Sugar and said, "I need to make a quick stop at the bathroom. I'll meet you by the cars."

I snuck off to buy something for the baby. I was drawn to pink, but settled for a *Lion King* golden yellow onesie with a matching hat. Boy or girl could shine with the sunrise behind Pride Rock. The clothes were so tiny. I rushed back and stuffed the rolled little package into my plastic bag full of nonsense. Grace, Sugar, and Red had gone to bring the cars to the entrance.

Anthony struggled to get his head over Giant Mickey's ear. He asked Santa, "Ma, we didn't even ask for these. Why we gotta carry them now?"

"It ain't all fun and games, papito. Sometimes you gotta work. Just sit tight and hang on to Mickey."

· · ·

We drove down to Miami from Orlando singing "It's a Small World After All" till we were sick of it. Our suppliers gave us the address to a furniture warehouse in Miami. It was at the end of a long, dark street lined by majestic palm trees. It was easy to see how those trees made everyone feel like they were living in paradise. Inside the gates, small details made it clear it wasn't only furniture they were storing. The guy on the walkie-talkie sitting less than a hundred feet behind the security desk, and the machine gun he was barely hiding. The sniper on the roof. Miami was in-your-face different. It was not our world.

We didn't take the kids to the warehouse with us. They were staying in a hotel a few miles away with Sugar, Remy, Teca, China, and Destiny. The plan was to swing through to pick them up when it was all packed and ready. It was only me, Santa, Red, and Grace. The idea of riding back through eight states with those kids, and whatever we were here to pick up, made me nervous like I had just discovered that was the plan. If all that we had done before felt like things we had just fallen into, this was clearly on purpose and full of will and hard choices we could blame on no one but ourselves. Once we were past the gate, there was no way to turn back without getting killed for being suspicious; even looking back felt risky. All our bodies shifted in the car as we moved toward what we knew might turn us into something not one of us had set out to be.

Grace got out first. She shook hands with a tall, skinny man standing behind a round table covered with take-out food. He waved us forward and Grace walked with him to the other end of the warehouse. There was nothing special about it. Only the guards in every corner with semi-automatics tipped you off, but you had to look for them. Santa was taking the lead as boxes were opened. She was sitting on a sawdust-covered floor surrounded by rows of furniture-sized cardboard boxes and metal barrels filled with cocaine and weed and bags of pills. Santa carefully cut open the seams of the giant Disney characters to fill them with the drugs we were taking. She added as much stuffing as was needed or could fit, then carefully sewed them all back together. She had the most wide-ranging skill set of any one of us, which made her useful in a hundred different ways. She was also calm and steady in everything she did. She sat there, in her Minnie Mouse T-shirt, sewing like it was the only thing she had on her mind. I bent over her and whispered, "How much longer?"

She looked up at me, annoyed. "I'm not a fucking sewing machine. I'm working as fast as I can. If any of these other bitches could do anything, I wouldn't have to do it by myself." I could have taken that personally since I was among the bitches who couldn't do half the shit she knew how to do. I was about to try threading a needle when a spasm down the right side of my back froze me in place. My body knew way before I did that things were changing on the deepest of levels.

In that split second there was a loud bang. All guns were drawn including mine and Santa's. Grace and Red had our backs as they stood by the driver side of each car. The suppliers had theirs out as well. They sent someone to check on the noise. Grace motioned for Red to follow.

Luis, the man that had greeted Grace, said, "Sorry about that. One of the trucks that came in banged up a barrel. Calma. No hay nada." The guy by the door, who was also holding the money, signaled his men to lower their guns. Red gave the nod that confirmed we could lower ours as well.

Santa went back to sewing, though her hands were shaking a little. I put one hand on her back and used the other to massage my side. I could feel our hearts racing as if they were both beating in my own chest.

Santa finally looked up and said, "We good to go!" The toys were heavy, and Luis had some of his men help us pile them in the vans.

He shook Grace's hand as we left, then looked at us and back at her as he said, "You might want to bring some extra help next time."

Right then a woman parked her car in front, opened her window, and waved Grace over. Grace signaled for me to get closer, but then held up her hand and motioned to stay back a little. It was the first time she had spoken to me directly on this trip, and she hadn't even used any words.

"Grace, hija de Doña Durka, no?"

"Sí."

"Cuídate mucho. La calle no es ningún relajo."

"Yo lo sé."

The woman motioned with a visibly veiny, unsteady hand for Grace to come closer. It seemed like a warning when she patted Grace's hand, rolled her window back up, and drove away. I had chills from head to toe. We all knew who she was. Doña Durka had told Grace the story, and Grace had told us. The legends were long about the woman running Miami and killing anyone who pissed her off or crossed her in any way, particularly ex-husbands and lovers. She wore a little white fedora that looked like Doña Durka's straw hat. Durka had sometimes described their encounter by saying, "No es lo mismo llamar el diablo que verlo llegar." That was the truth. Grace started repeating it, especially when I seemed surprised by something I was asked to do. It was not the same to call the devil as it was to hear her knock on your door, know exactly who she was, and open it anyway.

· · ·

At the hotel, the four of us waited with the vans outside while the others brought the kids down in their pajamas. The full moon coming through the palm trees no longer felt special. It felt like a spotlight on my back. I'd had enough of Miami. I was ready to be home, with or without Pete waiting for me. We had come traveling light and were returning with suitcases, souvenirs, and a new kind of stress I had never known.

Grace came up to Sugar and said, "I don't want the kids to go in the car carrying the stuff."

Sugar answered, "Too late for that, girl. If we do get stopped, even for a traffic light, it will look mighty suspicious to have all those toys with no kids in the car. We should spread the supply and the kids in every vehicle. We all be taking this risk together. We all carry it together." She added, "It's fine. I'll ride with mine in here," as she put each one into a seat and strapped them in with their seat belts, then called Destiny to ride with her.

Grace, Red, and Santa were driving the vans first. I rode in the front with Grace. We left Miami at three in the morning.

Serena was looking out the window. She tapped the glass softly with her glitter-painted nails and said, "I like how the moon is following us. It's like she's protecting us."

Grace answered, "Not everything that follows you is out to protect you."

. . .

After we switched drivers, I took over. Destiny gave me and Grace a little military salute and said, "It sure was a good idea to make us all get driver's licenses."

Destiny was the baby of our crew. Her taking notice of what it meant to be capable gave me the feeling that whatever Grace had in mind was working. It would all be worth it. I had to believe. Mostly, I couldn't sleep when anyone else was driving. Pete had made me stop drinking coffee, so face washing at every rest stop was all I had to stay alert. Grace wasn't sleeping much either and still hadn't spoken a word to me. She finally dozed off somewhere near Maryland and woke to sirens howling and pulling us over.

My heart was racing at a pace I did not feel I could sustain. The other cars had instructions to keep moving no matter what, so we only had ourselves to worry about. Grace turned around from the front and started pinching the kids hard in the back seat, which got everybody worked up and crying. By the time I rolled down the window, the kids were carrying on. The officer scanned the car, taking in Sugar's three crying kids, and the stuffed toys in the back row, before turning back to me.

"License and registration, please."

"Yes, officer."

"That's quite a racket you got going there. Whose kids are they?"

Sugar answered without pause.

"Mine, sir. I don't know what's got into them. They tired I suppose."

"You ladies are going pretty fast. Close to eighty in a sixty-five-mile-an-hour zone."

"I'm sorry, officer," I jumped in. "The truth is two of the kids were crying about needing to use the bathroom, and I might have been rushing to the next rest stop to avoid an accident."

"Yeah, well, you could have been in a worse accident as a result. Looks like you guys are coming from Disney. Did you have fun?" He looked over at the kids, all of whom had learned at a young age that cops are to be taken seriously. They nodded their heads as they dried their tears. His eyes rested on the back seat as Sugar moved to soothe them.

"Ladies, I'm going to let you off with a warning. You did a good thing by taking your kids to Disney and all, but you need to keep safety first. I'm calling your plate in, so if you go over the speed limit again and they catch you farther up the road, they will be giving you a ticket and a full workup. Lots of dangerous drivers on the road. No need to help them out by being reckless yourselves. Stay safe and try to get these kids to a bathroom." He smiled at the kids as he said, "My own kids drove me crazy on the drive back from Disney."

"Thank you, officer."

He handed me my paperwork and we closed the windows. As soon as we saw him climb back in his car, Grace hugged and kissed the kids and apologized for pinching them. Sugar started laughing.

"What the fuck is so funny?" I yelled between a laugh and a cry and a spasm in my back that felt like it might cripple me.

"'License and registration, please,'" Sugar repeated, and then added, "You almost shit that license right in your pants." Sugar laughed so hard and so much she almost got us all laughing.

"I don't know why the fuck you all laughing. That shit was not funny," Destiny, who we all thought had slept through the whole thing in the last row, shot up straight in her seat, tears running down her face. "That shit wasn't funny at all."

"You're right. It wasn't. Can someone else drive? I'm done."

Grace grabbed the steering wheel with her left arm to keep me from opening the door. "Nah," she said. "We all here to learn how to take heat. He's probably watching us too. Just pull out nice and slow. We'll change drivers at the next rest stop."

It was my own fault that I couldn't say, *but I'm pregnant*, and blame the stress or whatever. If I was here, I had to be here. My duty was to everyone, not me, and not my baby. I took a deep breath. Sugar squeezed my shoulder from the back seat for moral support. Grace never took her eyes off the road ahead.

5
❧

UN VERANO EN NUEVA YOL

Pete was home when I got back from Miami. I prepared myself for one hundred questions, and started planning one hundred lies. Instead, he met me at the door, swept me into a strong, warm hug, and killed me with kindness.

"You know, it felt a lot longer than a few days. It made me realize we haven't really been apart that much since we met. I missed you."

I looked at him all suspicious to be sure he wasn't faking me out. "You for real right now?"

"I am. Why? Did you not miss me? Did you at least bring me a souvenir?"

I pulled the baby outfit from my bag.

He pressed it to his face, kissed it, and held it up to his chest and laughed. "It's a little small, but I think I can make it work." Then he held out his hand to me as he said, "It's going to be okay. We'll figure this out." He kissed me on the forehead and added, "I know you're hungry, so I have chicken and rice with black beans."

Over dinner he went out of his way to ask me safe questions only.

"How was the weather?"

"Hot, humid, not really my thing."

"Did the kids have fun?"

"To be honest, we all felt like little kids there, and we all had fun."

"You just made eighteen weeks, you know. According to the book we could find out the gender now."

"I don't know. I think I want to be surprised. Like, have no expectations."

He looked disappointed. "Yeah, that sounds good. Let's keep things simple for now, smart. The book also says you're going to get even hungrier, but I guess you already knew that."

· · ·

That night in the dark, with no eye contact or aggression, only soft light and whispers, he kept working me slow. A foot rub, a shoulder massage, helping me unpack my bag, all given with the intent of landing in the same spot as always.

"I understand what this is for you, but it has to stop. They will still be your crew. You don't have to lose them." He was sprinkling me with his version of fairy dust, not that different from Disney's, a combo of charm and affection from the prince to the rescue. He drew on my belly in these beautiful designs, kissing any skin he hadn't already covered.

"This is not about putting in my letter of resignation. You know what I mean," I replied, still bracing for the verbal assault, but he was on a whole other kick. He climbed on top of me, careful not to press my belly, which was still sort of flat except right in the middle and extended my arms out wide across the bed.

"I know, I get it . . ."—he crossed each arm with kisses from top to bottom, then bit my shoulders—"I just don't want you to get confused. The world is a big place and that little chunk of it isn't the only one where you can be happy. You can be happy here, I think. No?" He didn't wait for a response. He kissed his way across my neck, tugging softly at my ears and melting any chance I had of answering or defending. "Pull away slowly. Don't do the most dangerous jobs. Spend more time with Grace and less with the business." He was trying to sound all kinds of rational and calm, talking about something he knew next to nothing about, while covering me in the coconut oil he kept in a small jar by the bed. "Getting out at least a month or two before the baby arrives. That gives you plenty of time to show respect to your crew, and to show some respect to your baby. It's too long for me, but I'm here with you, so . . . as far as I'm concerned"—he brushed my skin with his mouth between words and then with his oiled hands—"I'm not going to keep pushing and making you miserable. We deserve to be happy. I need you to be happy. Our baby needs to be happy." He pressed kisses all the way across my chest and down my belly, writing a whole new ending to who I might become if he just gave me some space. How could I not buy into that dream? I fell back into the soft feather-lined space he was offering. We both knew I had already bought into another dream that had no space in it for his, but in Pete's world, knowing you might fail was just one more reason to try harder.

· · ·

A few days after we returned from Miami, we had a drop-off in West-chester. The wife showed up at the house unexpectedly and found us in her living room because the dude had been too disorganized to come to the door with his checkbook. As the husband came downstairs to pay us, she started asking questions.

Her voice was tight with disbelief. "So what is it exactly my husband hired you ladies to do for him?"

Red turned on cue. "We're party planners. Hate to ruin the surprise, but we're here to talk about catering a surprise party."

It helped that we were wearing suits and pearls and carrying the right purses. The wife looked at us and then at her husband, who was frozen solid. He soon took our lead and sprang into action.

He added, "Yes, sweetie. It's not a surprise now, but I wanted to throw you a lavish birthday party."

The wife looked at him as if seeing him in a new light, but still through the fog of knowing him well. "That is not really like you."

"I know, but you have thrown so many celebrations for so many people, I thought it was about time I threw one for you." He leaned in for a kiss that she was happy to take.

She turned back to us and asked, "Why don't you have any sample books?"

The husband thankfully jumped in, "Honey, we did want this to be a surprise. Why don't you let them do their jobs, and they can send over a proposal based on what we discussed, and they observed. Then you can add to it if you like."

Remy scanned their photos on the wall, all from different ages and wearing Hawaiian leis, and added, "That sounds like a good idea. He talked a lot about your trips to Hawaii and how much you loved them. It has me thinking about extravagant tropical flower bouquets and an elegant hyacinth signature drink for the cocktail hour. A kind of midnight in Hawaii feel, dark blues, simmering heat, the elegance of the island after the hula dancers and the tourists are gone, and the beach comes alive in the dark."

It landed. I could tell by the look in the woman's eyes.

Grace and her relentless pursuit of expertise, via her little made-up school for lost girls. Her plan had been to teach us to be at ease with whatever came our way, which was really a way of being at ease with ourselves, the very person most of us had been taught to fear and loathe.

The briefcase we'd brought looked just like his and Red was able to leave it in his office when she slipped off to the bathroom. This is what we did that Toro, Nene, and his boys could never do. Some clients demanded a certain kind of quality that Grace had bred into us. Some wanted the party planned and the drugs woven in as if part of the decor, others wanted the front. It wasn't just looks, although that helped; it was the confidence that came from knowing so much about their world that you could believe you were really in it together. These were the ones we specialized in. It had been Doña Durka's great invention, but Grace had chiseled it into us so deeply that we were changed. We weren't drug dealers, and they weren't drug addicts. We were all just acquaintances exchanging goods and services: a network.

. . .

It had only been three weeks since we buried Doña Durka, and Grace was pushing us hard to prove we weren't afraid. It made sense that we had to solidify our presence now that Durka was gone, but I wasn't up for the increased intensity. I hated driving drugs into Manhattan. There were so many damn cops. The suburbs were empty and easy. Manhattan was increasingly tight and carefully watched, especially since 9/11, not to mention patrolled by police who had their own games running. They were sometimes more dangerous than the clean ones. The officer on the drive home from Miami had scared the shit out of me, but he'd also served as a sort of "poison is the medicine" vaccine. That small dose had immunized me against bigger fears that might have gotten me out sooner. I kept overriding my own doubts to the point where I felt like I didn't even have my own back.

Our next stop was on the Upper West Side in a building overlooking Central Park. When we arrived, Red asked, "Sure you don't want to join us? It's gonna be a good party." She was being sarcastic. She knew drivers never went in. I ignored her as Remy and China just laughed. They had their college girl look going, with expensive designer casual clothes and loose hair. China had braided her gray streak with a dark weave and some colored threads. It was amazing how ageless we could appear with more or less makeup, suits or jeans. Details were everything. We had become screens onto which you could project almost anything. I never felt disguised. Mostly, we all knew how to play our parts, and we were good at it. We had found each other because we belonged nowhere. That had made it easy for Grace to convince us we belonged everywhere, and that everything should be ours.

It was China's first physical drop-off. Grace had mostly kept her working on the numbers back at the apartment. I think she was being tested for her loyalty and her willingness to put her ass on the line with the rest of us. There were still a bunch of girls that didn't trust her and thought she could be there trying to win points with Nene by spying. Grace would only say, "Imma keep letting her see stupid little shit no one else sees and if it gets out, I know exactly who did it and what I'm going to do about it." Three of us were usually more than enough, two to drop and one to drive, but Red had insisted, since we were carrying a lot of shit and needed to be discreet. She described it as a summer stash heading out to the Vineyard in bags with beach towels and picnic baskets.

She asked me to drive with an accusation: "I know you don't like to get your hands dirty, princess, but we can't go in this building with suitcases. We need to divide things up nice and even. All you have to do is sit in the car and not need to pee every five minutes."

It was bullshit. I had done plenty of drop-offs, but she was right that I'd never liked them. I still had not made it public, so her saying "pee every five minutes" in front of Remy and China felt like she was threatening to expose me. Grace had taken some downtime and was staying at the safe house. She never asked permission or said where she was going, but I always knew, and after Red had gone away, it was usually me Grace left in charge. It never really meant anything though. Grace was in charge, even from a distance. Red seemed to be taking things a little too seriously. These were new clients from Chad. We never did new clients till Grace okayed it. But I wasn't sure Red was clearing things with Grace anymore, and I wasn't in a place where I could ask. Red was reminding me of that.

I dropped Red, China, and Remy off in front of the building. We never rushed. In and out drew attention. When a parking spot opened up on the side of the street, I took it. I felt like calling Pete, but he would have asked me what I was doing. I was trying not to lie as much anymore. I wanted to do my part too. Show some effort. I sat there thinking about Pete rubbing coconut oil all over me. His new game was working. I was not the "happy, happy" he was looking for, but I wasn't the low-grade furious exhausted I had been either. I pulled out the little book of "memories from conception to birth" that he had given me. It was small and delicate, which made me think it was something his mother had bought and then asked him to give to me instead. I opened it to the following suggestion: *Tell your baby a story about you today. Where are you? What are you doing? How are you feeling? How many weeks along are you? Take this chance to tell your future child about all the ways you thought about him or her before they ever arrived.* I slammed it closed. Twenty weeks almost. That meant I had twenty more to go. Still plenty of time to figure this out.

The job was taking longer than I liked, but our rule was never to call the drop-off crew. You never knew what they were doing and how it might blow the moment. I kept my knitting in my lap, a tiny scarf I never came close to finishing. I didn't love knitting the way Teca did, but I liked that I could just unravel it and start again. I kept my eye on all four windows and three mirrors, as usual. I was about to pull the little string that would bring it all undone, when I spotted a group of guys dressed in jeans and hoodies who were clearly cops across the street. They were undercover or off duty, but cops for sure. Grace had a few on the payroll and they'd taught us what to look for. These guys walked slow but prideful, their shoulders back and chests out like a team. They self-corrected the posture all the time, but it was a default position. Cops had a specific swagger too, and had just as much difficulty hiding it as thugs. The closer they got to the building, the faster my heart started beating. Two of them looked over at the car as if they were going to cross the street. I turned on the ignition and pulled out nice and slow without ever making eye contact.

When I turned the corner, I saw that one of them looked like Red's dad. It was too far to be sure, but he had the same longish jaw, and seemed to be limping. Her dad had walked with a soft limp ever since he was shot in the line of duty. It wasn't possible. He worked in the Bronx, but I swore it was him. I sent the cop code to China's beeper and drove around the block. Red, China, and Remy walked out of the building as I was waiting for the light to turn. I saw them ahead of me. I couldn't risk honking the horn. When they didn't see me, they flagged a cab. Red called my phone.

"What the fuck? Where did you go?"

"I had to move the car. What took you so long?"

"Long story. Meet us on 110th."

Red got in the car cursing. Remy's makeup was running like she had been crying. China was breathing heavy as she peeled her sweaty oversized sweater over her head.

"What happened in there? Did you guys run into the cops?"

"No. We got your message as we were going to the elevators, so we took the stairs. Those asshole kids were high when we got there. They seemed to think they were getting drugs, whores, strippers, and a party in a box. It was a real fucking scene. We kicked their stupid asses, but then we had to clean up the mess we made, while they cried like babies about what their parents would do if they found out. Real stupid shit. Where did you see cops?"

I explained what I had seen, but left out the part about Red's dad. I wanted to tell Grace before sharing with anyone else. We drove back to the Bronx in silence—with no music or shit-talk to burn the nervous energy, the danger felt amplified. I wanted to ask Red if she had seen her father since she got home, but it was too tense and too loaded a question in front of the other girls, especially China. It was time. Grace had to stop hiding out at the safe house. There were too many moves being made too fast.

When we parked, they all climbed out of the car and Red slammed her door. "I'm going to kill that little piece of shit, Chad. I swear I'm going to kill him."

I sat in the driver's seat calling Grace with my mind even though we had never been further apart. I pictured us little, holding hands, walking to the playground at Devoe Park. The image of that felt most charged with love and innocence. I used it to connect to her. *Come back, Grace. Come back.* It was a trick we used to practice in grade school in preparation for when our mothers would eventually return and separate us. We believed it worked because we had always found each other again.

• • •

My life was now being calculated in weeks with stupid images like, "Your baby is long and lean, like an ear of corn, and your growing uterus is the size of a soccer ball." Twenty-four weeks was very pregnant. Everyone was giving me space to come out and say it. Grace came back as quietly as she had gone away. It had only been a few weeks, but it felt like years. No longer room temperature indifferent to me, she returned ice cold to the touch. She would talk over, under, or across but never to me. She only gave me orders directly: "We have an important day tomorrow. We have new drops. We have another meeting with Toro and Nene. You and Red need to be here overnight today. We have a lot of shit to cover."

I went on a new drop to one of the big banks on Wall Street. Chad had arranged it so that right after, he and Grace would have a financial meeting. Grace had decided that she would not be having any more private meetings with Chad. Red, China, and me, or some combination of us, were to be included in all of them. I walked in through the front with Teca and Remy. Teca was transformed in her dark blue suit, sensible shoes, and wire-rimmed fake glasses. She actually did need glasses, but like me, only wore them as costume. Her Texas accent transformed her into a cattle rancher's daughter educated on the East Coast and handling some of daddy's money. Her pale skin and huge brown eyes took the attention off her full lips and long regal Mayan nose, so she could play the rich mestiza version of Mexican that banks did business with all the time.

Red and China were already inside and waved us over to the elevators. Red relished walking into banks, wearing long-sleeved, dark blue suits that covered all her tattoos, in high heels that made her look like a giant, with briefcases filled with drugs, walking out with ones full of money. She didn't like the dressing-up part, but she loved the game. There was no building she found too intimidating and no bullshit, pompous, high-as-a-kite rich kid or banker she couldn't keep under wraps. One way or another she always got her way. I had a look that could work in some places, but not the heart for it anymore, and I was getting fat for real. I'd never really had the "it" factor anyway. I'd always get stomach cramps and sometimes even cold sweats if the place was "too ritzy" or "too white." That's what Grace called my "nerves." If I had anything of value to contribute to the team, it was that I never failed to smell a rat, sense a trap, or feel the full weight of an omen when they came. It had been my gift, but I was off at every level and didn't trust anything I was feeling these days.

The offices had no big desks or fancy furniture. It was an open, windowless space where a small army of white guys in their early twenties worked cramped into desks next to each other, taking phone calls, talking over one another. It got me in my feelings for sure. Because I knew the size of the deal and the drop-off, I knew they were making more money than we would ever see, and it made me want more than I needed just because. I was looking right at them. They weren't special. If they could have it, so could I. Chad turned, and probably thought he was talking to Grace, as he said, "This is what you call ambition. They don't even go home some nights. We are the oil that keeps this machine moving." When he realized he was addressing me, he looked away to find Grace, who was standing close to the door, eyeing all the exits.

Remy was walking and talking faster than everyone in that room. Eyes darted quickly from the computers to her long, thick legs. Only the bosses dared speak to her. They tried hard to get creative: "If you stand there long enough, we'll all become millionaires just trying to get your attention." Remy was mighty in her presence and every desk she passed by went quiet for a second. She wore her body like a weapon only partially hidden behind the shield of her expensive suit. She also didn't give a shit, and she wore that like a crown. One young blond guy in a wrinkled shirt and loosened tie stood up to talk to her. He got as far as rubbing his hands across his mouth, then sat right back down as soon as she looked him in the eye.

Red though, she was the air they breathed, at least in the superficial ways that counted. She moved through their desks with catlike grace and precision, switching briefcases at the points where she had been told, signaling Remy, winking, and throwing kissy-faces at the boys who required ego games, and then cleared out.

Chad pulled me and Grace out of the big box room and into a hallway that led to a private elevator and up to the top-floor offices, which seemed more secure than even I knew how to recognize. Red and China were waiting for us when we got there. The heavy doors closed behind us without a sound.

. . .

Grace and I drove back together. Red and the others had gone off to do more drops. In the car back to the Bronx, I was hoping there might be a softening, an opening where we could talk for real about how she was or what she was thinking. I obviously had something to tell her. But Grace shut it down.

"We need to make a stop at Nene's house. He called me earlier. I asked if Toro was with him, but he said no and that he just wanted to talk to me. I don't trust it, so I need you to come with me. Yesterday, Toro called too and said he wanted another meeting of the four of us. Some shit is going on between them."

"Okay. Should we tell Red? Do you think we need backup?"

"Not yet. Let's just get there."

She turned on the West Side Highway. It was our favorite ride. The sun was glimmering on the Hudson River and the bikers and boats shared the river's edge of a city that was crowded end to end. I sat back trying to enjoy the water on my left and the Manhattan buildings giving way to vast stretches of leafy green trees as we drove further uptown.

Grace turned up the music. She ate some half-melted stuck-together Skittles out of an old, opened bag in a cup holder. There were candy wrappers everywhere.

Her first real words to me since Miami were, "Open the glove compartment and pass me the M&M'S with peanuts."

The glove compartment was always locked, as was the trunk. I took the key from the little slide pocket under the dashboard and opened it. There were several bags of candy stashed inside. I passed her the yellow one. She tore it open with her teeth and poured the M&M'S directly into her mouth.

"Are you okay?"

"I'm fine. Thanks for asking. You?"

I started to clean up the wrappers from the cup holders. She wasn't looking for an answer. She was looking for a fight. I bent to reach one on the floor, but the seat belt cut into my belly sharp, so I popped back up. She emptied the bag of M&M'S into her mouth then threw the wrapper in my direction without skipping a beat.

"Since you're in the mood to clean."

"Is this really how we are gonna start talking?"

She ignored me and stayed on her own track. "You know, Nene rarely, like never, calls me, so I thought something was up with Toro. Instead, he asked if I would go by his house because he had something important to talk to me about." She reached in the cup holder where the old Skittles had been and found nothing.

"I tried to get out of it, but he didn't ask or beg or back down. He just kept saying, 'It won't take long, but I got a few things I want to talk to you about and this is the safest place to talk.'"

"Safe is good, no?" I asked, and felt the baby flutter. We were all here together and none of it felt right.

"It feels bad. Wrong. Nene reaching out to me alone like that. It's not good. Doing it at his mom's house is a way to make it feel safe for me. You know. Like he would never do some crazy shit in his mom's house, but it feels fucked up."

"Yeah, well, hopefully it's not. I hope he doesn't want to talk about China. Because even I don't understand that shit."

Grace looked over at me and rolled her eyes before answering, "I hate when you act like a pura pendeja. Like, 'Oh no, I hope he doesn't want to talk about what it's obvious he wants to talk about.' I already explained the China decision. No use having her out there when I can control her in here."

I might be a pura pendeja, but Grace was nervous. Her candy was giving her away. Grace being nervous only felt good for like thirty seconds because Grace being nervous meant we were all fucked. I didn't really want to hear any more either. I turned up the radio another notch and Missy was giving advice on how to work it, reminding me that shit was changing everywhere.

I had never been to Nene's. He had bought his mom and sister a nice two-family house on a quiet street in the northeast Bronx near Pelham Parkway. His sister lived with her kids and husband and his mom lived alone in the second apartment. His dad had left when he was a kid. After things fell apart with China, he'd moved back in with his mom. When we pulled up, his sister was putting her kids in the car. She looked at us like she knew us but didn't smile or say hello. Grace knocked on his mother's door and she opened it, revealing a living room that could have been our abuelita's. Furniture still covered in plastic slipcovers and tables with lace mats. It made me smile a little to see that Nene still lived like a kid in his mom's house. It looked as if he wasn't in charge of anything here. His mother took us to the kitchen and offered café con leche. She was older than Doña Durka even though Nene and Toro were the same age. Nene was the youngest and the only boy. He had been her little milagro born after she turned forty-five, fifteen years after the birth of what she thought would be her last daughter.

She called out to him through a door right outside the kitchen. "Nene, llegaron tus amigas."

"Send them downstairs, Ma."

We climbed down a narrow set of wooden stairs to the basement. Nene's basement was a finished apartment with a small kitchen, bathroom, and a big living room he had turned into a recording studio. He had records everywhere, turntables, a computer, and mixers; it looked official. He had a poster in a frame of the Young Lords with *Pa'lante* written on it, and another one of Tego Calderón. He had his Puerto Rican flag hanging over the one small window. He didn't get up to say hello. He just nodded in our direction and pointed at the couch. He looked at Grace like he wasn't expecting me, but she ignored him. He was listening to someone on the phone, so I kept busy looking around. He had one of those old-school black-and-white notebooks with the word *lyrics* printed in graffiti letters on the line where his name was supposed to be, and a few books scattered around. I picked up the one on top: *A Puerto Rican in New York and Other Sketches* by Jesús Colón. I had never seen or even heard of it. Just below that was a poetry book by Julia de Burgos. I had heard of her but never read that one either. I wanted to show Grace, but she was looking at him and the papers on his desk. He hung up the phone. I was still holding the book in my hand when I sat down. He looked over at me and said, "Don't look so shocked. You think you the only ones who know how to read?"

Grace sat closest to him. "Nah, don't even play that. I've never played you like that."

"I'm not so sure about that. I always wondered why you had so much attitude with me. So much animosity. Like I did some shit to you. Or like I was too stupid for you to bother with?"

"Why do you even say shit like that? You know Toro never really liked to mix business with me. He liked me to kind of stay out of his stuff and away from his people, not to mention other guys."

"Yeah, but I always felt like we could've been cool, and you were always funny like you were hiding something." Grace squinted hard in his direction and moved around in her chair like she couldn't find a comfortable spot.

"Did you call me over here to work on our friendship?"

"Maybe. Something like that. I got a few things I want to talk about." Nene filled the space when he stood. His head almost touched the low basement ceiling. He sat again on the more comfortable-looking black leather chair across from the matching couch where I was sitting. A poster of Biggie with his crown on was framed right behind him. Grace had to turn her chair to make eye contact with him again.

"So, first I wanna say that, just like Toro, I don't feel this whole China getting down with you and your little Westchester crew or whatever you call yourselves. Especially now that your real protection is gone. That's my kids' moms right there and this ain't no shit she needs to be involved in. So cut her loose."

"Sounds like a conversation you should be having with China. That is a grown-ass woman, not some little girl." Grace looked far away and small. She stood up from the chair to lean against the front of the desk with her hands behind her back. She was struggling to claim authority in that room.

Nene rubbed his face and leaned forward in the chair with his arms on his knees. "So, you gonna play games?"

"No. I mean she does the books for the pawnshop and the music shop. We don't do much of that other shit anymore. I'm guessing Toro is planning to phase me out. Doña Durka set us up, so we didn't need that forever. Talk to China about how you feel, but I need a good bookkeeper and she is one."

"What happened to white boy Chad?"

Grace looked set off by that. There was no reason Nene should even know about Chad. I felt my phone vibrating in my bag. I peeked inside and saw it was Red. I wished she was here instead of me.

"Like I said, talk to China. You had kids with her, and now you need to talk to her through me? Do what you gotta do, but that has nothing to do with me." Nene's mother called down the stairs that she was bringing us some food and coffee.

"Ma, deja eso, it's fine, just leave it up there."

She came down the stairs as if she hadn't heard him. I served myself a heaping pile of white rice, maduros, and pollo guisado. I even took the little piece of aguacate she had wrapped in plastic on top. The tight skirt I'd worn to the bank was making it hard to breathe. It felt like it was about to pop a button. I had bought it two sizes bigger, but I hadn't gotten any maternity clothes yet. Nene looked at me like eating was the dumbest shit on earth before adding, "Buen provecho, that right there is some of the best food you ever gonna eat." He turned to Grace and said, "Okay, so let me tell you then that you ain't the only one with big plans. I'm working on some stuff. I'm finishing a mixtape."

"Really? I didn't even know you were still doing your music. That's great."

"Yeah, well. I heard you have some friends in the music business, so I was wondering if you would pass it along as a demo. You know, make it fall into the right hands."

I can't explain how he looked at both of us in that moment. He knew what he was saying. Grace taking it from him would have been the same as admitting he was right. He looked at her and held it out in his hand.

"I don't know where you heard that, but I don't have any connections. Doña Durka is the only one I ever knew with connections. You should have asked her before it was too late."

Nene flinched at the sound of Durka's name before plunging in, "Don't play yourself, Grace. This game ain't for pussies."

Grace started pulling away from the desk. Turning away from him, she said, "Right, which is why I'm in a whole other game. Good luck with the music."

"I been warning you. You take more than you can protect. You taking way too much."

Grace signaled me to follow her. She walked up the stairs banging her high-heeled shoes on each step. I left my plate of half-eaten food, wanting like hell to take it with me. I had gone from throwing up everything I ate to being hungry twenty-four hours a day. I was definitely losing focus. When we got to the front of the house, I was still trying to catch up to her.

"Nene makes music?" I asked.

"All those motherfuckers think they gonna be rappers someday. Nobody even makes mixtapes anymore."

I wished I could have heard his music. I wished his could've been a hustler-turned-rapper story for the ages. I felt myself wishing something different for all of us. The more I felt Grace turning solid around this thing she'd decided we had all become, the more I wanted to wake her ass up. This was not the dream. This was not even close.

She looked over at me and said, "Hurry up. We have shit to do."

6
❧

WEDDINGS

We'd found out I was pregnant at five weeks. My body was like a calendar in the dark with my period never missing a beat, so I got a test at the first sign I was late. That was back in cold and rainy March. Pete had decided we should go out for brunch, and the rowdy Irish bar scene of St. Patrick's Day was playing in the streets of Manhattan. He proposed on the spot, on one knee without a ring. The already drunk crowd clapped and hollered.

I said, "Yes, okay, but let's talk about this at home."

Pete started proposing to me every morning after that, for like a month. I kept pushing back, so he bought a ring. I said, "Just give me a minute. It's a lot." So, he did.

After Durka was killed, the fights began and then those turned into ultimatums. After Miami, it was the kindness games. The games felt like resting. I was tired of making up excuses. My timeline had become a circle, while his had a clear door at the exit that he was counting in weeks. Would I make it in time? I couldn't even think that far ahead. I just wanted a break.

I worried his kindness games were making me soft, and I'd recently made the mistake of telling him that Grace had been married to Toro all along.

"Seems like you ain't as tight as you think you are. That's not the kind of shit you keep a secret from your . . ." He never finished that sentence because he knew that whatever name he gave her—homegirl, best friend, comadre, sister, cousin—could never capture all that she was to me. He stopped midsentence a lot now. Like he didn't know what to say next that wouldn't set me off, or like he was looking for the magic words that might set me straight. What he didn't know was that I had found out weeks ago. I had put him off after each of his proposals by saying I needed time to plan, to get out of the life, to lose weight after the baby. That we needed to at least be fighting less to get married. After I got back from Miami, he didn't really want to hear that anymore. I think he thought getting married would somehow sever me from her for good. After his love and acceptance seductions, he wore the unhinged look of a man mad for a cause. I can't even lie, it was kind of sexy.

. . .

Summer in New York City was burning a hole of heat through the open window when I woke up. Pete wasn't a fan of the AC, and I couldn't live without it anymore. Mostly, he let me have my way, but as soon as he woke up, he'd turn it off, open the windows, and let in the light. The sun wasn't light in August though; it was fire. I had thrown up twice in the middle of the night, after I'd thought that part was done. I pulled the sheet up over my head.

He laughed and pulled it off me. I was wearing nothing underneath. His faded drawings still covered my belly, with new ones springing up around the sides. He had spent the nights since my return sketching his hopes and dreams on my stomach. I walked to the kitchen where the coffee I couldn't drink, but still craved and loved to smell, the eggs with cilantro and scallions I loved, but no longer craved, and the toasted bread with butter greeted me on his little orange and silver Formica kitchen table by the window.

"I wish I could marry you naked just like that. Twenty-seven weeks today. Next week you enter your third trimester. This is it. This is all happening."

I opened my mouth to offer one of my many tired pushbacks. It was getting under my skin the way he'd tell me the week and what was happening like what he was reading in some book could replace what I was feeling in my own body, transforming me from the inside out.

He shushed me with a finger to his lips. "Shhh, enough already. You already said 'yes, but . . .' like ten times, maybe twenty. We can have a huge wedding with the perfect dress whenever you want, if you want, and never if you don't want. That can be your call. But we are getting married today."

I took a bite of my toast as my mind scattered in a hundred directions. He looked manic. Would either one of us ever be hooked into the kid that way? I hoped so.

The best of Pete was kneeling in front of me now. His soft curls, his warm hands on my thighs, his prism eyes of gray and brown that saw a world full of color and magic everywhere he turned. It was the look that came over him when his paintings rushed out of him like a river of light.

He said, "You told me you didn't care as much about the dress as you did the veil. So I went all out on the veil. I actually made the tiara part myself and had the lady in the shop work it in the tulle."

This was the Pete that silenced me. I was in awe of him. It was wild to witness someone so reckless with his love and faith.

The veil he pulled out was a huge, stunning, tentlike thing with a crown of dried flowers and twigs sprinkled with glitter, crystals, and tiny pearls. The fabric itself had some sort of shimmer to it that made it look like the night sky in white with a hint of blue. I just sat there and stared at it and cried.

He put it over my head and took my hands in his. "I know you don't believe in any of this, and I know that you do. Maybe I can't fix anything, but I want to be here for you. So will you marry me, today, please?" He laid his head in my lap and kissed my thighs and never let go of my hands.

Pete was inexplicably determined to crack my code, to get through to what he believed was the real me. My heart was racing. He pulled out a beautiful ivory dress. It was simple and gorgeous, short and strapless with an empire waist that would easily hide the belly.

In the end, all I could do was close my eyes and whisper, "Okay." It was not, I'm sure, what he had hoped for, but he should have given up hoping by now.

"Today we get married in City Hall. You deal with Grace. Beep her. Call her. She can come. I really don't care." He looked away as he said the part about Grace, and I knew it was a lie. He did care. He did not want her there. On that they'd both agree, since she'd never have come anyway.

Then he added, "We do need two witnesses, so I called my parents."

Pete had parents to call. Of course they would be there. He had no idea how lonely this day would be for me without Grace. Without any of my girls. I wouldn't call anyone else if I wasn't calling her. I was getting married surrounded by no one that belonged to me except the one I was making myself, still quiet in the dark.

It was not a veil for City Hall. I looked like the women in those paintings that Grace hung all over the apartment walls—half tree with roots drawn all over my stomach, half tiger hidden behind the veil. I knew Pete's parents did not approve of me. They had no idea how much more there was to disapprove of, though his mother had grown to like me in superficial ways. We bonded over music, food, even art. All shit I only knew about because of Grace. His father was old-school annoyed by the fact that I had no parents or family, and offered no real explanation other than, "We don't really get along."

On the flip side, Pete was older than me, so his mother was relieved that he wasn't going to stay single forever, and no one could argue with the unifying power of a baby on the way. Pete came up behind me, his reflection cast against the backdrop of his half-finished deep-sea mural on the wall. He started unfastening the veil from the little twig and flower tiara, brought out a smaller version and held it out to me. As if he had read my mind.

"Better for City Hall, no? The big one can be for some pictures in the park afterward and the 'wedding wedding,' you know whenever that is. We could use it on the honeymoon. You do look good in that veil and nothing else." He was smiling like a little kid showing me his artwork. He stood over me, worked the bit of tulle into my hair with whispers of "I love you, Carmen. Don't hold back on me today. Let's do this."

I watched in awe as he folded the other veil into a bag. I tried to imagine what it was like to be him, to plan ahead, to envision: a veil, a picture, a baby's room, a future. To trust that what you hoped for was possible. He'd see a dream and work to make it happen. I could only see what was in front of me and bust my ass to make it work. The mystery of his love was still a secret inside me, an ache in my chest as strong as the one I'd had as a little girl feeling like my mother had never loved me. I had no right to reject the best love I had ever been offered, even if it didn't feel that way yet, or even ever. I had no right.

. . .

I married Pete that hot, bright, sunny Friday morning. All four of us took the subway from Brooklyn to City Hall, and people oohed and aahed the whole ride there. Hard-ass New Yorkers seem to bend a little when they see a bride on the subway or in the park. Many blessings were offered with smiles, glances, floating words like *beautiful* and *congratulations* and *good luck*. Pete squeezed my hand on the pole between us and watched me as if he was worried I might jump off at the next stop. We had lunch at the fancy boathouse place on the lake in Central Park that his mother loved. She looked beautiful in a royal blue skirt suit and chunky silver jewelry. Her curly hair was freshly cut into a bob. Pete looked just like her and it was clear they adored each other.

She smiled big when she asked, "Y mi grandbaby, how is everything in there?" She reached out in the direction of my belly but didn't go so far as to touch it. We weren't there yet, and she understood that.

"I love this restaurant. Manuel brought me here in the seventies after he took me for a boat ride. So beautiful. I'm happy to share it with you."

I had been there with Grace and Chad once before but acted like I had never seen it. There would be no way to explain. His mother won points by bringing a tiny Valencia cake with pineapple and guava filling. A nod to the old-school in all of us. The waiter took pictures and we smiled. There was a real photographer waiting outside after lunch. We did all the shots: the fountain, the rowboat on the lake, the little archways, and the bridges. The photo album, like all wedding albums, would tell an incomplete story of a happy and romantic day. None of the shadows would appear. It was, I think, the most I had ever given him. Walking through the park afterward, Pete and his mother held on to me—he by the waist and she with her arm through mine as if they both knew I still posed a flight risk.

. . .

The night of our wedding we had love sex and angry sex and cried and laughed and ate ice cream and leftover cake at four in the morning. I was on a roller coaster of emotion, sugar, hormones, and exhaustion. Pete was in a coma. Instead of dreaming about Pete or the baby or the future, my mind kept returning to how Toro had come for Grace when we were only fourteen, and how sometimes what felt like the solution was really a bigger problem in disguise. Getting married had maybe solved a problem for Pete, but without a doubt, created a bigger one we could not know in advance.

I spent those hours awake in the dark, thinking about Grace, and how our dreams had come for us in shapeshifting suits of never quite what was needed but more than what we had. The dream lady had taught us to think about our waking dreams as paths to revisit what went wrong so that we might fix it or know what haunting to release. My waking dream, as Pete snored softly next to me, took me back to the church where I'd always thought I'd get married, with Grace there beside me as my maid of honor. It made me want to tell my baby something I'd been taught to be ashamed of, but that I was trying to learn how to hold with neither pride nor shame. I got out of bed and dug the little book Pete had given me out of my purse. I began to write:

I married your father today, but I want to tell you a different story that most people will tell me I shouldn't tell you, but it's one I think you need to know.

Me and Grace used to love going to church. It had been our meeting place after abuela died. We'd hide there, till we had the strength to figure out what came next and ask the Virgin Mary for her love and guidance. As I waited for Grace, sitting on the front steps, I looked up at the stained-glass windows, which I knew would be dancing with that kind of light we loved on the inside. The windows were one of our favorite parts about church; we prayed more to the colors and the light than to the images of saints.

When I first saw her that day, I didn't even recognize her. Why would I? We had been feeling ourselves as the summer before high school started, but this was something I had not seen coming. She climbed out of the front seat of a Mercedes-Benz with dark tinted windows, wearing expensive sunglasses, hair fresh from the salon, and all new clothes. I watched her with the same curiosity we'd always had for girls like that. When I realized it was her, all I could think to do was pray: Dear God, please let this be a mistake. Dear God, no. The car pulled away and I never got to see who else was inside. I only saw Grace in her glory. Everyone turned to watch her climb the church stairs.

That felt like all I had for the baby, so I closed the book. There was more to the story, but it made me realize that the longer I stayed in, the more I would have to tell any child I brought into this world. What exactly did I want to say? I pushed the book aside, though I couldn't shake the feeling that what had happened on the church steps that day, and didn't happen, had so many roots in what we thought possible.

I'd jumped up from my seat on the stairs, half terrified, reached out to hug her, and then pushed her away, saying, "Look at you! You got anything you wanna tell me?"

She squeezed my hand tight and squinted her eyes. "Of course. I got a lot I wanna tell you."

I return to that moment a lot, run through it, over it, under it. I try to imagine all the things I might have said or done so things could have turned out differently. But the alternate endings have always been equally unsatisfying. How do you stop a train wreck from happening when it's already underway at full speed and you are on the train? How do you jump off?

"Let's skip church today. God answered my prayers. I can take a break now."

Still sure I had some say in this, I snapped back at her, "Last time I checked God usually doesn't send the devil to answer prayers."

Grace shot me a dirty look. "Toro is picking me up in two hours, so we don't have a lot of time."

"Okay, where should we go?"

"The park, silly. Where else would we go?"

As we walked from the church, we sounded like the fourteen-year-old girls we were—talking about the car he'd picked her up in, the music he'd played, how good he smelled. I couldn't stand the suspense and finally asked the question she wasn't even touching.

"So, did you do it? Are you having sex?"

She answered with her own confusion visible, "It's weird. I can tell he feels me like that. But he hasn't even tried to kiss me. He gives me a little peck on the cheek and a hug when he sees me, and when we say goodbye, and that's it." Her confusion seemed like genuine insecurity, but I was not convinced.

"Are you serious? No fucking way. Don't hold out on me!"

"Serious. I wouldn't lie to you. I'm having a crazy bunch of feelings myself like I might want to, even though I don't, but like, I've had my period since I was nine, so I guess my body is like what the fuck is going on out there. But we haven't gone anywhere near it."

"How old is he?"

"I don't know. I think he's in his twenties. Maybe thirty. I can't tell. He hasn't asked me about my age or what grade I'm in. He just asked me if I liked school, and if I was still going. He's been keeping everything kind of vague."

"Yeah, no secret there, jailbait." I elbowed her lightly in the stomach to make a joke of it, but she wasn't joking, and she didn't laugh. "Are you really sure you want to have sex with an old dude or even sex at all? I mean we both know who this guy is, right?"

"Don't hate. His mother is amazing." She looked away as she said it. Seeing Grace genuinely taken with someone shook me. I was suddenly fighting for both of us. If she fell, what would become of me?

"I'm not hating. I'm just wondering when you lost your mind. You been warning me away from guys like him since we were ten years old."

I sat there on our favorite bench facing the playground and listened to Grace talk for the forty-five minutes I was supposed to be listening to a priest. She was not her usual breathless saleswoman trying to put me on to her latest and greatest scheme. She related the story like it was a fairy tale. Toro had arrived and everything had gotten better. Magic Man, Red would later call him, after one of her favorite songs.

Grace stood up in a dramatic pose and shifted into a sarcastic, bitter, wicked witch voice as she proclaimed, "In a land far, far away there lived a princess who had been kidnapped and forced to live with a terrible witch who was also her mother."

I rolled my eyes and turned away like I didn't want to engage. I was so scared of what was coming and how much it might make me cry. I wanted to pull her back into my world and the application our teachers had given us for the scholarship programs to a local private high school. We were the only two girls in the whole school who'd been invited to apply.

I tried to interrupt. "I've heard enough. Did you even hand the application in?"

She ignored me and spoke louder. "Her prince was taller, healthier, cleaner, and finer than anyone she had ever stood that close to. He looked like an angel. He smelled so good. She knew some would call him the devil. She did not care. He had really nice teeth. He offered her food when she was hungry. He lived with a beautiful queen, who was also his mother."

I changed my strategy, interrupted her with rudeness she might recognize as her own voice of reason. "You live in a shithole, so that must have helped him look good." We shared a look that made me think we were finally going to talk for real, but then a beeper went off. I hadn't even noticed it hanging off her belt loop. It was hidden under her shirt. She looked stressed and grabbed for it immediately, but her pants were too tight and made her stumble. I couldn't resist pushing her a little more. "What's a matter? New pants too tight? He's slowing you down already." She shot me the look. It was full-on Grace; there would be no room for real talk anymore.

"Shit, he's coming back around. I gotta go. Come on, hurry." I tried one last time and yanked Grace by the arm. I stood as if ready to fight.

"I know you are not trying to fuck with me right now," she yelled.

"If not me, who? Who's gonna stop you from throwing your life away?"

"What life? Are you stupid?" She started walk-running. I followed.

"Could you at least fill out your application? Things could change. Don't throw in the towel like this."

She turned and faced me aggressively close. "I'm not throwing in the towel. I'm getting in the ring. I'm tired of living like shit and waiting on empty dreams. You should be too. That application is just another form of welfare. More begging for permission to fucking live. I'm tired. I'm out." She turned to make her way out of the park.

I yelled at her, "You're pretty fucking stupid for somebody so smart. Big words won't stop a bullet from going through your head." She gave me the finger as she jogged toward the street. I ran top speed to catch up to her.

"You don't have to do this, Grace. You know better than me what those dudes bring." I grabbed her hand, tried to get her to look me in the eye one last time. She never looked back. When we got to the exit, she opened her new purse.

"I gotta go. I can get here next week. Here's some money. Make sure you come. I'll ask him to take us both out to breakfast. This is just the beginning. Okay, just chill. I got this."

We hugged hard, if not long. She crossed the street, hurried up the side stairs of the church, and then came out the front doors with the crowd, looking like she had been in there the whole time. I stood watching from across the street at the entrance to the park as she disappeared into the car. Only after it had pulled away did I remember the summer youth job and the working papers application in my bag. It was supposed to be a way for us to make extra money in case we did get into that private school. At least we would have cash for some new clothes. But she already had new clothes and she was no longer interested in applications of any kind. She was not looking for permission to live anymore.

That was the beginning that brought me all the way to Pete, still sleeping quietly beside me on a wedding night I had shared with no one except him. I glanced at my beeper on the floor next to the bed, hoping one of the crew would come looking for me. We were still using beepers even though we all had new cell phones. Beepers in their hard little cases felt safe and anonymous in ways the phones didn't yet, and we had codes that had become our language.

As the sun started to beat back the humid dark, I felt like I was floating and drowning all at once. I wanted out. I wanted my own "this is just the beginning." Pete was offering to carry me out and take me as far as I wanted to go. But I didn't trust him any more than I trusted the life I had with Grace. Toro had come to take Grace. Out was a sham unless you walked there on your own two feet. As soon as I thought this, I could hear Grace answering me: "Unless someone is carrying your ass out of a burning building."

I was relieved when my beeper started vibrating. The flashing green light across the numbers revealed the date of Grace's birthday, code for meet me at church. We hadn't been there together in years. It almost felt like the old days when we were still calling each other with our minds. I only had to think about us in church and she could feel it, or maybe we had developed a default setting for how far each one was allowed to get out before the other one pulled her back in.

Pete turned over once or twice while I dressed in the dark. I snuck out of the apartment like I had stolen something. I knew leaving a note would be an insult; he'd assume whatever I had written was a lie anyway. I had given him what he wanted. We were married. That would have to be enough for now. I left for the Bronx just as the sun was coming in through the windows. I heard the birds chirping, but I didn't stay long enough to listen. I slipped my wedding ring into a zippered pocket in my bag.

7

SACRED

The heavy red wooden doors of St. Nicholas of Tolentine Church looked like they were sealed shut. The sun sprawled out on either side of the front steps in the early quiet. Across the street, Devoe Park was all the shades of deep summer green. Early-shift workers were waiting at the bus stop along with the drunks heading home after a night turned morning in the street. I kept looking for one of the many cars Grace might use, but instead she walked up and grabbed me from behind like a stalker, one arm around the neck, the other sort of dragging me back. I recognized her perfume, Samsara by Guerlain. It had been a gift from Doña Durka for her high school graduation and Grace had never used another perfume again.

"Grace, is that you? What the fuck?"

"Who else would dare come for you like that other than me?" She laughed her crazy high-pitched cackle as she turned me around and hugged me.

I pushed her back. "If people just heard you laughing, and couldn't see you, they would think you were completely unstable and dangerous at that."

She turned and spun in circles, laughing as she answered, "And they would be right, wouldn't they?"

I pulled away from the embrace only to fall into it again. It felt good to be with Grace alone, away from everything and everyone. She was back to being my Grace on the church steps, even if I had no idea how long it would last. The arm around my neck became an arm around my shoulder and another at my waist as if she had many arms at once. We walked up the stairs toward the entrance. I was surprised when the door opened right as Grace pulled it. I was nervous, as if we couldn't really go in there anymore.

"We haven't been in here in years. Are we really going in?"

"Yeah, there is someone I want you to meet."

We touched the holy water to our foreheads in the sign of the cross from the small marble basin at the entrance, as if we had been going to church every Sunday. Habits and ritual hold Catholics together when faith and action fail to deliver. All along the wall with the shorter pews, we admired the familiar stations of the cross carved in dark heavy wood. We sat in the front on the left-hand side. The church was mostly empty. It was early Saturday morning. Grace smiled in the direction of the confessionals.

She waved her arms around as if giving a tour and announced, "You gotta love a church that lets you sin on Friday, confess on Saturday, and take in the body of your god on Sunday morning! I mean, that shit is perfect really."

A few people began to filter in and scatter around the pews, still doing their penance from last week or praying for things they would never say out loud. It was that dark, cool, quiet version of church we had always loved. It had been a long time since I'd seen the stained-glass windows. I was lost in the color blue when Grace pinched my thigh.

"Are you even listening to me?"

"Sorry, yeah, I am. I just haven't been here in so long . . ."

"Yeah, yeah, would you like to go to confession? 'Father, forgive me, it has been many years since my last confession, and since then I have taken to dealing drugs in a pretty big way and I will probably move on to killing people soon.'" She laughed quietly and stared at me.

"What do you mean kill people? I've never killed anyone, and I have no intention of doing that shit."

"Yeah, but remember, my intentions are the ones that have gotten us this far not yours." She pointed to the statue of the Virgin Mary as she spoke. "You have to admit it was kind of brilliant the way churches were made to look like castles and priests to look like kings. To confuse the people. To lure them in. To make them loyal. To make them feel like they finally got inside the castle and could call it their own. To get them out of the woods and away from their devotion to the Great Mother."

The light from the stained-glass windows illuminated Grace from the side. I loved her as much as I had ever loved anyone in my life. We had held on to each other in this church during our hardest years. It was the place Abuelita had given us to turn to. It was all she had to offer.

Grace tucked one leg up on the pew and rested her head on her knee. She asked, "Did you bring your little notebook where you write down our dreams? I had a weird one last night. It was deep."

Dreams were a language for us. Depending on who you told your dream to, they would ask for numbers or colors or faces or animals. Remy's grandmother would use a dream to tell you what number to play in the lotto, and Sugar's Granma Helen would use it to tell you how to feel about how you were living or who you were loving or if you were sick. Dreams were also currency exchanged as a form of trust. It was a good sign that Grace was telling me a dream she had. I only wished I had the little notebook. I had started keeping it for the ones we shared with each other after the dream lady workshop that Grace had set up especially for me. I wasn't really carrying it anymore.

"So, what was it? Remember to tell it in the present tense so we can be in the dream together."

"Okay, so check it, I'm here in church looking to the Virgin Mary. I'm like, 'Mary, I love you and all and I pray to you, but I feel so alone. I feel like you don't really hear me, like I'm not good enough for you.' Then Mary opens her eyes and looks right at me and says, 'No, my love, it's not that you are not good enough for me. It's that I am not the right mother for you right now. We are all here to love and protect you, but some of us have different things to offer at different points in a woman's life. I am always here, and you are always mine, but I want to introduce you to my sister, my mother, the mother of us all.'"

Grace paused as if to check if I was listening, but also to see if I was judging her. I nodded and motioned that she should keep going.

"I'm sitting here like, holy shit, the Virgin Mary is talking to me—I gotta call Univision or something! And then like some stupid little kid I start thinking, wait, shit, no one ever told me about the Virgin Mary's sister, of course she had to have one, everyone had brothers and sisters back then. They used to have like ten kids. So, I'm sitting here waiting for some cool sister to come from somewhere, but it's actually the Virgin Mary herself transforming right before my eyes. The Virgin drops her blue-and-white outfit and veil and stands completely naked for a second, then a red-and-gold cloth covers her before her skin goes dark like blue, then brown like us. She is gigantic, the size of the whole church, and she stretches out her arms till there are arms everywhere. She has eight arms, then sixteen, then eight again, then ten, and every arm has a weapon or a tool. Her hair grows out long and black and thick, you know, it's hard hair like ours, and she has a nose ring and the bindi on her forehead. Of course I recognize her. It's Durga Maa. Who needs no introduction with me, right, but I'm sitting here just watching. Then her lion is right beneath her as her ride, and he turns into a tiger then back into a lion. The red-and-gold sari is fanned out at her feet, and she is wearing all the chains and bracelets. Illuminated like one of the windows, her whole body emits light.

"She is standing there in the middle of the altar with the cross behind her, but you can barely see it. She smiles at me and says, 'Oh, my lovely Grace, I am so sorry it has taken us so long to find each other. Well, so long for you to find me. I have always been with you, from the beginning.'"

Grace was chasing the words out like it was a race against the tremble in her voice. I opened my eyes and found her wiping tears away as fast as she could. She got so desperate she dried her whole face across her arm. I reached out and rested my hand on her thigh. Even though she was whispering, she looked around to make sure no one was watching or listening. All she found was the light streaming in through the colorful windows designed to make you feel both watched and protected.

"Just keep going."

"So, I have a thousand questions for her, but all I can do is kneel. I mean I'm Catholic, right, and that's what I know how to do, kneel. Durga laughs at me and says, 'You don't need to kneel. You are my daughter. Come into my arms.' Now at that point I'm a little freaked cuz despite her very calm, loving face, those are a lot of weapons, so I find myself reaching for my gun and she laughs at me some more. She has that look of total serenity as she says, 'You won't be needing that.' Then she sticks out one of the hands that doesn't have a weapon in it, only a little tattoo of a flower, and it's covered in gold rings and bracelets. Everything about her is reminding me of everything I ever wanted to be that I never felt—strong, calm, protected, powerful. Sacred. Then, just like that, I can feel it. My heart is beating fast, but I feel it. All of it.

"All the other arms with the weapons look like they are moving, but she picks me up with her one free hand, sort of the way King Kong picks up the chick in the movie, remember that? Then she pulls me right up to her huge chest and just presses my head against her and I start crying. She whispers to me like I'm a baby, 'It is hard to be so far from home, so far and without your mother. But your mother is with you everywhere you go, even if you never had her while she was standing right next to you.'

"I cry for a long time into her chest. She puts me back down and kisses me right in the middle of my forehead between my eyes. Then she blows on the same spot and another eye opens up right there. I am terrified, but also crazy-ass calm. Then she starts talking to me in a strong, booming voice, 'There is time for fighting, Grace, and demons to be killed, but don't become confused by what that means. Confusion is the biggest demon of all.'

"Then, just like that, she disappears. It's the Virgin Mary again sort of winking and smiling at me as she slips back into her blue dress. Then old Padre Juan comes in and she gets all statue-like again. He is coming toward me like he recognizes me. I just run out of the church and don't realize until I am outside that I left my gun inside on the pew. I couldn't remember taking it out, but I didn't have it anymore, and when I put my hand inside my pocket, I have Doña Durka's knife that looks like a small sword. I woke up sweating. Couldn't shake it off. Then I sent you the message to meet me here."

Grace leaned her head on my shoulder and I put my arm around her. We stayed like that, still, for a long time. Finally I asked, "Did it mean something to you? You must have had some kind of feeling when you woke up?"

Of course, I was fishing for what I wanted to hear, some version of: I think it means it's time for me to get out and give this shit up for good. I kept pushing her to see what I saw. She stayed quiet.

I asked, "Remember the dream lady who came to give us classes. You did it for my twenty-first birthday. The one with the beautiful Italian name, Scardamalia, I think."

"Yeah, I do. She was cool."

"Well, remember how she taught us to talk to each other about our dreams, right? Like if your dream were my dream, I would want to know more about what Durga meant about killing demons. That shit was deep."

"I guess," she said, and then sat up and pulled away from me. I wanted to pull her back. She went on, "For me, it was more about trying to figure out how to feel that loved when I'm awake. It made me think about what I need to do to let our crew know that we are bound by something much bigger than money or even loyalty. It made me want to claim what is mine and make it clear that we are here out of love for each other."

Grace stood and stretched her arms out, moved them around as if they were many. She touched her hand to her mouth in the sign of a kiss and sent it up to the statue of the Virgin Mary. She spoke out loud to no one in particular, but looked directly at the statue as she said, "I will never forget who my real mother is, and that she has my back and that I deserve to be loved exactly as I am." Her walk down the center aisle toward the exit was marked by a halting rhythm similar to a bride. That was my first sign that maybe she was playing games with me. The heavy wooden door creaked open as Padre Juan entered the church. Grace strode past him as if he had appeared to open the door just for her.

. . .

The moist, hot air hit hard as we came out onto the street. We had only been inside a short while, but Devoe Park was already filled with kids playing. Fordham Road was packed with the summer crowds of cars honking and people lining up at the Bx12 bus stop on the corner by Fordham Pizza with their coolers, heading to Orchard Beach. Grace waved at me to follow her across the street where she had a limo waiting in front of the park. It was not her way to be so flashy in this neighborhood. When we got in the car, she announced, "I sent everyone a message to meet in front of the church tomorrow morning, so you can all ride the Bx12 bus to Orchard Beach."

Grace rarely had us all in the same place after Doña Durka was killed. Since Miami, our dinners in the apartment were the only times we were all together, and even these were happening less and less. We hadn't taken a bus anywhere in a long time, much less to Orchard Beach. Everything felt dangerous when Grace started breaking her own rules.

"So, what's with going to the beach on the bus? Aren't we a little old for field trips?"

"I'll tell you what you need to know. The rest you will find out when you get there. But first, we're going shopping."

The limo pulled up in front of La Botanica San Lazarus on Tremont and Burnside. They must have been expecting her. As soon as the car stopped, four guys dressed in white from head to toe came out with several boxes they loaded into the trunk. Grace rolled down her window and spoke to them in Spanish. I was surprised by how well she spoke it. There had been a time when we both knew enough to communicate with our abuela, but not much more. She was giving them instructions about what to put in her trunk and what to put in the big white van behind us. They filled the van with conga drums and large standing vases bursting with flowers. A big woman with loose, wrinkled skin and foggy green eyes came to the car. She kissed Grace on both cheeks. Grace passed her a fat envelope then closed her window and our car pulled away.

"Okay. I'll bite. What the hell is going on?"

Grace took a deep breath and a shadow came over her face that made it hard to know what she was feeling. "Every girl on the block lives for the day some dumb fuck will put a ring on her finger and walk her down the aisle in a white dress. Even if she ain't seen a wedding in three generations in her family, she is still Cinderella sitting around with three kids waiting for her prince. Pure bullshit. Pure poison. And that shit is holding every single one of them back. I'm giving these girls something to aim for, something to do for themselves and their kids without waiting on some bitch-ass fool with his underwear hanging out and his pants at his knees who plays them dirty, fucks 'em, leaves 'em with kids and diseases, and keeps it movin'. Tonight, we're having a wedding. A different kind of wedding, cuz we gonna marry each other." She looked over at me with a smile that had *fuck you* written all over it.

"What are you talking about?" When she didn't answer, I left it alone. She knew about me and Pete. This was my punishment: her talking about those girls when she was really talking about me.

We were heading south on the Harlem River Drive in light traffic. We got out at 60th on the East Side and I watched the Saturday brunch crowd begin to take shape. I could not fully understand what Grace was doing. She was playing games with me that felt like a threat.

My stomach flipped when the car slowed to a stop in front of Tiffany's. We had crossed so many invisible barriers of wealth and class over the last few years—high-end parties in penthouses, Wall Street offices, mansions in Riverdale, Westchester, and the Hamptons. We had become who we were because we could move quietly in circles that would otherwise burst at the sight of us getting on a subway heading home to the Bronx. Doña Durka had opened the doors to these places, and though she found respect there, she was never comfortable. She passed the task onto Grace precisely because Grace was still young enough to develop a kind of fearlessness when moving between worlds, and the skill to do it easily. Grace had become an expert at wearing costumes like they were her skin. Her baggy Champion sweatshirt and Timbs were just as much a costume as her Armani suit. She wore it all with the attitude that she was all of it and none of it at once. I had learned to flow in places where we were expected or invited. Though I still had trouble doing what Grace loved to do, showing up at expensive restaurants, pricey boutiques, or car dealerships unexpected. No matter what clothes I was wearing, it felt like I wore where I was from, and who and what I really was, like a giant red letter A on my forehead. *The Scarlet Letter* was the last book I sort of read before dropping out of high school. I understood Hester better now. Could feel her plight. Grace loved playing games with the fluency she had in these different worlds, and her commitment to none.

"I want to pretend to be surprised, but I'm not. Where else would you go to buy rings?"

Laughing, Grace slapped my knee. "Girl, why not give them the little blue box that comes built into the stupid fantasy? By the way, I know your heart is beating out of your chest right now. Don't worry. They're expecting us."

The driver got out and opened our door. We circulated drivers pretty frequently, keeping everyone confused as a rule. However, today we had a young girl Grace had been using a lot lately. Her name was Flo and she had bleached blond braids that she wore up in a bun and long, thick legs she rocked under tight, black pinstripe pants. She never looked at anyone or smiled. I imagined that was part of her charm for Grace.

There was a representative from Tiffany's waiting for us at the entrance. A middle-aged man, with salt-and-pepper hair, wearing a dark navy-blue suit. He smiled and extended his hand to Grace. "Ms. De los Santos. It's a pleasure to finally meet you in person. Let's make sure everything meets your specifications."

We were led past all the display cases laid out beneath the soaring ceilings of the main public showroom. There was bling and glitter everywhere. Tourists eyed million-dollar necklaces while holding their fifty-dollar beat cancer or AIDS bracelets in the little blue box everyone wanted to take home. The elevator went down a floor and opened into a long hallway with several doors. Guards in black suits stood in the corners trying to look discreet. Even the doorknobs and glass surfaces shone like jewels. The man in the blue suit opened a door for us, and I suddenly wondered if Grace had her gun on her. I never carried mine when I was with her unless she told me to. It helped to have someone who could go in and out of places unarmed when that was needed, and I preferred to be that one. There were no metal detectors at the entrance, but I had to wonder about the private rooms. Fear swept over me and sweat began to soak my back, then I realized it didn't matter. We were already in. Whatever was waiting for us was underway.

The man pulled out two chairs for us at a table covered in large velvet boxes. A woman on the other side of the table looked us over once as if she, like me, wondered how the hell we had gotten this far. I was dressed in jeans I could no longer button and a loose T-shirt with one of Pete's blue oxford shirts open over it. My hair was untied, and I had my white-on-white Nike sneakers. Grace had not warned me. I had not prepared. Grace was wearing a black skirt suit and black leather pumps. She sealed the look with her hair pinned back, making her look older. I could barely pass for the unruly tagalong. The man in the suit nodded at the woman, who was staring at us. She opened three long, velvet boxes. Each one of them contained nine of the same things. In the first box, there were nine engagement rings with sizable diamonds. I knew nothing about diamonds, so carats and color were beyond me. Pete had given me a simple band of two ropes entwined in white gold. These rings were big and shiny. I had only seen them on the hands of rich girls who wore them like a badge that proved their worth. In the second were nine more rings, but these were in the shape of snakes coiled over three times with small diamonds across the full length and what looked like a tiny red ruby for an eye. In the last one, nine bracelets with eight small charms on each—a sword, a bow and arrow, a gun, and others I couldn't see close enough to identify. I had to assume all of it was platinum, which was the only acceptable upgrade from the silver Grace loved. Toro had, at first, bought her yellow gold, but as she grew into herself, she wore silver, white gold, and platinum. A few of the girls still wore yellow gold jewelry, but slowly she had turned each of them on to silver, then platinum as money had allowed. Grace had recently started talking about how China and Chad were reinvesting money in the "company" and the future. I wondered if it was all sitting in those boxes. It struck me, right then, that I had no idea how much money we actually had.

Grace took the engagement ring marked by a small tag with her initials. She slipped it onto her left ring finger where Toro's ring used to be; she held it up to the light like a bride might, with a smile just as big. Grace spoke to the saleswoman with a mix of authority and childish glee. She said, "My sisters will love this. We know it's unusual, but we really want to have the same engagement ring no matter when we get married or to who. Now that I am the first to marry, I'm making sure that their rings will be ready when their time comes. I don't want my sisters to ever have less than me."

I was sure she had concocted an elaborate story for why we were here, and this should be treated as if it were all quite normal. Latin American heiresses, rapper wives, who the hell knew, but it was still amusing to hear her tell it as if she believed it. Watching everyone around her believe it as well, or pretend to, was the most fun, even as the snake rings and the charms on the bracelets could not possibly fit into that explanation. Money has a way of making people look away and go, *Why the fuck not?*

"This is my sister, Carmen. I would like her to try hers on."

With that, she slipped the engagement ring on my ring finger, and the snake ring on what she had taken to calling my no-trigger finger because I had never actually pulled one. I wasn't sure she had ever pulled one either, but I was the only one who'd refused any target practice other than the basics to keep us alive, if it ever came to that. The snake fit neatly over the bottom half of my finger, and she placed the snake head facing up as if it were literally climbing out from inside my hand. I stood neck-deep in my double betrayal, of both her and Pete, wearing an engagement ring of that size on the same finger where Pete had just slipped the simple and beautiful wedding band I was hiding in my purse. A rush of power filled me, then quickly faded into feeling lost in my own lies.

"It's beautiful."

"Do you really like them? Do you think they all will?" Her face looked like Grace in that moment. She really wanted to make us happy.

"Amazing. We were never going to see anything like this in our lives without you."

"Great! Let's get all of this wrapped up in the famous little blue boxes, please."

The man answered, "The chains you ordered with the special designed medallions have also arrived. Will you be taking those today as well?"

"Yes, please. Thank you. You've done a beautiful job with everything."

With that she pulled out her wallet and put a credit card on the table. The woman asked for her ID, and Grace handed over her license. I had never seen her use a credit card before. I was burning with questions. I held tight. Those were dizzying heights; it was all I could do to keep my poker face and follow her lead.

Back in the car with her Tiffany bags lined up beside her, Grace looked like she was ten years old again with our stolen library copy of *Ludell* in her hand. She was glowing with self-satisfaction.

"I don't want to rain on your parade, and that was, by the way, impressive. Just walking in there and walking out with all those diamonds. Nice. But where did you get that card and how are you going to pay for it?"

"Chad has been making our money make us money in so many ways it's hard to keep up. I told you I don't plan to do this shit for nothing. I mean to make this money do something for me, for all of us. I'm going Kennedy clan on you, and you didn't even know it."

Her mention of the Kennedys made us both laugh. She had given me endless speeches on the Kennedys, and the mob, and cleaning money and going legitimate. How everybody who got rich in this country started dirty. Slave trade. Moonshine. Gambling. She used to love to say, "Even the Pilgrims fucked with the Indians to get what they got. Nobody who starts with nothing gets their something clean." It was something Doña Durka had put in her head. Between them they had a vast cache of ideas about how hustling was just a stepping-stone to something much bigger and that everyone had their version. I never really believed any of it. I mean, it wasn't a lie, but it didn't make sense the way they tried to make it sound obvious and inevitable. I repeated it to Pete just the same. Grace had been left to finish what Doña Durka had started.

She called out to the driver to take us back up to the Bronx along the West Side Highway, rather than the FDR on the east. She was in full celebration mode.

"Is that safe? Putting your name and our money out there?"

"You think standing on street corners is safe? Walking into banks and mansions with packages? None of it is safe, but neither was walking in and out of the building where my mother lived when I met Toro."

Any mention of our mothers made us quiet. We rarely went there, and when we did, we were careful.

"Okay, but I feel like there's a lot of shit you ain't telling us."

"That shit is going around, isn't it?" She looked at me hard, giving me my chance to come clean. I didn't feel like telling her any more than she could manage on her own. Instead, she went on as if that pause could stay there between us right up until I gave birth.

"How can we change where we come from if we don't even want it?"

"What does that even mean? Are you planning to talk to the girls about this? They are making the money and taking the risks. Don't you think you should put them on to what you're doing?"

She moved away from me and removed her jacket, let her hair out, and took off her shoes, then curled her feet up under her on the seat. Her long-sleeved blouse was buttoned at the wrists, which felt strange for summer. I kept looking at her trying to see what she was not telling me.

She responded with some hesitation. "I will tell them, but first I need to make them understand that this is bigger than any one of us alone. I'm trying to get them to open their minds. Remember the cars?"

We all remembered the cars. We always would. It was about a year after she and Red had finished high school and the full crew minus China was fully formed. We had gotten the apartment and Grace had started making us learn shit. When we'd first started, she would walk around the room while we were taking one of her endless classes, saying, "I'm only as strong as my weakest link. Which one of you is going to be that weak link?" Fear. Terror. Love. All of it wrapped up in her lessons: swimming, driving, computers, GEDs (Santa, Remy, Sugar, and Destiny all got them, all who needed it except me), martial arts (tai chi, MMA, karate, and capoeira), world religions, dream interpretation, energetic healing, and my personal favorite, cuz it was so out the box, knitting. Supposedly knitting would develop patience. It was all Red could do to keep from poking her own eyes out, she was so bored, though Teca took to the needles like a first love and made sweaters, hats, and scarves for all of us. It helped her become the best driver. Skills had ways of begetting other skills, and that was the thing Grace loved most. Knitting helped Teca find her calm and cool. She could now be counted on to just sit there in a car knitting and never rush or call anyone during a drop-off, when that had not always been the case. There was cooking too, which taught us culture and geography: Italian, Chinese, Thai, vegetarian, and French. There was opera, transcendental meditation, Puerto Rican history (the kind they don't teach you in school, as Grace liked to say), yoga, and the history of the CIA. That apartment, away from Doña Durka's big house on Grand Avenue and Toro and his boys, became an extension of her college life. It was a dorm-like gathering place after we did what we did and learned what was offered in each experience.

She had picked up one of those little brochures for the Learning Annex in Manhattan during one of our first Upper East Side drop-offs. She brought it home and read it out loud for us. She was awestruck as she said, "Can you believe people pay good money to just learn shit like for no reason? No degree, no job. Just to learn." She was always looking for ideas to bring home to us. Though she was the only one who actually kept going to school regularly, she invented "no child left behind" before that was a thing. She'd hire people she met in college or seek out experts as her connections to the larger world expanded. They were always a little shell-shocked when she sent a car to pick them up and they were dropped off in front of what they might consider a scary-ass building in the Bronx, then faced with us around a table rapt with attention for whatever they had to offer and well skilled in asking probing questions. We used community rooms and small rented spaces for the floating annex, even the back rooms at the pawnshop, and it became an integral part of our work. Grace would always give us a pep talk before one of the lessons, saying things like: *Ask questions, bitches. The only stupid question is the one you keep to yourself and never find the answer for.* It was Sugar who called it what it was: "This right here is Miss Grace's School for Lost Girls."

How did we have time for all that? Truthfully, we had plenty of it. There were frequent pockets of waiting in our line of work. Toro kept his boys busy watching *Scarface* on repeat and memorizing every single line, ordering Chinese food, smoking blunts, and hanging out with girls. We watched *Scarface* once as part of a film series on depictions of gangsters in the American cinematic tradition led by a grad student from NYU film school. Grace knew what she was doing. She even had Sugar's and Santa's kids in after-school programs and had a team of women from the neighborhood on call for after-hours childcare when that was needed. We could drop references about skiing, scuba diving, and museums that made our customers feel elevated, among friends. Every new thing made us feel that much more fluent in the worlds we were being asked to move through. It gave us confidence. More important to Grace, unlike the money we were making, the skills would never disappear.

Grace was unique, not in her appetite for extravagance or acquisition, but in how she spent her money and what she acquired. Some we knew of had collections of exotic animals or expensive cars, chains, or sneakers. I knew a girl who used to run the business with her father and brother, and she collected Jordan sneakers. She had every pair, special edition, and color. She bought two of each, so she could wear one and keep the others in a glass collector's box like Cinderella slippers—her reference, not mine. She had a cousin, still running the business after she got caught and put away, who was still charged with keeping the collection every time a new pair was released. Grace collected abilities. It was like she thought someday what we knew would become like a new skin that would let us shed the old one and walk away, without anyone even noticing where we had come from. Our trip to Tiffany's was maybe a dress rehearsal for that afterlife.

Grace dropped me off by the garage on Jerome where I had left my car. I couldn't face Pete yet. I called Sugar. She asked no questions. "You don't need to call, just knock on my door."

. . .

Early that Sunday morning, I rode with Sugar and Destiny. We gathered in front of the church. Mass was in session, so we had the stairs mostly to ourselves to get organized for our trip to the beach.

We had to hurry or the crowd would come pouring out all at once and overwhelm us. The girls with kids were whining hard about riding the bus. The bus to Orchard on a hot Sunday felt like a sweaty clown car filled beyond capacity. Red tried to get philosophical. "Grace wants us to remember where we come from. She wants us on the bus for a reason, so bus it is."

Sugar just said, "It is too hot for this shit."

We also knew we were going to the place where Durka had been killed. No one was going to say it out loud, but it could not be ignored no matter how hard we tried.

If you were lucky enough to have a window seat, you could watch the dense population of people, cars, and tightly packed clothing stores all along Fordham Road give way to the leafy green of the Fordham University campus, the Bronx Zoo, the Botanical Garden, then the open stretch of trees along Pelham Parkway, and finally the beach. By the time we got to the stop by the Bronx Zoo on Southern Boulevard, buried in a tangle of legs and arms of strangers who all wanted our seats, we were drenched in sweat no AC could cool. Everyone started cheering when the bus made the turn onto the bridge toward the landfill. We knew the route well enough to know it meant we were close. A man in the back row turned on his radio and filled the bus with old-school salsa: "Si te quieres divertir . . . un verano en Nueva Yol." I understood exactly why Grace had us ride the bus. It wasn't about remembering our suffering; it was about remembering that we were not alone.

. . .

The sounds of Orchard are not waves crashing but guys on the boardwalk catcalling girls, seagulls eating french fries, the ice-cream truck, lost kids being announced over the loudspeaker, handballs and paddle balls cracking against concrete walls, giant boom boxes and tiny radios battling for dominance with house music in one corner, old disco in another, hip-hop in pockets, and salsa everywhere. The sun warms coconut suntan lotion and fried food in one giant cauldron of summer steam. Families went to Orchard Beach to cool off, teenagers to hang out, and the OGs mostly to be seen and to see each other feeling free. For many of us, it was all we would ever know of what it meant to be Boricua on a tropical island surrounded by beaches. It stood as affirmation of our birthrights: sand and sea. We were happy there. Grace had taken us all down to Puerto Rico for the first time right before Red was sent away. On Luquillo Beach, I felt what made us so alive on Orchard Beach in a way we never felt anywhere else. I sensed the roots of that attachment to a place that held the memory of other places that had once belonged to us. I didn't know what Grace had planned, but it was no accident she had chosen Orchard to do it. We had a mystical bond with this place that stretched beyond Durka's tragedy, and I thought maybe she was trying to heal or restore that. It had been two months since we buried her.

We had been instructed to leave our weapons at home. It felt both light and scary to know we were all together and unarmed in the same place Durka had been shot. Grace called doing things that scared us *eating fear*. "Just open your mouth and eat it. Once you swallow and don't die, you won't be scared no more." There was no plan for swallowing and actually dying.

It already felt ten degrees cooler than it had on Fordham Road. My shoulders dropped with every deep breath I took. Even Pete and the growing weight of my belly turned soft and hazy. I let myself hang in the space where I could pretend this was a party with my girls that they didn't know was for me. We stopped at the stairs that spread up and out from the garden planted in a semicircle in the drop-off parking lot closest to the bus stop. People were moving fast trying to get to the best shady spots or picnic tables before they all disappeared. You could smell the salty air, but you couldn't see the water until you hit the top of the stairs.

All stairs were kicking my ass these days, but these had a gift waiting at the end, so I walked faster. Once I hit the platform at the top, the horizon and the beach stretched out as far as I could see left or right. The blue sky, the ocean, and the smell of salt came into sharp relief after the dark, cramped bus ride. It was the thing in front of us, the beauty of who we already were and already had, that Grace could always somehow make us see clearer.

She greeted us on the platform wearing a white scarf tied around her head, her giant bamboo hoop earrings, with *Grace* written in script across the middle, and a long white skirt. I had not seen those earrings since high school. They glittered in the sun with the dreams we had back then fully realized all around us. The entire landing at the top of the stairs was a carnival of "give it to me, I'm worth it," with everything from cold drinks to fresh empanadas; several women on hand equipped with shovels, buckets, sand toys, and water bottles; and a piragua man, parked behind Grace, shaving ice and filling paper cones for the kids on demand.

Sugar wasted no time as she approached him and said, "Tamarindo, por favor."

The kids all ran up the stairs to Grace as soon as they saw her. Santa's kids, Anthony and Julissa, clung to her skirt. She picked up Anthony to hug him. "Chacho, when did you get so heavy?"

Serena, Sugar's oldest, was almost as tall as Grace. When she came in for a hug, Grace pushed down on her shoulders and joked, "Girl, you can't grow taller than me, that is a rule. Did they not tell you that?"

Serena talked back in her newfound sweet sarcastic style, "My mom is taller than you."

"Yeah, but I found her like that. I met you tiny, so different rules."

Serena smiled proudly. "You just saw me at Disney. You always act like I grew."

Grace shot back, "Do you know for sure you didn't? I mean last night even? Could you prove that? No, so maybe I see you bigger every time because I can see you growing in ways you can't."

Serena gave an exaggerated little shrug and curtsy, then ran off to play with her brother. Sugar had done a great job of keeping her young. It made my heart ache to think that Grace had moved in with Toro and Doña Durka when she was just a little older than Serena. She must have seen it on my face.

"What is it, crybaby? You look like this is a funeral. Lighten up. Have some fun. Does Pete not let you have fun anymore?"

I ignored the Pete comment because I was honestly tired of them both. When I wasn't dying of love or loyalty for one or both of them, they reminded me of middle school girls fighting for a boy who didn't want either one. "No, honestly, this is beautiful. All of it. It's just that Serena . . ."

"Yeah, I know. She is hitting that age that scares the fuck out of me, but I aged in dog years, so I can't really relate. Sugar got it, though." She pinched my waist and added, "Wepa, chichos. Pete must be feeding you right. Old as I am, I ain't even the one getting fat, go figure." She didn't let me respond, but laughed and started dancing with Santa and Red.

There was a DJ mixing old-school salsa, hip-hop, and Mary J. Blige, playing the soundtrack to how we loved each other. One by one we each kissed Grace and received the depth of her hug. She held each of us longer than we would have dared hold on.

She pointed at some bags from Bloomingdale's with our names on them lined up against the far concrete wall and said, "Go change. We can't be out here looking like bums."

Teca looked offended and said, "Well, maybe if you didn't make us get here on the bus ride through hell . . ."

Grace just put the bag in her hand and sent her to the lockers.

The lockers had been closed for years, but Grace had somehow managed to donate, agitate, and raise enough money to renovate and reopen a small section. The columns still had the faded blue and white Greek meander pattern that you see on all the to-go coffee cups in New York City diners; it made them look like an ancient Greek temple. Grace had read to us from books, the whole history of Greek coffee cups, then Robert Moses and Orchard Beach, over several dinners at the apartment after our first visit as a crew years ago. Grains of sand she was always throwing to strengthen and expand our internal shorelines.

The locker rooms were empty, even though the beach was packed, indicating just how much influence Grace had used to get us here. We opened the bags to find waves of white that resembled wedding gowns. Each of us had a long, white, cotton skirt. Remy's had a long slit on either side. Mine had ruffles and a long train with a short front. Santa's looked like a multilayer cake with each layer hiding a color beneath it. She was a rainbow in motion when she spun around to make the skirt flare out.

Destiny called out to Remy, "Yo, did you see the hats?"

They pulled big, glamorous, floppy hats over their heads and strutted like peacocks on a runway. Teca pulled a Panama with a thick, black band out of her bag and nodded with approval.

Sugar had a church lady hat with lilies and a little veil. She grabbed the paper it came wrapped in and made herself a fan, then waved it as she giddily announced, "Child, this is not your mother's church on Sunday, but damn, this feels good. If only Granma Helen could see me now."

Red laughed as she pulled a white-on-white Yankee fitted out of the bag that looked like it came straight from her closet. Tucked inside was a white Janis Joplin concert T-shirt. We all stared at it as she held it up to the light. The picture of Janis, eyes closed, singing in ecstasy under her name in giant letters. It was exactly the same image as the one that had faded on Red's mother's original. She pulled it on and said, "That concert might literally have been the happiest day of my mother's life."

China had a little white straw fedora with a pencil sticking out the band like a bookie. Grace had saved the eerie shit for me. I pulled a little flower tiara out from my bag that looked way too much like the one Pete had made. I wanted to burst into tears. She stood in the doorway of the lockers framed by the columns and lit up by the sun. We locked eyes only for a second, but everything in me went cold. She came over and secured the tiara on my curls with two bobby pins with the plastic end protectors removed. I had watched her pull those pins from her hair and chew off the ends, then spit them into her hands, since we were kids. She shoved the exposed metal edges hard against my scalp in a way that let me know what she really wanted to do to me. I drew back and touched my head looking for blood. I glanced around to see if anyone had noticed, but they were all laughing and spinning and dancing. I reached for her wrist as she turned.

She yanked her arm away and whispered, "Don't even fucking think about it. I got nothing to say to you right now."

We had spent a lot of time learning how to be invisible, so standing out on purpose was confusing. Once we were all dressed, we looked at each other and made faces, but only Destiny spoke. "We look like the brides of magic."

Red poked back, "Well, the brides of Christ we most definitely are not." She took one of the drinks in red plastic cups waiting for us on a tray by the door and raised it in a toast. "We all here, and here we are. Ready or not . . . let the Fugees take it from there."

Back outside, the people getting off the bus and crossing the platform to the stairs watched us. There were whispers, no doubt, but all the chatter was tinged with awe and fear. Some nodded in Grace's direction, but they all kept moving. Walking the world like you mattered, that was the Kool-Aid we drank and it kept us coming back for more.

. . .

The stairs down to the boardwalk spilt off on either side of the platform, forming a wide gentle spiral where we were standing. Grace had lined the area with flowers. Orchard Beach had layers and Grace had us crossing them like thresholds. She waited for us at the bottom with beaded necklaces, smaller versions of the medallion she wore, with Durga on one side and the Virgin Mary on the other, and draped them around our necks.

Yemaya, our Great Mother of the Ocean, was everywhere. There was a small statue of her with a candle and flowers at each of the little white metal tables arranged like miniature altars all facing the sea. There was an altar for Oya in the front, closest to the stage, separated from everyone. She was a mystery to all of us, but her statue had appeared in Doña Durka's house after her cancer diagnosis. I imagined that Grace added her out of respect for the unknown storms ahead. The murti of Ma Durga, as Grace had taught us the figures that held Her were called, was set off to the back at the last tree in the wooded area to the left of the open path. It was placed on an elaborate and beautiful stand covered in handmade gold cloth that had Teca's signature stitching on the bottom. Someone had put up a big red beach umbrella as a cover that gave the whole stand a reddish glow. Overlooking all of it from the fierce seat of her lion, Durga looked so much like us, covered in gold chains and rings. Her clarity and consistency sustained me. Grace had put some of Durka's real gold chains around her neck too. Hindus called her Maa, and we called her Ma, the way we called each other. "Oye, ma" added to any request or comment made plain we were all little mothers to each other in some way.

I was pretty sure Toro and Nene weren't invited, but there was no way something this big and in your face would remain a secret. I searched the crowd for them or any of their boys. What would it mean to find them there? I was too swept up in the spell Grace was casting to linger in the fear too long, but it flickered in and out.

Grace led us to a round blanket at the front of the grassy area closest to the view of sand and sea. She signaled for us to sit down and smiled as we arranged ourselves around her. Lovingly she said, "We might come from different mothers and fathers, but we are sisters before the mother of us all. This is not about what we do, but who we are." She paused and let her words sink in before continuing, "Today we dance, we eat, we drink and sing as the Daughters of Durka. Mothers have been stolen from us or us from them, but we can reclaim the one that belongs to all of us. It is a bond deeper than marriage, and we commit to loyalty, honor, and love. We are the D.O.D., the Daughters of Durka."

A soft murmur of hope, love, and fear grew louder as it rose up through us. Sugar and Destiny leaned deep into each other, shoulder to shoulder. Teca and Remy swayed to a beat in the background, arm in arm.

Red whooped and hollered, "¡Que viva the D.O.D.!"

Santa raised one hand and called back, "¡Que viva!"

Only me and China stayed quiet, but China looked like she might have been wiping tears.

Grace sat still at the center of the circle and took in all the energy, offering hugs or kisses or high fives, but never standing. I felt quiet inside. It was powerful to be seen and given so much that was real, but I was no longer enchanted. I felt entangled.

Our name, the D.O.D., was a reference to Las hijas de María. They were the teenage girls we had watched from a distance serve in the church as the Daughters of Mary, dressed in white with red ribbons around their waist, especially around the Ascension of Mary. They were also the daughters of prominent women who never welcomed us. These were not rich people, but the people who raised their own kids, worked hard, went to church on Sundays, and always looked at girls like Grace and me as some kind of contagion, as if we carried the stain of our mothers' neglect. We were not, according to their laws of decency and family, fit to be the Daughters of Mary, and back then we couldn't afford the clothes anyway. Grace was reinventing us as the daughters of mothers who'd claim us no matter how wild or scary we became.

The congas in the corner started a slow, steady rhythm that turned into a single pulse connecting us. Grace turned slowly and took off her shirt to reveal a full back tattoo we had never seen. It was still shiny with Vaseline, indicating it was recent. Red smiled. It was clear she'd had something to do with it. When Grace extended her arms out on both sides, we saw it went across her arms as well. It was Ma Durga in extraordinary detail. She had eight arms, each with a weapon in hand, two ending above Grace's wrists. It was then that I recognized the charms on the bracelets: they were Durga's weapons, except for the gun—that was Grace's. Durga sat upon her tiger, stretched across Grace's lower back, claws wrapped around each hip, surrounded by lotus flowers with our initials at the center of each one. The two lotuses closest to Durga's feet were me and Red. My eyes watered and my stomach tensed. Grace stood and turned it up by flexing her arms and her back muscles. All the girls whistled and cheered. The drums picked up the pace and we made our way to the dance floor by the bandstand.

A group of older women were already dancing in a circle. These were the familiar faces Doña Durka had helped that would now offer their loyalty and gratitude to Grace. It was not a traditional bembé, although there were clearly real practitioners present. I didn't know how far Grace or Doña Durka had gone in their faith, but I knew that they had deep reverence for the lineage of Mothers the religion had sustained over thousands of miles and centuries of slavery and abuse of every kind. Orishas worshiped in the Yoruba culture were still known and loved by name on a beach in the Bronx and across the world, because it had held on to us even as the world had tried to erase us. This much we had been taught to revere no matter our individual beliefs, which ran from Red the atheist to Santa the lone still-practicing Catholic among us. Maybe the rules had been bent for Grace, as they often are for the powerful, or maybe she was deeper in than I knew. Ma Durga was not part of that tradition, and yet she too had claimed us and come to us deepest of all.

My belly tensed, reminding me that I wasn't here alone. The desire to pretend that I was, and that my actions only had consequences for me was still strong, but it felt like parts of me were peeling off like old paint. La India, the main concert performer, came on the stage to cheers and screams. She opened with her song to Yemaya and Oshun, from her first album, which had come out when we were just starting with Doña Durka. We danced like it was our first night on a dance floor. We danced like we might destroy the world and make it new.

. . .

We were all high in one way or another, something Grace rarely allowed, and so we had no habit of doing together. I didn't drink or smoke but felt a kind of elevation and freedom I hadn't experienced in a long time. Beach security made its way through the crowd to announce the beach was closing as the sun dripped honey-colored light across the flow of liquor, food, and music that hadn't stopped since we'd arrived. Back on our little circle blanket, Red played "Love Alive" on her guitar and we sang it loud and proud. Sugar wrapped her arm around my lower back and squeezed. Santa leaned over Sugar and kissed me on my forehead. For right now, we were enough, and all I had that felt real. The servers Grace had hired for the day began to clean and pack up around us.

Teca smiled and said, "Finally, we leveled up from cleaning after ourselves."

Grace rolled her eyes and handed a security guy an envelope of cash to cover her after the park closed. It took hours to empty Orchard as people packed and slowly left. Except for the guy she'd paid, and a few extras watching our personal belongings, we were finally alone.

Grace signaled for us to follow her toward the water at the end of the boardwalk. Section 13 was the rocky end of the beach farthest away from the parking, bus stop, food, and bathrooms. It was liminal space, in the same way the dream lady had told us dreams were. Spaces between worlds that had meaning beyond what we could know, even when we thought we knew everything.

We crossed from the boardwalk into the sand with our skirts blowing in the wind like sails. Grace must have consulted the almanac for this party because a perfect full moon rose out of the water in the east as we walked to the edge of the ocean along the rocks in the dark. When we reached the wet sand, Grace asked us all to kneel and gather in a circle shoulder to shoulder. We were close enough to feel water lapping around us and slowly our skirts grew wet and took root in the mud. She opened a white towel she had been carrying and spread the little blue boxes out across the towel.

"There ain't a man alive who will ever do for you what I will make you able to do for yourselves. And once you know how to do it for yourselves, there ain't a man alive you can't love because you won't be waiting on him to save you."

Beneath that fat slice of moon still climbing up out of the ocean, Grace was transformed. I no longer recognized her as she put a ring on each of our fingers and the bracelets around our wrists. She added ankle bracelets I hadn't even seen. They looked like she might have brought them directly from India, with the small bells and curved S-hook clasp. She kissed each one of us hard on the mouth when she was done. I was as transfixed as any of them. She saved me for last, which I took as a sign of honor. Then she pulled me in close and whispered, "I bet that motherfucker didn't give you a wedding like this. Don't get confused. You belong to me, you always have, and you always will. Go play house if you want, but remember you wouldn't even know him if it wasn't for me." I slipped back and almost fell onto the sand, but her hand held mine and pulled me back up to my knees before she finally let go.

Grace took off her skirt and her bikini top and stood naked before us. She turned to give us her tattooed back again, arms up and out in victory and acceptance, which were maybe the same thing. Most of the girls were on their knees. Slowly, each one stood, took off her clothes, and followed Grace into the water. Some were looking at their rings and some were crying. We had all taken swimming lessons at a YMCA years before. I stood at the edge, still dressed and staring out across the dark, asking Yemaya for guidance. I refused to get in the water. A force greater than my love for Grace began to fill me with the sense that maybe she was only one aspect of the world, and maybe there were other plans for me. I could hear them singing "Love Alive" without me and I cried hard as I turned and walked away.

8

SAFE

Sunday's midnight drift into Monday was almost underway. I looked in my bag and saw at least ten missed calls and beeps from Pete. I was not going home to a warm welcome. I had to ask the guys still putting stuff back in the van for a ride out from the beach to Pelham to catch a cab. The tree-lined streets of Pelham Parkway were empty and quiet but for a few scattered families on either side of the green sitting outside for fresh air. I had never even called Pete. I had left the house in the dark on Saturday morning, the morning after we'd gotten married. I hadn't called him once since or even kissed him goodbye. I was wearing a giant diamond ring meant to be worn, as most are, like a price tag on my loyalty. He would be worried and angry, and he had every right. I felt like a rubber band pulled tight that finally snaps, landing far away in some random place stretched out and useless. I had to go back to the apartment in the Bronx to get my car keys and change. Maybe I would call him from there. Maybe I would stay in the apartment and never go back to Pete. I changed my mind with every step I took.

· · ·

The apartment was usually buzzing with movement, even when I'd lived there. There were small windows of quiet in all the energy, but nothing like the empty of being there alone not knowing what to do next. I stuck to the routine of hanging my keys on the nail by the door, walking through the hall quiet to make sure no one was there who shouldn't be. Security had the apartment to the left and they hit the wall to see if I would knock back in our code. I did.

The apartment was mostly empty space to keep room for all the shit that had to move through there. It had traces of home. It could never be home. It was the truest home most of us had ever known. I was the only one who had lived there, my personal stuff stashed in a corner of the bedroom that we mostly used for packing. Grace had started collecting paintings and slowly covered the walls with images of girls and women turning into trees or wolves or the sea itself. She didn't talk about the paintings or the artists, she just kept bringing them in and hanging them on the walls. Santa had picked out the dining room table and kept us stocked in scented candles. Sugar had picked out the eggplant purple couch and Destiny the sandy gold cushions and curtains. I had picked out the dish set Santa demanded we buy for our dinners. Remy, Teca, and Red had declared themselves "women who didn't care about none of that shit," but there was a hand-knitted blanket from Teca on the couch, a framed picture of us on our bikes that Red had hung in the kitchen without saying a word, and an old pilón and rice pot Remy brought in one day, saying, "These were my grandmother's. I'm never gonna use that shit, but she had sazón, so maybe we should keep them here." China had not yet left her mark on the place, at least not visibly.

I swore I heard Red's fierce whistle, and peeked out the window, though I knew she wasn't there. Even in my head the sound of Red was a warning that made me move faster. I went to change in the back room. I opened the door with my key, but the closet door inside was swung wide, blocking the entrance. It was the one with the many locks and the safes that only Grace, and most recently China, had the keys and combinations to, standing open and empty. No drugs, no money, and no forced entry that I could see.

I backed away as if it were a dead body. I didn't want to touch a thing. I didn't want to know. I left the pile of white clothes in a corner with the tiara in the middle. I thought twice about leaving my gun. I kept mine under my old bed. I went back for it. Leaving didn't mean I was out, especially if no one even knew. I had no way of knowing if Grace had done it or someone else, but calling her would be like asking permission to come back. My heart was racing. I did the knock on the wall to let security know I was leaving and ran down the stairs. Through. Through. Through. The only way out of this shit was through. I was fucking through. I could not stand the idea of leaving Grace in danger, but she never had a problem putting me in danger. This was how we lived. Red was back. She had a partner. I would not be leaving her alone. We tell ourselves so many stories. My leaving was just one more.

I saw the flashing red lights of police cars through the glass top of the door at the entrance to the building, turned at the mailboxes on the ground floor, and went down the small stairs to the basement. I was almost 100 percent sure it had nothing to do with us. Cops who came to that building knew to look the other way. But everything was changing fast. Panic was rising. I went out the back entrance across the yard to the other building. It was a route we had practiced. I walked the eight blocks to the garage where we kept our work cars, nice and slow, trying to breathe through my nose. *If you calm your breath, you calm yourself.* I could hear the yoga teacher Grace had hired repeating it over and over. *Breathe deep anyway. No matter what happens. Breathe.* At the garage, I found the attendant who worked for us. I asked him to give me the keys to a car that was registered in my name. I gave him the keys to my personal car, told him where it was, and asked him to bring it in off the street. I wasn't going back to that block or that building. I wasn't going back.

. . .

When I walked up to my apartment—our apartment—in Brooklyn, I saw from outside that all the lights were out. Pete usually left one on for me. It wasn't even midnight yet. He never went to bed that early. Realizing that my danger was his danger, and how reckless I had been with his safety, struck a blow. I peeked up the stairs hoping to see light coming from under his studio door. I was listening for his music, old records from his uncle's collection that he sometimes played while he painted: Orquesta Broadway, Fania All-Stars, Raphy Leavitt, Pete "El Conde" Rodríguez.

My body, already heavier than I had ever known it, landed on our floor with a dull thud as I sat on the top step. No light from his studio. No sounds. When I opened the door to our apartment, I pulled my gun. Instincts were as they were, and everything felt off. I went in every room and turned on every light till, finally, I found a note taped on the wall of the half-painted mural. I took a breath, put the gun away, and locked the door. I sat on the edge of the bed reading his tiny print. It was more of the same till the end when he wrote: *I'm scared, Carmen, for you and for me and for our baby, and I wish you could understand that my reaction is the normal one.*

Normal where? Normal for who? What the fuck did he know about my normal? If this is what normal people did, run when the shit gets crazy, then I had no use for his normal. I knew many ways this could go wrong for me. I ran over them like a shopping list in my mind. But it didn't matter. He left first. It was the door I needed. I took the basics with me. I left the ring he gave me inside the tiara that was on the dresser. Fuck this. I didn't need it. I was in my car, but I had no idea where to go. I was too scared to go back to the apartment in the Bronx. I headed for the safe house, pretending like I didn't know there was no such thing as safe. As I drove away from Brooklyn in a fancy convertible registered in my name, but only ever used for work, it was clear as hell that even my getaway had Grace written all over it. Even Pete had Grace written all over him.

• • •

The year 2000 had seemed like the big future when we were little, but it came and went as more of the same, except for the arrival of Pete. Nothing crashed that New Year's Day, even though everyone was waiting for it. That summer we were doing all the things we had ever wanted to do. One night Grace asked me to go on our favorite drive down the West Side Highway. We drove all the way from Dyckman to the Brooklyn Bridge. Brooklyn was not our usual territory as far as I knew back then. Grace would normally turn at Battery Park and make her way east to the FDR or circle back up the West Side Highway, or if she was feeling in her "Manhattan State of Mind," she'd go straight up Broadway, then other streets when it turned one way, only to get back on first chance she got. It was a long, inefficient route of miles upon miles of red lights and pedestrians and yellow cabs. A nightmare to most, but it was the heart of New York City, and she would drive it from lower Manhattan all the way up into Washington Heights and the Bronx till she hit Riverdale. It made her feel alive that there was such a street, one with as many personalities as she had, running through the city. On that night she drove over the bridge into Brooklyn. She hadn't said a word since we'd left Durka's house. I didn't dare say anything either because of Doña Durka's last comment to me as we'd left: "Don't let her go soft on me."

Without taking her eyes off the road, Grace said, "Cancer. Fucking cancer. Dodging bullets and beatings her whole fucking life, and it comes down to this bullshit."

"Durka? What kind? I mean how sick?"

"Stage four. They're not even sure where it started, but it's everywhere. Her lungs, her liver. The whole fucking thing was full of little black spots, like bullet holes all over her." She couldn't keep talking as the tears came and she drove faster.

"Maybe you should pull over. You know. I'll drive." But she just kept going. I didn't know what else to say.

"Where are we going? I mean we don't really do Brooklyn."

This made her smirk a little. "Listen to you. We don't do Brooklyn. Girl, we do the world. You should know that shit by now."

She spent the rest of the ride wading in and out of anger, trying to find her way back to the place where she made shit work. She had a pocket full of candy and popped Skittles the whole drive.

Finally we got to a warehouse-looking building with an odd assortment of people kind of mingling around outside. From where we parked, you could see paintings on huge white walls.

"Is this another one of your educational adventures? Cuz it's a weird time for that shit."

"Bitch, do I look like I'm trying to waste my time educating you. I gave up on that a long-ass time ago. This is strictly business." She cleaned herself up in the mirror, and with no further explanation got out of the car.

It wasn't until we were deep inside the stupidly too cool but kind of interesting art exhibit that I recognized Chad. He was all blue pinstripe suit, red power tie, and conspicuous blond hair in a crowd of arty punks, hippies, and the self-proclaimed avant-garde. Weirdos and chilled-out white people gathered in front of walls covered in art much the way viejitas gather in front of altars. Chad looked surprised to see me, but his face lit up at the sight of Grace.

"What brings you to dirty old Brooklyn? I've invited you to like a hundred of these things and you always give me, 'The Bronx doesn't do Brooklyn.' Very, very nice surprise." He leaned over to kiss Grace, who had her biggest "I am ever so full of shit" smile firmly in place.

"Let's just say I got tired of saying no."

"Let's hope that spirit spreads to everything I've ever invited you to do." He bit his lower lip as he said it.

I couldn't resist poking holes in his stupid. "Don't they teach you any game in prep school? All that education and you still look like a sex offender trying to kick it to a girl. Why?"

He twisted his face into a creep grin and said, "Hi, Carmen. Always a pleasure."

Grace ignored me. "Yeah, well, don't get ahead of yourself. I came to talk business."

He looked around as if confused, "This is not exactly the kind of place where I can talk business with you."

"I know, but I have a situation and we need to make some changes pretty fast, so I figured I'd come early and keep you from getting drunk or laid and then we could work out what needs to be done."

"Okay, but I need to hang around a little while. I've developed this artist, Pete Gonzalez. I've pumped like a hundred grand on getting the space ready to show his work. I've been letting him live upstairs in a loft/studio to keep him focused. I actually think he's pretty talented, and super interesting. Let's walk around. You'll do wonders for my image." He threaded his arm through hers as he said it. He barely looked at me as he muttered, "Well, I guess you're coming along too, no?"

"Yeah, don't hurt yourself being awkward. I'm good."

I walked ahead into a wall of huge faces made of hundreds, maybe thousands of tiny lines. They were paintings you could look at for hours and never stop seeing something new. Then there was a two-story Santeria altar in a back corner. Tall, dark, salt-and-pepper, curly-haired Painter Pete, as Red would get us calling him eventually, was standing there talking to a group of people next to congueros in the corner playing music. He was explaining how altars were an art form that had always inspired him. I could see Grace trying to edge Chad in that direction, but he was busy working the room, so I drifted closer on my own. Pete gave off a warm light in a room full of empty small talk.

He looked over at me and smiled. He was older, but I wasn't beyond a good flirt. I smiled back at him. When I nodded my head to let him know I was into the work, he excused himself from the crowd. Pete came walking toward me in his white linen guayabera shirt looking fly as hell.

"Hey, I don't think we've been introduced. I'm Pete."

"Hi, Pete."

We awkwardly shook hands, both of us leaning into the electric charge it gave off. It was that strong chemical thing from minute one. Not that many people bring it like that. Just raw wordless attraction. No matter all that came after, it never really changed, the power of that current between us. It took us both a minute to sort of step back from the pull of it.

"Is it weird to ask what you think of the art?"

"Weird? I don't know. Isn't that what you show it for? I like it. I mean, I'm not an art show expert or anything. But I like the vibe in here. I like looking at those faces. It feels like I could just keep staring at them for hours."

"Thanks. That's kind of what you want to hear. That people want to look at the work and have a hard time turning away. I'm kind of having that experience myself right now." Pete was like that from the start; his game was upfront. He stared at me until I had to look away.

"Yeah, well, what about those altars. They're pretty different from the paintings. What are you trying to say with that? They are things people actually believe in still, not just props."

"Slow down. It's not like that. They started as a way to pay homage to my grandmother, Abuela Tuta. She owned and ran a botanica here in Brooklyn when I was a kid. I used to go there after school. I really think I became an artist there. All the colors, the beads, the statues, the candles. It was this very esoteric and ethereal place that people came to with the most mundane shit. Like I would be sweeping the floor or unpacking the herbs and I'd hear people telling her about their problems at work, or with their husbands or mother-in-laws or trouble getting pregnant, and I was always confused. It took me a long time to understand the connection between the stuff in the store and why the people told her all these random secrets about their lives. The altars started out like that, you know, just thanking my abuelita and the Orishas for my art. Then I got really into the idea of altars as art, the aesthetic, the symmetry, the colors, and the intention to evoke emotion and meaning. Shit, did I just give you the long-ass answer that makes you think, *I have to get away from this boring ass . . .*"

I shook my head and said, "Nah, nah, I asked the question because I'm interested."

"Yeah, I'm a little out there right now. This is a big night for me. I gotta admit, you're kind of throwing me off. I guess I'm just trying to put it out there that I'm not some arty bore."

"Or you're tryin' to say I look hood and you tryin' to keep it real."

"No. I'm trying to say you look good and I'm trying to keep it together." We laughed and leaned in, touched shoulders or arms. Even now I can feel the tight electric impulse straight across my body that made me think I would find a way to go home with him even if it meant ditching Grace.

"I don't want to keep you. Lots of people look like they want to talk to you. I'm here . . ." As I was about to go on, Chad and Grace walked over. Chad clapped Pete on the back and started talking, which was never a good thing.

"I see you've met the next Keith Haring. I mean, is this guy incredible or what? He has his finger on the pulse of urban frenetic energy, but he brings it up and out of chaos into order, beauty—in short, magic through his connection with the ancestors. Powerful. We've already sold three tonight, and we're hoping to sell at least five to keep him working and making progress."

Grace saw me rolling my eyes and gave me the "behave yourself" face before she asked me, "What do you think about it?"

"I love it. I was just telling him how much I like the faces."

"Great, so we'll buy them all."

Pete looked stunned and suspicious. He started looking Grace over, taking notice of her shoes and her bag and her jewelry, trying to check on the DL whether she could actually afford the pieces. He innocently fell into her favorite trap, the one from which no one was ever sprung without a little bit of humiliation and sometimes a lot.

"Have you seen the price listings? I mean, I'm totally excited that you like the work enough to want to buy it—" He didn't even get to finish before the knives were out and sharpened.

Chad just looked up at the ceiling knowing as well as I did what was coming.

"First off, I didn't say I liked your art. She does. I also wouldn't be that excited if I were you about being compared to Keith Haring, who basically appropriated graffiti and made it white and fun and lovable and made a fortune from what Black and Latino youth created from the absence of choice and canvas, and the need to make themselves visible. And last but not least, I own the building you're standing in, and most likely the one you live in, if this fool is the one who put you up and is helping you out, and if you think he has money, just realize he was a broke-ass kicked out of his trust fund college student before he met me." She turned from Pete to Chad in a clear signal that there would be no response expected. "Chad, I'd really like to get moving, so if you could have someone work with Carmen so she can pick the ones she wants, that would be great."

Her crazy *I own all these buildings* talk confused me. I assumed she was speaking on behalf of Doña Durka. I did go home with Pete, not her, and it wasn't even that hard. She was in explosive mode, and taking it all out on Chad.

Pete hated her from that first humiliation and never budged, not an inch. I think it became part of his appeal to me. He was the only person I ever knew who didn't fall into the magic haze of Grace. He couldn't win, of course, at least not with me, but I liked that he fell only for me. As soon as she walked away, he turned to face me.

"What the fuck was that about?"

"Hard day. Long story. Too much information. You pick."

"What are you two? Sisters?"

I knew he was asking something else, but he didn't dare go there. "Not exactly, but pretty much. We're cousins, but more like sisters."

"Oh, and she just buys you thousands of dollars' worth of art for fun?"

"Sometimes. But I could buy it myself. She did it more to piss you off, and to piss off Chad, not that he cares as long as money is involved and he gets his cut."

"So, you know Chad like that?"

"Not like she does, but I know enough. Anyway, you sold your art. I love it. Let's just leave the rest alone for now, unless you're already tired of looking at me."

He hesitated. I saw it. Instinct works like that, but once you doubt it, it leaves the building and you're on your own. Had he listened, he could have been spared. Instead, he put his arm around me and squeezed.

"Yeah, not quite. Let's go choose your favorites. I'm curious about which ones you're going to pick."

At some point Grace came by and half whispered, "I'm guessing that suddenly you do Brooklyn. I'm sure you'll manage to get yourself home, or not."

. . .

I fell hard into the midnight blue of Pete's dream about who I might be. It was a tumble down a magic tunnel with twinkling lights where I was quiet, smart, mysterious, and gorgeous. It was a place where Grace was not stronger than me.

When we got to his apartment, I saw his full name on a phone bill on his kitchen table: Pedro Albizu Gonzalez. Named after a famous radical Puerto Rican writer and revolutionary Grace had made us study in her "Know Your History, Since You're So Damn Proud of Your Flag" class. It was a name that indicated he had interesting parents. I picked up the bill while he poured two glasses of wine from a bottle he pulled out of his fridge, which I noticed was surprisingly full of actual food.

"So, Pedro, how'd you go from Puerto Rican nationalist to Williamsburg Pete the artist?"

"Damn, girl, you already going through my mail. I haven't even given you the keys to my place yet."

We hadn't kissed, though the tension of it had been building. He lived in a walk-up. I remember thinking that if we had taken an elevator we probably would have kissed there. It was irrational chemistry that had been simmering for hours by then. He laughed as he put the glass of wine down, took the bill out of my hand, and pressed me against the door to kiss me.

. . .

We woke up around five in the morning to the sound of garbage trucks. He rolled over toward me. My instinct sent me away from him to check my beeper to be sure Grace or one of the girls wasn't looking for me.

"Damn, so much for snuggling."

"Yeah, I'm not big on that."

"Well, you're big on a lot of other things I like way more than snuggling, so that's cool." But he reached out and pulled me close anyway. "So, am I allowed to ask questions?"

"Not until you answer the one you pulled out of my hand a few hours ago."

"Oh, that, yeah, my parents were the Pippies. Puerto Rican hippies. They did the Young Lords radical movement, they occupied Hostos in the seventies, and they both got PhDs. My dad in Puerto Rican studies and my mom in Latin American history. Amazing people. They named me Pedro Albizu, but seriously, by the time I was six or seven years old, I was Pete. They had all this Puerto Rican nationalist identity going on, but I mostly went to all-white schools. I don't know what they were thinking. If they wanted me to feel like a Pedro, they should have made more of an effort to surround me with Puerto Ricans. I guess they thought family, Brooklyn, and Abuelita's botanica were enough. In a bunch of ways, they were. But you know it's hard out there trying to hold all your worlds in your mouth, your hair, and your name all at once. Some things fall away, but hopefully, the good stuff remains. They didn't even know people called me Pete till middle school. They got all pissed off too. My uncle was cool though, he told them that was awesome cuz now I was named after his favorite singer Pete 'El Conde' Rodríguez, who had to have been a Pedro at one point too."

"I guess I should pay attention to how I ask you questions cuz I'm gonna to have to always expect the long answer."

He looked a little embarrassed, but also determined as he got closer to my face and said, "You see. I knew it. Fine. Now I ask the questions. How do you and your cousin have so much disposable income?"

I laughed before answering, "Don't be afraid to cut to the chase or anything. Did anybody ever tell you it's rude to ask people about their money?"

"No, I mean, I know it's rude, but it's kind of the elephant in the room. I just had sex with my biggest benefactor. I feel a little confused."

"Aww, do you feel cheap? Like you had to sleep with me cuz Grace bought all your paintings?"

He reached over, pinched my ass, then bit my neck before he rolled on top of me. "Yeah, well, for all those paintings, I mean, that's like a lot of sex you're entitled to. I mean, I'm sort of like an indentured servant." He looked down the length of my body and added, "Tell me, en qué le puedo servir."

"Do what you do best, just be creative."

We went on like that for two whole days, from bed to couch to kitchen. We took food in bed and sex in the kitchen. I think we took a shower, but I can't remember the soap, only the sense of being soaked from head to toe and inside out. We talked endless amounts of bullshit, but he steered clear of that original question. He came back around to it a week later, but those two days were the honeymoon we would never have.

Grace sent Red to pick me up on the third morning of my descent into Brooklyn. She knocked on the door. Sweaty, wild-eyed Red, with her long uncombed hair, leather pants, motorcycle helmet in hand. It was clear from his face that she took him by surprise.

"Rise and shine, sleeping beauty. It seems your Prince Charming here put your ass to sleep instead of waking you up. You have work to do. Our queen has sent for you."

She walked right past him down the long hallway into the open loft living room. It was artist-messy with paint and canvas leaning against the walls. I could see her from the bedroom, which was only separated by a sheet, as she looked around for my clothes. She collected them in her arms from various locations around the apartment—and in her very dramatic Red way, used a fork she found on the floor next to an empty Chinese take-out container to pick up my panties and throw them at me from behind the sheet curtain. She then popped her head in and winked at me as if to give her approval before announcing, "Okay, kiddies, enough with the fun and games. I'll be waiting downstairs." She walked out and smiled at him while he was still standing at the door. I had to laugh.

I jumped up and started getting dressed.

I called out to him, "Yeah, well, I think my carriage just turned into a pumpkin. A large red-haired pumpkin to be exact. I better go."

Pete was not amused. He was a grown man. I felt that difference between us when he stood in front of me and gently put his hands on my shoulders. He looked me in the eyes like he wanted to see something there. Like he was expecting to find an answer.

"You got like a lot of weird friends, but I'm not going there right now. I just need to know if this was a little game for you, because it wasn't that for me. Be straight with me. I can take it, no bullshit."

I backed up and pulled my shirt over my head. "Chill. I've been here two days. My girls are just looking out for me. I'm lucky to have them. This ain't no game, at least not any more than everything is, right? You're cool. I like you, I like your paintings, and it's cool. Is that enough?"

"Does that mean I can call you, see you, what?"

"Yeah, I mean, I'm not a painter or anything. I work for a living you know, but yeah, let's hang out again on Sunday. I'll come for dinner. I can tell by your fridge that you cook. You even have homemade sofrito. I expect rice and beans, papi."

He relaxed a little then pulled me into his chest and said, "I hope you don't break my fucking heart." He kissed me in my hair before walking away toward the bathroom. "Pull the door closed behind you and be here at seven. I hate cold food and I don't own a microwave."

Red was waiting for me on her motorcycle out front. Grace knew I hated riding that thing, which is of course why she had sent her on it. Pete had become a path away from her, but it was path that always led me back. Even now, two years later. To leave Pete, I was heading toward Grace. This is what it meant to be trapped. Feeling like there was no way out even as the car keys were in my hand.

• • •

If Doña Durka's house on Grand Avenue was a chaotic blend of street and money that had been built piecemeal, then the safe house on Long

Island was pure money from the wooden floors to the wall-to-wall windows overlooking the ocean. Durka had purchased it as soon as she found out she was sick. She had put Grace in charge of decorating, so every room spoke Grace's name in some way, but also Durka's. Cherrywood ceiling fans, expensive handmade bamboo and wicker furniture, enormous paintings, and statues of Goddesses from all over the world paid homage to the many worlds Doña Durka had opened for her. The library resembled a temple with curtains, artwork, and four-corner altars built neatly into walls of books. Grace had even installed small stained-glass windows, turning the library into her own version of church. It was everything she deserved. It was everything we all deserved. The colors were deep blues and purples like a dream of the twilight skies and the Caribbean Sea our grandparents had been forced to leave behind. I knew Yemaya was everywhere the ocean was, but everything about this beach still smelled of complications.

The front door was locked. I could see lights on in the back rooms. I had not expected Grace to be here. I thought she'd be out with the crew after the intensity of her ritual at Orchard Beach. I put in the security codes and the door opened.

Grace called out our code, "I got ninety-nine problems, but a dick ain't one."

I jumped back a little at the sound of her voice. Grateful not to be alone, I sang back to her, "If you got boy problems, girl, I feel bad for you, son." We laughed before we even made eye contact because, of course, we both knew I had boy problems if I was there.

I found her lying on the couch in sweatpants reading a book. It was strange to see her there with three books on the floor, one in her hand, and no makeup or jewelry. Her curly hair loose and still wet. The sight of the Grace I loved and admired and would do anything for made me ashamed of how I had shut her out.

She sprung up when she saw me at the door and hugged me as if she hadn't seen me in years. As if I hadn't just disrespected her hours earlier. She was shaking a little and squeezing me too hard. It should have scared me, her eagerness to let it all slide, that was not her way, but it was such a relief to feel the love. I let myself float in it for a second. I also needed to fake that I was expecting to find her there, like I had come looking for her, which I hadn't.

Alarmed, she asked, "What are you doing here? Why didn't you call? Is everyone okay?"

"No, no, everyone's fine. I just needed to talk to you. In person. Alone. You know, looking at your stupid ugly face."

She grabbed me and pulled me down on the couch. "Who told you I was here?"

"Nobody, I just felt you calling me with your mind."

She put her arm around me and softened. "Aw, you miss me. I miss you too, you stupid little bitch. Brooklyn been sucking more than your pussy; it be sucking away your mind and all your free time. You make no sense anymore." She started laughing, but when she noticed that I wasn't really laughing or hugging her back she pushed me away a little and stared at me hard.

"I don't want to talk about the beach. Not now."

"Me neither." I accidentally kicked the small pile of books as I sat on the couch. I noticed *Ludell* on top. I hadn't seen that book in a long time. The little yellow paper hanging out the side looked like the summer youth job application I had gotten for her when we were fourteen.

"Are you here to talk to me about Brooklyn? I already know and I don't care. Don't expect a fucking baby shower like this shit is great and all. It's not."

I sat there in silence.

"Are you keeping it? Having it? I mean, you know you don't have to. We can get this taken care of right away. How far in are you? I mean you are fat as hell, so probably too late." She looked me dead in the eye as she said it.

I answered, less confident than I wanted to sound, "It wasn't an accident. I mean it wasn't exactly on purpose, but we both knew what we were doing. We sort of wanted it."

"Sort of wanted it. Is that what you're gonna tell your kid when she grows up? That you sort of wanted her. Nice. I guess that works. Our mothers probably sort of wanted us too."

The agitation escalated quickly. It went from hot to unbearable.

"Can I open the window?"

"What? What the fuck are you talking about windows for? I don't open windows here at night. Why do you want to open a window?" Her anger was rising and irrational. She opened the windows here at night all the time. Something wasn't right. The sight of her face marked by rage over my baby infuriated me.

"What is wrong with you? I'm twenty-four years old, I have a man who wants this baby with me who is grown and a college graduate, which supposedly you respect. I have more money than I ever imagined. What the hell do you want from me?"

"That is the wrong question. What the fuck do you want for yourself? That is what I been trying to get you to focus on your whole damn life. You're a high school dropout dealing drugs and the only money your man has is the money me or Chad have given him, which essentially you have earned hustling. You might do it carrying fancy briefcases and guitar cases, but don't get it twisted, we the same as Toro and Nene."

"Yeah, and whose fucking fault is that? You, with your college and plans for graduate school and all your books, haven't gotten us out of all this yet, so what does that make you?"

"Same as you, except I ain't going around pretending I can be someone's mother."

What she flung at me hung between us like the dead. Whether present or absent, our mothers were eternal mirrors in our minds.

"Yeah, well, talk on the street is you ain't someone's mother cuz you had a missing piece of some sort. We all know more than one Toro baby out there." As soon as I said it, I knew I shouldn't have. I knew it was stupid. Grace had never been one for accidents. If she had no babies, it was intentional, and if it wasn't, this was no way to bring it up. Everyone did notice, and talk about it, when fear didn't keep them quiet. It was clear Doña Durka wasn't having an underage mother in her midst in the early days, but Grace was long past that stage and hustler with a wifey and no kids wasn't what we'd come to expect. Boys half Toro's age had kids, some with multiple baby mama drama, and yet he had none he could claim openly. At one point there was talk of some girl on the side whose kid looked like Toro. She started coming around and trying to be down, but Durka wasn't having it. The girl was called into her office one day, then walked out quietly and was never seen again.

"Word on the street is I kill people for saying less than that. Get the fuck out of my house. Or did Painter Pete kick your ass out too. Is that it?"

"You ain't never killed nobody."

"Tonight might be as good a time as any to start." Her face went slack as she said it, and she seemed on the verge of tears.

"Oh, and you're going to start with me and my baby? I can't believe you would be such a bitch that you can't be happy for me. All those books haven't taught you shit about how to treat people."

"Out! Get the fuck out! I don't have no kids cuz I know I can't protect them." She was screaming at the top of her lungs in a wild unfocused rage that made her sound exactly like her mother when she'd yell at us. I stood there knowing I wasn't leaving and trying to figure out the shortest path to saying it.

"I left him. I left Pete."

The dancing whirl of anger and love that was Grace turned as if on cue. This was the version of me we both could work with: injured and needing her. This was what she really wanted to know. Who would she be in relation to me and this baby? Pete being out of the picture was something she could handle. She turned away and walked toward the deck doors that led out to the beach. She pulled one open and let in a gust of air that sent a few papers flying and the curtains swirling behind her.

"What happened to 'we sort of wanted it to happen'?"

"What happened to 'I don't open windows at night'? What is wrong with you anyway?"

"No, this ain't about me. Seriously. What happened?"

"We did, but I don't know if we can happen. I'm scared and I'm tired." I threw myself down on the couch and felt relieved. I finally said the one true thing I knew. I was scared and I was tired.

"Well, you always have been a scaredy-cat, haven't you?" She threw herself on the couch next to me and pulled me in close.

"You could live here. No one knows about this place yet. Just go about your business quietly. Take different routes to come home. Go to the apartment when you need to but do most of the work in fewer days. Don't work when you don't feel like it, but make sure shit is covered. I'm not running a home for unwed mothers."

I flashed the ring she had given me and said, "I'm not exactly unwed, am I? I got married twice in one weekend."

She laughed with so much energy it felt forced. I wasn't sure why, but she had a tremor to her voice that didn't sit right. She asked, "Anybody else know about the belly openly? I mean everybody knows looking at you, but who did you tell before me?"

"Red figured it out at the airport, and I think Sugar knows because she always knows."

"Red, since the airport, huh? She's been holding out on me in so many ways lately."

"You know I never like to say anything about her because you always think I'm just hating on her."

"Mostly because you are." Grace pulled my head down on her lap and started playing with my hair. The breeze from the window was cooling off all our heat. I started to relax, but her hands were trembling.

It felt like time to let her in on what I had been noticing, "But there is something going on with her and Chad. It's like whenever she talks about him it's personal, and she is the one who has to deal with it. I don't know, but you need to follow up on that." I turned over on my side, my head still in her lap. I looked down at the books and noticed a little pile of banana Laffy Taffy wrappers. I reached out, picked one up, and threw it at her.

"Laffy Taffy, like shit is real up in here. What is going on with you? I haven't eaten those since I was like twelve."

She didn't hesitate to come for me. "Yeah, but funny enough, you're the one who looks like that is all you eat." She slapped my ass as she said it and pushed me a little. She got serious and added, "There's a lot I need to follow up on right now. This belly of yours might help us loosen people up a little and see what's what. I'm going to see Toro tomorrow. I want you to come. It's supposed to be some new information they have about who killed Durka. I think it's bullshit, but we gotta go."

Grace looked out the window and didn't say any more. It was a thing she did when she lied big: she would go quiet and wait to see if anyone had the balls to defy her. She had the upper hand because she would have me any way I came—pregnant, crushed, floating out to sea. I'd have to pay for what she didn't like, but she would never turn her back on me. I missed Pete already. His smell of paint and funky botanica oils. His heat. Still, I knew by how relaxed my body felt, despite all the real danger around me, that Pete made me work too hard to be with him. I was everything right, then nothing good, when he couldn't just write over who I actually was with who he thought I should want to be. Choosing me over everyone, even my baby, felt like rest. This was a rest stop. I could believe that for a minute. I deserved a place to rest.

Grace got off the couch and walked toward the kitchen. I went to the master bedroom. I loved the view. Every room had a different angle on the ocean, and the bedroom suite felt like it sat right on the edge.

She came in with toasted ham and cheese sandwiches, which we ate sitting on the side of the bed in silence, looking out toward the ocean even if it was too dark for us to see. There was so much neither of us was willing to say or ask. When we finished, we laid across the giant hand-carved wooden king-size bed, with the sound of waves outside the window, the same way we slept in Abuelita's tiny apartment: hugging the same pillow between us and telling stories about what we would be when we grew up, to avoid the stories we were standing in.

I finally asked, "So what do you want that you're working so hard to get more? Like what is next? Is this it?"

"I don't know. A lot of things. I want to run a community center in honor of Doña Durka mostly. A place where every problem under the sun might walk through the doors. If I help solve even one, that would be kind of cool. That is what she did."

"Yeah, it would be cool. I mean, she caused a lot of suffering too. No?"

In the pause before she answered I could hear Grace breathing through the tears that were already pushing hard.

"We all cause suffering, girl, all of us, no matter how hard we try. That baby in there, I promise you, she will suffer, and some of it will be because of you. Not on purpose, but most definitely. And she will make you suffer like no one else has. Así e'."

She dragged her hand across her eyes and lay on her back to keep any more tears from coming. She felt far away, though we were closer than we had been in months. We had traveled a long distance in time, circling each other instead of being together. It felt like my Grace was already half gone.

As she looked up at the ceiling fan she asked me, "So what do you want?"

"I don't even know. I can't really remember wanting anything anymore. It's weird. I have everything, but it all feels like nothing." After everything I said about her and babies, I didn't want to mention wanting the baby, but it did feel like the one clear thing. I wanted this baby to know me, and I wanted to know him or her. It was a simple want that felt stupid hard.

She squeezed my hand tighter. "Don't worry, ma. It's all gonna be okay."

I didn't really believe that anymore, but I rubbed her hair with my free hand and kissed her cheek. I imagined doing that to my own baby. The tender in us can be born anywhere.

• • •

When I woke up, Grace was gone. I planned on a slow morning just getting myself back in working order. A rest. Grace came and went as she pleased, so not finding her did not surprise me. What I could not shake was the feeling that finding her here last night meant she no longer felt safe in the Bronx. Maybe she left early because she had decided to go see Toro without me. I hoped so. I honestly never needed to step foot in that house again. The kitchen was flooded with sunlight like our thunderstorm had never happened last night. It was possible to imagine, for a second at least, a beautiful day at the beach.

I wasn't planning to look at the beeper or the phone, but I was already doing that shit of hoping Pete was looking for me, so I peeked in my bag. Red had put 911 on the beeper. I hesitated. Not every emergency had to be mine. But we were all still in danger and it felt stupid to leave myself out of the loop that might give me information I needed.

When I called her back the frenzy in her voice crackled as she said, "Listen to me. Toro and Nene were both found dead. Grace said to call you and tell you not to leave the house. Stay there till she gets back. She won't be answering for a minute, so call me if you need something. Don't call anyone else. Don't tell anyone where you are. Not even Painter Pete. Are we clear? Hello, are you fucking listening?"

The answer, of course, was no. This was not the sexy work of helping rich people get high. I was not prepared. I was not there. My whole body was taking flight. I grabbed the table with both hands and held the phone in the crook of my neck. This was Pete's warning tracking me and now I was trapped for real.

"Yeah. I'm here. I mean, I don't even know what the fuck to do."

"I just told you what to do. Nothing. Stay calm. Don't move and don't make calls. Me and Grace will be down there tonight. Set the alarms and stay the fuck inside."

The Daughters of the
Wild Mother
According to Grace

1992 – 2002

9

CASTLES IN THE BRONX

Toro knocked on the door to my mother's run-down rented room like an answer to a prayer. I was *harta,* a word that has no translation but described exactly how I felt. I was not myself. I was done. Over all of it. Some days the strong that Abuelita always said I had would just up and leave me. She would say it often: "Esa, esa sí. Con esa no puede nadie. Esa e' fuerte como mi mama." Abuelita wasn't around anymore to remind me of how strong I was. On another day, I would have been at school or the library. He caught me on a bad day. He would not have been able to catch me on any other kind. I waited to see if the knocking would go away. It didn't. I pulled myself up and out of the bed I had in the corner, piled high with all my shit. This was the smallest place we had lived in by far. I opened the door in a T-shirt that came to the top of my thighs and no pants.

Toro was only a little taller than me, but he carried himself like a king. His hair was a close-cut Caesar with flawless edges. He shined from the diamond stud in his ear to the rows of three gold chains that got successively longer and thicker. Staring at me through his dark, deep-set brown eyes, and long, dark eyelashes that appeared almost wet, he looked amused and gentle. How you see a thing has everything to do with where you see it first. On the street, I would have looked away, labeled him a two-bit hustler. Un maldito cabrón. I felt superior like that sometimes. In my doorway, up close and personal against the backdrop of my shit life, he was everything beautiful. He smiled. Magic lit the doorway.

At first, in a fake cheesy voice, he said, "You are definitely not the woman I am looking for today." He paused for dramatic effect before adding, "But you may very well be the woman of my dreams."

I followed his eyes down to my legs. On a strong day I would have tossed him like I did all the old dudes on the block. I might have said, "You got young dreams if a fourteen-year-old is the woman of your dreams." But I was half naked, and the door was already open, so I tried to get behind the wheel and drive. I put my hand on my hip and rolled my eyes.

"Is there something I can do for you?"

"Too many things to name, mami."

"Any I might be willing to do without a gun to my head?"

"Funny. Brave too. I like that."

His smile was so perfect and his teeth so straight it made me want to cry. Everything he said sounded better coming from behind that smile. We would see guys like him on the block from a distance, but you rarely ever got close unless you were invited. I never looked for that invitation, but when it appeared on my doorstep, all my carefully cultivated hard core collapsed like a row of dominoes. He might as well have slammed his hand on the table and yelled capicú. His hand was already won. I fake smiled and raised my eyebrows, trying to look like I didn't care.

"So happy to have been a pleasure for you. Look, I'm about to close this door, so if you have something you really need to say, go 'head and say it." He put his foot in the doorway and raised one hand as if to slow me down.

"I'm looking for a crackhead named Evie. You know where I might find her?"

"No, unless you plan on killing her, in which case I would be happy to tell you exactly where she is." We both laughed when I said it. "Why are you looking for her?"

"She owes me some money."

"Well, as you can see from the splendor that surrounds me, she doesn't have any money."

"You talk funny. You sound white and shit. You got a white daddy or something?"

"I ain't got no daddy. Is that better? Do I sound familiar now?"

"No need to get so tight. I was just saying. You don't sound like you from around here is all."

"Well, here I am. Anyway, I can't help you. I haven't seen her for days."

He poked his head a little farther in to look around, coming close enough for me to breathe him in. He smelled so good that it felt right to inhale as long and as much as I could. He snapped back and looked at me like he'd caught me.

"You hungry?"

I wanted to be able to say no, I really did, but I was hungry in too many ways to hide.

"Actually, food being the scarce commodity that it is around here, I am. Why would that be of any interest to you?"

"Damn, girl. I'm gonna need a dictionary to talk to you. I like that shit. It gives me energy."

"That's weird." I eyed him like I knew exactly what he meant by that and wanted no part of it, with the one ounce of resistance I had left.

"Yeah, well, maybe we both weird. Let's go to breakfast. I know a cool diner. Get dressed. I'll wait for you downstairs."

He walked away sure that I would follow. I didn't close the door until he was all the way down the stairs. I had never felt whatever it was I was feeling at that moment. I wouldn't go so far as to say it was love, but if I had to call it something, I'd have called it hope.

When I went downstairs, I thought he had left. The only car down there was a black Mercedes-Benz with dark tinted windows. I understood, as he lowered the window on the passenger side and waved me in, exactly who he was and why he was looking for my mother. This was no scrawny kid dealing dope on the block. This was the guy who owned the block. I hadn't been on this new block long enough to recognize him. Evie had been playing his team for some time. I heard her conning them left and right. Telling them story after story, giving them whatever she had to till she could give them a little money. This guy was coming in to play the enforcer. I loved the idea of climbing into the car with my mother's enemy. I slid into the soft leather seat, smiling.

. . .

Toro took me to the diner on the corner of Kingsbridge and Jerome across the street from the armory that me and Carmen had always called the castle when we were kids. We had lived on Webb Avenue, only a few blocks away, across the street from the VA hospital, for the few years Abuela had been able to keep us together. The Kingsbridge Armory was a huge brick "castle" that took up more than four square city blocks and hid its secrets behind a tall black iron fence circling the perimeter. We had made up hundreds of stories about going inside, marrying a prince, living there, and all the adventures to be had from one end to the other: we would roller-skate to breakfast, ride bikes indoors; we imagined the space as freedom from rules because we didn't yet understand that castles have rules of their own.

High above the ordinary streets and the elevated 4 train, the armory pushed past the images in the picture books we read about the princesses and their castles in the woods. It had an empty moat and its own subway and sometimes reminded us of Mr. Rogers' neighborhood with the subway operating as the trolley. As we got older, we started calling it our castle in the hood. We learned about it in school from our teacher Sally Sunshine, who loved the Bronx and everything in it. She told us that the towers at the top were called turrets and that it was on record as one of the largest armories in the world. We spent months making a classroom replica using wire hangers painted black for the gates, dry mini pasta dipped in red for the bricks, and cut-up cardboard for the turrets.

I was surprised to see it because Toro hadn't mentioned where we were going. It felt like a good omen when we got to the Capitol Diner, and they sat us in a window booth with a perfect view of my castle. It was sunny and the sky was storybook blue behind it. I had no way of knowing it was only a couple of blocks away from his house on Grand Avenue. Toro was no prince, and the armory was no castle, but he had brought me to the one place in the Bronx that had always felt like home. He was close enough to all that I was missing to confuse me on sight.

The manager called out to him from behind the register. "Your table is always ready, pa." Everyone who worked at the diner said hello to him by name or pa. It didn't matter that it was a tiny place under the rumble of the 4 train on Jerome Avenue. It felt like a world stage. Toro had an audience and it felt good to be seen.

I tried to play it off. "I take it you're a regular around here." I was still nervous and pretending I wasn't. I read the menu as if it held secret codes for how to proceed and make this whole thing work for me.

"Yeah, it's like a home away from home. Food's good. Order what you want."

A waitress in a skintight white T-shirt with a deep plunge that put all she had on display walked over and ran her hand across the back of his neck. He pulled away.

"You didn't pull away last night. What's your problem?" She looked over at me with disgust as she added, "I didn't know you had a little sister."

Toro raised his voice and answered, "There's a lot a shit you don't know and you don't need to know. The question you supposed to be asking is what the fuck is my order."

The manager behind the counter noticed the tension and hurried over. He nervously asked, "Is something wrong? What can we get you this morning? The usual?" He waved the waitress away.

Toro was still pissed and looking at the waitress over the manager's shoulder. He finally answered, "Yeah, the usual."

Then the manager looked at me. "What will you be having?"

"Pancakes and bacon, and a burger with fries."

Both the manager and Toro looked at me and then at each other. Toro just nodded at the manager, as if to say, give the girl what she wants, so I threw in, "I'll take a vanilla milkshake too."

Toro finally laughed. "Hungry?"

"Why else would I be here?"

"Ouch. You know how to hurt a guy's feelings. I have my pride, you know."

"I ain't tryin' to diss. You know how you look. The waitress seems to be looking for more." I smiled as I said it, then stopped to watch him.

He laughed again and looked at me like I was the most interesting person he had ever met. It was hard not to fall even faster than I did. It was also new to be in the company of a man who was paying attention to every word I said, so I kept talking.

"There are a hundred good reasons for me to be here including free food. The real question is what can you possibly want from me that you can't get better somewhere else?"

"Slow down, mami. Ain't nobody talking about getting nothing from nobody. I just wanted to take a pretty girl out to breakfast. I wanna get to know you."

"Know me? Yeah right." I was young but not stupid enough to believe that. "Okay, what do you want to know?"

"We could start with the easy stuff like your name."

"Grace. Altagracia, actually, but they call me Grace."

"I like that. A pretty name for a pretty girl. So, you like school or what? You sound like you love that shit."

"Truth?"

"Nothin' but."

"I do. Two square meals a day served with an endless pile of books to read. What's not to love? My attendance fucks me up sometimes, but my teachers cover my ass a lot. They get it. They know the deal."

"You don't get bored and shit?" The look of genuine interest on his face was startling. Toro was curious in ways that bound us from the start.

"Sometimes, but boring beats the fucked-up crazy of my house any day of the week."

"Why you ain't in school today?"

"It's a long story you probably already know. What about you?"

"Me? I never liked school. Not even kindergarten."

"Who doesn't like kindergarten?"

"All the kids the teacher hates from day one hate kindergarten. That was me. Moved too much. Talked too much. Asked too many questions. Touched everything. It was a hassle, man. I dreamt about dropping out like some people dream about graduation. I threw a 'finally out' party. My moms was pissed, but she signed me out at sixteen cuz I was driving her crazy and the school counselors were getting on her back too, and she never liked that kind of attention."

We both knew I wasn't asking him about school, but we were already practicing how to talk to each other. What to ask, what to accept as an answer, how to circle what we did not want to talk about just yet, all steps in a dance I was just learning. His smile was bringing down brick walls in every corner of my body. I could feel I was in trouble. My body was rattling inside like it was going downhill in the supermarket shopping carts the delivery boys would give me a ride in before going back for the next compra. It was bumpy as hell, with no brakes, a crash landing once they let go, but a joyride I could never turn down. Terrifying and fun as hell was a combination my body recognized.

"That's too bad. School is just about the only place I have ever been happy. School, the library, church, and the park. Pretty stupid pendeja shit, but true."

"Nah, that ain't stupid. You also most definitely don't look like a pendeja. You're like those little miracle plants that grow out of cracks in the sidewalk. All bent and shit but growing where they ain't supposed to."

"Nice metaphor."

He shook his head and squinted his eyes in something like awe, as if I was talking physics, before answering, "You're gonna be a lot of fun to talk to."

The manager brought the food over himself. The table was so full he had to put the syrup and ketchup on the next one over. I reached for the syrup and a french fry at the same time. I was diving into the food as much for the distraction as anything else. I was happy to have the smell of bacon overpower the scent of Toro, if only for a while. With my head bent over my plate, I said, "If you're thinking about trying to use me to get to my mother, it won't work. If you try to hold me to get your money, you should know that she doesn't really care—I mean, not like that anyway. She would be glad to be rid of me."

He reached his hand out across the table and touched my cheek. I shrank back a little, but the connection was already there.

"I can't imagine anyone being glad to be rid of you. But also, I ain't trying to kidnap you. You be watching too many movies."

From the start I needed Toro more than he needed me, but he wanted me more, and so in some ways we were even. At least I told myself that because I had never been told that a grown man and a fourteen-year-old girl are never even, no matter how big her tits are. I had that old-school training that if you could keep his attention then you were his match. He looked at me for a long time before he lifted my chin with two fingers and said, "I don't want nothin' from you. I have everything I need. I just wanna be your friend."

"Then you want something. Wanting to be my friend means wanting something."

He leaned back a little, raised his hands in surrender, and laughed. He lit the room up with that fucking smile. It made me nervous. He took a long sip from his coffee like he might have been asking himself what the hell he was doing having this conversation with a kid. His tone changed like he was dropping down somewhere he didn't go often as he answered, "Okay, you win. I wanna be your friend. Ain't nothin' wrong with that."

• • •

All the lights were off in his house the night I went to stay there for good. It was only a few months after we met. From the sidewalk, the windows were dark as we crossed the entrance with a lion on either side. A lot of the buildings and the houses had those white concrete lions, but these were painted deep red to match the red metal gate. I was a lot of things when Toro came along, but not an atrevida, not yet anyway, though that too would come. Carmen might have something to say about that claim, but no one ever knows you like you know yourself. From the small hallway just inside the door the smell of steak with onions, rice and beans, and tostones drew me in. I saw it covered with clear plastic wrap on a plate next to a bowl full of pears and apples. All of it on the kitchen counter and lit up by a night-light shaped like a crescent moon plugged into the wall. It was the only light on that floor of the house. I had wanted to eat from that bowl before, but I didn't dare. Like I said, I was no atrevida. I knew my place. I had only been inside a few times before and I still felt like a stranger. I had never even been upstairs.

Toro held my hand as we climbed the stairs. I could not stop thinking about the pears and the apples and how I was going to live in a house that had fresh fruit in a bowl. I heard Doña Durka's bedroom door creak open. When I got close enough, I saw she was standing at the door wearing a bright red satin robe, with her curly hair loose and thick like a black mantilla around her face and over her shoulders. She was still wearing her dark eye makeup and wine-red lipstick. Heavy with gold chains, beaded necklaces, and bracelets, she extended her arms out to me inviting me in for a hug.

Toro gave me a little push toward her.

"Camina," he whispered, "show some respect."

Crossing that narrow space felt like walking down the hallway in a dream, the ones that get longer the more you walk or run. She appeared wilder, but also softer than her usually pulled-back bun or braids; in daylight she was fierce, but in the dark she was beautiful.

I hadn't been hugged by a grown woman since Abuela died when we were twelve. My head was pressed against Doña Durka's chest like a child, which I guess I was, even though I hadn't felt like one for a long time. Her gold Virgen de Guadalupe medallion marked my cheek from how hard and long she held me. I didn't dare move or talk.

She pulled my face up and looked at me with tears in her eyes. "Yo sé lo que es vivir sin madre. Pero tú tienes una madre en mí."

Whatever kind of hard I thought I was in the world felt far away as she kissed me on my forehead then turned and walked back into her room, closing the door behind her. I turned to Toro, tried to play it off like it was all normal and I was all good. I was always frontin' stronger than I knew how to be, cuz I knew one thing for sure: no one was interested in weak. I put on the flirt expecting him to take me up to his room and finally have sex with me. I had assumed that was the setup. That's what the guy always wants. Exchange of goods and services. The barter system. I learned that shit in history class.

I felt ready mostly because I didn't know any better. I was nervous too, but kind of looking forward to getting it over with. I figured it would all get better once we got the first time out of the way. Then there was that nagging feeling I carried of never having been pure to begin with, so having nothing to protect. I knew a few girls who had done it, and our English teacher had said Juliet was probably only about thirteen or fourteen years old. I could play Juliet to Toro's Romeo. It wasn't like I wasn't feeling him because I was. Carmen had been asking me every time we spoke. She was surprised he hadn't even tried yet. I was too, and I figured time was up and he was making his moves. Instead, he opened the door to a room down the hall from Doña Durka's that was a pink and purple palace only a fourteen-year-old girl could love.

I turned to him. "This can't be your room?"

"Yo, don't diss. You don't know me." He laughed and started tickling me.

I laughed till he kissed me on the mouth. He looked good, smelled good, tasted good. Even salt and sand taste like cotton candy when you're being rescued.

"No rush, mami. My room is upstairs, but Moms wanted you to have your own room. You know, underage and all that. She went all out. She never had a girl, so I guess she has something she wants to get out of this too, but it ain't gonna be nearly as good as what I'm gonna be getting." He kissed me again then turned and walked up to his room on the top floor.

He called to me from the stairs, "She almost never cooks, but she made dinner for you. The food is on the table if you get hungry."

. . .

I heard him go out later that night, but I knew from the start I wasn't there to ask questions or feel any type of way about his business. How we met, and the wordless deal we struck, made all that clear. I sat in the canopy bed wondering if there had been a dead daughter and I was going to be dealing with ghosts. Truth was, I didn't give a shit. I was happy to replace a dead daughter if I would be treated even half as well. Espíritus be damned. I would consult Walter Mercado if I had to, just to make this work. What I didn't know yet was how it felt to live right and how much it might cost. I wasn't sure what that even meant, but it was crossing my mind like a warning sign I didn't know how to read. I hung Abuela's Puerto Rican flag behind the canopy. I sat for a long time just quiet. I was here. Here was better than there. That was gonna have to be enough.

I went downstairs to eat because there was food, and it had been saved specifically for me. I was exploring the edges of this new world. I took a pear. I ate it slow on my way back up the stairs from the kitchen. The pear was so juicy it kept spilling down my chin. These were not the pears in plastic containers they gave us in school. This was the real thing. I couldn't imagine Toro buying or even eating a pear. The pear felt like an offering left by Doña Durka for me. I started building a story about what being loved would taste like with every bite I took.

On the first floor, there was a black velvet poster of Elvis on the wall across from a life-size wooden sculpture of Christ on the cross. There were statues and sculptures in every corner that ranged from Catholic saints to the Buddha surrounded in pennies, a full-size black panther, a Goddess with many arms, and a masculine figure with a belly as round as the Buddha's and an elephant's head. There was a small front room where the furniture was white and red velvet with gold paws and hard plastic sofa covers. That was the room where the black panther stood guard by the entrance. It was a weird combination I had no name for, but I loved it all. I stopped to look at the photos of Toro's brother Jimmy on the wall. His was a life of uniforms from his earliest pictures. Toro had told me that he was sent away to school after their father died. When I finished eating the pear, I couldn't figure out what to do with the core. It wasn't hard like an apple. It was a soft, skinny thing with a few seeds and a small stem. I was so worried about not making a mess I thought about just swallowing it. Instead, I put it in my pocket, afraid to make more noise on the stairs. I figured I would remember to take it back to the garbage in the morning. I climbed in under the canopy with all my clothes on and fell asleep thinking not of Toro's kiss, but of Durka's beautiful and frightening hug that smelled like té de clavo y canela.

. . .

"So how was school today? What did you learn? ¿Qué tienes que contar?" Obvious questions to ask a kid, but no one had ever asked me till I arrived in Doña Durka's house with nothing except two garbage bags filled with stuff Toro had bought for me. It was the first time we were alone in the house without him. I felt shy. I didn't know what she was expecting. Toro had insisted on paying for an all-girl Catholic school and it felt like she might be checking in on the investment.

"It was great. I liked it. Everyone is real serious. We got to work right away."

"Did you learn anything?"

The question felt like a test. I was good at those. I scrambled hard to figure out what would sound like a smart answer, but something in me felt like this was a different kind, so I kept it short and honest.

"I learned that I know a lot more than most of them because I read a lot more, and most of the nuns care more about how we behave than what we actually study." She smiled and I saw where Toro got his from.

"Good, nena, you're paying attention. Just be sure to pick something up every day. Especially if it looks like something they don't want you to know. No dejes pasar ni una. In or outside of school."

The two women who worked in the house, Maria and Dolores, called me into the kitchen and served me a toasted ham and cheese sandwich and fresh-squeezed orange juice. I ate it quietly. Doña Durka was taking calls in a small office right outside the kitchen. Eventually she closed the door with a smile and a wink. I felt like someone's daughter at that table. I already knew that being treated like shit for too long can convince you that you'll only ever be treated that way and you should accept and expect it as a way of life. Turns out that getting hooked on the first person who ever treats you well is equally dangerous. Toro made me feel good, but Durka made me happy. It made me want to make her happy right back. She also asked great questions. It was like we were made for each other. So many small things fascinated her. She loved the idea that the winter solstice was the literal return of sunlight in tiny incremental amounts. She loved it even more that they didn't teach it to me in school, that I had asked a librarian in the public library.

"So, what made you ask that question, nena?"

"I was curious why the calendar in the library said winter solstice right before Christmas, but the one in our school didn't have that. I asked Sister Kenneth and she said, 'Don't worry about it. You will learn about it in science class. It has to do with the seasons.'"

"Okay, and it does, no?"

"Yes, but her answer felt like she was annoyed I was even asking, so that made me want to really know. When I asked the librarian, she got crazy excited and got me all these books to explain astronomy and the sun. Then she looked at my uniform and asked me how much I really wanted to know."

Durka laughed out loud when I said that, then added, "Por supuesto, you said, 'I want to know everything,' right?"

"Yeah, pretty much. That is when she gave me the books on the pagans and the Catholic Church and the way all the Catholic holy days fall on the calendar right around the old pagan ones as a way to convert them, and then she said, 'If you really want to learn about who is teaching you in that school, and what they are still hiding thousands of years later, read these.'"

Durka jumped up and laughed, hugged me, and danced a little salsa with me in the kitchen. "Eso, nena. Don't let them keep you from getting your answers."

Doña Durka loved the random and the mysterious. She loved learning something she hadn't known before, finding unexpected flowers, and burning incense while planting seeds in her garden; knowing something somebody was trying to keep to themselves. Then there were the things she didn't care about. I never saw her with a man. She also didn't give a shit about my grades. She never asked for a report card, and after my first few times of handing it over with pride, only to have her wave me off and throw it on her desk, I stopped showing it. She never asked. She went to the parent-teacher conferences because it was required in Catholic school, but she only asked the teachers what I was absorbing and understanding. In her soft and fading Spanish accent she would ask the nuns who were busy telling her I had hundreds on everything, "But does she ask good questions?"

She reminded me of Ms. Sunshine, who said things no ordinary adult ever said to eight-year-old kids, like, "If the sun won't shine through your window, you've got to paint it on your wall." In Ms. Sunshine's third-grade classroom a rainstorm once produced twenty-six brilliant suns in as many sizes, shapes, and shades of yellow, orange, red, and gold. We covered the walls in sunshine that would last. "The point of being alive, my children, is not just to survive, but to thrive." Most of us were in that struggle day and night, even in the third grade when we didn't have the words for it. She knew it and gave us the words.

Ms. Sunshine was a Black woman from South Carolina with gray-streaked hair pulled back in a tight bun, a pearl necklace, red lipstick, and a smile full of perfect teeth at a time when my mother, who was half her age or even younger, had already lost hers. I remember being impressed that una vieja could have such perfect teeth. I made a note to myself in my notebook to brush my teeth at night, as she'd advised, so I could keep them longer than my mother had. Thriving was serious business in that room, and everything, from the barley seeds we planted in mud-packed little egg containers to our paintings of the sun, and later the phases of the moon in silver and blue, vibrated with the power of it. If we want to blame somebody for all my reckless ambition, we could start with Ms. Sally Sunshine.

Then again, you can't really blame a third-grade teacher with a beautiful smile for not knowing that all that thriving business gets complicated pretty fast. She knew the hard and fast paths to danger that ran through our lives like the Cross Bronx Expressway ripped through the heart of our hood, but she could only do so much to keep us from the danger at our doorsteps, and nothing about the danger behind those doors once they closed.

One of the first things I noticed about the house with Doña Durka and Toro was the quiet. Toro's parade of people made plenty of noise, but mostly he took that elsewhere. There was always somewhere to go where quiet could be found. Sometimes for days it would be only me, Doña Durka, and Maria and Dolores, moving from room to room with little contact till dinner. Whoever was in the house at dinnertime sat down to eat, including the two ladies who cooked. If Toro and Durka both had to be out, then Maria and Dolores would sit and eat with me and talk to me in Spanish. I only had traces of it from Abuela, but talking to them over dinner eventually made me fluent. They even helped me with my Spanish homework. Any time I went into the kitchen I was offered food, but other than that, I was left to myself.

There was the quiet and then there were the smells. The scent of sofrito bubbling up in a pan made me feel at ease almost immediately. It made me think of me and Carmen at our grandmother's house. The second, more intense layer was incense and candles, strongest in Durka's office and bedroom and the small spaces right outside those rooms. It was church, botanica, y cocina in a combination that felt protective and safe.

Toro would say stuff about it sometimes like, "Ma, why you always burning shit in here? You gonna burn this house down one day."

She would look at him, smile, and say, "Bueno, mijito, you better just hope you're not home sleeping the day it happens."

The strongest were the scents of Toro and Durka. His was a dark, musky mix of any one of his colognes with smoky wood and rain that came off his skin like a mist. No lies told, it was intoxicating. If I had to guess the thing that drew chicks in before they even knew what hit them, it would have to be that. It was an aura that walked out in front of him. Doña Durka had what my imagination grabbed onto as the way a mother should smell. There was all the surface stuff of skin creams and shampoo. For her, those were Nivea and Herbal Essences, which she never changed no matter how much money she had, and then the deeper stuff that makes each mother unique. Durka's innermost layers reminded me of cinnamon tea even when there was no cup in her hand.

· · ·

When school ended for summer break, I had been living there a month. I had lots of free time. I could just lie around in my bed, reading or watching TV. I didn't go out much those first few months because I wasn't really sure what was expected of me. I snuck off to meet Carmen once and then ran right back when she didn't show at church. It was Doña Durka who came to my room and asked, "Don't you have any friends your own age? You can't stay locked in here all summer."

I answered shyly at first, "Not really. I mean I know people, but people bring a lot of problems. I have my cousin Carmen. She's the only one I really hang out with."

"Well, where does she live?"

"El Barrio."

"Let's pick her up and go to the beach soon. ¿Qué te parece?"

"That would be great. I miss her."

She moved in from the doorway and sat on the edge of my bed. Her long red nails and heavy rings looked harsh against the shiny purple satin as she smoothed out some wrinkles on the bedspread. She looked up at me and gave me a warm smile.

Then her tone shifted. "I'm sure you have a lot of questions about why you are here or why I am doing this for you. The easy answer is Toro. He could not stop talking about you when he came home the day he met you. He kept on about how smart you are and how beautiful, of course, and unspoiled. How it was such a waste. Men are very drawn to the pure. It is one of their many weaknesses." She stopped and stared at me, testing the waters to see how much truth I could take before continuing, "But your age is a problem. I told him he would have to be patient or it could cost him, me, everything. You could say taking care of you is another way of protecting myself."

"You don't have to worry about me. I know how to keep things to myself. I'm careful." She kissed the top of my head and pulled me in for a hug. It was still awkward for me to have physical contact or affection from her, but it felt good.

"I know. I just want to make you feel at home and safe. This isn't only about Toro. My mother died when I was born. I had my abuelita, but then she went back to Puerto Rico. I know it's not easy for girls out there alone. Just don't ask too many questions. You will get answers as you need them. Try to understand that Toro is a grown man. Men have needs you can't and shouldn't be involved in yet. There are lots of things here you don't need to be involved in yet, and each will come as you are ready, but don't rush."

"Okay."

I didn't really have shit to say. I was so damn happy to be lying around well fed and in peace that it hadn't really occurred to me to ask any questions. I was curious, but it was also not an unheard-of scenario on the block. The guy who can have any chick always wants the one that is off-limits: the married one, his best friend's girl, or the Goody Two-shoes. Underage is often the kind they want. Needy and unprotected are usually the only kind of "too young" they can get. That was me. I knew who I was in the food chain. You learn it young. Doña Durka was something new and it would take me a long time to figure out what she was getting from the arrangement. Durka's rules were easy to follow. Toro's rules were another story.

It had been his idea to enroll me in an all-girl Catholic school. According to him, it was for my protection, but according to Durka, it was to keep me away from other guys and under tight surveillance. I didn't care. I loved the whole fantasy: the uniforms, the rules, the quiet in the hallways, church services once a week. I was going to school with girls who had parents who weren't rich but were willing to pay for school even though it could be had for free. I, like them, was now someone's priority. It was a whole new world. A big green campus on a hill full of trees. Still in the Bronx, but like another planet. There was a gate you had to pass through to get in. School had always been a place to rest for me, and now it felt like a resort. I know it wasn't like that for a lot of people, but it was for me. Some of the nuns were mean as hell, but some of them were smart, deep, caring women who talked to us about doing good in the world. I was into it. I really was. When we asked one of them, Sister Kenneth, why she became a nun, she paused for a long time. Then she looked at us. We were all expecting some story about God or Mary coming to her and calling her into the church. Instead, she said, "I couldn't really picture myself married. I didn't want to cook and clean and take care of little kids. I still wanted to do some good in the world and this seemed a clear way." I liked that answer. I could relate.

10

THE HOUSE OF NEW RULES

I met Nene, Toro's best friend and second in command, at Toro's thir-
tieth birthday dinner on City Island. Nene was tall and dark and thick
where Toro was short, light-skinned, and thin framed. Toro wasn't
skinny; he was muscular but slight. Toro and Nene together looked like
a featherweight and a heavyweight. Most small guys don't pick a big
dude as a best friend because it makes them look smaller, but these two
went all the way back to elementary school. According to Nene, by the
time he was taller than Toro in junior high, they had won too many fights
together for Toro to back out of being his brother.

Nene scanned a room with eyes that flickered and rested on details
that everyone else missed. He was smart and fast and funny. Nothing
anyone said went past him or over his head, and if it did, he stopped you,
asked a question to clarify, and then you could go on. Guys sin complejo
like that always stood out. Some people called it charming. He was just
real as hell and not embarrassed about who he was.

At the dinner, Nene sat on one side of me and Doña Durka on the
other. She didn't let me sit next to Toro when we all went out together.

Nene broke the ice between us with my favorite topic. "So, Toro tells
me you like to read. What kinda shit you read?"

"I don't know. I like everything, really. Maybe novels and history the most."

"That's cool. I like to write poetry. I mean, now I write raps and lyrics, but back in school I always used to win the prize for poetry. Toro used to try to make me feel stupid and call me a sissy and shit, but it was cool."

"I like poetry sometimes. Mostly I like when people play with words until you can't see the thing you thought you saw, and you can only see what they want you to see. Poems usually aren't long enough for me."

"Yeah, see, and I always liked it because it could be short and to the point, but deep. You like the books that break your back coming home from school. I like the little ones I can carry in my back pocket."

We laughed. He leaned into me, as if he was forgetting I was Toro's girl, like he might just touch me. Instinctively, I moved back a little.

"Maybe, but I think mostly I love getting lost in a long book full of words I don't even know. By the end it's like I have a whole new way of saying things, even thinking about them."

He leaned back in his chair, watching me intently.

"Exactly, it don't pay to be stupid or tongue-tied in this world. Especially if you among the ones nobody wants to hear. You feel me. You gotta find ten ways to say a thing to get one damn person to listen. Stay in school, mama. Don't let nobody throw you off track. Not even my bro over there. He gives you any shit, you send him to me." He gave me a warm look with a slow smile and elbowed me in the arm a little.

Toro, who I always kept in my side vision, had started looking at us funny the more we talked. I took it as my cue to get up and go to the bathroom. When I came back, I sat facing Durka. She noticed it too and made a point of putting her arm around me. She looked directly at Toro as she did it.

Toro threw a fit when we got home from the birthday dinner. He slammed the front door as soon as we got inside and started yelling, "Why you trying to make me look stupid in front of my friends by flirting with Nene? I know he got fancy words like you, but you need to know your place."

He carried on cursing and shouting for like forty-five minutes. I was running a maze in my mind. I sat on the couch looking down at my feet. I could not say the things I really wanted to, but I could not stay quiet. I was hitting dead ends every time I tried to say anything. I'd never had a real boyfriend, never mind a man. I was shocked they could turn so easily on such a loose and weak hinge.

I sat there doing my fake crying thing while I was boiling inside. Now I knew I could feel about Toro as I did about my mother, and it scared me. I always understood there was a part of me that could cut anybody off to save myself. It was how weak he looked yelling about such bullshit. It was pathetic. I was falling for him in some kinda way, but that night he turned me just a slight angle away from him and back to myself. Durka was in her office. I knew she could hear. She wasn't doing anything to defend me. That pissed me off too. I had been tested enough to know I was being tested again. If I couldn't handle him, she wasn't going to take my side over her son's. My days in that house would be numbered if I couldn't figure this out. I got up and walked over to him with all the authority I could pretend to have.

"It won't happen again. I didn't want to be rude to your boy and I just don't know enough about a lot of shit. You don't need to get crazy. Just tell me shit and I'll get it."

He was disarmed. I didn't defend myself. I quietly reminded him of my age without accusing him of anything. Even then, I knew he enjoyed the power trip of me saying there were things only he could show me. He pulled me into his chest. "Don't fuck with me, girl. I'm changing all my rules for you. Just don't fuck with me. Que tú no puedes conmigo."

It took me two months after Doña Durka's offer to get in touch with Carmen. I hadn't seen her since that last day when she came to my mother's house and Toro arrived to pick me up for good. I needed to feel secure about who I was in the house before I let her see me again. I knew how she felt about what I was doing. I couldn't stand her disappointment. Failing was easier when no one who cared was watching. I wasn't sure I was going to be able to make this work in a way that would convince her it was a good idea. When I finally showed up at her grandmother's house, I dressed like it was a date. I wanted Carmen to see on the outside how good this was feeling on the inside. I was wearing two of Toro's smaller gold chains, matching bracelets Durka had given me, and giant doorknocker earrings with my name in them and a little diamond in the G. My sneakers were fresh out the box, and they matched my shorts. I changed three times before deciding. I was nervous as hell.

We had our usual reunion of hugs and tears. Carmen was a little llorona sometimes and could pull the tears out of me fast. I noticed she was pulled in deeper and closer to herself. She had grown taller, and her scrawny was turning into the curvy skinny that some guys love. She had decent clothes and fairly new sneakers. We both understood how dark it could really get, and for that split second, we looked like a sunrise.

She grabbed my hand and started with her usual questions. "What the hell is going on? You look amazing, but I need details, girl, like right now." She added, "Are we going to church today?"

Carmen was my spirit guide in so many ways. She had a way of looking at me like she could see right through me, and it felt good. Who else could look at me like that? Who else knew me like that? Who else had loved me from the start? She turned her mouth to the side and rolled her eyes as she said *church*. I loved her face. I had been staring at it all my life hoping it could show me the way. I pulled her in for another hug, then whispered in her ear, "No church today, we're going to the beach."

"The beach? You crazy? How are we getting to the beach?"

"Act like you never took the twelve bus, mi loca? Anyway, we have a ride. Get a towel and a bathing suit."

"I don't have a bathing suit. I haven't had one since we were like twelve years old and Abuela last took us to the beach. Remember?"

"How you don't have a bathing suit? Aren't you like a camp counselor or something this summer?"

"In training, cuz I'm too young, but also, I don't swim, so they call us dry fish. We stand at the edge of the water in our camp T-shirts and make sure nobody gets out the water and gets lost."

"Okay, dry fish, we'll just have to buy you one then."

"I'll bring shorts and a tank top. Let me get my bag."

Carmen's grandmother on her father's side couldn't stop gushing over how beautiful we both were. She gave us a blessing that was also a warning; our viejitas know trouble long before it arrives. "Que Dios me las cuide, mis hijas. No se dejen llevar de lo que brilla y de la palabra bonita. Tengan mucho cuidado por ahí."

We went down the stairs two at a time like kids do. The minute we hit the sidewalk all eyes were on us in ways that made it clear no one really saw us that way anymore.

She saw the white BMW and looked at me confused, but also annoyed. She didn't want to get in. I opened the back door.

"Come on, get in. Don't embarrass me."

I got in the front.

Durka smiled and turned back to Carmen. "Grace has told me so much about you. My name is Doña Durka. I'm Toro's mother. I guess you could say I'm Grace's mother too, now." Durka gave me an affectionate pat on the hair as Carmen buckled her seat belt, looking like a prisoner.

. . .

Orchard Beach was famous for being our beloved "Riviera of the Bronx" and for dirty diapers and syringes washing up on shore. It was a reflection of a city divided over how and when to abandon the Bronx. It was only ever as clean as the city would pay to keep it. It was also the beach anyone could get to on the bus or even ride their bikes. Still, we had only been a few times by the time we were fourteen. It was like that. Money was a deciding factor, but it was also a matter of family culture. There were those who prided themselves on never stepping foot on Orchard because it was ghetto. For the rest of us it was a paradise where we didn't have to pretend to be other than who we were to be carried and healed in the salty water. Even the poorest managed to save up bus fare for three or four kids, pack a cooler, and hit the beach at least a few times every summer. Our summers had often been too chaotic and disorganized for that. This trip was a sign that things were changing.

The music was louder than the ocean and still separated by sections, the same as when we had come with Abuela: the Puerto Ricans rocking salsa in section 5, the Italians with their disco or house music in sections 6 and 7, and the Irish who were still there, only a few left, playing classic rock from sections 9 to 13. Hip-hop was on the move, blaring from boom boxes across the boardwalk, though it never settled in one spot. Me and Carmen were off to the side sitting on the wooden rails overlooking the sand. She elbowed me softly in the ribs.

"What's the deal with this Doña Durka woman? She's a little scary, isn't she?"

I watched Doña Durka out of the corner of my eye. I wanted to be careful what I said to Carmen. Doña Durka was not a single thing or way. Every environment I saw her in revealed another aspect or quality. She always had the heavy jewelry and makeup. I had seen her in pant-suits for my school meetings, tight dresses to go out at night. I hadn't yet figured out how to say that she could look and be scary and not be scary at the same time. To the beach she wore high-heeled sandals with tight cutoff denim shorts and a Panama hat. She had the toned legs of a young woman, and her thick waist and full breasts squeezed out on all sides from underneath her halter top. In some places people would have seen her as an older woman trying to look young. The way people came up to greet her with love and respect made her seem more like a mythical figure surrounded by admirers and supplicants. *Supplicant* was a word I had learned from one of the nuns. It came to me as I watched the way people approached Doña Durka with a quiet need and want that hummed from a distance. I knew I was the main supplicant, but it was nice to see I was not the only one swayed by her magic. I tried to share it with Carmen.

"Doña Durka is awesome. I can't figure her out. She's like a real mother worrying about food and keeping order in the house, but she's also not. She's like his boss in some ways, and she is heavily involved in the business."

"What business?"

"His business."

"Hustling? His mother gets down with hustling drugs?"

"Shh. Shut up, loca. She hears everything. Yeah, she goes into rooms with him and his boys. She takes a lot of calls and gives orders. I'm pretty busy during school, but you know me, I'm always trying to figure shit out. When I'm in the house, I'm mostly in my room, which is amazing. You have to sleep over. Anyway, she also has a room where she sees people, and no one is allowed in. I'll get in there eventually, but for now I'm steering clear of trouble."

"Well, that's new."

"Funny."

"Do you feel safe?" It was a stupid question that hung between us like a flag signaling the distance already separating us.

"Have I ever? Have you?"

Carmen looked away, knowing there was no need to answer that question.

We ate, we danced salsa by the handball courts, walked along the boardwalk, then crossed over to the sand. We went up to our knees in the water. Neither one of us knew how to swim. We built a sandcastle with some young boys who were too excited by teenage girls giving them time and attention. We were not sandcastle experts, but they didn't care; they were just happy we had built it so fancy and impressive in the first place, using shells and seaweed for windows, doors, and gardens. It was constructed out of things they had right in front of them, but they had not yet learned to use what they had. Still, we'd built it too close to the water, so when the tide came in, it washed away.

We went back up to the boardwalk to meet Durka by the paddle-ball courts, and couldn't walk more than two minutes without being stopped by people of all ages coming up and hugging her. They called her madrina or comay. She smiled as she introduced us to everyone. Sometimes she would take them aside and listen as they whispered close in her ear. I wanted to watch her, but Carmen was distracting me, pointing out women in thongs, old men in Speedo bathing suits, and cute little girls we both knew reminded her of us. When we went to the bathroom, Carmen came with the questions again.

"What is the deal between you and him? Is she okay with it?"

"I'm not sure what it is. He still hasn't made a move on me. He takes me out less now that she's in charge. She takes me out more, and she keeps me busy with watching kids around the neighborhood, house stuff, shopping, but she never bothers me if I'm reading or doing homework. It's not like I have to work. She has two ladies who help her. It's like she makes me do things she wants me to learn. He flirts with me. Every so often we hang out in a guest room and make out and watch TV. He treats me like a girlfriend and a sister at the same time. I don't know."

"Do you have any idea why they are doing this for you? Have you heard them talking or anything?"

"No. I mean she said a few things about Toro being obsessed with me, and her trying to protect him and herself, and her mother dying when she was young. Unlike you, I don't want to come off as ungrateful or nosy or pendenciera by asking too many questions. You know what I mean."

She smirked and looked up at the ceiling like I couldn't possibly be talking about her.

"But enough about me. How's work? How's life? Got a boyfriend?"

It was our turn to go in the bathrooms. There was no time for Carmen to answer.

I was in charge of the radio on the ride back. I made small talk with Doña Durka. It was amazing to watch if you knew how we had been treated all our lives. I kept watching Carmen in the rearview mirror. She was looking out the window. The whole ride she didn't make eye contact with me. She dozed in and out of sleep in the air-conditioning, but kept popping up startled. I wrote it all off as jealousy, which was easier to swallow than what she might really be thinking. But what could she say? Be careful of the scary rich lady who buys you everything and treats you well. Maybe you would be better off with your mother? Carmen had a place to go. She could judge me all she wanted. That shit was not going to change anything.

When we dropped her off at her grandmother's building, she hugged me hard for what felt like a long time.

"I could ask my grandmother if you could stay here. There are five of us now, but I could always squeeze you into my side of the bed."

"Come on. Let's not do this. I'm finally somewhere that for whatever mysterious reason, I am wanted. I'm not trying to go back to being an unwanted burden. Anyway, you saw those papers when Toro picked me up that time. She has legal custody. It's all legit. I would have to get my mother to fight to get me back. I'm not leaving you behind. I'm just trying to figure a way out for both of us, okay." Carmen was sucking on her upper lip and looked like she was about to cry.

"We were supposed to do it together, you know. Figure this shit out without making it worse," she whispered.

I couldn't handle it. Carmen was not going to crash my party. "I'll be in touch soon. If you need me, call this number." I pressed a piece of paper with the house number into her hand and a hundred-dollar bill. I ran back to the car before she could say anything else. I tucked my new wallet back into my purse, but not before catching a peek of the picture of us with Abuela when we made our first communion. Both of us wearing borrowed white dresses and veils; only the shoes and socks that Abuela bought us at Alexander's had been ours. I remember mine were too tight. In the photo, I am holding one foot off the ground like a flamingo, trying to protect the foot that hurt the most.

11

THE HOUSE OF RAIN

I heard Durka yelling as soon as I opened the door to the house, thunder crackling behind me. I was shaking out my hair and soaking wet in my uniform after getting stuck in the storm when I got off the bus. It was just after my sixteenth birthday. I already referred to the house as home. Toro always opened all the windows and shades when it was raining, which set Durka off.

She was hollering at him from her office, "Mijo, ha'me el favor and take your National Geographic Wild Kingdom rain and thunder show to your room. Esta casa se va inundar." She almost never raised her voice, but this was a way they both acted out. The flash of lightning lit up the living room like an exclamation point on her sentence.

Toro met me at the door and pulled me up the stairs behind him, holding his fingers to his lips to keep me quiet as he called back to her, "Okay, okay, Ma, I got you. Imma close the windows."

We had done a lot of things around that time and it seemed like we might do more. I had the feeling it would happen soon, and I was relieved. My body was sending me all sorts of mixed signals, but it felt like sex was a good way to seal my place in the house. Even though Durka was already making it feel like my own, I still worried I was only welcome as long as Toro wanted me there. My body felt primed to be offered as bounty. It didn't feel right, just less wrong than a lot of other shit.

We went up to the attic where all the windows were open. It was a big triangular room and he had knocked down most of the walls, leaving the supporting beams and windows with a church-like door at the entrance.

"Wow, I'm finally getting access to the penthouse suite."

He smiled as he slipped a key in the door and said, "That's your reward for never trying to get in before I gave you permission."

"Did it always look like this?"

He shook his head and filled with pride as he said, "Nah, this attic was like three tiny little rooms when we first bought the house. Me and Jimmy each had one and shared one where we kept our toys. After my pops died, my moms sent Jimmy away to that school, so little by little I turned it into this. He held his arms out open. "I did all the work myself." He winked at me when he said, "I'm good with my hands. You'll see."

All the predictable movie posters were on the wall: *Scarface, The Godfather*. It looked like a shrine to Al Pacino, but I didn't say anything about it. There was also a poster-size picture of his dad in a big old-fashioned golden frame. He was looking off to the side, wearing a white straw Panama hat and sunglasses. He kind of resembled Héctor Lavoe. You could see his gun strapped under his jacket, only a hint of it though, and his chain with the huge medallion of the Virgin Mary, which I recognized as the one Doña Durka wore. You could tell he had posed for the photo because it didn't reveal much about the man except that Toro didn't really look like him.

A giant round bed covered in black satin sat on a platform in the middle of the room. The black sheets were moving like storm clouds caught in the crosscurrent from all the open windows. Toro put on some old salsa, the slow sonero stuff his father had loved, on a record player he'd attached to nice speakers. He had thrown me bits and pieces of his father over the years like crumbs to follow. He never told me stories, just random details about what his father loved, what he hated, and what he had wanted to teach Toro. I had never seen any pictures or heard his record collection, which Toro was always talking about. Toro usually came to my room, or we hung out in the little guest room on the second floor. His room was always locked. It looked like a museum devoted to everything Doña Durka had erased about his father from the rest of the house. There was even a wedding picture of Durka and his father on the dresser. The girl in the picture was sad, skinny, and vulnerable. She had not yet grown into her beauty. I must have looked something like that to Toro the day he showed up at my mother's place. If we saw a girl like her on the block, we'd have called her a jíbara.

He pulled me over as close to one of the windows as we could get beneath the slanted roof and started kissing me. The wind was blowing a fine mist through the window. I felt it on the backs of my legs. I had goose bumps all over as he kissed my neck and lifted my skirt, mixing his touch with wind and rain. It was October and cold, but he was hot to the touch. It wasn't gentle or rough. Toro was strong and muscular, but his use of force was measured and careful. He grabbed my flesh and pressed and pinched and pulled. He did all of it in a rhythm with the music that felt like dancing. I didn't believe in the fairy tale anymore. I don't think I ever did. I believed in the castles and the jewels, if not the happy endings. I wasn't waiting to get swept off my feet, but I definitely believed in being lifted off the ground in strong arms with a storm as the backdrop. The room was dark and damp at three thirty in the afternoon. We danced and he rocked himself gently but unstoppably into my world. After it was all over, he rolled me onto my side and started writing with his finger on my back while I stared out the window.

I asked him, "What's with you and the rain?"

"The day my dad was killed, it was pouring outside. People coming in and out of our house and everyone soaking wet. There was a long line of big black umbrellas along the hallway making puddles on the floor. I sat by a window watching the rain and I remembered something he used to say to me when I was a kid. 'Mijo, rain is life. Don't sit there hating it, go out and play. In Puerto Rico we would run and dance in the rain. Go jump in some puddles and make your mother angry, but don't hate the rain.' I had never listened to him when he was alive. The day he died, the rain felt like a way I could be with him."

I tried to turn around to face him, but he held my shoulder in place and continued drawing shapes on my back. His grief felt present from his voice to his fingertips.

He kept going. "That day I ran outside and played and cried in the rain. I was sixteen years old, but I ran around like a kid. I got soaked and dirty and no one even noticed. It felt good. I felt alive. Now rain always feels good. It's like I can feel him. It calms me and reminds me that I'm okay. I'm alive."

"Really? I wasn't expecting that," I answered quietly, not sure what I could say.

"What were you expecting?"

"I didn't know your thing with the rain was so deep." He turned me around to face him, pulled my hair back from my face.

"Don't make the same mistake as my mother. Don't underestimate me. I ain't book smart like you, and I ain't power hungry like her. She has a plan for every single thing. Me, I'm a simple guy. Just remember you never know how deep a puddle is just by looking at it. Sometimes it looks like a little splash of water on the surface, and then it soaks you up to your ankles."

"I ain't trying to underestimate you. Nice metaphor though." He looked at me with that same curious face he wore the day he'd asked me about school in the diner.

"What's a metaphor? You've said that to me before. I remember hearing that in school too, but I never understood it."

In that moment I realized I had a choice. He was open in a way I had never expected. If I made fun of him for admitting he didn't know something, he would shut down. My instinct was strong to humble him after what he had done to me with Nene and repeated a bunch of times since. According to his jealousy, I was trying to have sex with everyone from the bus driver to the mailman to the plumber who once came to fix the sink. Durka had only ever told me to learn to handle him. I had a pile of grudges already. I don't know how I knew or where the message came from, but it came clear: controlling my impulse to humiliate him would bring him closer and make me stronger.

"Yeah, it's a funny word like that. It's like you know it, but you don't. It's just what you said about the puddle being like a person, you know, deep in ways you can't see from the surface. It's like that. Using images to explain ideas. You actually do it all the time. Like the time you said my hair smelled like a rainforest after a storm. You ain't never been in no rainforest, and me neither, but you sort of imagine it as being like my hair when it's clean and loose."

He was touching my face and wearing his big, beautiful smile.

"I'm gonna learn a lot of shit from you. I like that. I also like what I'm gonna get to teach you." He ran his finger along my neck and shoulders, tracing my bones. He turned me over onto my back, climbed on top of me again, and the smell of rain and Toro became mixed in my head as one and the same. He whispered in my ear, "You were definitely worth the wait."

I whispered, "Just don't tell your mom, I don't want her thinking I'm trying to disrespect her house."

"No worries. We can keep it quiet. I don't go around giving my mother the play-by-play, you know. Besides, you're in my house. You're here because I brought you here. You don't need to be worried about anybody else."

He slept hard after that. I watched the little puddles under the window where the wood was already buckled from the many storms before this one. I didn't feel shame or pride. I felt quiet. It was kind of a relief to finally let my guard down, let my body respond for itself, and stop having to think about protecting it. The chill from the rain and open windows mixed with the heat of his body felt like lying on warm sand after coming out of the cold water on the beach. I didn't really believe what he had said about this being his house. Not like what he said was a lie, it just wasn't the whole truth. I turned to slip out of the bed, but he lifted his arm over my waist and pulled me in. It felt good, so I stayed.

12

THE D.O.D.

The rules became more complicated as I got older. I saw Carmen regularly, even though I hadn't brought her to the house yet. I didn't make new friends beyond the school grounds. Toro didn't want me riding trains. I took the bus to school, but I had to ask for rides to go anywhere else. Durka would drive me, but she was busy. It was her idea to sign me up for driver's ed the fall after I turned sixteen. I was so excited about learning how to drive that I called Carmen and told her to meet me at our favorite bench in the park across the street from church.

"I have exciting news!"

She whispered into the phone, "Are you pregnant?"

"Are you crazy? That shit is nothing to be excited about right now, if ever. Hell no."

"You're so dumb. Babies are cute. Can you give me a hint?"

"Just get your ass over there. So impatient."

I was always excited to see Carmen. Meeting at our old survival grounds in Devoe Park made it even better. I asked Durka to drop me off to make sure Toro wouldn't be able to wreck my mood with some bullshit attack about where I was going or what I was doing.

Durka just said, "Okay, but I think you ladies are getting a little old to be hanging out in parks. If you trust her, you should bring her to the house next time."

Durka dropped me off at the back entrance on Father Zeiser Place. Carmen would be watching the big stairs that came down from University Avenue. That was the entrance to the park across from the church that we almost always used. I was early. That's how shit always starts. You get there early, and you see what nobody means for you to see. I walked across the field slow, not because I was looking for anything, but because it made me happy. I would be the first woman in my mother's line to learn how to drive a car. None of them, from my mother to my grandmother to the great-grandmother in Puerto Rico Abuela sometimes mentioned, who I was supposedly just like, had ever driven. It was sad to say it in 1994, but it was true.

Once I hit the middle of the open field, I saw Carmen sitting on our bench and some dude next to her. She had mentioned liking some guy named Rapture, Rap187 was his tag, who did graffiti. I wasn't expecting company, so I was already annoyed. As I got closer, I could see she was looking up at the stairs and then back at him as if trying to make sure I wasn't coming. When I saw the smoke between them, some shit they were passing back and forth, I broke into a full-speed run and knocked his ass off the bench before either one of them knew what hit them.

I jumped on him first and punched him till he grabbed me by the arms and threw me off to the side. "Yo, what the fuck? I don't hit no bitches, so whatever this is, figure it out, Milky Way." Then he ran off.

The first thing I did was grab Carmen by the hair and pull her up to my nose. I inhaled deep and said, "You smell like our fucking mothers. You stupid, stupid little bitch. Of all the things you could have gone and done, this has to be the dumbest. Fucking Milky Way. Is that shit supposed to be cute?"

I pulled her down to her knees, yanking her hard by the hair, which I had wrapped around my fist. "What you crying for? Do you even know why you crying? I'll give you something to cry about!" Words both of us had heard before a hand landed across our faces, as if physical pain were the only justification for crying. Words lacking everything we prized most, even back then: dignity and reason. I slapped her as hard as I could, back and forth, till my hand felt numb.

I rolled down and over her. I kept hitting her as I yelled, "Fucking defend yourself. Do something. You can't give up, bitch. I can't let you." I was boxing her ears, kicking her shins, punching her face. My whole body remembers that beating good and clear, the shock of looking down and seeing Carmen. It was a force I had, until that day, used only to defend and protect her. It terrified me how hard I was hitting her, but I couldn't stop. Mixed with my fear was my awesome love, as well as a little bit of ego. How could she do this to me? To me?

Once she tasted blood from a split lip, I think she started fighting back. I couldn't really hear anymore as we rolled in the dirt screaming and crying, but pieces of what I was saying mixed in with what she was saying. "You stupid fucking little bitch, is this all you want for yourself, hanging out on a park bench with a bitch-ass fool smoking weed or whatever the fuck that was?"

Silence filled with blood-thumping, heart-stopping fear was punctured by her voice again. "Why you think you so much better than me? Why? You just selling pussy for food. At least I'm out here having fun. Being me."

"Are you fucking crazy? How could you? How could you be so stupid? Pendeja. You know there's nothing out here for you. You know it better than anyone."

"Yeah, but who knows, maybe your man or his mama sold it to me?"

We unleashed from places in us that had been slashed and burned long ago and fought with everything we had. A puño limpio. I don't remember how long we went at it, but we fought ourselves raw. At some point the switch went off, it wasn't even Carmen anymore and all systems focused on causing pain; there was nothing but rage and clarity. I was going to fucking win no matter what. We both hit the point where you fight until someone or something pulls you apart or knocks your ass down for real. That feeling of being alive from end to end that everyone who gets hooked on fighting is really hooked on. Finally, someone must have called the police. The sirens coming from a distance pulled us back.

"I'll kill you before I let you become like them. I'll kill us both if I have to. Act like I won't and see. Que la Virgen nos cuide because if she won't, I will." I pulled her up and we both limped away toward the exit on Father Zeiser, taking the long loop up Sedgwick to Kingsbridge.

I couldn't look at her. We had both done some real damage. The road ahead felt like such a waste of time if it was going to be more of the same.

I had thought we were so different with our love of books and school. Now we were just two girls on the block beating the shit out of each other. It felt like insurmountable odds stacked against us. It felt like failure. My whole body throbbed and jerked with sobs I tried to hold in, the pain rising fast as the adrenaline began to wear off.

I had to keep it moving. I picked up my pace and dragged her along. I kissed the cheek that was still bleeding from the cut I had made on her face with my ring. She tried to pull away then, so I pulled her in harder.

"Don't worry, Carmelita, everything is going to be okay, but we have to stick together. No more fucking up."

She pushed my arm off her shoulder, but I was glad it had been there.

I whispered in her ear, "Let's go to my house. Just let me do all the talking. I'll tell Doña Durka we got jumped. She'll look out for us. I got this."

We must have looked pretty bad because more than one person stopped to offer us help. We kept walking until we were within a few blocks of the house. Instead of turning in on Grand Avenue, we turned right at the diner on Jerome. I kept looking around and kept us walking in what felt like circles till we turned at 190th and then onto Davidson Avenue, where a few of Toro's boys held court and handled business. I needed an audience and a distraction. They started making noise and pushing people out of the way as soon as they saw us. They surrounded me and announced to the world that someone was going to pay for what had been done to Toro's wifey. I could see the shock on Carmen's face. I was the chick that had a grown man on lockdown. I was someone she didn't know. I noticed Carmen fall back a little and pulled her along at my side.

The corner house on Grand Ave was always referred to by those on the block as La Casa de Doña Durka. Since I had been living with Toro and his mother, Carmen didn't have any real sense of my physical environment, or the way I was living, other than it was better than what either one of us had ever had. Her knowledge was based on what I told her. I'd never invited her in because she'd never really pushed for it, and it felt safer to keep her out until I knew where I really stood. She had only met Doña Durka when she took us to the beach and seen Toro a handful of times. We were escorted to the house by a bunch of boys that looked like a street gang trying to be a security detail. Doña Durka was already on the porch and her face registered little reaction to the commotion.

The two boys started talking at once until one deferred to the other who spoke for all of them. "Don't worry, Doña, you know Grace is like a little sister to us. We'll find out who did this, and take care of it. You know we will."

Doña Durka's eyes fell on me. The hairs on my body stood on end and a cold shiver ran through me. Se me pararon lo' pelo'. She already knew what had happened. I remembered all the people who'd said hello to her at Orchard Beach. If she was that well known in a random collection of strangers gathered far from home, it was impossible that she didn't know what had gone down less than six blocks away. She had probably gotten two or three phone calls with blow-by-blow accounts. People called her before they would have called the cops. I couldn't believe I had been so stupid. The salt from my sweat was making the scratches and cuts burn, but I didn't dare move, not even to wipe my own face.

Doña Durka instructed the boys, "Don't do anything or even talk about this until I tell you. Entienden. Nothing. I'll speak to Toro myself."

They nodded, turned, and walked away. She waved us in and closed the door behind us. I prayed harder in that hallway than I'd ever prayed in church, and all I could think to pray for was mercy.

"Let's get you girls cleaned up. Then you can tell me all about it."

She led us to the downstairs bathroom and said, "Carmen, you use this one. Grace, you go upstairs and use the one near your room."

I knew she was separating us for a reason. Maybe she wanted to corner me first. I locked myself in the bathroom and decided not to come out till I was called. I sat at the edge of the toilet, letting the water run in the sink long after I'd washed my face. I couldn't stand my reflection, or the idea that it was Carmen who had done this to me. My whole body was throbbing. I had a massive headache coming on, but nothing compared to the terror in my stomach.

Doña Durka knocked on the door. "Are you okay in there?"

I called back to her, "Yeah, thanks. I'm fine. I just have a deep cut I'm trying to clean." She didn't move from the front of the door. I half expected her to knock it down. As soon as I heard Carmen open the bathroom door downstairs, I shut off the water and opened the door. I didn't even look at Durka's face as I race-walked past her down the stairs, though I could feel her eyes burning the back of my head all the way to the bottom.

The kitchen was filled with sunlight that snuck in through the glass door leading out to the backyard. It was my favorite room in the house other than mine. It had bright yellow walls and matching white appliances, copper pots and potholders, dishrags and ceramic jars all with a rooster pattern. I had only ever seen a kitchen like that on TV, and now it was where I ate my meals. Durka didn't cook often, but she loved order in her kitchen. The floor tiles were sparkling white like no one ever went in there, and it smelled like food was constantly cooking on the stove. I knew I would find Dolores and Maria in there. They didn't even turn around as we walked by, though usually they'd hug and kiss me hello. Everyone knew. I was done. Doña Durka opened the small door to her office. It was the only room in the house that I had never been in. It was always locked, and when she was in there no one ever knocked. You waited to be called in. I had never been called.

The walls were painted the orange of the Vietnamese Buddhist monks' robes we sometimes saw on Fordham Road. There were fresh flowers everywhere. Her desk was against the back wall, surrounded by a shrine to la Virgen de Guadalupe in one corner, and an altar to the many gods and goddesses of the rest of the world in the other. It smelled like incense and there were candles burning beside every statue. When we sat down, I ended up next to a female figure sitting on top of a tiger. I counted eight arms, with a weapon or tool in almost every single one of her eight hands and one holding a flower. Another had a tattoo on the palm and was open, facing forward the way the priest gives the sign of peace in mass. She wore a bright red Indian sari, a red dot on her forehead, and a fierce nose ring. You could tell straightaway that she was not playing. She resembled the figure Doña Durka sometimes took outside in the garden and kept on a stand in a covered cove, though a bunch of details were different: a tiger instead of a lion, eight arms instead of ten. The sound of Doña Durka's voice brought me back into the room.

She handed each of us an ice pack and stared at us hard. "Well? Who's first? What happened to the two of you? Cuéntenmelo todo."

There were a thousand lies either one of us could have told. I was easily more prepared to lie than Carmen, but one of us could have thrown a rope and the other one would have latched on. Doña Durka would not have believed any of it though. It was so quiet I could hear the squirrels on the drainpipe along the side of the house, the birds chirping in the giant tree in the yard. I kept peeking back at the figure on the tiger, praying for that kind of strength.

"I'm waiting."

I looked out the window and turned back to Doña Durka with tears in my eyes. Only Carmen could have known how fake those tears were because she had watched me perfect that trick of looking out the window and thinking of something sad to get pity, mercy, and attention when we were in grade school. I was an expert at crying on demand and I had more than enough sad to draw upon. Carmen was an expert in crying for real. I let the fat, fake tears roll down my face and took a deep breath. I could hear Carmen sobbing and I knew it was all too real for her.

"Doña Durka, it's a long story. But I'm sorry. I'm sorry to bring problems to your house when all you have done is help me. I'm so ashamed."

I lowered my head into my hands and started sobbing in earnest. Crying was a great relief even when it was fake. There was plenty to cry about, and by that time my body didn't know the difference.

"Enough with the tears, coño. Who did this to you?" she asked, staring only at me and waiting for a lie that would have undone everything I had built with her.

"We did it to ourselves because we should have known better." I looked over at Carmen to make sure she didn't try to talk.

"Grace, look at me. Why did you bring problems into my house? Into the house I have opened to you? I should beat the shit out of you both so you can really know what it feels like to fight."

Silence filled me from end to end and I tumbled around in it, hearing echoes of our mothers till Doña Durka spoke again.

"I don't know what you thought this might help you do, Grace. It was stupid."

"I know."

"Is this how you treat the people you love?"

These were the kind of questions she was always asking me. Questions that had no one answer, though definitely a right and a wrong one. I held my breath. I needed to get this one right. Instead, she lifted her hand in my direction as if to say stop, no more bullshit. I've heard enough.

"I will give you a way to make it up to me for bringing such disgrace to my house. Más nunca, me oyes. Never again will you act like the street trash you come from."

Doña Durka had never talked to me like that before. I didn't like it even if I deserved it. The number one rule in that house was to bring no problems inside its walls. Keeping a low profile was the air we breathed. I had fucked up. Had the cops caught us, they would have brought me to her very door. The more I thought about it, the more ridiculous I felt about what I had done.

"Go upstairs and change into a clean school uniform. Give Carmen one too. Use some makeup to cover all that bullshit. Then take this backpack and drop it off at this address. Don't open it. Don't put it down.

Don't touch it till you get to the address and the person on this card. Don't fuck it up. I'm watching you. That much I think you know. Since you seem to be looking for trouble, let's give you something real to do."

That afternoon we quietly put on my uniforms. I don't know why we didn't talk or why Carmen didn't ask a hundred questions. I think it was a combination of fear and collusion. She had decided she was down with it all no matter what, so why ask questions. Maybe she was ashamed. What she'd said about me thinking I was better than her surprised me. I didn't think it was true, but maybe it was. Maybe I had decided that my brand of hard was really the only brand that mattered. It had only been weed. It wasn't like she was smoking crack. I had overreacted. Maybe. It was all overwhelming. Too much to think about, never mind talk about. Quiet was the only choice that wouldn't bring more problems. We covered as much of the bruising and scratches as we could with makeup. We looked both stupid and hard-core depending on how you looked at girls who would willingly walk the street looking that fucked up. I gave her a pair of Ray-Ban sunglasses from a drawer that had at least ten pairs. That helped even us out some.

"You can keep them."

"Thanks."

In the mirror, I pulled her in close and lifted both our sunglasses to the top of our heads and laughed.

"Maybe you think how I'm living is fucked up, but this is different. I might be living crazy, but I'm moving forward, not backward. You'll see. Now you'll get it. Let's make a promise that no one will ever do this to us unless we doing it to each other."

Carmen hesitated then said, "Yeah, okay, whatever, but I don't think we need to do this shit again."

· · ·

We rode the Bx12 bus along Fordham Road into upper Manhattan, passing our old church along the way. I stared at the building and asked God to protect us and the bag on my back. I kept praying out of habit even when I wasn't sure I believed anyone was listening anymore. We changed buses on Broadway and 207th Street and caught the Bx20 to Riverdale. The bus ride felt long and slow as we crossed a small bridge back into the Bronx that veered west into Riverdale, the part of the Bronx that had never really been. I went from cold and bored to paranoid in shifts. For long stretches I forgot about what was in the bag, or at least what I thought was in the bag, since no one had actually told me. Then I'd remember and imagine everyone could see in it, or at least knew what we were up to. Carmen probably thought I had been doing this all along, but Doña Durka had never given me work. It was my first time too. I was just playing it off like I was the expert. Once we hit Riverdale, a group of girls in uniforms wearing expensive sunglasses and carrying designer bags like mine got on the bus. It was perfect. Doña Durka obviously planned it. We fit right in. Most of the girls were white and blond, but I could pull off the whole attitude, which was way more important. I even pushed one of them a little, to make a point, as we made our way out at our stop.

We got off at the bottom of a steep hill and climbed a long tree-lined street with huge houses on either side. There were only about six houses where twenty stood on Grand Avenue. I asked Carmen for the card, looked at the number, and then gave it back to her. We walked a little farther up and turned left onto a large circular driveway. Pushing a button on an intercom, I said, "I have Mrs. Orlington's delivery from Our Rosary of the Holy Mother." The gates swung open, and I walked through sure-footed and calm. I felt my stomach flip over and my heartbeat sped up a little, but I really did feel like this was something I could do.

Carmen tugged at me. "What are we doing here? This is crazy. This ain't no around-the-block shit, you know what I mean."

"That is exactly the point. We ain't no around-the-block shit. Just breathe and pay attention. We'll be fine."

We walked the rest of the driveway and met a tall, skinny bald man at the door. It was the closest I had ever been to that kind of money and luxury. I was stunned. It is not the same as seeing it on TV. I calmly opened my backpack and gave the man a box wrapped in brown paper with *Our Rosary of the Holy Mother* imprinted on it and a set of rosary beads stamped right beneath in black ink.

He smiled and passed me an envelope. "Be sure the parish gets our grateful contribution, and here's a little something for your trouble. It's a long walk from the bus stop."

There was a hundred-dollar bill under the envelope, which I handed to Carmen with a smile just after he closed the door.

It was late fall and the walk back to the bus was alive with red and yellow leaves that I had been too nervous to notice before. It was the way the world looked in the books we'd read when we were little: falling leaves spinning to the ground that parents then raked into piles, so their kids might jump into them when they got home from school. My senses were charged as if I had done the drugs instead of the drop-off. Everything felt so intense. We walked along quietly, and the leaves crunched beneath our feet. A cool breeze swept in off the river, which you couldn't see but could smell in the air. The throbbing in my face and head was still there, but I suddenly felt possible. Possible. Like I might leave my mother and all the trash Doña Durka said we came from somewhere far behind. I had never had that feeling of true possibility before. It is, without question, as addictive as any drug.

· · ·

Little Red came next.

The first time I ever saw Rhiannon McGuinness, she was beating the shit out of a poor Italian girl that had the stupid luck of calling me a dirty spic. As soon as I came down the long, tree-covered, gated entrance to the school, I saw Carmen leaning against a parked car. She had started meeting me after school when we had work or plans to hang out. I never went to her school. She waved at me and then pointed at some commotion going on down the hill. We followed the noise to see what was up.

Carmen laughed and said, "I heard the dark-haired girl say your name and *spic* in the same sentence, and before I could even say anything, the redhead came out of nowhere and dragged her ass down the hill. You got bodyguards up in here already?"

"Nah, I don't even know that girl."

Little Red was all dark, obviously dyed red hair; checkered green skirt; white knee socks; and pounding fists as she bent over the girl, pinning her down on a corner only two blocks from the school. I had no idea Catholic girls got down like that. I had been picked up and dropped off for the first two years and was only now going home on the bus and getting to know the scene outside our gates. I was impressed. Still, I had to set her straight.

"I don't need no one fighting my fights. Get off her."

Little Red just kept at it until she drew blood. Then she stood and pulled the girl up by the collar. The girl was crying and carrying on about how her brothers were going to hear about this, and Little Red pulled her close and said loud enough for everyone to hear, "You bring me those little guini bastards and I promise I will fuck the ones I like and beat the shit out of the rest, and just in case, I'll bring my five brothers, who are all cops and love arresting Italian boys with big chains and small dicks."

Carmen looked over at me. Our eyes gave away that we were dying to laugh. We had never seen anything like it. White on white and getting crazy like we did. It was a whole new world.

Red then topped it off. "Unless you're planning to leave this school and never come back, you go home and say some girls from public school jumped you or you will get a beating like this every day of your fucking life until there is nothing left. Remember, I'm the orphan Irish girl on the basketball team. All those Irish nuns in there got my back. You'll have to find yourself a nice guini school on Arthur Avenue if you're look-ing for sympathy." That last part she said with a fake Irish accent, and we did laugh. I couldn't help it. She let the girl go and we watched her run down Bedford Park to a few friends waiting far down the hill. The girl clearly had no back.

"What the fuck was that about?"

"Listen, I heard her talking shit. You and I both know she could get you kicked out of this place, but I can get her kicked out. You know the racial totem pole in there as well as I do. Anyway, I hate her and all the stupid bitches like her with their big hair and ridiculous makeup. They make me sick. It was just an opportunity. I didn't mean anything by it."

I laughed and asked, "You really got five brothers who are cops?"

"No, just my dad. But everybody thinks all the Irish are cops and drunks, and so I use it when it helps. I got three pussy little sisters, and I gotta fight for all of them."

Carmen asked suspiciously, "Orphan?"

"Mother dead. Father cop. So might as well be."

"Are you hungry?"

"Sure."

"I know this cool diner. I got a tab my man pays for, so you could come with us. His uncle owns the place."

We took the bus to the diner and me and Red talked about teachers, classmates, boys from the neighboring Catholic school. Carmen watched with nothing to add. There is chemistry to friendship the same as there is in love; me and Red had it from the get. Carmen had probably never seen me like that with anyone but her. I don't know what possessed her to get off before our stop, but she just stood and said, "I'll see you later. I got things to take care of. Have fun." I stared at her hard, but she got off the bus anyway. I gave her the middle finger behind my head out the window without even turning to look. I knew she'd be watching.

· · ·

Going to Red's basketball games opened a world within a world I thought I already knew. I invited Carmen a bunch of times till she finally agreed. We had never cared about, played, or even known girls that were into sports. We knew who they were growing up. We just weren't in those circles. To Carmen, it was stupid and boring. I was curious. I was surprised by how many people were there. Parents, teachers, and students from both schools, mostly girls watching other girls play. I was sitting with a group of girls I knew. We were all in our uniforms and I could tell Carmen felt pushed aside before she even saw me.

She stopped at the entrance to the gym and looked like she might turn back. Red spotted her and pointed to where we were sitting. I pulled Carmen down next to me on the bleachers. We listened to the other girls chatter on about teachers, the upcoming dance, and midterm exams. I was in deep in this environment. I tried to play it cool to keep Carmen from feeling left out. We were also already doing several drop-offs a week for Doña Durka at that point. Carmen knew enough to make it all feel as fake as it was. I was not one of these girls, no matter how well I blended in.

Red was all power forward, running full speed down the court, throwing elbows and shoulders and ugly faces at every girl who dared stand in her way. It was a breathtaking sight. It felt like she made every shot she got close enough to the basket to take. She played a low game against three girls who were taller than her on the other team, and spent most of the time down by their knees with her elbows out in front of her. She was fast and angry. I was on my feet screaming and cheering. I even got five girls to start chanting, "Little Red, Little Red, Give 'em Hell, Give 'em Hell," till two nuns made their way across the court and told us to sit down and stop invoking evil. Carmen had been sitting there looking bored but had to laugh when the nuns came. She looked at me and said, "Invoking evil? She has no idea."

• • •

After the game, we waited for Red at the exit from the gym. She came out red-faced and sweaty. "You guys wanna come to my house?"

I answered for both of us. "Sure."

She lived in a nice enough building on Bainbridge Avenue near the school. It was a part of the Bronx that the Irish and the Italians were still trying to keep for themselves. The hallways were well lit and smelled clean, which had nothing to do with the tenants, but was a sign the supers were paid well and actually required to work. Her apartment was another story altogether. The absence of a mother was clear. There were piles of clothes on every chair, the couch, and two open ironing boards. Shoes and dolls were scattered across the floor, and the whole house smelled like cat and beer. I looked at Carmen to see if she would register any disapproval, but she just looked straight ahead.

Red's room was right out of the after-school TV movies we loved about rebellious teenagers. She had clothes everywhere, two guitars, basketball sneakers, basketballs, and a huge stereo system with speakers mounted on the walls covered in posters of rock bands and singers I didn't even recognize. Me and Carmen stared at the posters with similar confusion.

Red gave us a tour of her own Rock & Roll Hall of Fame. She pointed as she announced each one, "Janis Joplin, the strongest, most rebellious bitch to ever self-destruct. Hendrix, the king. Led Zeppelin, rulers of the kingdom. Pink Floyd, masters of the mind fuck. Rolling Stones, the legends. Heart, the baddest chicks to ever pick up the guitar. And Joan Jett, just plain badass. Most of the posters and records were my mother's, then I just kept adding on."

I walked over to the guitar in the corner and asked, "Do you play?"

"Yeah. My uncle taught me. He gave me that one over there, the acoustic, for like my tenth birthday, and he gave me that electric beauty for my sixteenth. He lets me play with his band at the Irish bars on Broadway sometimes when I can sneak out. My father would kill him if he knew. He calls my mother's family a bunch of leftover Irish witches and gypsies."

Carmen finally perked up and asked, "Left over from what?"

"I have no idea, but I think it means he doesn't like them."

I asked in a fake shy way, "Can you play something?"

"What do you want me to play?"

"Play something you love."

Red threw some clothes around and made room for us on her bed. Then she sat in a chair by the window and picked up the guitar. She plugged it into a small black box and fiddled around with the knobs for a minute. The ability to actually do things well was something I craved and respected; between punching out the Italian girl and playing basketball and guitar, Red was just about the most accomplished person I had ever met. Definitely the most accomplished person our age, never mind being a girl.

She moved her fingers along the guitar and filled her room with music. She sang to us, more whispering than belting out, a song that she could not have known, but might have imagined, was as much an anthem for me and Carmen as it was for her. When her playing picked up power and speed with a huge surge of energy, Red became the sun and moon. She should have had her own poster on that wall as far as I was concerned. She gave the struggles we were all living a place to work themselves out in the strings of her guitar: *You need a whole lot more than money, You need more than to survive. You gotta keep your love, keep your love alive.*

13

NO ONE ON THE CORNER HAS . . .

Doña Durka started us out small and simple. Pick it up, drop it off. Go here. Go there. Little to no details were exchanged. It made it easier to pretend we weren't really doing anything wrong. We went to the neighborhoods the boys couldn't without drawing attention; eventually, we found out they didn't know much about our end of the operation. Doña Durka kept it secret. I was a senior in high school when we finally formed our own crew.

Durka invited me into her office and opened a safe. She pulled out three guns and put them on her desk. She held my eyes for what felt like forever, squinting hers the whole time as if trying to decide if I really had what she thought she saw in me. She said, "Hold each one in your hand and tell me which one feels right." They were heavier than I expected and cold. I chose the one in the middle. It was small and felt like it was made for my hand. She smiled softly as she said, "Good choice. That is not a gun for showing off or shooting long distance. Two things you don't ever want to do anyway. Just remember that when you pull this out you need to be prepared to use it. Shoot to kill because the people you'll be pulling it out on won't hesitate to kill you first. Given the end of the business you're working on, you will never use it for enforcement, but you never know when you will need it for protection."

Durga sat in the orange-walled office surrounded by candles, with Durka's many saints and spiritual protectors on either side, her chains and bracelets covering her like armor. It should have felt dangerous. It didn't. It felt safe. I felt protected for the first time in my life. Durka gave me bullets and taught me how to load and unload it. She gave me a tender look that turned stern and fierce as she said, "This is not what little girls dream of when they grow up. But it should be. Mostly, they dream a lot of shit. Pura mierda." She sat behind the desk after she said it. I didn't respond. In so many ways I agreed with her, but I was still dreaming a lot of shit. "You can start your own group to expand the kind of things I've had you doing. We won't be competing with Toro, but never say more than I tell you to say." As I turned to walk away, she added one last thing: "Make sure you show Toro the gun and tell him I gave it to you. We don't want him thinking you're trying to be the man or anything. Tell him I told you to ask him to take you to practice out in the country where he takes his boys." Then she laughed and signaled for me to close the door.

Laying on my pink and purple canopy bed, I tried to imagine how many people I might kill and under what conditions. I played out scenarios in my head. Armed and dangerous. Intrusive thoughts of shooting my mother kept appearing. No real reasons why, just various encounters of pulling out my gun. Sometimes it was a mercy kill like when you shoot a horse to put it out of its misery. Other times it was pure rage. I had not seen or heard from her since the day I left. Toro probably knew where she was. What felt hard and impenetrable in me was directly linked to pretending I didn't give a shit, and so I kept adding layers to the lie. The only thing that ever made me think of my mother was my fear of running into her randomly on the street. So far it hadn't happened.

I fell asleep wondering what might make me point it at Toro or Durka. The gun felt hard under my pillow. It wasn't loaded, but I wanted to keep it close; I needed to feel it and know it was mine. I was almost out of high school and Durka had put a gun in my hand and a roof over my head. I knew how to drive and owned a car. Toro had agreed to let me go to college. It felt possible to have and keep all those things. Having them all made me want more. Who doesn't want more? That melancholy salsa that my grandmother loved rang in my head: *Pronto llegará, el día de mi suerte, sé que antes de mi muerte, seguro que mi suerte cambiará.* Doña Durka had changed it all.

• • •

I invited Red to the party Doña Durka threw for my high school graduation. Inviting her to the house was a sign of trust. It was mostly Durka and Toro's friends and family. They gave me expensive jewelry, perfume, gift cards, and cash. It also felt like a coming-out party. Like there were people there Doña Durka wanted me to meet. She introduced me to everyone as her daughter or Toro's fiancée.

Graduation parties had been rare in that house and Toro looked uncomfortable. He pulled me off to the side of the kitchen and kissed me. His eyes were watery and red. A combination of liquor, weed, and emotion that made him soft to the touch. As he leaned on the counter, he reached out and pulled me in close. He hugged me instead of pressing up on me or kissing me hard like he usually did. Then he held me by my arms a short distance away from him as if he was trying to see something that wasn't quite there.

"I saw all this that day I met you at the door, you know. So beautiful. So smart. So fearless. You have something, Grace. Something big. Just don't get lost and don't forget who made you. You were the one who told me that without Michelangelo, *David* would have been just another piece of rock."

I had said that after a lecture in my art class when the nun had shown us a slide of the seventeen-foot statue and explained it was made from a single slab of marble. I was amazed. I talked about it for a week. He had been listening.

Toro hugged me again. This time he whispered in my ears, "I wish you could have met my father. He loved this kind of shit. He would have been proud. But you probably wouldn't even be here if he was. Doors open for some when they close for others." He kissed me on the top of my head like I was a kid.

All I could think to say was "Thank you."

He nodded, walked away, then half turned back to say, "Come up to my room tonight. Don't be shy. You can sleep in there now. Come out and dance with me."

He came back and grabbed my hand.

Toro had taught me how to dance salsa. I was slow and clumsy at first, though my body seemed to remember it from my own mother teaching me when I was too young to know what it was. We went out to the living room, and they were playing a new song by a young kid everybody was talking about, Marc Anthony. "Hasta que te conocí" was the Juanga song all the abuelitas loved. The new kid singing it over salsa riffs made it ours. I stepped onto the dance floor with Toro and met his every step, held his every turn, and felt my body learning its own song. Fuerte. Esa muchacha e' fuerte. I felt it, what my grandmother had said about me. I felt it bone deep. In salsa someone always leads, usually the man, and someone follows, usually the woman. The one following has the most power to disrupt the flow, to throw off the lead, or to fix the flaws and make them seem like part of the dance. People cleared the floor for us and clapped and called out *wepa* as we glided like one body. I could see Carmen watching. Doña Durka was smiling from ear to ear.

After the party ended, I let Red and Carmen sleep in my old room. I went to sleep with Toro. They had no way of knowing it was the first night I was actually sleeping in his bed. My relationship with Toro was a mystery even to me. It had been revealed in layers over years, and always looked one way when it was really another. We had been having sex for two years, but I had been told by Durka that I wasn't allowed to sleep in his room until I graduated from high school and turned eighteen. Later that night, I came down to wake Carmen and Red. We got drunk on forties that I snuck from the kitchen.

I asked Red, "Do you have a plan for your future?"

Red got quiet and answered, "Do I look like I have a plan? I'm not even sure I have a future. All I've ever wanted was music and basketball. Not much of a plan."

I put my arm around her and made my offer. "Well, you have a future with me if you want one."

Red just looked at me for a long time, then laughed. "Crazy is as crazy does. My mother used to say that all the time. Count me in."

Carmen rolled her eyes and pulled the quilt over her head. Carmen never could hold her liquor. She yelled, "This is bullshit!" then fell asleep. Me and Red laughed till we almost peed ourselves.

• • •

Red made things undeniably easier. A white girl in the crew always does. It opens doors, eases tensions, keeps eyes off and ears shut in places where that matters. That she was the daughter of a much-loved cop was a shield of sorts, but also a problem because he wasn't one of the cops that played nice with Doña Durka. She didn't like it, but she'd trusted me to do my own thing and so stepped back. Red was useful in big and small ways and helped us make our first big money deals on our own. She started out doing the bus rides to Riverdale for drop-offs with me and Carmen. Once we got driver's licenses we started going to Yonkers, then deeper into Westchester, to what they called the river towns, and finally, to Long Island. It was always large estate-like private homes, small- to medium-size boxes with the rosary stamped on the outside and small deals. We didn't know how Doña Durka connected with these clients. We basically went where we were sent.

The summer after our graduation we started going more often. Sometimes we did three or four in a day, and they were all pretty good tippers, in addition to what Doña Durka was giving us. So we were easily pulling in more in a day than we would have in a week doing any other jobs girls our age could get when we could even get them. There was a tangible shift in life expectancy for all of us. Ours was not a scary job as long as you didn't think about it too much. We weren't like Toro's boys out on the corners yelling out and running from cops, wearing what we did like a giant white T-shirt. If they were the soldiers—and that is what they liked calling themselves—we were the special ops: in and out, as invisible as possible, with information received on a need-to-know basis. We never went to the same place on the same day or time. We rarely met the people who lived in these places, mostly maids, drivers, butlers, and nannies. It was Red who noticed a magazine addressed to a famous music producer on the steps to one of the houses. She recognized the name because she still wanted to be a rock star and followed the business. On the drive back she started asking questions and spitting out ideas.

"How does Doña Durka get to know these people? Why do they trust her?"

I answered, "I don't really know. She hasn't let me in that far yet. I think she will, just not yet."

"We need to make contact with that guy. Music studios are full of drugs. Every one of those artists and studios needs some very discreet drug delivery. That could be our corner of the market."

Carmen weighed in with sarcasm, "You say that like someone isn't delivering them already. I think the music industry has been pretty efficient at getting drugs for some time now."

Red looked like she wanted to punch Carmen in the face, which was a frequent look for her. "No shit, Sherlock. But the whole thing is built on relationships. If this guy trusts Doña Durka for his drugs to be delivered to his house, then she can expand into his studio or his artists. Networking is how people get replaced. It's all about who you know. Take my uncle, he could expand us into the pot and acid scene with struggling musicians, except I can't tell him what I do for cash without him beating the shit out of me and getting my father to throw me in jail. But if I could, he would."

I was driving but listening, taking it all in, thinking about how to turn it into something more than what Red had intended. Doña Durka would know. I admired Red for taking the risk to think bigger than what had been given to her.

Carmen sat back and hissed, "I think it's stupid. It's going to draw us into trouble with people who actually do this shit for real. We're already making enough money."

At the same time, me and Red both said, "Enough money for what?" and laughed.

Then I said, "This ain't enough money for anything but fun and games. And for the record, once you do this shit, you do it for real. If you get caught, you can't tell the judge, 'Oh, but I'm not a real drug dealer. I just do it, you know, for fun, on the side.' Even you know that. I'll figure out a way to talk to Doña Durka about it. But I'm going to have to say it was my idea. She won't like that an outsider is trying to do her thinking for her."

"I don't mind, as long I get to be the one going to the studios."

"Deal."

That moment in the Honda Civic Durka had given me as a graduation gift marked the beginning of us as a crew with a purpose. I didn't have a name or a plan for what we were doing. I was doing it to be with Durka. It also felt like we were moving toward some unimaginable future. Carmen had quietly left high school before I could stop her. Living with her grandmother and like six cousins who rotated in and out of a tiny two-bedroom apartment, she hid most of her money in sneaker boxes under her bed. She gave her grandmother small, reasonable amounts and told her she was working at a clothing store. To Carmen, that much money at seventeen, with no guy attached to it, was all the money in the world. It pissed her off every time I asked her about school, so I did it often. I was not trying to let her turn any way but my way.

"So, since you ain't doing this for real for real. What are your plans for the future? Tell me again what it is you plan to do without a high school diploma?"

"I know you are not trying to give me that speech in this car. I don't owe you any explanations. You ain't my mother."

I wanted to say, I am all you have. But it wasn't true. She had a family that had claimed her, and I didn't, so I kept on poking.

"Just get your GED at least. I mean put some of that magnificent brain to use."

"You can stick your big words and your fake-ass compliments you know where. I don't want to hear it. If my high school diploma is a requirement for this job, then fire me."

"Okay, ladies, break it up." Red pulled us back into focus. "We need a name. You know, something to identify what we do for ourselves."

I responded as if I had been thinking about it for a long time, "We are the D.O.D. The Daughters of Durka."

• • •

True to a dream I once hid close to my chest, I enrolled in college. The nuns tried to tell me I could land a scholarship to some of the best schools in the country. Instead, I went local, public, and low key. I decided I would make my way quietly. It wasn't like I couldn't leave, but it made no sense to start over. Again. I kept trying to figure out how to do the sustainable thing, the thing I could still do even if Durka and Toro threw me out the next day. I no longer really felt like that would happen, but I needed to prepare for it anyway.

After my first day on campus, I couldn't wait to tell Carmen about a new GED program they had. "You gotta do it. You prepare, then take the test, then register for college right there in the same place. This is your chance to pick up the pieces. Let's do this together."

It bothered her that I wanted her to go back to school, but didn't care if Red went to college. She didn't take it as love. She took it as judgment. I had never made any big moves without Carmen. I just wanted her next to me. She went with me against her will. It was all over her stupid face. I dropped cash like Toro did at the strip clubs. I paid several thousand dollars in money orders for my tuition, and several hundred in cash for books. I even bought a T-shirt and a hat with the school's name on it. Carmen had an attitude, but I looked like a kid in a toy store with birthday money. I felt like some girls did spending that kind of money on a purse or a pair of shoes. But unlike those shoes and that purse, this was an investment that would pay beyond what I could even imagine, and I was imagining a lot.

"This is it, Carmelita. This is the beginning of the end of crazy for us. Do it right and we leave here completely free and different." I believed it. I really did. We all did at a certain point. We were going to open restaurants and music stores and become rappers or rock stars. No one grows up with the dream of being a drug dealer. We grew up with dreams that needed support we couldn't find anywhere else. School for me wasn't a dream about a job; it was a dream about transformation. It didn't matter if it was useful or produced a job or career; it was about being changed, somehow altered. It was about what Sister Mary Ellen called the alchemy of learning, and how it could turn whatever you were born with into gold. I needed to believe that learning could do that for me, and it felt like Durka believed it with me. I had turned to Toro so I'd never become my mother. Going to college felt like a path to becoming something I could not yet name.

. . .

On the first day of my Introduction to Psychology class, Teca walked in. Everyone was staring at her, and she stared back hard at every single one of them. She never looked down or away, and for that alone I liked her. She looked far from home. She was wearing a flannel shirt buttoned to the top, baggy jeans, big hoop earrings, and dark red lipstick. Teca sat alone at the back of the room. I got up and moved my seat so I could be next to her. As the teacher called our names, I waited to see how she'd respond. When she heard Maria Barrios, she raised her hand halfway.

The professor asked the class, "How is psychology present in your everyday life?" We were all quiet. She went on, "Has anyone here ever done anything you swore you would never do?" A few hands went up. Teca just looked out the window. "Have you ever wondered why you did it? That is the foundation of psychology. Every psychologist is trying to understand why people or animals do what they do, and some are trying to figure out how to help them change when they want to make changes."

I tried not to stare. I couldn't resist though. Teca was beautiful, but so hard you could feel the borders of her personal space as if they were made of concrete. Her clothes and makeup gave her away only because we had all seen the Tupac videos by then. We understood West Coast even if we didn't really know what it meant. Compton didn't mean anything to me other than not the Bronx, and similar in ways that might make it familiar. I was curious. We didn't get many California transplants. It turned out Teca wasn't exactly one either. Class ended and I stood up before she did.

I looked her over and said, "You look like you don't know where to get good food around here yet. You wanna get something to eat? The cafeteria is terrible, but I know a good diner."

Teca looked at me like she might slap me. When I didn't flinch, she broke out into a crooked half smile. "Nah, I got another class now. But maybe some other time."

"What building is it in? I'll walk over with you."

Teca's long, big black hair smelled like apples and hair spray. I later learned she was obsessed with some apple shampoo, but on that first day it was a weird combination.

"I'm Grace."

She was guarded and not really feeling my college girl introduce yourself vibe, and answered without looking my way, "Teca."

"That's a cool name. Is it short for something?"

"Yeah, so I gotta go. I'll see you around."

The way she cut me off and walked away gave me all I needed to know about her. We were going to be friends.

• • •

Teca came around slow. At first she only said a word or two to me after class; then she asked about places to eat, and we went to the diner. It was a far walk from campus along an almost straight line through the Aqueduct. She marveled over the trees in between the rows of buildings. Once we came out on Kingsbridge, she noticed everything as we moved through the neighborhood, commenting on clothes in window shops, accents, and even cars.

She remarked on every little girl that rode past her on a bike. "That shit was my favorite, riding a bike made me so damn happy when I was a kid. I miss my bike."

Walking with Teca through the Bronx was like seeing it for the first time. She had only been in New York a month. She had gone from California to Chicago to live with family, then to New York. Both of her parents were in jail, and she was staying with her mother's youngest sister, who was a bilingual kindergarten teacher going to law school at night.

When Teca talked about her family, she shrugged and said, "We got a little bit of everything. My great-grandparents were ranchers, but they lost their land. My grandparents picked grapes, my aunt is a teacher with big dreams, and my parents rejected all of it."

"At least they care. At least you have them."

"I know, but I'm not sure I believe any of them. You know the whole hard work bullshit. I'm not sure I believe that. Even my parents write that shit to me in their letters from jail. Like work hard, mija. Like for what? I don't know."

"Yeah, I know what you mean, but you gotta try, right?"

"I guess."

Teca made it all seem new—the Bronx, college—and for a minute I thought I was turning away from the house on Grand Avenue. But I was learning that gravity pulled even when you couldn't see it holding you down. Getting away with shit had a flow. It built momentum that made me feel safer than we were ever going to be, and it was good for business. The more me, Carmen, and Red did and got away with, the more I wanted to do. It turned out that the army wasn't the only one recruiting on campus. I was expanding my vision of what we could do with every class I took and every odd but useful person I met.

I met Chad after the first day of our Introduction to Business Management class. He opened with a ridiculous one-liner. "The only business you will ever need to manage is the business of being beautiful." He was stupid like that. No game. Zero. That never changed.

I laughed and said, "Yeah, well, I been handling that fine all my life.

I don't need no classes for that. What I need to pick up is how to manage money. You got any ideas about that?"

"You got any money to manage?"

"I might."

"Sounds intriguing. What's that ring you're wearing?"

"It is what it looks like. Lockdown. That change your mind about teaching me what you know about money?"

"No. I'm just disappointed is all. Beauty beheld is not the same as beauty held."

Chad walked with me along the long and winding path that made our campus a place where TV shows and movies liked to film and fake the Ivy League with all our statues of famous white men, even though Chad was one of only a handful of white men who actually went there. We were standing between heavy black iron gates beneath a quote inscribed in concrete that read: "Be filled with joy that those within were born" and some shit about the greatness of these men.

I read it out loud and asked him, "How many of those men do you think owned slaves or abused their wives and kids? What joy is that shit supposed to bring me?"

He raised his eyebrows in surprise. After a pause, he answered, "There is a stormy sea beneath all that calm water you portray."

· · ·

We went on like that for months. He would talk crazy Shakespeare kind of shit to me, and I would smile and play sort of flirty stupid while I tried to figure him out. His story came out slow and a little different every time he told it: kicked out of too many schools, bounced around between two very rich parents, therapy, pills to focus, pills to relax, a rich kid sob story, but still pretty fucking depressing. I never understood how so much privilege could do so much damage. His last round of trouble had been closer to the ground, and more like something I could relate to—his parents had stopped giving him money, so he found ways of making it himself. Except he got caught. His parents hired lawyers to get him off and gave him the ultimatum of going to community college to get his grades up and his act together. A first round of opportunity for most of us on that campus was his last resort. It was easy to hate him and hard to understand why I liked him. He was a proud white boy with his chino pants and blue blazer. He was never trying to be down. I did respect his commitment to being himself even where that shit wasn't reflected back to him as appealing in any way. Then again, those statues affirmed him at a whole other level, so he didn't really need my approval.

By the end of the class, we were the top two students with a somewhat friendly rivalry. He was also starting to figure me out. We never talked about my money or his money, but we began to see each other for what we were. I was drawn to him, not sexually, but like I had found some alter ego version of me. Proof I might have been what I was, even if I had been given everything from day one. It was like having Chad be bad somehow made me less bad, if not downright good. The more I learned about how fucked up the rich were, the more what I did made perfect sense. I begged him for stories about "stealing" in broad daylight and what he knew of it.

At the end of our first semester, I made him a proposition.

"I have some money my mother won in a lawsuit. I have some ideas about how I want to invest it, but I could use some help. Are you interested?"

"I don't know much more about money management than you do. Why would you trust me?"

"You look like you know people who know more about money than either of us do, and you seem like you have an axe to grind, you know, like you want to make a point. Maybe prove something."

First, he looked at me like he could not imagine what I was talking about. Then he smiled as if we were old friends.

I went on, "I figure you want to make money all your own. I respect that kind of energy."

"Yeah, and from what I figure, we should just agree that you don't need to tell me where your money comes from. Just how much more of it you want to make and what you're willing to risk to make that happen."

. . .

Durka decided that Toro and I should get legally married. We didn't make it a big thing, but she wanted me to be protected if anything happened to her.

The apartment had also been Durka's idea.

She had loved the plan of me going to college and presented the whole thing like I was moving into campus housing. I wasn't actually going to live there, but it was a way to spread my wings.

"You have a lot going on and you need a separate space that no one except your crew will know about. It has to be in a neighborhood where Toro doesn't have anything going on, but in a building where people will be happy to look away and no rival crews are working."

I decided early that Chad didn't need to know where it was. He and I would meet on neutral territory. Durka's real estate people found us a small place. I moved Carmen into the apartment, and out of her grandmother's house. It was off Fordham Road, on Valentine Avenue. It was a small, crowded street that had enough traffic to make us going in and out seem, if not normal, no big deal. If you walked straight up Fordham going west, you came to our old church, and if you went east, you came to the Bronx Zoo and the Botanical Garden, and if you kept going after Fordham turned into Pelham, you'd eventually get to Orchard Beach. It felt like sacred land between places that had always made me and Carmen feel if not safe, somewhat at ease. We did not feel that way often, but we were always looking for it. We'd stopped going to church, so the land itself became our protection. We rented spaces in two parking lots on Webster and Jerome Avenue that we used for the cars. The D.O.D. was up and running. We had no idea what that meant other than the fact that it was the best any of us had ever lived.

. . .

Durka took me to family court when I was eighteen. She had to do all of it legally because I wasn't her biological child. I never really understood what she had done, but she had lawyers keeping everything official in case my mother ever came looking for me, which she never, that I knew of, did.

I met Santa on my last day in family court. She was sitting on a bench crying, which irritated me. I hated the whole "ward of the state" shit to begin with, and we were there to declare me free. Her crying reminded me of all I had escaped and never cried over. I was avoiding sitting next to her, but it was the last seat left and Durka waved me over so they could see me. According to her, our name being on a docket meant nothing. She wanted to get this whole thing over with, and my being visible to the guard was somehow going to get us in faster. I sat there quiet and a little repulsed by Santa and her sobbing.

Then she just looked at me and said, "I will never let my kids go through this shit again." Santa looked young to be talking about kids in the plural. She was thick and baby-faced and had two names tattooed in script on her arm: Anthony and Julissa. I had nowhere to turn, and she seemed to be waiting for conversation.

"How many kids you got?"

"Two."

"Wow." I realized after I said it that I didn't have anything else to say. It was not shock, more like disdain. Santa was everything I was hustling not to become.

"Yeah, a lot of people got a lot of shit to say about that, but ask me if I care."

She took my silence as permission to talk and told me all about herself. Finally, she said, "All I really want to do is stand up and take care of my kids, you know. Like I get it that maybe I made some mistakes, but I don't want to trap them in holes I dug for myself."

It took me by surprise. Had my mother ever had a thought like that and no one listened? I wasn't sure, but it was enough for me to give Santa my number and tell her that maybe I had work for her. She hugged me like I had saved her life.

. . .

The first time Santa came to the apartment, she brought a bag of groceries and started cooking. We all stared at her. All we had ever done in that kitchen was fill the fridge with beer, wine coolers, and soda. We had take-out menus for Chinese, Dominican, and pizza. I still ate most of my meals at Durka's or the diner. When she arrived with her bag of groceries, there were take-out containers on the counter and no plates, cups, or forks.

She turned around and looked at us. "Grace hired me to feed you bitches, but not to clean up after you."

Teca looked over at me and called out, "Is that what she told you?"

"Yep, and what the fuck ever. I don't care what other shit I do here cuz I need a job, and she pays right and in cash."

Santa sent Red out to the store to buy paper plates and plastic forks, but in her big brown bag she had rice, beans, plátanos, potatoes, cilantro, onions, oil, lemons, garlic, adobo, tomato sauce, salt, and meat. She might as well have set out the ingredients to make explosives for all we had ever collectively or separately done in a kitchen. Some delivery guys came in right behind her. They carried in, and set up, a huge dining room table and chairs that she had asked me to buy. She said she wasn't cooking for people to sit around on couches eating the food like it was garbage out of a box. I loved her vision. It was the only other furniture besides some mattresses we used as sofas during the work hours and Carmen's bed when everyone went home.

I clapped hard. "Get up off your lazy asses. Santa here is going to show us how to cook."

Teca, always quick to question, jumped in. "What the fuck do we need to know how to cook if she's going to be doing the cooking for us? I got more than enough money to eat. I don't need to become no kitchen slave like my abuelita."

"Cooking ain't about being a slave. It's about being free. Free to eat what you want, how you want, when you want. Free to know what the fuck is in your food," Santa responded quietly but forcefully as she looked at the fast-food wrappers lying next to us on the floor.

"Where did she learn how to cook anyway? We don't even know if she cooks any good."

I shot Teca the look. "I know how she cooks and that's all you need to know, so go wash your fucking hands."

And so it began. The smell of home-cooked meals eaten at a table together. People think I invented that shit, but it was Santa. Not every day, but several times a week we ate dinner like a family. We all took turns helping, doing dishes, buying groceries. We set the table and cleared it. Some of us had never done any of these things, so at times it was met with resistance, but in the end, it made us feel real. At that first dinner there was lots of talking smack around the table until I shut everyone up and started what would become the familiar but often mocked dinner talk.

"I ain't gonna sit here and listen to you bitches talk garbage and ruin my appetite. Dinner talk has to have some meaning to it. Some order. No yelling and carrying on. No gossip. Talk about something productive. Something interesting. Or don't talk. Quiet is good too."

"Next thing you're gonna say is we can't curse," Teca added with an eye roll.

"Nah, I mean it's up to you. Your language is your own. I don't want no one putting words in my mouth, so I ain't trying to take any out of yours. I like choices. But I'm talking about topics. Ideas. You know. We should enjoy our food and our conversation."

At first no one spoke. There were still some empty chairs. Santa's food, which was incredibly good, was also a good excuse to ignore the sudden and awkward silence

Red said, "Those rules make talking sound like homework. I never much liked homework even when I liked school."

"Nobody likes homework," Teca answered. "It's like a punishment for having gone to school."

I added, "Quiet is better than bullshit. So it's fine if you don't feel like talking."

Santa was the one who broke the silence deep. "One of my foster families had a dad that was a short-order cook. He learned to cook from his abuelita in Adjuntas as a kid, then he added to his skills cooking in the merchant marine. When he came out, he got jobs in diners. He worked at the Riverdale Diner when I lived in that family. I was the only kid in the house who asked him how he made stuff and told him that it tasted good, so he taught me how to cook. He used to say, 'Cooking is like living. You can do it good or bad, but you can always learn how to do it better.'"

. . .

The first building we bought was an old warehouse in Williamsburg that Chad set out to turn into loft apartments. Doña Durka approved. He had already turned the first floor into an art space, which he said was a way to lure people to the neighborhood. Before they were ready to live there, they would need to feel like it was a place to go. To me it looked like a place full of people already, but he wasn't talking about the Puerto Ricans who lived there. We were sitting in the little office that must have been originally used by the warehouse managers. It struck me that my grandfather or grandmother might have worked in a place like this when they first arrived from Puerto Rico. They were old factories and warehouses that had long been abandoned and were, according to Chad, about to become the next big thing in real estate. I couldn't see it, but the people he knew did. The office on the second floor had not been renovated yet. It was still greasy and smelled like old food, but you could see the bridges in the distance and Manhattan just beyond from the dirty little windows. As I tore down some walls in my imagination, I could begin to see the high ceilings and vast spaces he spoke about, but I also felt the steel and concrete weight of a building where people used to work that was now empty of purpose. The idea that we would own it was hard to believe.

Chad only said, "Well, getting used to these things takes time, so you need to be patient. Just act like old money. Like you never have enough, and more is all that will ever satisfy you, except of course it won't."

Chad was a living lesson in the huge difference between making money and having it. If you've always had money, spending it was never as exciting as making more of it. If you'd never had it, spending it felt so good the pile felt endless, so making more of it never seemed necessary. He also always knew someone who knew someone who was perfect for what we needed next—long tangled networks of bankers, accountants, and lawyers that were impenetrable unless you had a friend already in. It helped me to see the real value of an Ivy League education. It was about who you met, since we could all read the same damn books.

I told him, "I know. I'm working on that."

"Well, do it as fast as you can. The more grows fast. The building can be held by all of you equally. We can form a management company in all your names. Given your incomes this past year, and Doña Durka's assets, you should look like you had the money to invest as a group but not as individuals, so it's neat and clean, and these apartments are going to sell for big money when the renovations are done. After that, you will be legitimate millionaires, at least on paper, and money will be even easier to move and hide and grow. The more you have, the easier it all gets."

He said it with no hint of sarcasm or apology. I already knew I was swimming in shark-infested waters and only pretending to be a shark. I would never have the ease Chad did around the invisible mobility of money, but I had sharp teeth and that would have to be enough. I brought Red along with me because she had no greed and tons of fire. For her, the money was the same as fighting. It was all about power.

Looking over the papers he had created, he laughed and said, "Those are some mighty good strippers and cleaning ladies you got working for you, but they could make a lot more money 'stripping' and 'cleaning' in private schools, colleges, and Wall Street. Are they ready for up-close-and-personal delivery that involves more than dropping it off at the door?" He was looking at Red, opening doors to his world slowly. Durka didn't trust him, but she had deferred to me with just the one line: "Control your people."

Red seemed curious, but pointed at me and said, "Talk to the boss."

He smiled at me and added, "Are you ready for a high-level expansion? I have ins, but you need to be ready to cross those lines."

I stood and pretended to move some old boxes from the front of the window and saw what I thought I would find under the desk: a pocket with a gun. We were still getting to know what the other was capable of doing. All this talk of expansion into worlds where Chad felt safe, and I didn't, made me want to know without having to ask.

I turned back to him. "Aren't you worried about your parole? Why would you want to drag us into that corner of the world that knows you so well?"

Chad could hold a silent pause longer than anyone I knew. I had learned to wait him out. He leaned over the desk and rummaged through some papers. His hands were thin and delicate, but they were big with long fingers and nails he bit to the bloody, raw edge. His dark blue eyes darted back and forth across the desk. His face looked as if he was having a conversation with someone I couldn't see. He clasped some papers in his hand and made a big show of putting them in order, then throwing them back down.

"The thing about us that works is that we don't know much about each other, right? I mean we know what we know, but we don't pretend to really know anything except what we see on the paper. Let's keep it that way. Let me keep helping you help me. When I say enough, then you move on to someone else, but I have access to markets that you don't, and frankly I'm impressed with the way you ladies move."

Again, he was looking at Red. As soon as he said he was impressed, I was suspicious. He had never said anything like it. Never.

"I'm not sure about this. It feels like too much at once."

A mouse darted out from a corner. Red sprang to her feet and jumped up on the chair. He laughed when she did it. I could tell he was charmed.

"Big bad Red afraid of a little mouse?"

"I don't fuck with rodents. I mean, I will kill a rat if I have to, but I'm not going to pretend I like it."

He smiled harder this time. She just looked away.

He let out a long breath. "I'm letting you know that you can expand what Doña Durka started beyond what she imagined, but you will need to work fast. You are not the only swimmer in this pool." He talked as if he knew what she had imagined, when he didn't know the half of it. I wasn't sure I trusted him with any more than he already had. Chad, like Doña Durka, had gravitational pull. I could follow the money talk, but he could follow the trails in the dark you had to be born into to access. Who but him was I going to follow there?

"Okay. If you ain't scared, then I ain't."

Red looked at him and then at me, and said, "We can be scared. We just can't act scared." She put her feet back on the ground as she said it and stomped them around a little to make sure that mouse knew she was wearing boots.

• • •

The move to buy the building with Chad was a threshold we were crossing. There would not be much room for expanding our inner circle once we crossed it. I'd never had a set number or idea about how many of us would be included. I had watched Toro and Durka carefully. I noticed who they trusted and how, what they shared and what they kept secret, even from each other. Toro had Nene. Durka was alone at the top. It made sense that at a certain point the solitude becomes its own logic. I also knew I had not come this far to be more alone. What I understood from the start was that Carmen was my home, but I needed protection she could not offer. I also needed ground under my feet and wings at my back.

Sugar came like an answer to my prayers and just in time. She approached me at the diner one night while I was waiting for Toro. Durka had me and Carmen meet with him as if we were just another arm of her empire, when she was helping us build an entirely separate body.

Sugar walked in the door and came straight up to me like she knew me. I slipped my hand over my gun as I watched her. She stood there at the edge of the table looking mean as hell.

Then she said, in her sweetest voice, "Somebody on the block told me you could help me."

I just looked at her. "Who said that?"

"I don't know her name, but some crazy white girl with red hair and a bad attitude. Hangs out at the strip clubs sometimes." If Red had a signature, bad attitude would have to be it.

I asked, "You hungry?"

"Always."

That made me and Carmen laugh. Sugar didn't look hungry. She looked rather well fed and at ease, which I admired. I slid over to make room for her in the booth. I asked her what the situation was.

"I got a little sister getting herself into some mess. She got crazy Gucci taste. And it's Dolce & Gabbana this, Fendi that. Bitch is turning out just like our mama. I need to put a stop to that shit. She has taken to the pole, and I want her off and people tell me you know who put her there."

"I could talk to some people, but what you gonna do with her? Lock her up? She's gonna do what she wants. You got a plan?"

"No. I work as a home health aide for minimum wage, and I got three kids of my own, but I can't watch her go down like that. It was bad enough with our mother."

"Is that all she's doing? I mean, dancing is not the worst thing out there."

"I think so. She comes home a little high or drunk, nothing too wild yet. That's why I gotta get her outta there soon. It's not like I don't want her to dance and shit, I just know that world. That life took our mother. It ain't taking my sister on my watch."

"What exactly are you looking for from me?"

"Get the people who give her work to fire her. Spread the word if you can that she is not to be hired elsewhere. Maybe give us cleaner work we can do for more money. Any of it or all of it. Whatever you can manage."

"I ain't got cleaner work. I got more lucrative work, but I wouldn't ever call it clean. What do you actually want? Like for real."

Sugar paused. She was confused by the question and the sincerity.

"Maybe a nurse. My grandmother was a midwife in Georgia and her mama too."

"Good credentials." I smiled. "I'll see what I can do about your sister. But if I give you a job, you gotta go back to school and try to become a nurse. I don't know how smart or stupid you are, but you gotta try. What about your sister? Does she want something?"

"Who, Destiny? Other than another designer bag or some Jimmy Choos or some shit, not that I know of. She young and confused and stupid like our mother. Too pretty for her own damn good and thinks it's gonna do some work for her. But I ain't given up yet. She just got growing up to do."

"Good. I never give up either."

Sugar was light in all directions. It was her gift and her danger. She illuminated paths that were meant to be hidden, but she also made it seem anything in this world was possible, if you had the balls to ask for it and the courage to receive it. Sugar also calmed Carmen down. At the diner Carmen was doing the whole biting her lower lip raw shit that she does when she's nervous. I gave her shit about it all the time. It made her look like a kid. Sugar pulled out some Juicy Fruit gum and handed her a piece.

"Here," she said, "give your teeth something to do other than destroying your face. We all gotta work with ourselves."

"Is Sugar your real name?" I asked.

She looked at me like I was not nearly as smart as she had been told. "Who the fuck names their kid Sugar?"

Carmen said, "Dulce is a pretty common name in Spanish."

"Do I look Spanish? Did I say Dulce? I said Sugar, I think," and for emphasis she banged the glass sugar dispenser on the table and pulled out her high school Spanish, which I loved more than anything. "Also, *dulce* in Spanish means sweet and even candy or pastry, I believe the translation for my name would be *azúcar*, you know how Celia says it. Does anyone name their kid azúcar?" Sugar smiled with self-satisfaction and smirked with bravado that guaranteed she was down.

Carmen fake evil-eyed her. I could tell she was annoyed and charmed. "Well, since you know about Celia Cruz you know we look all sorts of ways. So, you could in fact be 'Spanish' but like, for the record, none of us are that either."

What I had from the start with Red, it seemed like Carmen was going to have with Sugar.

"Yeah, okay, but no. I'm sweet as hell, as you can both see, and my grandma Helen gave me the name cuz, according to her, I was sweet as candy from day one. My name is Mavis if you really need to know."

"I love it! Like that is the name of an actual grown woman if ever I heard one." Carmen said it with a little clap. Carmen charmed was a great relief.

We laughed and buried ourselves in hamburgers and french fries. Toro came in, but when he saw me surrounded, he turned away and sat in his booth by the window with Nene. We were still laughing and talking when he stood up to leave.

He stopped by our booth and said, "You got a lot of new friends up in here. I'm gonna have to start making reservations just to be sure they have a table for me."

There was always a table for him, but I could see in his face a kind of distance. The more confident I grew, the less interested in me he became. He gave me a cold kiss on the mouth, holding up my chin and making a big show of how he could and there was nothing I could do to stop him. He never even looked at anyone else and said, "I'll see you at home."

• • •

When I went home, Doña Durka, not Toro, was waiting there for me. I always checked the hall for the light under her office door and stopped to say good night if she was awake with the door open. She was sitting in the front living room by the black panther statue with a few candles burning on the table.

"One of my people died in jail. I want you to take his mother a check. She won't want to see me, but she will accept the check. Do that first thing tomorrow. It's on the table. She likes to talk, so be sure to give her some attention and listen." Durka pulled a blanket out from the shelf under the coffee table and wrapped herself in it. She looked a way I had never really seen. Her hair thinner than when I met her, her skin softer at her chin and neck. She had lost weight. I had not really noticed any of it till now. She was still beautiful with a fierceness that lit her up from within, but she would not make eye contact with me. Finally she reached for the remote to make sure I knew it was time to go. Something was off. I could not name it or know it, but I felt it coming at me. She waved me off with the gesture I had always thought was her coldest, a little sleight of hand to send you off because she was done, even if you were not.

. . .

Remolino came to us like the stormy name her great-grandmother gave her. Me and Carmen went to the woman's house to drop off the check. We took Teca with us so she could sit in the car knitting one of her many scarves. We thought it would be easy, in and out. Instead, the old woman greeted us in a dark apartment with food and a long, sad story about her lost children. I got up to leave many times and she found a hundred ways to make me sit back down. Carmen just sat there eating.

Finally I stood to go to the bathroom and came out to stand by the door. "We really have to go now. I am so sorry for your loss."

The woman grabbed my hand and answered, "Yo tengo una nieta. No puedo con ella, dile a tu jefa que ella es la que hay que cuidar."

I promised I would mention the difficult granddaughter to Doña Durka, but insisted we really had to go.

Outside, I found Teca in a screaming match with the very granddaughter la viejita upstairs had asked me to protect. Her real name was Cassandra, but her grandmother said the family had given her the name Remolino because she used to have these tantrums as a little girl back in DR where she would literally spin herself into a fit, raising dust and dirt all around her, doing everything she could not to cry. Furiosa would have been a good name too. Eventually, we shortened it to Remy. She was fancy like that, smooth like cognac, and could spin you upside down with her words like one too many shots before you'd even noticed.

Teca was yelling at her, "You're like the Tasmanian devil and shit. You confuse me. Shut up already!" Teca, who never said much when she fought, kept shouting, "Somebody shut this bitch up!"

A beat-down from Teca was never fun—she always went for the face, which made no one want to fight her, but she was always fair. She stood back and gave you time to get back on your feet before she started punching you in the face again. Her trip wires were well hidden, but not that hard to set off.

Remy made noise. It was all arguments and fast-talking, switching from Spanish to English and back, raising hell with her mouth. The fight, according to some little kids watching from the front of the building, had started when she told Teca her hair was stupid. It was dumb girl shit, and Teca was ready to ignore her because she knew Doña Durka did not like us drawing attention to ourselves on the street like that, but Remy just kept talking shit and laughing. Me and Carmen thought the minute Teca turned and punched her that would be the end, but Remy shot back up and started talking even more, throwing punches and pushing and shoving. She wasn't exactly a good fighter, but she was relentless. All the talking was throwing Teca off until Carmen stepped in and separated them. I told Teca to get her ass back in the car. Remy was looking back and forth between me and Carmen and the car and calmed down long enough for me to walk up to her.

I asked her, "¿Qué lo tuyo?"

Remy looked me dead in the eye and said, "Lo mío e' joder porque no le tengo miedo a nadie."

I laughed at her. "So what? The real question is: Is anyone afraid of you?"

"My own mother is afraid of me. I think that says something."

I liked that answer, and Remy was brought on as raw power and raconteur. I knew Remy was going to make excellent dinner talk, and she did. She would unfurl her stories one by one like so many tiny flags of belonging. She had a million anecdotes about her mother, her grand-mother's life as a political activist in DR, her great-grandmother's farm. I loved that Remy knew every member of her family on both her father's and her mother's side for generations back. Sometimes I would ask her to name them as if that alone was a story. Back in DR she had five aunts and three uncles and thirty-two cousins. She could name every one of them. Remy did always make me wonder how someone with so many people could get so lost. Me and Carmen had so few names that we knew, and no people we could call ours.

• • •

Six months later, with Doña Durka as our cosigner, we closed on the building in Brooklyn. The D.O.D. was officially in business. We closed a millennium in 1999, with a crazy New Year's Eve party in the empty warehouse building in Brooklyn. It was ours. The land, the building, even the fucking bricks. So were the problems, but we weren't thinking about those yet. We were poppin' bottles and dancing in a room with a tiny greasy window that had a view of the Manhattan skyline. Nas was singing to us loud and clear: "The World Is Yours."

14

THE MOTHER OF SEEDS

Durka had been planting the seeds of her own death for a long time. As it all unfolded, she began tending it, cutting back excess to reveal and make space for it, like it was one of her plants in the garden. Even the day she had told me felt like a setup in hindsight.

"Ven, siéntate aquí conmigo." She had put her arm around me and kissed the top of my head, grabbed my hand, squeezed it, and then let it go. All of it was affection that came easier to her as she got sicker, but I didn't know that yet.

"I'm going to say some things to you now and I want you to keep yourself together. Toro does not know. I need you to know now, but to wait until I tell him." She had taken a deep breath and exhaled a whisper. "I have cancer."

I contemplated pretending I had not heard her. I didn't dare make her say it again. I was stuck in a single loop of fear, running circles in my head trying to find what to say or how. "What the fuck? What do you mean?"

She looked at me as she had always done when I was acting beneath what she had trained into me. Doña Durka had mothered me mostly with her eyes, which she did til the very end.

"No empieces. Yo no soy una de tus amiguitas. We are not going to curse and carry on. No somos babies aquí. Ni tú ni yo."

She had moved away from me on the couch, taking the corner spot where there was an old and tattered cushion that had once been her grandmother's. She folded her feet underneath her, put the cushion on her lap, and said, "What you need to know is that I will fight and I might lose. I have not lost yet, but I am prepared for the fact that I might. You need to be prepared too. We can talk more tomorrow. Ya."

I had wanted to throw myself on her lap and cry. She was not having any of it. I got up as slowly as possible, hoping it would give her time to change her mind. To say more. Instead she gave me the heartless hand wave to leave. My whole heart ached with a love I had hoped never to feel again in this life. Love for a mother I could not save. Except with Durka I was sure I would die trying.

. . .

Durka responded well to the treatments and lived in a sort of stable holding pattern for about a year. It was not remission. It was what the doctor called a longer than expected pause in the progression, but the disease was recently back on the march. I drove along the tree-lined stretch of Mosholu Parkway that Durka loved.

She called it Cathedral Drive. "This is my church, nena, look at the beauty. There is not a church on earth more magnificent than a gathering of trees."

Driving to chemo, like sitting in the garden or staying up late talking on the porch, had become a kind of confessional for Durka since she'd gotten sick. She would talk and talk and then go quiet. Random memories. Stories of her childhood in Puerto Rico. Driftwood that washed up randomly and then floated away. I was collecting all of it, trying to gather her up and hang on. Sometimes she would say, "Pa' que sepan quién fui, so someone will know me, you know, who I was." Other times she tossed stories like shells and trinkets so I might do with them what I wished. I asked questions, but they went mostly ignored, only to pop up later as an answer in another story, somewhere I had to work hard to find. Lately, I felt as bold as she felt weak. I wanted answers. Like, there was shit I needed to know.

"What about Hector? What was he like?"

She didn't even pause to register surprise. "Hector loved animals and flowers. We had the house. I thought we could sell and start over somewhere else. We had enough money, I thought, to get out and start something small and simple. You know, a restaurant, a flower shop, I even thought of a pet store because that was the dream back then, and I guess some people still have it. I see these kids, grown men too, and they think this life is glamorous. This. No one wants this. It makes no sense to only want this. It's empty. It is a life where you can get stuck, feel trapped. Yo entiendo what it feels like to think you have no choice. I would have been a good florist, I think, maybe even had one of those nursery places in Florida where you can grow all year."

I thought of her in her garden surrounded by roses and zinnias and morning glory vines that wrapped around the fences, forming a kind of throne behind her little round table. She was a mother of seeds, filling mini brown envelopes labeled for each color of morning glory. She rolled the thin-skinned bubbles that formed and dried along the vine between her fingers, catching the hard black centers that looked like mouse droppings in the palm of her hand. She caressed them before slipping them into the envelopes for next year like she was tucking small children into bed.

She stared out the window at her beautiful green cathedral. I drove slower, drifting up to each red light so she'd keep going before we reached the hospital. She never felt like talking on the drive home. It was now or wait till the next time. Finally she picked up again. "I wanted us to move to Florida. I actually believed he was considering it when he took me out on a trip with him. We stayed in this beautiful apartment on Miami Beach, and I thought he was giving me some kind of sign. So, one night I asked him, 'Papi, it's time, don't you think? I love Florida. I think this is good. You're here and can talk to your people in person.' He came close to me and grabbed my face, soft at first. Then he squeezed it hard and said, 'I don't understand why you can't shut the fuck up and mind your business. I don't see you complaining about how I make my money when you spend it.' Me prendí. I started talking as if he was going to listen. 'It's not that. I just don't know what you're scared of. So many people get out. What is it you're so scared of? We don't need any more than we have. This is not a life for our boys, Hector.' His eyes, mija, were dark, solid like rocks. No feeling in them. He stared at me like he had never loved me and said, 'Who the fuck told you I'm scared? Is this worse than the roach-infested apartment I pulled your skinny ass out of? Mujer, por favor.'" Durka shifted visibly in her seat and moved to open the window even though it was windy and she was always cold.

"Qué se yo, I don't know what got into me that night, but I was tired. I knew his temper was hot. I knew I should've left him alone. He had been sniffing and drinking and had to go to a big party later and he always had a hard time with those things. He hated having to talk to new people. Mucho complejo about his English . . . about his Spanish. That's why he loved the block so much. There he was king and he never had to explain himself or compete. I sort of knew I was pushing, but I couldn't help myself. I pushed some more. I whispered right into his hand that was still tight around my face, 'I'm leaving. I'm not going to sit around waiting to get killed or to see you go off to jail. I've had enough. Estoy harta.'

"It wasn't the first time he ever beat me. He was into that, though it wasn't an everyday sort of thing. I think he liked to keep me guessing and confused. He'd go months, even years, without touching me, then start beating me over any little thing. I never really understood that. Hector was a guy who loved music, animals, nice clothes, and good food. He loved to dance. He was a gentle spirit caught up in a life and then, like so many, like me even . . . it ate him up and he never really came back. It was like he didn't know how to be in the world any more like an ordinary person, sabes. Bueno, I didn't understand him then, but I understand him a little better now." She looked at me as she said it as if to make sure I understood I was no different from Hector either.

"He went to that party without me, and I snuck off to the doctor.

I never did it before because I knew it would draw all the wrong kind of attention. I mean I had my kids and it was dangerous to have people investigate the house, but I was in so much pain, and since we weren't home, I figured it wouldn't go any further. My ribs and my sides had me bent over. My face. I couldn't even look at it." Durka's voice shook and she shuddered like she was still looking in that mirror in Florida. "So, I went to the ER, and I got a beautiful Indian woman as my doctor. She had the small red dot on her forehead and the tiny nose ring, and she was so gentle. Her skin was the same warm brown as my abuelita's, and even as she spoke, it felt like a hug from far away. She wore a red silk scarf under her white coat.

"After she examined me, she pulled me into an office away from the emergency room beds. She reminded me of my grandmother even more once she got close because she smelled like clavo y té de canela, you know. It made me feel, que sé yo, safe. She looked up from my chart and said, 'Hello, I'm Dr. Gupta. Your name is Durka?' I just nodded my head. She turned and picked up a figure she had on her desk. 'In my country we have a Goddess. Her name is Durga. She is a warrior Goddess. You must be very strong to have such a name. My mother gave me this murti when she sent me here to study. Durga protects women who are sent far from home, far from their mothers, and all who need protection. She is no good luck charm. She is a fighter; the strongest one we have. The Mother of us all.' La doctora put it in my hand. I was holding it, a little bit confused. In my life I had never seen something like that. A woman with all those weapons, all those arms, so much power sitting on a lion like it was a horse. She was so strong and beautiful. I started to cry. I wanted to be that strong, you know, to fight and stop being the one getting beaten. Then the doctor went on, 'My mother told me that Durga teaches us that sometimes there is fighting to be done, and only a woman can do it.' She stopped as she said that and looked me in the eyes. 'You don't have to allow this to continue. You have three broken ribs.' She turned around and filled out some papers. I just sat there holding the statue and staring. She left the room, and I swear it felt like Durga filled the whole room with the sound of a lion's roar and swords clanking in the air. It was powerful, muchacha. It was not my tradition, but Abuelita had always taught me to respect the traditions of others. She said there was too much that had been stolen and lied about to think that what we had in our tiny hands was the whole truth or even true at all.

"By the time Dr. Gupta came back, I wanted to steal the Durga figure. I mean, I didn't want to give it back, but I knew that was not the way to get the power I was hoping for. As she was handing me some papers, she said, 'Keep it. Let Durga guide you out. She will help you slay the demons in your world and protect you through your most difficult times. Keep her clean and in places of honor and respect.' She took my hands and looked into my eyes with so much love and compassion. I couldn't imagine why. She didn't say anything else. She gave me some painkillers. Some phone numbers. But there was no judgment, entiendes. She didn't look down at me. She looked me in my eyes like they weren't swollen and black and blue. Like I wasn't pathetic. It was shocking, pues, the respect she showed me. I left there thinking all sorts of things about how to get out, fight back, fuck him up, get revenge. You know, ya tú sabes the loquera we feel when we get it in our heads that we are going to do something; somehow we think we are going to do everything, except the thing we actually end up doing."

I saw the hospital ahead and thought about turning the car and going in circles. My hands were wrapped tight around the steering wheel. Her breathing was heavy and I had a sudden panic that she might die without finishing. It made no sense, but the thought crossed my mind. My mother had never told me the story of my birth, her labor and delivery. This felt like my beginning in some twisted way. I wanted it more than any story I had ever heard, even though I knew the ending could not be good. I sat there frozen until someone behind me honked the horn. I hadn't even seen the light turn green.

"Muchacha, pay attention. You can't get us both killed. Anyway, we stayed another week in Miami. It was time I needed. I thought I was planning my big escape. I even went to a real estate office. On the last night he said we were going to an important party. The most important one of his so-called career. It was one of those things where you only get invited if they intend to reward you or kill you, and you never know which it's going to be, but you have to go in thinking it's a win. No other way to live this life. You never know who is coming for you. That much you better have learned by now." We pulled up in front of the hospital and I kept the car running. I wasn't going to be the first one to signal she should stop.

She closed the window again, looking tired. The sunlight revealed a map of struggle in the lines of her face. She took small shallow breaths and kept going as if she wanted to be sure it was done and over with too. "I was still quiet and planning. I wanted to have Toro and Jimmy in my hands before I said or did another thing, and they were back in New York with Hector's mother, so I covered my bruises with makeup and put on an evening gown. I watched Hector through the mirror getting dressed, surrounded by stacks of money and his gun. It was like that back then. Everything was always laying around like it was some kind of movie or something. Ridiculous. A mí me da hasta vergüenza pensar how we were living. He looked off, like he was nervous, but I had it in my head that I was only getting through the night. I had the little Durga murti wrapped in one of my abuelita's handmade pañuelitos that I always took wherever I went. I switched it to the small silk bag where I kept my rosary beads, so I could carry it in my little clutch purse to the party because she was a comfort to me. She felt like protection. I would rub her arms and touch each weapon and pray for that kind of strength. You know, I kept thinking, if I had weapons, if I had the balls to use them, ese cabrón wouldn't lay a finger on me. Pero na', it was all just trying to get strong to leave him. That was where my thinking was. The demon of confusion was still very much in charge.

"Bueno, this night was the classic Miami drug scene in the eighties. It was that big show of look at me now, with white clothes and big houses on the water. It was nothing like New York, where you could show off a little in the summer, pero mostly it was hard, dark, and grimy. You knew you were living on the edge, and getting stuck in a snowstorm doing a drop-off reminded you in case you forgot. Not Miami. That place made this life look like Hollywood con las palmeras and the beach. The whole thing. The people too, they were different, más sinvergüenza, ya tú sabes. It was like there were no police. Killing cops was the same as killing anyone else. We went to this house on the bay that was amazing. As soon as we got there, Hector went off and started talking too loud and dancing with other women. He was high. You could tell it was making him uncomfortable to be there, but he didn't have the kind of respect in that room he wanted. People weren't calling him to their table. The whole thing made him look awkward and it made me nervous."

Durka looked at her watch. She'd be late for her appointment if she didn't get out soon. I still had the car running close to the front entrance, so she wouldn't have far to walk. She looked over at me and said, "In the end, I turned out to be no better than him, but that is where you have been helping me. You have made me better. Un poco más decente. You let me feel like a mother again." She put her hand over mine. Hers was cold, bony, dry, and covered in scabs from the needles and IVs of her chemo. My heart was racing. Durka held my hand so tightly, looked ahead, and jumped back in like she was plunging off a cliff, reminding me that I was going over the edge with her and there was no turning back.

"I walked away from Hector at the party. On top of the beating and the abuse, the way he had no self-control in front of people was humiliating. I went out onto a balcony overlooking the water. The moon was almost full. La luna has always been kind to me, and I stood under her light, remembering mi abuelita and taking in strength. A woman in a tight white pantsuit and a hat was making her way through the crowd on the other side of the balcony. It was clear that everyone there paid their respects to her. I had heard something about her, but you know, it was still like a legend then. The woman running Miami. Imagínate eso. The men didn't want that story coming out, so they all played it down. She came over to me and smiled. I smiled back and told her it was a beautiful house. She said, 'You look like shit. Pareces que caíste bajo un tren.'

"'Pues sí. Así mismo fue. Bajo un tren descarrilado.'

"'I know what this is. I know who did it and I can fix it. I've solved this problem for myself and other women too. He is trying to fuck me around in my business too, and no one fucks me around. I could solve a problem for both of us.'

"How can I explain this to you, Grace? Or anyone? Esa mujer was clear that she knew me, and she knew Hector, and she was choosing me. Why? Qué sé yo. Why did I choose you? Eso no se sabe. She knew I had kids. She also understood that if she pulled me in, I wouldn't be leading the call for who killed my husband. No era pendeja, obviously. She was doing major expansions and what was I? One more that might work or one more she might have to kill down the line. It was like that. I knew a few things, but I did not see myself as she saw me en ese momento. So I answered her, shy and confused, 'Lo mío no tiene solución. I have two small boys at home.'

"'Let me take care of this. I can get you started on your own. You just show up to the same supplier Hector used. I will let them know. It's not that hard. If I have your back, no one will fuck with you, but keep in mind it's kill or be killed. No in between. Te tienes que poner fuerte. And if you can take a beating like that and put on a gown and show up here como si na', well, it looks to me like you are strong enough.' The image of Durga came into my head. I know that is not what that doctor had in mind when she gave it to me. But it felt like an answer to a question I didn't know how to ask. Al final, pues, she pulled me in for a strong hug and said, 'If we don't put a stop to this ourselves, it will never end. Entre hermanas vamos a ir resolviendo poco a poco. One by one. Until there isn't one left who dares lay a finger on us.'

"When we got back to New York, they killed him within a week, and just like she said, she hooked me up with his supplier and sent one of her men to have a meeting with all of Hector's guys to let them know I was the boss. They fought back a little, claiming I didn't know shit about the business. A few of them left, saying no woman was going to tell them what to do. I never saw those guys again. She sent me word to phase out the older ones or send them to her, and to start my own crew and start them young. To raise them up as mine, so they'd be loyal. I can't explain this even to myself, but all I ever come out with in the end is that if it was that easy for me to just slip right into it, I must have had it in me all along. Tú sabes, la maldad. I must have had it por dentro all that time. I mean, I killed the father of my children sin pena. Not with my own hands, but close. It is easy to think she was probably going to do it anyway and I just made it work to my advantage. Maybe. Who knows? But really, it was sin pena. I mean it was hard for me to watch the boys mourn, especially Toro, because he was close to his dad. But I never missed him. Not even one day. I was never sorry he was gone. Never. I knew what she said to me was true. Kill or be killed. What was I going to do? Run and hide? Where? With what? No. He might have killed me had I waited around, but for sure he would have killed me if I tried to get away with his sons."

The car was dark and cold, the engine still running even as time stopped. I felt like I would explode if I spoke. All my instincts went into hyperalert. I could not have been more terrified had she pulled a gun on me, and now it suddenly felt possible that she could. What had I been expecting? I don't know. I had felt prepared for anything, but somehow not that. I stayed quiet. I wasn't sure I could even move. Before she stepped out of the car, she looked back at me and said, "I learned a lot of things. The most important one is to take control of your situation. Even the end. Make sure you know who is coming for you and why you might deserve it. Don't look away. Decide how you want to go and don't let them take you by surprise. También, aprende, mijita, not to ask questions if you don't really want the answers."

I was trembling and hanging on to the steering wheel as if I might float away. I watched her walk through the hospital entrance. Nothing about her slow gait or bent posture under the clothes that were all baggy on her now gave any clues that she was who she had just revealed. I had repeated that so many times to Carmen and the girls when they looked shocked or pissed, that nothing was as safe or easy as it looked. It was the wrong advice all along for all of us. We had gotten lost following instructions when questions, and answers we didn't want, were what we needed most.

15

TODO TIENE SU FINAL

Durka's cancer treatments were wearing me out. I had gotten into a bad habit of curling up on the couch in the front room closest to the door before taking her for the next round, trying to hide from everything I felt closing in on me.

Carmen was floating away from me into a world with Pete that I'd created but could no longer control. Toro was picking fights every chance he got. I didn't have the nerve to ask Durka anything more about what she had told me in the car. That'd been almost a year ago and it made me feel a twisted softness toward Toro that he was using to just drag me every chance he got. Doña Durka was vanishing right before my eyes. "The World Is Yours" felt like a promise when I had nothing, and a punishment now that there was so much to deal with. I kept closing my eyes to nap or to daydream or merely to catch a break.

When the banging started on the door, I jumped up off the couch and pulled out my gun, my eyes still closed. Nene was the first to come through the door and grab me, talking me down as he took the gun out of my hand and held me against his chest. I still didn't understand what was happening. Toro went to the back with three of his "little brothers," which is what he called the young ones who followed him around like puppies waiting for orders. He didn't even look my way, just left us stand-ing there, but I could hear him crying. I turned my head up toward Nene and saw real fear. He held me by my arms a small distance from him so he could look me in the eye. I was shaking in his hands.

"What the fuck is going on?"

"Doña Durka. She's gone."

"What? The cancer? She died during chemo? I don't understand?"

"Nah, nah, man, they shot her up. Bullet holes everywhere. They left her in the front seat of her car in the parking lot at Orchard Beach."

I fell to the ground in the split second he let me go. I didn't faint or lose consciousness. I simply could not stand. Crumpled like paper you throw in the trash, I cried and carried on till I could not breathe. I should've been with her, and if someone killed her, it was because they knew I wasn't. They had even taken her car, which would have made her think it was me picking her up. Who the fuck had the balls and the access to do this shit? It was the last question on my mind before I was dragged out into waves of grief that were harder and stronger than I knew how to ride.

I sat on the floor with my back to the couch. Nene bent over me. "They stole her car. We looking into it. You know that. You gonna be aight. We all gonna feel this one, but you got family." He buried his face in my hair for a minute. I could feel his tears running down the side of my face.

After dark, the house filled with people like a fog that blurred the edges between grief, fear, and rage. Someone called Carmen and she called the girls. They huddled around me until I wore myself out. Toro never came near me that night. He hid behind a wall of noise about finding whoever did it and what they would do to them. They drank and smoked and talked revenge. It was all wrong. No one was talking about how they got her car or why the beach. They were just throwing around names of rivals that had long ago learned to play nice with Doña Durka. It made no sense. My mouth was dry. I had so many words. None would come out. I had my period and the dense fog in my head that came with it. I had been reading a book about goddesses for my anthropology class, which Durka loved me to read to her from. I was still going to school, and she was still asking me what I had learned. The book was on the floor where it had fallen off my chest. I had been planning to read it to her while we waited at the hospital.

I be saying, "Don't be sleepin' on me" to my girls all day long, and then that is exactly what I did. I slept on some of the biggest shit to ever go down on my watch. I was waiting for Durka on the couch, so I could take her to chemo, the round she'd decided would be her last. The remission had been short lived, the treatments drawn out and painful. I fell asleep with a book across my chest like a dumb-ass kid. I pictured her pulling the white cotton summer blanket over me and letting me go on sleeping, asking one of the guys on the block to drive her. The last thing she did was tuck me in. Something no one, not even her, had ever done. She left the note on the table of where she would wait and what time she'd be finished.

. . .

Right after Durka's burial, we all met up at the apartment. When Sugar asked for words, I realized I didn't have any. I wasn't trying to touch the grief. That had to go in a lockbox for some other time. All I could think to do was hold on to Red. Red would let me walk through silence till I found my words again. Carmen was the sentinel watching guard over us all. I could feel her wanting to stay. It was the one gift her fear always gave us. Carmen never let her guard down even when she could. She always asked too many fucking questions though. I couldn't keep her close. I wasn't sure how vested she was in holding the line anymore. Red would sit around all night without saying a word, if that's what I needed. She'd never ask questions unless I opened a door to them. She would tell me random-ass stories if that's what I wanted to hear. I sent everybody home except for Red. After she locked the door, I stretched out on the couch, looked up at the cracks in the ceiling, and tried to imagine a way around that would lead us forward. It all felt like a vicious circle surrounded by flames. I called out to her in the kitchen, "Tell me a story."

She turned to look at me through the little cutout into the living room that Santa had requested, so she wasn't left out of the fun while she was cooking. Red was doing the dishes and smiled. It was so good to have her back. "One you know or one you don't know? I got a lot of new shit from my travels."

"Give me my favorite."

"I can't believe you ain't tired of that shit yet, but okay."

She started in on a story she had told me a hundred different times in a hundred different ways. I never got tired of it. I had no idea why my mother had named me as she did or where it came from. Naming felt powerful and all important. The story of Red's name struck me as beautiful just because it was a story that could be told. Someone had even bothered to tell it to her.

"Most people don't know this, but my father calls me Collie because he wanted to name me after his mother Colleen. My mother hated his mother and refused. She said the old lady had tried to get him to abandon her, claiming the pregnant belly wasn't his. My father had wanted a boy and would have named him Collin after her, but I was born, and my mother looked at me and named me Rhiannon. My father was furious. He called me Colleen anyway. Then he shortened it to Collie. All my life he's called me Collie, and my mother refused to even list it as a middle name on my birth certificate. You'd think not being able to agree on the name of your first kid would maybe make you think before having another, but my three sisters came one right after the other. He finally won with the little one. My mother named her Colleen Ann. I think she did it because she had already kind of given up on living, but maybe she did it because she knew she was leaving us soon and his mother would have to fill in the blanks. Who knows? But he never has stopped calling me Collie, so the little one is just always full-on Colleen."

"So, who named you Red?"

"Some crazy bitches, of course. Not even that creative," she answered through a huge smile that she peeked back out of the kitchen to share with me as she dried her hands on a sunflower dishcloth that Teca had recently bought for the kitchen and then embroidered cuz she'd gone needle mad.

Teca was knitting, crocheting, even sewing. It was fun to watch, and every once in a while I liked to remind her of an old dream she had. "You could be sewing up bodies, girl, you are real precise." She'd look up, roll her eyes at me, and return to her needles.

Red threw the dishcloth on the table and came out to join me in the living room.

"Speaking of the old man, does he know you're back?"

She moved around the room putting things in place. She was moving cushions around and stopped at the window to pull down the shade before answering me. "Not by my mouth, but it doesn't take long for people to spot me and call him. He will find me eventually."

She turned to face me and asked, "Can I finish my story?" She knew how much I loved the next part. It was a dance we had been doing for a long time. She had some of the best mother stories, so I made her tell them over and over. I closed my eyes and waited.

"My mother named me Rhiannon and even gave me a theme song sung by Stevie Nicks. She would play the song for me and dance me around the living room."

I opened my eyes and saw she was swaying from side to side the way she always did when she told this part.

"Even when she was drunk or high, which I couldn't always tell back then, she was so beautiful, and she loved me. I could feel it as she sang the song to me, even if she was mostly singing with her eyes closed. She was only twenty-six by the time we were all born. I could never imagine being a woman with four kids at that age."

She always added a little something new. This time it had been her deep faith in her mother's love and her growing empathy for her struggle. It was a path we were all on, slow or fast: the older we got, the more our rage against our mothers turned to sadness about what we now knew they'd faced. It wasn't forgiveness exactly. It was a kind of understanding you only get from seeing your mother as a woman before she became your mother, but you have to be a woman to get there. I hadn't seen my mother since I'd left but had started wishing I might after Durka told me about Hector. I was looking for something, a sign for how to move, though I was pretty sure it wasn't coming.

Red had grown while she was away. She was leaner, with a dark reddish tan and darker freckles from her time in the sun. I was fascinated by all the mystery behind the solid I knew and had always counted on. I could have just stayed there listening to the sound of her voice all night. She started dancing around the room slow and sad and played Joplin's version of "Summertime" on the old stereo she'd brought to the apartment from her childhood room. It still worked. No one had played her old records and CDs since she'd left.

Red floated around the room in a slow-motion circle singing along. "She always danced alone to 'Summertime.' That was the song that meant she was trying to get away, even from us." Red was in her own world with her mother—and Red's mother had done all the shit white girls aren't known for, but do plenty of, from heroin to cheating on her Irish husband with a Puerto Rican on the block, maybe even falling in love with him. The way Red told it, her mother died from an overdose they disguised as breast cancer just in time because her father might have killed her had she kept on dancing in her red platform shoes. Red still had those shoes hidden in some closet. I watched her dance and tried to imagine where all of this was coming from and where it might go.

Then, as if nothing, she looked at her beeper and said, "Shit. My little sister. I gotta go. I'll call you." Red walked away firm. No hesitating. She kissed me on the cheek and never looked me in the eye before heading straight for the door. It slammed behind her. She had left the record playing. I had to get up to turn everything off.

She was not the same and it should have scared me. Instead, it made me soft. I felt abandoned and started plotting ways to bring the crew back together as I lay across the couch. Staring at the ceiling again, I came up with a million paths across the sky and landed at the little patch above the radiator where the paint was peeling.

I declared to an empty apartment, "We should all go to Disney World." It was something my mother had said more than once when our backs were up against the wall. I never forgot it. I had believed her. Maybe she had believed it too. It had stuck in my mind as a thing to do or say when you got in trouble and had no idea how to get out.

16

PRESENTE

Me fui porque me fui. Sometimes you take off and you can't even say why. I went away to the safe house a week after we got back from Disney World. We felt solid. We had faced a challenge and a surprise. I needed to go away because people only show who they are when they think you aren't looking—and I needed to see who was who if I was ever going to figure out what had happened to Durka. Maybe I was also checking to see who I was now that Durka was gone. I told Carmen and Red that the expansion was keeping everyone busy. I had business elsewhere and they should hold it down. I gave Carmen her usual job of paying attention; even if she was more distracted than usual, she could be counted on for that. I gave Red the keys to the kingdom because there was really no one else. Sugar would have been my first choice, but she had been letting me know in a thousand ways that she was done being out front in the danger zone and would only do what she knew she could do carefully.

Then I put on my shades and went to the beach, fed myself on sand, sea, dreams, and jelly beans. It was the thing all this shit was supposed to make possible: a beach house, a vacation, a fucking break. Grief did not get a lot of space, but sometimes it made demands. I was cracking on all sides and going away was my humpty-dumpty move. I had to put it all back together again. Never mind that all the king's horses and all the king's men couldn't even do it. I had to try. After that, there was rest and dreams of Durka telling me stories in her garden about her childhood. The last nightmare was my sign that it was time to come back. It shook me. It felt like Carmen calling me with her mind.

· · ·

I first stopped at China's place before making my way to Chad's. Before I left, I'd asked Remy and Destiny to work with their real estate contacts to find China a place near Van Cortlandt Park. My instructions were a view of the woods and easy access to the playgrounds, in her name. I remembered her saying she'd never had a lease with her name on it before, and it was one of the first points of showing good faith, building loyalty between us. Her name on the lease made it clear I'd look out for her, but that I wouldn't try to own her. Durka had taught me that you never owned the people who handled your money. You were better off trying to make them need you, love you, respect you, or some combination of all three. You definitely wanted to make them rich. Scared of you was a distant fourth because the same fear that made them loyal could make them turn when someone else scared them more. Durka had never met Chad. Once she asked, "Should I worry about him?"

I answered, "No, I know what he wants, and he is getting plenty of it."

"I let you pick this one because this expansion is on you. You're moving in places where I never fit. Just know your people."

I talked to Durka now that she was dead almost more than when she was alive. I called her name with my heart. I asked questions, filed complaints, then listened. I heard her voice clear as day. It wasn't eerie or supernatural. It was plain and ordinary. All those movies and TV shows where a character talks to a dead person like they are sitting next to them made new sense to me. That shit is real. Doña Durka was everywhere, now more than ever. It didn't make me want her actually here any less though.

I sent her a missive from China's door: "If you really sent this girl to me, make it clear today. It's getting wild out here." I threw up a kiss and rang the bell.

China opened the door and hugged me. Her kids were on the floor putting together a puzzle. She was beaming with pride as she swept her arm out in welcome. The sunken living room was a large, sunny open space decorated in beige and white furniture with a dash of yellow in the curtains and cushions. The serenity prayer in a frame by the door and a picture of the Virgin Mary were the first signs of religion I had ever noticed in China. She pulled me in and closed the door.

"You haven't been here since I moved in, have you? Welcome back. What do you think?"

"It looks great. Feels like home."

We sat at her dining room table where she had fresh flowers in a vase. China didn't strike me as the type to buy herself flowers.

"Nice flowers. Housewarming gift?"

She twisted her mouth as she decided how much to reveal. "Look, he sent flowers. He bought the kids some bedroom furniture. He came by. You didn't think Nene was going to just let me move his kids away from his family and not check where they'd be living?"

"No, but you're like the original ride or die. I can't have Nene knowing you down with me. How did you explain how you could afford the place?"

She smiled wide like she knew she had the right answer. "That was easy. My uncle has had a lawsuit against the city for like fifteen years. Nene has always known about it and called it the poor man's pipe dream, saying that people dreamt of winning a lawsuit like they dreamt of winning the lotto. I told him he won, and he bought me the apartment for all the help I gave at the gym and with the paperwork for the case all those years."

"Can your uncle keep that story under pressure?"

"Yep, cuz he did win, and he did give me some money. He also hates Nene for cheating me out of a fighting career. He's happy I'm on my own and still doing his books. Plus, I'm not really asking him to lie. He thinks he did this too."

Her gray streak was braided back in with the rest of her hair. She looked younger and stronger without it hanging in her face. Her tank top and shorts revealed that every inch of visible skin was resting on muscle. She looked at me and said, "And for the record, I ain't no ride or die. I have never known anyone other than my own two kids that I was willing to die for, and definitely no man, so just shut that down, please."

"Okay, but it's on you to keep it clean with Nene. I brought you in cuz you showed up with permission from the dead, but we clear that I'm not playing games. What you got for me based on what I gave you?" I made space by pushing the flowers away as she pulled out two boxes from under the table.

She drew out folder after folder with each of our names on top. "I took the money you showed me in the apartment to expand our official financial identities. On the books we're in cash-heavy roles like strippers, bartenders, waitresses, and nannies holding down two or three jobs at once. Chad had set that up. Under him we have bank accounts in our names and pay taxes and social security on the half of it you already made visible with the building. The hidden half you gave me we are keeping in the Bahamas, investing in small businesses and real estate outside of the US, where claiming shit is not really an issue. Spreading it out and keeping it low. These are the new accounts and records. Then this is the files with the hotels that Durka was working on that you told me to check out. It all looks good. Red was out there setting up the door-to-door delivery service for the rich on vacation looking for full service they could trust. Chad looks to be expanding it to the kids on spring break. Kind of genius. It runs on automatic once you have the people inside, but I would need more information to give you better numbers."

"That's good. Do all that legitimate shit—retirement funds, CDs, savings accounts—on the surface. Keep this stash growing quietly. I'm going to arrange a meeting with you and Chad. I want you to figure out exactly what he's doing, and how we can eventually do it on our own. All of it."

"Well, like I told you before, I'm not there yet. I need to build some skills to take it further. I also need to talk to Red or go to those places myself. I need to understand the ground game, and Red is not exactly approachable."

I laughed and grabbed her hand. "No, but you aren't exactly the vie-jitas church welcoming committee either."

She rolled her eyes like she couldn't deny it but refused to accept it. Then she changed the subject. "Yeah, well now that I can pay off what I owe from the last time I was in school, I can register for next semester. I mean, I'm not sure if that is where I will get what I need, but I also need background. You been working on that in this crew. I can tell. I need some ground under my feet. It's heavy getting this deep in money so fast."

"But you're good. No?"

"Definitely. I just want to be better."

Her son walked over and put his head on her lap. She picked him up, snuggled his head against her neck, and wrapped his long legs around her waist. He was already too old and big to carry while she was stand-ing. China was pure muscle, but only a full five feet two inches of it. Sitting down was probably the only way she could still carry him.

"I think he's tired. Set up the meeting with Chad, but try to get me access to the paper where the real numbers live. People talk a lot of shit in meetings, but numbers can be made to sing out loud if you see them on paper."

"Got it. In the meantime, start reading all those business magazines and sections in the newspapers. Get your head in that world and learn their ways. Learn the language."

She nodded and sighed deep at my instructions to read. She kissed her son's shoulder and buried her face in his hair. He had China's sharp chin and Nene's big dark brown eyes and thick eyelashes that were flut-tering as he fought sleep. I had Chad and money on my mind. Watching China with her boy made me think about Carmen and what she'd gone and done, and still had not told me. I lost a little bit of Carmen every day she lied. Nothing scared me more. Not even dying. What the fuck were we going to do with a baby in this shit? I stood up to leave. Keeping it moving felt like the only way to stop from crumbling one minute to the next. Every step I took made it clearer that Doña Durka was gone and no one had my back. All my girls were counting on me as I had counted on her—and Doña Durka's were not shoes I felt ready to fill yet. I had no choice but to leave blood on the floor trying.

. . .

When I got to Brooklyn, the D.O.D. Management Group sign on the door reminded me that Chad still answered to me, even if he thought he didn't. I threw my shoulders back a little. I had relied on him because we clicked, but also because I didn't know much. I wasn't willing to keep letting that be the dynamic between us. His assistant didn't even blink as I walked past her and into his office unannounced. He looked up, surprised.

"Well, did you enjoy your break? Vacations are good. I love the beach. The Hamptons are my favorite." He wasn't supposed to know where the house was, and it annoyed me that I couldn't tell if he was fishing or revealing.

"Well, I went to the mountains. I needed some clean air and inspiring vistas."

"Did you go hiking? How high did you climb?" He smiled as he said it.

"I'm not here for chitchat, so let's get to the shit we know how to talk about."

He swiveled toward the windows he had reconstructed to offer floor-to-ceiling views of the Manhattan skyline. The missing Twin Towers still felt like a gaping hole, but also a world away from the problems I had at my feet. He had watched the whole thing from the window and only ever said one thing about it: "My parents got me an internship in that building. I guess it's a good thing I never showed up."

Me and Durka had watched the news, made some adjustments, but mostly we'd been hunkered down in her cancer. It was like that. All those memorials and pictures all over the city, ordinary people still dying and fighting for their lives every day. All of it death. All of it mattered. All of it inescapable.

Chad broke the silence. "Yeah, okay, so let's talk."

"I have a new girl that comes directly from Durka. She will be working with the numbers, and I want you to train her. Give her access to everything we have."

"You trust her like that?"

"Well, no more or less than I trust anyone. Her name is China."

"As in Nene's ex? Isn't that a little close for comfort?"

"She's a woman with an axe to grind. You know I'm a fan of that shit."

He looked at me and fell into one of his long silences. He folded and unfolded his hands, then stood and leaned on the window. I tried to imagine how he was as a little kid, and if he did this kind of smug stalling shit back then, how impatient that must have made his teachers and his parents.

He answered, "Okay, let's set something up and meet with China. Then we can decide on new directions."

He was watching me and looking past me at the same time. "You didn't bring this girl in to watch me or anything, did you? I'm not sure I like how all this looks right now. Red is pretty pissed off too. Have you talked to her about this new girl?"

I stood up to leave. "See, this is where you always get it wrong. You see a corner of the picture and think you can see the whole thing, but that is not your job, is it? Stick to what you know, and you can be sure that Red is not among those things. I don't talk to anyone about who comes in or out. Those are choices I make alone."

He put his hands up as he answered, "Yes, yes, the street code and all the things I don't know. Yes, well, truth is I don't need to know. You are right about that. Just make sure the girl you are sending me is good and ready. I'm not on the payroll of your little learning annex in the hood."

Outside, the sun burned after the cool dark interior of the building. I was already exhausted and had only been back a day. I didn't really understand grief, the waves of it washing over, through, and under me, in and out across the days. One minute I relished the hits and obstacles just to feel my bounce-back, the next instant every impact felt like it floored me. My back was a tangle of knots and pain. My mind felt stiff too, crowded and sticky. I wanted to turn and walk away and never look back. It was a dangerous feeling. So many people would be left out to dry, so much money unaccounted for, so much shit my girls would have to pay for in my absence. Chad would be the big winner in it all. That was a definite no. It killed me that I couldn't trust Carmen anymore. At least it felt like I couldn't in the same way. I even had a girl tailing her, pretending to be the super's cousin from Puerto Rico and mopping floors in the building where Pete had the apartment.

The girl called me as I was getting in my car. "I'm not sure but I think they might be getting married. I saw him carrying a bag from a bridal shop."

I had dreamt a lot at the safe house. Awake and asleep, always picturing us, as a crew, at Orchard Beach, a kind of wild wedding. Now I had an excuse. I made a quick call to Chad.

"Hey, can you do me a favor and set up a private meeting with a jeweler at Tiffany's."

"What happened? Are you outgrowing the jewelry stores on Fordham Road?"

"Why you always got to make it feel like work to talk to you? Just do what I asked. Thank you."

"You need a budget to get a private showing. You know, above a certain amount."

"Well, just figure out what that is and double it." He was laughing as I hung up. I would not be letting Carmen go off into happily ever after without me.

. . .

We came out of the water at Orchard Beach born again into whoever the fuck we wanted to be, including bitches walking across the sand in the dark in white bathrobes and diamond rings. We piled into the limo waiting for us in the almost empty parking lot clinking champagne glasses. China and Sugar were quiet, but no less relaxed and at ease. Remy and

Destiny were popping in and out of their seats, holding their rings up to the light. Red stayed in the car with me till we dropped the last girl. If there was a shadow hanging over that night, its name was Carmen, but everyone was careful not to mention her.

Red came at me like she had been waiting for the last one to get out of the car to make her true feelings known.

"I love your whole we are all married to each other bullshit, like that is supposed to make me feel some type of way"—she looked at her ring like maybe she wasn't sure she even wanted to be wearing it—"but do you even know what is going on with Toro and Nene? You think dancing in public with their money is a good idea? Is that the new plan?"

"No, it's not. That was the point. It's not their money. We are not hiding from them. We also need to smoke out their plan for us. Whatever they think they are going to do, they need to go ahead and try."

"What about what happened to Doña Durka? Do we really need to be enemies with Toro, if the people who went for her look at us like we all the same?"

"I don't think of Toro as an enemy, just not a friend. Not to be trusted to protect us, that's for sure. He needs to know we ain't scared of him is all."

"Looks like your girl Carmen grew some balls. Didn't even play in the water with us at your beach party. Rolling up with her big-ass belly not saying a word. What's up with that? You sure everybody is still in line? I mean, that's what this was all about, right. Roll call?"

Red opened the window and let the breeze in. The sky was crackling with the sound of summer thunder still too far away but coming. Lightning lit up from a distance. She wouldn't look at me and kept tapping her own knee. I slid closer and laid my hand over her hand.

"It was a lot more than roll call and you know it, but we need to solve some problems, so when we leave this game it's with real money and not bodies in bags and jail cells."

Her most cynical laugh filled the car. She slapped my hand before I could pull it away.

"Who are you now? Carmen? Going soft with dreams of escape.

We already got a body in a bag. Jail cells full of low-hangin' fruit. Doña Durka sent me out there to get us deeper in. She saw that big shit is coming. Doña Durka was way ahead of her time."

It annoyed me that it felt like Red knew things about Durka's plans that maybe I didn't. Neither one of them ever kept secrets from me, though both had accused me of going soft when Durka got sick.

"Well, if you know shit I don't, tell me then."

The car had been full of energy when we were all together. Now it was quiet and empty. Every word like an echo. I kept looking at the divider to make sure it wasn't open and the driver couldn't hear us. I was waiting for Red to turn and look at me, but she never did. She just kept looking out the window like she had never seen the trees or the traffic before. Her voice sounded like it was boring her to have to fill me in. We were getting close to the garage. I needed her to finish before she got out of the car. A garbage truck turned in front of us like a well-timed stall. We slowed to a stop behind it.

"Before sending me away, Doña Durka said some things to me. I'm still not sure everything she knew and saw coming, but she said it plain to me. 'Governments are getting tired of small heavily armed empires running without paying taxes. Little by little all this is going to get legalized; we have to get there first.' She sent me out there to the islands to watch white boys learning shit they plan to do legit back home, but also to trademark our service. The way we make people feel about the drugs they do. You know, the 'traveling apothecary,' 'we feel good when you feel good' thing. She was not trying to get us out, she just wanted more legitimate ways to stay in."

Red was talking over me in a way she had never done before, acting like I was the innocent one. She knew more than me, even more than she might tell me. I pressed her.

"Okay, but Doña Durka is dead, and as much as her plans were always my plans, we also need to change what we can't or aren't willing to do without her. I mean, nobody loved her more than me, but I ain't taking orders from the dead."

Finally she looked at me for a second with the face of a big sister scolding a child. "I have no problem being your ride or die, but you must know I can't be messing with dreams and la-la land bullshit. All your classes and your studying have been very good for business. So I'm down. But this is our business. You know we ain't getting out. Carmen ain't getting out. Ain't nobody getting out. Out where? Out how? I mean, we might get jobs as pharmaceutical reps. That is the closest to our skill set. But really, where we going?" Red laughed at her own stupid joke, turned the music up, and looked back out the window. The garbage truck moved, and our driver took a left at the next light.

When we pulled into the garage, Red broke the silence with information she was hesitant to reveal. "I saw my father last week, and it wasn't a good visit."

"How'd that happen?"

"I think my sisters told him I was going to visit my grandmother in the nursing home. He showed up as I was leaving."

"Anything I should know?"

"I'm not sure. He was cagey. Saying the usual, like he knows things and this is my last chance to get out, etc. . . . the same shit I been getting and denying for years. But something about him sat wrong with me. Like he was sad more than he was angry."

"Like maybe he was about to do something he might regret?"

Red's hair was loose, still wet from the beach. It made her seem soft, but her profile revealed nothing. I knew she had given up her life with her father and sisters for me, for us. I didn't have much to begin with and so I had little to lose, but she did. She gave her sisters money and looked out for them, but they had to sneak around to see her and felt torn every time they did. She had nieces and nephews she couldn't even see. Colleen was in college on Red's dime, but Red would never be able to go to the graduation. The sisters had decided to tell their father she'd won a scholarship. They called from time to time to keep Red informed, but she was locked out of the family life of baptisms, birthdays, and Christmases that they all shared.

She went on, "I only went because my sister told me the old lady was dying, but she looked the same to me. It makes me wonder if my sister wasn't in on it. They all think there is some magical kind of way for me to become something I have never been and for all this to get better."

"Maybe there is, maybe they are your motivation for out." She looked at me like I was ridiculous. I kept pushing. "I know he's your dad and all, but cops are cops. Should we be worried?"

"Maybe, but give me some time to figure out if he is just pulling the usual or it's worth worrying about. I don't think he really knows anything. He can't know what he has never really wanted to know." She stopped and took a deep breath. "He has too much pride to let other people in his precinct know what his daughter is into, even if they all talk behind his back. How much can he really get on his own? Plus, he's old as hell. He can't have the kind of contacts he would need. But I'll follow up."

"Maybe Doña Durka getting shot in broad daylight spooked him into taking some action. He might be afraid that same shit is coming for you."

She lowered her voice before she answered, "I doubt it. It would probably be a relief to him if I showed up dead somewhere. One less thing to worry about."

All of us had felt that way at one time or another. Like who could possibly care if we turned up dead? That changed when we started to matter to each other.

"I don't think it works like that with your own kid; it's possible, but I would say unlikely. I'm sure some people in there are worried about their 'overtime' salary too. It has to be a lot buzzing around him."

Red looked tired and annoyed. I wanted to comfort her, but I couldn't let her off so easy. I had to push till I felt sure there wasn't more to know. "What if your father sort of goes in with Toro? Nene and Toro are going to keep paying the guys who have their back on the street."

Her face changed, a new anger creeping in. She answered roughly, "Toro is your fucking problem! So deal with him. You know my dad has never played that game and now he is about to get cozy with Toro? That is some stupid shit. He might at any point turn and go after us. That I can buy. But slide in bed with Toro against us? Nah."

"I didn't mean it like that. I meant he would be trying to find out who killed Durka." But Red wasn't listening anymore. I honestly didn't know what I was saying either. I was circling around an idea in my head that this wasn't street work. That killing Durka had come from some deeper place, someone close. I hadn't even been thinking about Red's dad till she mentioned seeing him. I was just grabbing hold of whatever I could.

The drivers were all trained to wait till we knocked on the divider to get out and open doors for us, no matter where we were or however long we were parked at our destination. We were all trained in the careful art of waiting for instructions, moving slow or fast depending on what each moment required. I wanted more time. Red stretched across the empty space in the middle and knocked on the divider. The door was opened on her side first.

She drove off without so much as saying goodbye. As soon as I got in my car, my cell phone was going off with Toro's number. It wasn't shocking to get a call in the middle of the night from him. He had called a few times since I'd left the house, even more since I'd gotten back from Miami. He was usually drunk. This time he sounded kind of high on coke, which was not normal for him. His voice was all edge.

"Come home, Grace. I need to see you. I didn't think you had it in you to stay away so fucking long. I should have known you could. We been underestimating each other for a long time. Come home, Grace. The house is crazy empty without you. I'm crazy empty."

"Toro? Are you okay? Are you alone? Where's Nene? Should I call him for you?"

"Come on. I call Nene when I need to. I'm calling you, Grace. I need you, not Nene. Don't say no. Just come."

Every woman alive knows exactly how I felt at that moment and what I did. I was 100 percent sure that he and I had been done for years, and that going there would be a huge mistake. That it was dangerous. Still. I told myself the long, long story about how this was good. I had paperwork in the house I needed to get. I had books and pictures, and how maybe we could find some closure. Maybe he wanted to talk about a clean divorce. Maybe we would have crazy, weepy hectic sex. Not for a reconciliation, but like a goodbye gesture. Anything was possible. Maybe we could be friends. We had been friends once. I wasn't a threat or even his competition. Maybe I would get information that would be useful in closing in on Durka's killer. These were the long fault lines of thousands of years of history crushing female wisdom and telling me not to trust my instincts, not to listen to my one true voice that kept saying, *Stay the fuck away from that house.*

I drove in one of those ridiculous summer rainstorms, lightning and thunder that seemed to come out of nowhere. I had seen some clouds at the beach, and the far-off action from the car window, but it hadn't felt like this level of rain was coming so close so fast till I was driving through it myself. I thought about turning back a hundred times. I kept telling myself the story. I had waited too long as it was to get my stuff. It would be good for us to talk one last time. I felt alone too. Toro and I had both lost our mother. Maybe he had finally gotten to the place where he cared about how much I was hurting. Had I taken even five minutes to breathe, think, or call one of my girls . . . but we never call our truth tellers when we really want to do what the fuck we want. Red or Carmen would never have let me go in there alone. Had I taken a second to even contemplate Ma Durga plunging her spear deep in the demon's heart, who was of course disguised as a bull, I would have turned my car around. Instead, I drove through a storm that made me weaker by the second, if only because I already knew how strong he felt in the rain.

17

MATADOR

I ran the short walk from the driveway to the front porch. The door was unlocked. I went around the back and found that one open as well. There was no security at either door, or right inside, where Durka usually had them. The kitchen was dark. Light flickered beneath the door to Durka's office. The wind was blowing the rain in through the open windows. I pulled out my gun before walking past the office. The door was closed. Unlike cops who are always kicking doors down, we waited to see what came out from behind closed doors. Sometimes whatever was in there wanted to stay hidden and it was just as well for everybody that it did. I was sliding sideways, looking in both directions. I never gave my back to closed doors if I could help it. I wanted to turn around and leave, but if some shit was going down, it was bound to come for me. It had called me here.

I found Toro sitting in the half-dark living room, an empty bottle of Hennessy at his feet. Only the lamp in the corner was on and throwing shadows everywhere. The window behind him blew the curtain around his head. He sat there like a ghost staring at me through a storm that was just as strong inside the house as it was outside.

Toro's voice quivered. "Too bad she ain't here to tell me to close the windows, right. I can still hear her voice everywhere. You were smart to leave. Aquí no hay paz."

The sound of Héctor Lavoe's "Ausencia" filled the room with despair. Toro was moving his head to the slow rhythm, eyes closed as he mouthed the lyrics of Lavoe's eternal grito to loss and pain. Scattered lines of coke were laid out on the table next to him, getting wet from an empty glass turned on its side, an ice cube melting. The chill that crossed my body then had all my animal instincts on high alert. I brought my gun out in front of me, aimed low, but in his direction.

Toro didn't react or move anything other than his mouth.

"I never pictured us like this, Grace. I tried to keep what we had special. Unique. Único. You know. I never touched you till you were old enough. I never hurt you. I mean, that night after my mother's funeral, that doesn't count. We were both fucked up."

He bent forward and rested his forearms on his thighs. His movement made me pull the gun up a little higher and my own body further back. Lightning filled the room and then tossed us back into the dark. So fucking unstable. I tensed the muscles in my legs, lowered my shoulders, and worked to calm my breath. Focus on a single point. Those were the instructions we had been taught for staying in rooms and situations that made us want to run. I am not lost. I focused on the gold-framed mirror to the left of him. There were two, one on either side of the window. I was visible in the one to the left of his head, a shadow in the dark. I am here. I am alive. I am leaving here alive. My breathing hooked into the mantra. I lowered my gun to signal I was listening. I didn't put it away.

His voice wandered around in self-pity but swung out in rage by the time he finished the sentence. "Look at you pointing a gun at me in my own house." Toro was licking the wounds of his public humiliation and his heartbreak like they were one and the same. I had always known that was the greatest danger I ever faced in this house. I couldn't see his gun yet, but I knew it could not be far. I shifted my eyes from his face to my own in the mirror, and then to the room behind me to make sure no one had popped out from behind.

"A gun my own fucking mother gave you. That's some shit, isn't it?

She'd been trying to kill me since before I was born. Did you know her grandmother tried to give her some herbs so she would miscarry? Did you know that? When she found out how my father afforded all the nice things he gave her, she tried to help her get rid of me. Well, surprise, surprise. I wasn't that easy to get rid of." Long, loud thunder rolled through the house from every window. I jumped a little, which made him laugh.

"I thought you would have been over that by now. We been in a lot of storms together, mami. Scared of thunder but holding a gun ready to shoot. Qué mierda, ¿ahh?" His eyes narrowed under heavy lids. He looked around wildly, though his movements were slow and thick. His body was like the bars of a cage holding him in as he turned his head from side to side. He opened his mouth wide, a lion about to roar, but all that came out was howling pain.

"Yeah, she killed my father and would've killed me if she could've. The dudes in Miami tipped me off by saying some shit like, 'Be careful your wife doesn't turn out to be like your mother and take you out to get hers.' You know what that felt like? My mother. My father. My wife. Everybody I loved. And everybody seems to know, while I'm just the pendejo sitting around comiendo mierda. You can't know. You can't fucking know."

He threw the tipped-over glass in my direction. I ducked back less than an inch. It landed quietly on the throw rug at my feet. Then he threw a bottle against the wall closest to him. It shattered. The noise gave him energy. He focused on moving his hands around the couch like he was looking for something.

I slowly backed into the opposite end of the room in case I found a chance to run for it.

I took a deep breath and hooked in: *I am alive. I am leaving here alive.* I lowered my voice, maintained eye contact as I said, "You don't even know what you're saying right now. The street is full of stories that are only ever half true, if that. You taught me that. You're the one who told me people talk shit when you live on top. Forget all that. Calm down." The wind was blowing hard behind him.

He went to stand and fell back on the couch like he'd been pushed.

I noticed he was tugging on his nose and the remnants of a few lines on the table. Toro had never really done drugs. A little weed and drinking had been his limit. Getting high on your own supply was actually way more common than most people knew, but not when you intended to make big money or when Durka was running your show. Had he been paying attention to me all these years, he would've known better than to let me see him looking like my mother. He mattered less to me by the second, and that made it easier to square off.

His energy shifted as he unfurled his arms as if to announce something grand. The lightning felt like it was moving through my body. I no longer needed to check my back in the mirror. *I am leaving here alive* was vibrating in my cells.

Toro was always touching his face. He'd smooth his eyebrows, tug on his chin, pull on his lower lip. It was mostly soft and mindless but could sometimes be a warning that his anger was rising and he was containing it, though not enough or for long. He was high and sloppy as he ran his hands across his forehead, pinched the little bit of extra flesh between his eyebrows, as if to stop his eyes from releasing tension into tears.

"You think I don't know what you and my mother were up to? It wasn't bad enough she killed my father and taught my brother to hate me. She had to take you too. She took you and everything my father worked for and tried to leave me with a bullshit street game, while she left you an empire. With the future. What the fuck kind of mother is that? But you know the worse part, Grace? The very worst thing she did, she tried to get me to kill her."

My shoulders pulled back even as my chest caved a little at the sight of his pain. He ran his hands across his head. I tried to convince him to see it some other way. "Where do you get shit like that? That is coke paranoia talking. You hear me."

"¿Y tú que sabes? That has always been your fucking problem. You think you know every fucking thing. You don't know shit. My mother was not trying to go down bit by bit, piece by piece, with chunks of hair in each fist. I drove her to the hospital that day you fell asleep. I was fucking happy you fell asleep because it finally gave me a chance to be alone with her."

I shook with chills. My breathing was uneven. The weight of the gun faltering jarred me back. I straightened, pulled up again, made sure it was pointing in his direction. He saw me do it and shook his head at me.

"I drove her and talked to her about getting better. She handed me her gun and said, 'Mijo, you know what you need to do, and you know how to do it. You pick the time and place but do it soon. I would ask Grace, but she doesn't have it in her.' I looked at her like she was crazy, right. Like those fucking cancer drugs were making her nuts. I said, 'Ma, don't even go there.' She looked straight at me and said it. She said it like it might make me pull the trigger. 'Yo te la debo, hijo. It was me that had your father killed. I mean they were going to kill him anyway, but I agreed to it and never warned him.' That shit, I mean, she had to know it was only going to make me want to pull the trigger on myself. I mean, what the fuck?"

Toro buried his head in his hands; he cried open and loud in deep communion with the storm that was giving him the courage to grieve, to say what he had never said. Every bone in my body wanted to go to him and take him in my arms, but every instinct held me in place. I was as hyped on adrenaline as he was on coke. We walked a tightrope together, no safety net below.

My body started shaking uncontrollably. I used the breath to bring it back and hold it steady. We had trained for this shit, but it was impossible to know how it would feel until I felt it. I made tiny movements to soften where I was rigid: the small of my back, my knees, my neck and stomach. Agile. Stay agile. I leaned in to see where he might have left his gun. The way he had been running his hands across the couch made me think it was there, but his head stayed in his hands. It was too dark to really see anything clearly.

I tried to offer something soft again. "Look, you're drunk and talking crazy. Just let me help you get to bed. Why are you alone? Where's Nene? Should I call him to come over, so you won't be alone?"

Toro lifted his head. The look on his face made me think that Nene was already here somewhere. Toro's eyes darted back and forth.

"You don't know the damage you done, girl. You broke my heart, but that ain't shit. She broke my heart for real. Why did she think I could do that shit? She never would've asked Jimmy and he probably would have done it easier. But she was wrong about you. Falling asleep made it look like it couldn't be you, right? But your girl Red hadn't been seen in a long time. Word was my mom didn't want her around anymore. Sent her ass away. Everybody knows she was capable of stacking bodies, and suddenly she's at my mother's funeral. Maybe she got here a few days early?"

Thunder filled the room again. Heavy rain hit the windows like bullets. If I could have gotten out without turning my back, I would have left. I could tell he believed what he said about Red. If he did, then there was no way he was letting me leave here alive.

I tried again, slower, more careful. "You know in your heart that I would never. You know it. It would be easier to talk without guns. Can we just cool it? Maybe wait until the storm is over, go outside. You like walking in rain. It clears your head."

"It's too late for all that." Nene's voice boomed from down the hall. It echoed like he was still in the kitchen. I knew Durka had the place wired in weird ways, so she could listen to every conversation or whisper, and to protect her own.

I also knew this house by the sounds in the dark. I had come to live here as a kid. It'd be a lie to pretend I had not been terrified. I'd sat by my door for weeks listening to every creak on the steps, every door that opened and closed, every voice, muffled or clear, angry or sad. Information mattered. When I heard the squeak of his sneakers, I knew Nene had stepped on the linoleum indent right outside the pantry door. He was walking slow. I closed my eyes for a second, pictured him stepping out from the kitchen onto the worn-out rug that ran the length of the long hall. I remembered the bulky, heavy wooden cross hanging on the wall. I listened for a scrape against it when his broad shoulders came through. Scrape. He was closer. I checked on Toro. He was again searching the couch, fucking aimless with grief.

Even years into living here, I'd stand in doors and hallways in the dark—my eyes closed, but my ears wide open. I had learned that shit with my own mother. She would shush me with her finger up against her mouth, hold me tight against the door to see if the sounds on the steps were coming for her. Here I was listening for what I knew was coming for me. Toro looked down at the table and picked up his drink. I stepped back, deeper into the dark end of the room. I slid behind the big statue of the black panther Durka had in the living room. I heard the loud groan of the weak wooden plank near the stairs. He was just outside the living room entrance.

The small puddles forming under the open windows were sending water along the edges of the crooked wooden floor that rimmed the room and the center area rugs. My knee got wet the minute it touched the floor to find a more stable position.

Toro went to get up, then fell back again.

Nene was now standing front and center at the entrance, pointing his gun at him. Nene was looking at Toro and into the mirror for a rear view of the rest of the room. I felt safer with every move I could see coming. The room was too dark to offer him any information.

Nene swung around in both directions but didn't move. I stayed crouched under the panther. It was safe but limited my view. I could see his white, black, and yellow Jordan 17s, a gift China had given him for his birthday on behalf of the kids. I could see Toro's bare feet under the table. I would have to close my eyes and listen.

"Sorry, bro. I wish it didn't have to be like this. I know I'm supposed to be here to deal with Grace because you don't have the heart. The problem is that you don't have the heart for a lot of shit we need to be doing. Your mom called me after you left her on the sidewalk. I knew if she was leaning on me last minute there had to be more to the story. I wasn't going to do that shit, but she was clear it had to happen. She told me to let some people know, who she knew had her name on their list, her whereabouts. My only job was not to tell anyone."

To hear it revealed in the dark didn't make it easier to take. Durka knew not only that cancer was coming, but others were coming for her as well. She pulled her own strings, as always. She gave Toro a chance to get even. Release her guilt, maybe. Nene would have never done it, but she knew he wanted things Toro didn't want badly enough. My chest caved a little to think of Toro. He might, it was now clear, be the one not leaving here alive today, even if he managed to survive.

. . .

The leather couch creaked, and I knew Toro had stood up. His voice echoed more from disbelief than shock.

"What the fuck are you saying? You knew who took her out all this time? You helped them? I don't understand. What the fuck are you saying?"

"She took herself out, pa. She got me to tell the new Dominican crew her location. She told me exactly what to say. 'Diles that you left my car with the keys in it parked near the hospital, tell them why I'm here, que estoy debil, and that I will think it's Grace picking me up and I will just get in the car. Eso' tipo me tienen gana'. They're young and hungry. That combination makes people wild and reckless, but also strong. Lo único es that they will ask you why you are turning on me. They will only trust you, and maybe let you live, if they believe you and agree with what you say. Tell them you just got tired of being bossed around by a woman.' She knew exactly what it would take. When I said it, the dude laughed and answered, 'No hay problema. Esa la entendemos toditos.'"

Toro let out the wildest scream I'd ever heard. I swallowed mine deep, clenched my teeth hard. If there was a moment of leaving my body, this was it. My body, left alone to its own devices, knows only one thing: live.

As soon as Toro stopped to take a breath, Nene yelled just as loud, "It was what she wanted! I was her soldier for life. Somebody had to do it, but it was her choice. She had that right. The last thing she said to me was 'Todo tiene su final, mijo, try to be in control of yours if you can.' You keepin' me from that, bro, like you got no idea what it means to stay in control at this level."

Toro was paralyzed. He took one step forward right onto the glass from the bottle he had broken earlier. He didn't scream but fell back on the couch. Nene moved in a little closer and looked over his shoulder into the dark. I was on the floor looking up. He stopped and stayed quiet, listening for me in the room. I was out of the range of the hall light, but the space wasn't big enough to hide me for long.

He tapped the wall with his gun. He called out, "As for you, Grace, you can hide, but you ain't leaving here alive. You got too greedy, and in this business, it never pays to take more than you can protect. I warned your ass more than once. I was here from the start, and everybody trying to lock me out. Nah."

Nene pointed the gun at Toro and then swung it out wide in the dark. He was nervous. He was talking a lot of shit, but he was scared. Telling Toro that story, true soldier as he tried to make it sound, was breaking him down from the inside. I could see Toro's face as he bent forward over the table. The sliver of light coming down the hall showed he was frozen in grief and confusion. He looked up and it felt like he'd somehow made eye contact with me.

He leaned back and stuttered, "What are you talking about, bro? What the fuck is this? You making moves. Quítate tú pa' ponerme yo shit?".

Nene was talking fast, hyped. "You been sleeping on me, bro, and I ain't got time for that. You may not know how to read much, but I do. From what I been putting together, these bitches are cleaning up big-time while we hustle small shit and risk our asses out on the street. And I'm sure I only found the crumbs. They pulled China in too. Now that bitch won't even take my calls. Drops the kids off at my mom's house and keeps moving. These bitches got no respect."

A giant crack of lightning was the first shot fired. Nene aimed the next somewhere between me and Toro. I couldn't tell if it was a warning or if he'd missed. I couldn't tell where Toro was or if he even had his gun yet. I also couldn't sit around waiting to find out. I slid out from under the belly of the panther and aimed for Nene's knees.

Toro, still slow, went for his gun under a cushion on the couch like he had always known it was there. He started shooting randomly in my direction. My body burned whatever fog of fear I had left with chemistry and heat. A racing heart is for flight, to pump your blood faster for running. The clarity and strength of adrenaline are for fighting. I had no choice. I had to fight.

I crouched behind the black panther again, aimed for thighs and knees, then ankles and feet. They fell like rag dolls in a pile. Toro was stumbling and easy to keep down. Nene fell but got off a few more shots. The thunder clapped close and loud over the sounds of them both screaming. I jumped up and slipped in some of the new puddles forming, blood running into water. I steadied myself, breathed deep. That was the training.

I kicked their guns away from them. Toro reached out his hand to grab my ankle. I looked away to make it easier to kick him in the face. I picked up the guns and hid them on the stairs behind me. I kicked their pockets to look for phones and took Nene's. Toro's was on the couch. Nene grabbed my leg. He was still strong. I shot him again in the shoulder. He let go. My breathing was steady in the way I had learned. My pulse was fast but weak, like my heart was beating far away from me.

I went into Durka's office and stuffed papers and pictures into a big black garbage bag. A lot of the papers were already scattered around since Nene was going through them. All old shit. Leave no trail. Act like you belong here. Leave no room for doubt. All my instructions vibrated like tiny lights on a runway leading me to safety. I thought about setting the house on fire. Fires were careless, brought attention, did not belong here. Instructions rang clear and I followed.

Nene and Toro were still screaming in the living room. Their voices were growing weaker though. I was desperate to shut them up, but once it was clear they couldn't get back up or hurt me, I couldn't get myself to go back in there. I'd hit their legs, high up and close to the groin, avoiding the muscle. It was only a matter of time. My mind kept clicking. They were bleeding fast. It would be over soon enough. The storm was louder than they were. I grabbed the remote Toro had in every room and cranked up the volume on the music Toro was playing. That would be familiar to the neighbors. Not that anyone would call the cops. Gunshots were a sign to lock your doors and pull down your shades. Nene and Toro had been friends since grade school. They were more like brothers than Toro and Jimmy. That could easily have been me and Carmen on the floor. The image was cracking the door open on panic. It was the music that made me feel in control again.

Toro's new toy, the iPod, had long mixes that would just move from one song into the other for hours, mixes you didn't expect to hear together. It shifted unexpectedly from salsa to hip-hop, from nostalgia to survival. Nas rapping our world to the beat of "Carol of the Bells" locked into my heartbeat and settled it. Eat the fear. Get the fuck out. I climbed the stairs two then three at a time. I pulled what pictures were left on the wall and grabbed *Ludell* from the dresser. I took down Abuelita's Puerto Rican flag, full of rage at ever having hung it in this house. I went to Toro's room but found nothing of mine there. I peeked in Durka's bedroom as I went out the back. I left the same way I had left my mother's apartment the day Toro came for me. I was sure there would be no turning back, which didn't mean I had found a way out.

18

NO SUCH THING AS SAFE

I don't remember driving to the safe house, only the sound of Lauryn Hill playing on the radio in the background. I do remember burning all my clothes in the firepit outside. It was covered with an aluminum thatched roof that sat on tall wooden beams that Durka had built so she could listen to the rain as it sounded in her abuelita's house in Puerto Rico. I don't remember the sound of rain or even getting wet or walking naked back and forth from the beach to the house in a pattern only my body knew. But I did all of those things, and I know I did, because I found the evidence later.

When I could think, I was thinking about China. About Red. About Carmen. There was so much about to come in my direction. I didn't know where to start. I went back to the beach. I threw a chaotic offering of fruit, flowers, and candles I grabbed along the way from the fridge to the garden into the water for Yemaya. I prayed to be cleansed of my sins. I knew I did not deserve it. I swam naked in the dark. I drank whiskey, smoked cigarettes Red had left behind, paced in circles like a sick animal. I grew agitated in stages, spiraling in and out of terror with each realization of how hard it would be to keep us safe.

At every stage my heartbeat raced out of control. I practiced the breathing techniques. I slowed my heart and slowly cleared my mind. It was done. I had done it. I would have to bring the girls together. I would have to make it clear it had not been me. There was no turning back. If I didn't pull us in, we would all be in more danger, and they weren't ready to follow me as a killer. Maybe Red, but not the others. China would be the biggest problem of all.

More or less danger was all I could really wrap my head around. I couldn't stay still. Swimming, then pacing then back into the safe house. I laughed every time I imagined *safe*. What the fuck was that even? Where had it ever existed? I knew for sure I had no idea what it was.

Hard and vicious as I had wanted to be, thought I was, acted: I had never been a killer. Toro and Nene had to be dealt with before they dealt with me. It had been coming for some time. I had built a life I could not sustain if I wasn't willing to kill or die for it. I couldn't let my girls pay for my weakness. I made a choice. I walked the spiral of excuses and justifications, imagined Carmen looking at me and never being able to love or respect me again. When you do stupid shit, reckless shit, you never understand that the consequences won't be the ones you imagine or fear. They will always be worse. I calmed down enough to put on my sweats. I finally fell asleep on the couch with a stack of books by the fireplace where no fire had ever burned since we owned it.

. . .

The sound of a car pulling into the driveway woke me and lit me up with fear. I jumped and stood by the window with the lights off. I held my gun at my side. My first thought was cops, but there were no lights or sirens. Maybe detectives? Only Carmen, Red, and Doña Durka knew about this house. Headlights on the circular path made it clear it was not a ghost. I was hoping it was Red.

As whoever it was stood and climbed out of the car, it felt like I was seeing Carmen for the first time in years. She was hit by moonlight that pierced a light fog coming in off the ocean as the rain cleared. I had been looking right through her since Doña Durka died, and it was written on every inch of her that she was pregnant. She was beautiful. It was terrifying. I ran to the couch where I had my books all spread out, looked for *Ludell* and threw it on top. I needed distractions from all the feelings her being here was about to stir up. Nostalgia for who we had been felt like a good place to start. I tried to act surprised when I heard the security system open the door. I called out our code. She sang it back to me and we laughed. *I got ninety-nine problems, but a dick ain't one.* He was all of them.

**Lost Mothers and
Found Daughters
According to Carmen**

2002

19

THE WANING MOON

My third trimester found me trapped in the safe house with no contact with the outside world for twenty-four hours. The last thing I remembered from the book was that my baby might have eyelashes by now, maybe even saw light filtering in through my belly. Was I remembering that right? It didn't seem real. Nothing did. I moved through the unfamiliar rooms of the beach house like Goldilocks, struggling to find even a corner that felt safe. I tested every space from the little temple room Grace had set up to the pillows on the floor along the walls of books in the library. I forced myself to eat but wasn't hungry for what felt like the first time in months. I took a nap after that but was racked with nightmares. I wrote the details down in an empty notebook I found in the library. I started a fresh Carmen's Book of Dreams that felt like it would be a book of nightmares. I labeled and dated it and tried to pour out my fear by pretending it didn't mean anything. It was all a dream. I wanted to capture the specifics, so I could tell the girls later. It was bloody and we all had been in it. This helped convince me that I'd see them again and that we'd all be okay. I put the notebook on a half-empty shelf in the library.

The enormous living room windows opened out onto the ocean like a monument to how far we had traveled and gone exactly nowhere different. I felt exposed. It stunned me to realize that even a house like this could be a cage. If anything was going to help me propel out, this should have been it. It had to be.

Instead, I was sitting on a couch following Red's instructions. Not calling Pete. Not calling anyone. Holding my ground as I had been trained. I picked up *Ludell* from the stack of books. It was strange to see it here. Why was Grace suddenly reading this favorite from our childhood? I tried not to focus on what I felt in the pit of my stomach. That even if not by her own hand, Grace was behind this.

I opened *Ludell* and tried to find our story in hers again. This I realized was another thing I'd want my baby to know about us. I showed my belly the cover just in case it was true she could see through there.

Our life of crime had begun innocently enough in the public library. Me and Grace were in fourth grade. Neither one of us had ever owned a book in our lives, but you couldn't tell by how much we loved them. Our favorites were the ones about little girls who lived in houses, rode buses to school, and went to their grandparents' farm for the summers—books so far from our daily lives they might as well have been science fiction. We read the same ones over and over and hated giving them back. Holding our favorite, *Ludell*, by Brenda Wilkinson, was like holding hands. We'd loved this book as a way of trying to learn to love ourselves. I held it up to my nose now and tried to find my way back to us.

The story was about a little Black girl from Georgia whose mother left her with her grandmother. Ludell, like us, lived with her grandmother while her mother tried and failed to figure herself out.

We each took turns taking *Ludell* out of the library until finally we stole it.

Grace had just looked at me one day and said, "Put it in your bag. They'll never know."

I never questioned her. I never refused. It's impossible to say how people get that kind of power or how others give it up. I had no reason to doubt her. I also had no reason to think she was fit to decide for both of us, but I'd picked her.

She quietly slipped the book into my bag. We took a bunch more to the desk and checked them out, walked out cool and easy. This was before they had those electronic detectors at the door. We didn't run until we got to the corner, then we ran all the way home. We pulled it out of my bag in front of the building where we lived with Abuela for our longest and happiest period like Ludell. But we weren't living there together with Abuela yet. We were just visiting. We were still with our mothers and that meant we didn't always get to see each other except at school. We stared at the cover. There she was, Ludell, sitting with her best friend and smiling.

We laughed and hugged.

I said, "Okay, who gets to take it home first?" Then added, "I was the one who carried it in my bag. I should be first."

"Yeah, you did, but it was my idea. You would never have thought of it yourself. I'll take it first, and we'll trade every week."

I was mad, but she took the book anyway. Exactly seven days later she brought it to school. As she gave it to me, she said, "You can keep it. Now that it belongs to us, I don't need to have it as much. I'll ask you for it when I want it."

Would Grace tell this story the same way I remembered it? For as long as I've known both memory and fight, I have been fighting by her side. With her. For her. At the beach, when I wouldn't get in the water with the girls, I felt like I was drowning on the sand. Like maybe all along Grace hadn't really been on my side, so much as dragging me along in a current I now had to learn to navigate alone.

· · ·

Red came to the safe house that night after the call about Toro and Nene. I had been praying it would be Grace; that I could look in her eyes and be sure she'd had nothing to do with it. I'd spent the whole day clinging to us as kids, convincing myself there was no way we could have floated so far from each other. When Red showed up, she threw her keys on the table, cursed under her breath, and then threw herself on the couch.

She handed me a big bag of McDonald's. "You shouldn't be eating that shit, but I'm pretty sure under the circumstances you deserve it. I even got you a Happy Meal, so you can start playing with toys." She scrunched her nose and stuck out her tongue at me, then wiped her hands across her face. It looked like she was doing it to keep from crying.

I sat next to her. There was no way to comfort Red, at least not for me, but sitting next to her was something.

"We stay here till Friday. Then we go to the funeral. After the burial we are having a meeting here." She was talking, eyes fixed on the high ceiling. Every word spoken like a prayer because underneath was the obvious catch: *If we are still alive. If we are still alive.*

"I'm not going to that funeral. I don't even know what's going on. Where the hell is Grace? I need answers. I need to go." My voice was cracking, even thinking these things was overwhelming.

She turned to look at me with tender bloodshot eyes. She patted me on my knee awkwardly, like she wanted to calm me down, but also knew that was impossible. She seemed genuinely curious as she asked, "Why did you even come back? I figured your move at the beach was Custer's last stand and shit. How did you end up here?"

I had nothing to say. Where would I start? The empty safes? Pete not being there when I needed him most. My own feeling of being lost at sea without Grace. I had no idea and Red knew it.

"Well, whatever the reason, it's too late to think about getting out. You're not safe alone. None of us are. You gotta hang on. Go get some rest. We gotta buy you big-girl clothes for the funeral, fatty."

"I'm not fat, I'm fucking pregnant." I yelled unreasonably loud and full of terror that had nothing to do with clothes.

She laughed hard and said, "Good, I just wanted to hear you say that shit out loud. I feel like you haven't actually said it, you know, 'I'm pregnant,' to maybe anybody other than Pete. Own that shit. Also, fat is an improvement for you, flaca, best believe it." Red poked me in the side, then put her arm around me. She was trying her best.

The ocean was a loud threatening force right outside the windows. I wanted the familiar quiet waters of Orchard Beach, overlapping with the loud music and seagulls. Nothing about this house felt safe at all.

...

The funeral for Toro and Nene was so chaotic the cops actually had to shut it down. Where Doña Durka's funeral had been men and women, old and young, cops and politicians, Toro and Nene's looked like a small army of child soldiers in T-shirts with the picture of Toro and Nene on the front as little boys, and on the back, smoking cigars leaning against their first Mercedes-Benz with their arms around each other.

It was a sea of white T-shirts and calls for everything from revenge to redemption. They banged up against their own reality like bumper cars. Play fighting and slapping each other around, an attempt to reassure themselves it would never be them in there, but it also quickly deteriorated into real fights.

Most of them were so clearly children with no childhood to return to, only a fake premature manhood to dangle from in midair. I felt sorry for them. Both their general and his captain were gone. There was no one left in that crew that could rise to the top with ease, and so it was open to outsider invasion or total disruption. They were scared. They were sad. They were lost. I understood perfectly.

The thought of losing Grace like that was not even acceptable as a nightmare. It was what held me here still, even as the bodies piled up around us. As I watched those boys, it crossed my mind that Grace could die, and I burst into tears. I'm not sure why it did not occur to me to think that I could die, but she felt so much closer to the danger.

It looked like I was crying for Toro and Nene. A sixteen-year-old boy rubbed my back as he said, "I know, mama, we're all going to miss them. They was the real deal. You know." He hugged me and I felt guilty for everything I knew that he didn't.

They were the real deal. Toro and Nene were hustlers in the tried and true tradition. They were the look-at-me-now American dream in all its nightmarish neon brightness. They shined and they shared with people who never got offered a cut of that dream; it made them magnetic in their appeal even as you could see the skull and bones over their heads. I had watched Toro, through Grace, transform our lives with ease. I knew how these boys felt deep sorrow and gratitude and fear and love, but I could weep and mostly they couldn't. Some could have wet eyes, but none would dare throw down with the tears and heavy sobbing. Me and Destiny cried for all of us. Maybe it was being pregnant, but crying felt good. Crying felt powerful. I didn't feel weak; I felt like a force of nature. If we were lost, at least we could cry about it. These guys had to swallow hard and look up and punch someone. Maybe later convince themselves they had to shoot someone. Their options were, in some ways, even more limited than ours.

When Nene's family arrived, they looked confused. Their faces reflected that either they didn't know what Nene was up to or they had buried it so deep they were genuinely shocked to see it live and in person. Some people who lived on the periphery of the game liked to act above it, even as it fed them and their dreams. They had given all control of the funeral arrangements to Grace because she'd offered to pay the expenses, so some part of them knew, but that kind of fake half in/half out pretending was something I lived with every day. Pete had that "I love you, but not what you do" thing so hard, and we'd never once talked about where he got his money or apartment because that would have brought too much real to the table. Just like I had not yet been able to look Grace in the eye and ask about her hand in any of this.

Grace was in full effect too. In her tight black pantsuit she offered long hugs across the room, giving off cold and warm at the same time. People tried to comfort her, but really, she was comforting everyone else, and no one looked comforted. She didn't seem sad enough to be believed, but scared was close enough, and she had two pockets full of candy. I tried to stay close to her. People were saying all sorts of crazy shit in quiet and not-so-quiet whispers. She was not seen as the grieving widow. In a weird way, the other girls and women in Toro's life gave her an opportunity to get back in step with who she was as the place slowly filled up with them, all carrying babies and toddlers. There had to be at least six kids, ranging from a few months to around twelve years old. The oldest woman, closest in age to Toro himself, had a teenage boy who looked just like him. It was hard to watch the boy walking around, being high-fived and hugged as some kind of replacement for his father when he knew no one in that room. He had Toro's small frame and pale skin, but he was taller and wore glasses. He looked like the kind of quiet and shy kid Toro might have been if he'd been given the chance to discover himself at all.

His mother came up to me and Grace. She extended her hand. "Hi. We've never met, but you must be Grace. I'm Elizabeth." She was pretty with a serious face that gave little away.

Grace smiled and held out her hand. "Hi, Elizabeth. It's nice to meet you. You have a very handsome son."

Elizabeth gave a tight-lipped half smile that registered fear, distrust, and a certain level of disgust that we'd come to recognize as people telling us how they felt about how we lived, and what we did, without having the balls to say it. She answered slowly, "Thanks. Toro didn't see him much. That was probably for the best, but he always looked out for him at Christmas and his birthday. He paid for school. He bought him clothes. I can't complain about that. He's in Catholic school. Honor roll. Really good kid. I'm gonna have to get a second job to keep paying for it, but I will. He deserves it."

"Don't worry, he's been taken care of in the will. His uncle Jimmy will contact you and he will have more than enough to pay for high school and college and even to get himself a little car when he graduates. Nothing fancy, but a good start."

"Really? Toro had a will? He put him in?"

"Doña Durka made sure all of her grandchildren were accounted for even if she could not do it publicly, but Toro wasn't trying to leave him out either. It was safer, I think. The distance, you know."

"Toro always told me you didn't know about the kids. Doña Durka would see him once in a while, but never at the house. She was good to him, but like you said, from a distance. I thought Toro would just leave it at that. He gave us some money when Doña Durka . . ." She struggled to finish that sentence. No matter the hard feelings, the death of the father of her kid and his grandmother had to bring her face-to-face with the danger she had gotten herself and her kid involved with.

Grace reached out her hand and gently touched the side of her arm. "La' mujere' siempre sabemo'. Sometimes we pretend, but we always know. The kids are always the ones that pay, and I don't agree with that. Anyway, Jimmy or the lawyer will call you in a couple of days and get everything straightened out. I'm guessing Jimmy is going to want to get to know him too. They are all he has left."

Elizabeth stood there uncomfortable and awkward. "Yeah, sure. I mean, yeah, I think he would like that. They never met, but Doña Durka talked about him. I don't even know what to say. I guess, thank you, right? It's not what I expected. I brought him because I wanted him to be able to say goodbye to his father. I wasn't looking . . . for handouts."

She seemed nervous, like she was done and ready to walk away. Before she did, she looked right at Grace and said, "I have to admit to hating you for a long time. You know, like why you and not me. I was first. I had his first son, and he didn't marry me, never let me live in his house. I even asked him once, why you? He said he could never explain it, but it was something about you that made him want to be better and he was counting on it to save his own life. Too bad it didn't work out that way."

Grace looked away. When she turned back to us, she blinked and took a long minute. "Consider yourself the lucky one," she said, then quickly hugged Elizabeth. Grace grabbed my hand and squeezed it so hard it hurt before walking away.

We moved toward the coffin in a room that was still steeped in the memory of burying Doña Durka. We turned to kneel in front of the casket but remained on our feet when we saw Jimmy walk in with his son in his arms and a gorgeous woman holding hands with their daughter. The girl had two long braids and looked a lot like the only picture Doña Durka had of herself as a young girl with her grandmother. It had been taken at JFK airport with her grandmother when they'd first arrived in New York City.

We had never met the wife and kids, though we had seen pictures. Grace kept staring. Jimmy didn't look her way even once. Then she turned and bent into the coffin and wiped Toro's face as if she saw something on it. She was crying quietly and shaking. She lingered there just looking at him in a way that felt like genuine loss. I didn't even see Jimmy coming toward us until we turned back around.

He grabbed Grace by one arm. "Can we talk for a minute?"

I took her other hand and said, "Not right now. It ain't time for whatever this is. Also, get the fuck off her."

Grace looked over at me, surprised at my stance. "It's fine. Let's ask Octavio to take us into the back room. Carmen, wait for me outside in the hall. This won't take long. Bullshit never does."

I didn't want to let her go with him alone. I also didn't want to be alone with the fact that I was slowly becoming convinced she'd killed Toro and Nene. I didn't want time to think about the implications for her, for me, for all of us. Toro's blood would be the blood that bound us no matter what came next. If she had done it, we would all pay. I was rubbing my belly that still didn't show as much as my tits, which were spilling out everywhere.

The last time we had been alone together at the beach house, we talked late into the night till we fell asleep holding hands. Grace kept saying cryptic things. I wrote it off as having something to do with what happened at Orchard Beach, maybe taking on so much new responsibility, spending all that money on the jewelry. I made excuses for her weird uneven behavior as I always had. I wasn't sure when she left the house or even got up from the bed where we fell asleep. None of it fit together anymore. All the pieces of the puzzle were scattered and a bunch were missing.

Still, I couldn't accept it even as my whole body knew it to be true.

Remy came with China and her kids, and the crowd opened for her as if Nene himself had been resurrected from the dead. Nene's son, who looked more like China than Nene, struggled with a funeral T-shirt that was too big for him, but that he clearly wore with pride. Nene's mother ignored China as she took the kids into her arms. Remy stood by China waiting for her signal that she was ready to go to the coffin. China knelt beside it and lowered her head, sobbing. Her two kids ran to her and sat on the little bench crying into her sides. Remy tried to pick up the younger, but he clung to China's skirt. She put her arm around him and held her face with the other hand. All her muscles were straining under the weight of those tiny little bodies. We would all pay, and some of us had already started.

My body was in full-scale rebellion as blood rushed veins that felt studded with land mines. I had a throbbing pain in my back like an echo of my heart pounding. Sugar was holding on to Destiny, who was bent over in a corner of the hallway looking weak and sick. Red was standing next to Santa and Teca keeping an eye out while I waited outside the room Grace went into with Jimmy.

As soon as she saw Grace come out alone, China handed the kids to Remy and went straight for her. Red and Teca tried to cut her off. She moved right past them, bending sideways and back in a smooth boxer move. The place was getting loud and rowdy. Guys who smelled like weed and forties brought a wave of negative energy that was spreading. I tried to reach Grace as fast as I could, but I was slow even getting up from a chair.

Toro and Nene were both dead. There was fear and greed and suspicion in every heart. This was a dangerous room filled with the wounded and confused. Right as China got to Grace, a fight broke out between two young guys at the entrance, pulling the crowd in that direction. Remy and Sugar grabbed all the kids and took them to a back room. Red held her post close enough to Grace to intervene if she had to while giving them space.

China, on the verge of tears, grabbed Grace's arm and said, "Why couldn't you just take out your own man? Why Nene? I don't give a shit what you say to anyone else. I know you did this. You play some complicated fucking games, but you had no right."

Grace tried to pull her arm out from China's grip, but it only grew visibly tighter.

"I don't know what you know or think you know. I also don't care. Don't even go there unless you want your kids to be fucking orphans by tomorrow morning. Just be quiet and careful. Nene never gave you what I did, and he never gave a shit about you, and you know it. I didn't do shit to him, and I won't be fucked with. You know that. So cry and feel fucked up and then get over it and get back to work. Unless you don't need to work because Nene left you a stack in his will. But we both know he left all of it to his mama, and now she will own you and your kids."

China withered under that truth and released her. "This shit is coming for you, Grace. You can be sure of it. Lo tuyo te va llegar, tarde o temprano."

As if saying that one true thing was all she had left, China turned to Sugar, who pulled her in and let her cry into her chest. Sugar looked over at Grace and lifted her chin to indicate that Grace should leave. Grace stood her ground. Several fights broke out at once and Jimmy's cop friends called in more cops, and everyone but immediate family was escorted out of the funeral home.

Octavio was getting ready to close it all down. He came to me first and said, "Take Grace out the back, there are still people roaming the neighborhood and standing around in Poe Park across the street. Y también los gangsters en uniforme, así que, ya tú sabes. Ten cuidao saliendo por ahí."

China moved from Sugar to Remy.

Sugar stopped us as we turned to leave. "We're gonna need to keep an eye on China. She is talking a lot of mess."

Red answered from behind her, "I got this. I'll go around the front and wait for her. Me and Remy will stay with her tonight. Talk her down some. She'll be fine."

Before we could separate, the front doors of the funeral home opened and a cop who looked like an older male version of Red walked in. I had only seen him up close once or twice shortly after we graduated from high school, and from far away a couple times after that. It always made me uneasy, how I felt like I saw him everywhere, but really couldn't say what he looked like. He had Red's thin hair, only darker, like the blondish brown of her roots. His had gray streaks. His green eyes were sharp and attentive, darting around, sizing everyone up, but overshadowed by the puffy dark circles beneath them. He looked like he had been a good-looking man once. Now he was just angry. According to Red she took after her mother, but seeing them in the same room together, there was no denying she was her father's daughter. They were the exact same height and had the same boxy shoulders.

Grace tried to turn and leave. I grabbed her. This was the shit we needed to know and could not run from. He had two other cops with him who stood by the doors as he came straight for Red. I could only see her from behind. He reached out to grab her in a fatherly embrace. Red bent her head forward slightly but didn't give in to the whole hug. You could see he was furious.

"I don't imagine you came to pay your respects, sir."

"Well, it's been a long time since you could even claim to know anything about respect. Never mind caring about it, kid. That's all done and over, isn't it? What exactly is there to respect in this room in any case?"

"What then? Why are you here?"

"I came to tell you that you and your little friends are standing in a mess you can't quite handle. I came to give you one last chance to come home."

Red arched and threw her shoulders back, cracked her neck from side to side, opening and closing her fists at her sides. If he had paid any attention to her growing up, he would know, as well as I did, that she was getting ready for a fight.

"I don't think that's why you came here. I think you want to scare me and make me look like an ass. You know I'm never walking out of here with a bunch of cops who buy houses in the suburbs with the money they make off the bosses of the kids they throw in jail."

His face and fists clenched the same way Red's did as he answered,

"Did you grow up in a house in the suburbs? Did you? Don't pretend to know more about my world than I know about yours. Do you even know what you're doing here, kid? Leave with me or on your own, but this is no good and you know it. What do you think it's doing to your sisters that you chose this over them?"

Red was rocking back and forth on her toes trying to contain her energy. She went a tiny bit soft at the waist at the mention of her sisters.

He turned from Red and looked back to make eye contact with me and Grace. "I hope you know that keeping her around doesn't guarantee you any kind of special protection. I'm just one cop and not a very important one because I don't play games, and I owe too many favors already. Some people respect me, but you've stuck your fingers in a lot of shit. She can't help you, and I wouldn't, even if I could."

He looked like he was about to cry, his voice trembling. "First your mother and now you? You weren't born for this, Collie. You know you weren't." He grabbed Red hard against his chest, for the second or two she let him.

Then she pushed him away and said, "How the fuck would you know what I was born for? You don't even call me by my name. You only made plans for a boy."

After Red's dad left, Grace sent code blue on the beepers, the number of Red's father's precinct. It meant spread out, don't go near the apartment, and only go to the pawnshops in twos, so no more than two could ever get caught, if any. Grace sent me back to the safe house and told me to call everyone there in three days. She had a lot to do and it was best if I didn't know where she was.

More than anything I wanted to call Pete, but we were on full alert and that would not be possible. This was when self-preservation trumped anything you might think you were attached to because, at the end of the day, you were most attached to staying alive. It was the mantra our meditation teacher had given us for moments of panic and extreme fear. *I am here. I am alive. I am leaving here alive.* She told us to breathe it in and out till our breath slowed to the rhythm of the words, and to say the words slowly to calm the breath when we were afraid. I am sure she had no idea how intensely we'd need it. I fell asleep to it every night in the safe house.

I started thinking about Chad and how little I had seen or heard of him in the last few months. He was never a face around the way. It wasn't like we expected him at funerals or parties, but Grace not even uttering his name made his absence more like a presence.

I drove myself to Long Island and had to resist turning off the Triborough onto the BQE and begging Pete to just fucking rescue me, though I had made that impossible. The rescue fantasy clings hard even when you know no one is coming. And even if they came, there ain't a thing they could do that matters. Through is the wall you climb by yourself.

WALKING IN THE DARK

October was covering me in darkness. Every day darker, colder. Even the beautiful sunny days covered in leaves and Halloween decorations announced that time was passing, and I was still here.

In the two months since Toro and Nene's funeral, I had started working less. Getting bigger made spending time alone in the safe house the best option.

I lived there, though I sometimes spent nights at Red's or Sugar's place. I only ever called Pete when I was in the Bronx. I wanted to be able to tell him the truth about where I was and keep him informed about the pregnancy. I let him meet me at all my appointments and the birthing classes.

He had stopped trying to make it work and was sad and hard to talk to most of the time.

Grace stayed away longer than she said she would. She was only in contact with Red and Chad. I missed the crew, but it wasn't safe to be together all at once, so we laid low and did what we did from separate spaces. I came back in, but from a distance. I did a lot of paperwork and phone calls as instructed by China.

Teca had knitted me a beautiful open sweater with deep pockets. I would walk along the beach and filled them with shells and rocks, giving each one a dream to hold for me. A safe birth. A good relationship with my baby. A way to get along with Pete. Protection for me. Protection for Grace. For all of us. A way out that made sense.

That was the biggest rock.

The table next to my bed was covered in shells.

I offered, out of some weird loyalty, confusion, restlessness, or a desire to prove I was still in it with my crew, to do some Long Island drops. China laughed over the phone. "I admire your get down with it, girl, but if I got your weeks right, you need to pee so often at this point you might have to start asking to use people's bathrooms, not to mention the sight of you would make our customers uncomfortable."

She was not wrong. There was plenty of work to be done securing the expansion. Also, Grace had a whole double books system going, where Chad got one set of numbers and China got another. I was the filter keeping track of what went where. China was always checking my math, but I was organized, so it worked.

Red kept me company and sometimes busy.

"You coming, prego? I have a long meeting today. Gives you plenty of extra time to pussy around the old neighborhood." Red liked to make jokes, though I could feel her getting protective of me. "Come on, you know you can't stand being alone so fuckin' much. Let's go to Brooklyn."

I drove Red to Brooklyn once in a while. While she met with Chad or did drop-offs, I circled the building where I hoped Pete was still waiting for me. I never went in. I would just drive by and look up at the windows. I was a well-cared-for refugee in the safe house, but there was no doubt I was on the run. I was dreaming like a shaman in my last trimester, and filling my little book with visions of everything from what I most feared (according to my dreams: death, dying, tigers, and snakes) to what I still had the courage to dream possible (leaving here alive with my baby in my arms).

We made several stops in Long Island along the way, and finally in front of the building where Pete and I had met. Chad was standing inside the door. He opened it for Red as she approached. I hung around more out of a slow and sticky nostalgia for that first night than anything else. I also felt a kind of pull to stay close. I drove around the block to make it seem I had left, then parked a block up where I could still see the building.

I wasn't sure what I was looking for, but intuition was something we'd trained into a sharp and precise point as a crew. The more you listened to it, the more it told you. It grew accurate and exact if you trusted it, though it could also just as easily bubble over into the kind of paranoia that did people in. Without it you were a walking target, but it needed care. Being pregnant had made me foggy for a minute, then all the shit going down shaved me to my sharpened essentials. I was feeling fear I trusted about what Red and Chad were getting us into on their own.

Our encounter with Red's father at the funeral hadn't helped. It was like he came out of nowhere, but it also sounded like he'd been following us from the start. The idea made sense to me. Now that I had my own growing inside of me, I didn't imagine it was easy to walk away and watch your own kid dance at the edge of her grave every day. Most of us didn't have anybody. Red did. That had to be complicated in ways I did not understand.

I tried to inhale clarity and exhale confusion. I was working to eliminate distractions, zooming in on what my intuition was trying to tell me. When I first felt the baby kick around the end of summer, it had been like a tiny muscle spasm inside my stomach. As they'd grown stronger, those kicks came to feel like wake-up calls. Reminders that I was not alone. I stayed super still, looked down, and felt another pop. They were visible now and made my shirt move like a wave.

I wanted so badly to call Pete right then, but I didn't. I could tell him very little other than that I needed time alone anyway. I felt better than I had with him, so I tried to let it be. The baby had to live with me for now. I didn't plan on keeping them apart forever though. I was learning to sit with wanting everything at once and just letting it ride for a minute. Stillness was its own medicine like that.

I glanced over at the building and saw Red's dad. The second I realized it was him, blood came rushing to my face and ears in hot fear, flooding my chest, and my heart rate sped up. My stomach clenched in self-defense. I couldn't even slide down in the seat because my belly was too big, so I pushed the button to push the seat back a little. I still needed to see though, so I ended up on my elbows peeking over and sweating like crazy. He looked to be going inside, but then he took a call and turned back around and left. What the fuck was he doing here? Did Red know? Did Chad? Who the hell could I talk to about this? Fuck calling Grace with my mind. She was the whole reason we were in this deep.

I had to pee, and pregnancy pee has no patience. I waited till I was sure Red's dad was gone. I was supposed to wait till Red called but decided to just walk into the building rather than pee on myself in the car. The bathrooms for the first-floor gallery were right by the entrance, the same doors I'd gone through the night I'd met Pete. I could still see his paintings hanging on the wall even though they weren't there. His sales that night had sent his work through the roof. He showed at other galleries now; he also refused to be associated with Grace or Chad. Grace called him ungrateful. There was something of the hypocrite in what he did. They put him on the map and then he pulled them out of the profit. I knew he was doing it to separate me from them too, but he had to know he was only getting away with it because of his connection to me.

I pulled on the bathroom door. It was locked. I was still looking over my shoulder to make sure Red's dad wasn't lurking when I heard Red and Chad yelling at each other from the floor above. The pressure to pee was urgent, but I had to get closer to listen.

Red was talking loud and getting louder as the agitation in her voice grew. "I don't know why I keep trying to deal with you. Grace is having a hard time right now and I'm trying to keep her from killing what could be a good deal, but you are a slimy bastard. I can't trust you. I don't know why I ever thought I could."

Chad responded calmly, "You know as well as I do that Grace looks out for herself first and Carmen second and you are a distant third, if that. You're here because you know what's good for Grace is not always going to be good for you."

I was staring at their legs through the handrails to the next landing. They hadn't seen me yet.

Red turned to go down the stairs. Chad grabbed her arm. "You don't need Grace. We could do—"

Red stopped Chad midsentence with her hand in the air and pulled her arm away from him. "I've been wanting to slap the shit out of you for a long time. But we don't have time for games no more. You don't know anything about me and Grace, so just stick to what you know. She might get pissed at me, but she will be done with you."

"You don't get it, do you? You're never done with the people who know your money. You're never done till they are done with you. I'm not as easy to get rid of as Nene and Toro."

"Fuck you, asshole."

Red went straight for the stairs. In her rage, she didn't see me till she was a few feet away. I looked up at Chad, who smiled at me, shook his head, and rubbed his belly as if to indicate just how pathetic he thought I was. He didn't seem to give a shit if I had heard them or not. The baby kicked again.

Red narrowed her eyes at me. "What are you doing in here?"

"I had to pee." She looked at me as if trying to see what I knew or thought I knew. She grabbed my hand and pulled me along. Once we were outside the building, I tried to redirect her attention to the thing she liked most about me.

"I felt the baby kicking strong in the car."

"Good, cuz that baby is gonna need to be a world-class ass-kicking champion."

"The bathroom was locked. I still need to pee. Can we get the key from Chad?"

Walking fast down the sidewalk, unwilling to look back, she said, "Nah, we're done here. I'll take you to McDonald's."

. . .

We drove back to the safe house listening to music. Red's phone was vibrating nonstop. She ignored it. I was trying to decide how to tell her I had seen her dad or if I even should. It felt like something I should only tell Grace. I decided to dance around the edges to see what I could get.

"That shit with your dad at Toro's funeral was weird. Have you talked to him or seen him since?"

She waited a long time to answer, maybe deciding what to say, maybe waiting to see if I would let it go. "I don't really feel like talking about that."

"Okay, then what do you feel like talking about?"

"I don't know. Why don't we talk about the pregnant runaway bride and her abandoned groom Painter Pete? Maybe you needed to pee or maybe going in that building was part of your pilgrimage? Let's talk about that."

We were sitting in the kind of traffic that made me wonder how the hell people did this shit every day. Part of our job was to make sure we were never stuck in places we couldn't get out of with ease. Sitting on the Long Island Expressway at rush hour was a reminder of how very stuck we were.

Red had decided she wasn't going to talk. My head was still in Brooklyn. Though by now I should have understood that my body was carrying Brooklyn in ways I could not just drive away from.

THE BIRTH OF ARTEMIS

The week before I gave birth, I began staying with Red in her apartment in Yonkers. It was closer to the Bronx and neutral territory. I decorated a tiny corner of the spare bedroom she gave me with the outfit I'd brought back from Disney, my packed bag for the birth, and a little stuffed Snoopy that Sugar had given me for the baby.

Sugar had organized the baby shower at her house to be old-school: no men, no liquor, homemade food that Santa rocked like a catering professional, and store-bought decorations. It was a combo stork and Halloween Snoopy theme that made us all laugh. Sugar said, "Snoopy is the realest, keep him close," before giving me the box, which was one of many.

Only the gifts let you know there was any money running though that room. Baby Jordans in every color, a tiny sheepskin coat, designer clothes and baby bags. There were gift certificates and endless stuffed animals, some made from real fur and delivered in every size from FAO Schwarz. Grace's only appearance at the shower was a tiny blue box from Tiffany's with a silver spoon inscribed D.O.D., and an azabache protection bracelet.

She had also built me a nursery in the safe house, painted and furnished to her specifications, but never once showed her face since the funeral. It didn't even bother me that she hadn't asked what I wanted. I knew she had never asked before. Nothing had changed. Only I had changed. This would be a temporary place. I would have to leave both the hand-painted mural Pete was making and the palace Grace had built, but not yet. First, I had to survive giving birth.

When I wasn't working, I was lying around Red's apartment reading that stupid book about what to expect when you're expecting, as if it could tell me anything about what I should be expecting given the kind of life I was living. I was obsessed with it now that Pete wasn't around to tell me what he knew. It had pictures and warnings about all the bad things that could happen, the classes only taught me how to breathe, which made me laugh because I'd been learning that shit for years.

Still, none of it felt like preparation once it really started. I went into labor the day before Halloween with no signals I could see. No dreams. No signs. I had just hit thirty-eight weeks. I was sitting on Red's cream-colored couch when I felt something pop. I looked up at her and said, "Oh shit, I think my water just broke."

Red was calm and focused. "Well get the fuck off that couch, cuz only more shit is gonna start coming out." She grabbed my little bag from the room, took me to the bathroom, and helped me change my clothes. I just sat there kind of in shock, looking around.

"Move it, girl, we don't want you having this baby in the toilet."

Me going into labor in Red's apartment felt ridiculous. We had to put all our guns away in a safe before we could even leave. Suddenly, everything about me felt wrong. But what else did my baby have? I would have to be enough. I was already sure I wasn't.

Red called Pete and told him to meet us at the midwife center on Burnside Avenue. I had decided I wanted to have the baby there instead of the original maternity center where Pete's mother had taken us on Ninety-Second and Madison. They were still connected and shared midwives, but Burnside felt closer to home at a time when nowhere was home anymore. I heard him say, "Thanks for calling," but he didn't sound grateful. I really couldn't blame him anymore. I wasn't sure I'd have told Red to call him, but she wasn't really letting me make decisions anymore. She knew I wanted him there.

We got into a cab thinking it was no good to drive. It was easy to see that Red had experience. She'd been handling babies and pregnancies since she was a little girl. She was another version of herself as she breathed with me and wiped the sweat off my forehead. As much as I wanted to, I could not stop thinking about my mother. The faster the pains came, the more I thought about how it must have been for her. She had only been nineteen and already addicted to so many things. She probably felt the same sense of failure and stupid hope that I did, thinking that somehow she'd be different for a baby. So many women were changed when they became mothers, but what if I had the same faulty gene, the one that just couldn't let go of the bullshit? What if I turned out to be exactly like my mother? What would that even mean? That was my last thought before my body took over. Red's voice drifted in and out as the pain grew more intense. I did hear her say, "Let me find out you are giving birth to a little witch or warlock on Halloween. We need one of those. It is time to bring the magic."

• • •

The room where I gave birth was designed like a bedroom. The medical supplies were hidden away. It was dimly lit, and I could light candles and play music if I wanted. The women—I had noticed as soon as I started going to my appointments that they were all women—surrounded me and started giving Red instructions. Pete had been attending the classes with me, but Red always dropped me off so they knew her too.

I cried out and squeezed her hand. "Please don't leave." I didn't say anything more. I just kept holding her hand.

Red put on the music I had chosen for the birth, a group called Zap Mama that Grace had played for me the night we met up by accident at the safe house. She had learned about them from a woman she met at college named Mareeka. I had never met her, but she had made a strong impression on Grace.

When I asked if she'd be inviting Mareeka to join, Grace had looked at me and said, "Nah, Mareeka comes from a stronger place than you or me, she ain't having none of this shit."

I had been playing their songs for weeks as I read my what-to-expect book and practiced my breathing and stretches. The music zigzagged like my breath. It was from somewhere else and helped me imagine leaving all the places I had ever known. I think at one point I tried to call Grace with my mind. I never heard or felt anything in return. By the time I was deep in labor, I had totally let her go. She'd finally left me when I needed her most, and by doing that, she set me free.

I figured out how to let the sounds carry me from one contraction to another. I moved through the room in slow motion. Red and the midwife guided me from one position to another. I was bending and standing, squatting and rocking back and forth. They walked with me and held me up on either side or sometimes from the back. I floated in and out. The pain blinded me into uselessness and compliance. At some point all I could feel was my own exhaustion. I wondered if I could stand it. I had faked hard and strong all my life, but this did not feel like something I could survive. I heard Pete's voice in the hall. Red looked at me as if asking if I wanted him in the room. I nodded yes, cried out, and squeezed her hand. Gritting my teeth, I said, "Just don't leave."

Pete cried as he kissed my head. He asked if he could stand where Red was standing. He washed his hands, put on a gown, and the midwife gave him directions. I was sorry he had already missed so much. The way he leaned into me, skin to skin, made me feel he still loved me. Red stepped aside to let him take my arm. She stood back, but never left. At some point the air in the room changed; the smell and the consistency shifted. I could taste metal in the space between life and death. The midwife eased me toward the pushing and comforted me.

I threw up, then yelled out, "I can't do this!"

The midwife only smiled. "Oh, honey, you are doing it all right, and you're doing a great job. Just keep going."

• • •

Artemis arrived in the world covered in blood and screaming mad. We cried. We laughed. We sat in awe of a baby girl who'd only stop crying when I took her in my arms and put her to my breast. She mostly fell asleep the second I put her there. I had seen a lot of shit in my life up to that point. A lot of shit some people will never see. But I had never seen a woman breastfeeding a baby, and it broke me down to even try. I was feeding her from my own body. Even though it felt like nothing was coming out, I was all she needed to stay alive. Pete asked to hold her. I couldn't look at them when he did. He cried into her little cotton cap and kissed her head a thousand times. I had only the vaguest memory of my father. She would know hers well. I would not make her live my life again. The midwife came back to check on me. I was curled around a body pillow at the edge of the bed.

When Pete handed me the baby, he asked gently, "Is it okay if I call my parents and tell them to come?"

I nodded yes, but wanted to say no. To say I thought of my mother then would be to misuse the word *thought*. As I ached for my mother, I broke open for my daughter. Artemis's ears directly over my heart calmed every cry except for hunger. Had I ever laid my head against my mother's heart? There was no one alive who might be able to answer that question or who could be trusted to tell the truth. The thought of seeing Pete's mother hold her granddaughter only reminded me that mine never would. That it was better for Artemis to have everyone and anyone who loved her be part of her life was obvious. That didn't mean it was going to be easy for me. It was already so much harder to be alive with her on the outside than it had been when she was tucked in my body like a secret.

. . .

The first few weeks back in the safe house were quiet except for Artemis's high-pitched wails, which echoed through the enormous halls. The quiet was matched in intensity by the smells. I was rancid with milk, blood, and unwashed hair. I was keeping the cuarentena. Forty days of not washing your hair after childbirth to allow your body to "close" back up. I knew my abuela and her friends would have insisted on it if they had been there. It was my only scrap of female legacy from my own lineage, something I remembered hearing a pregnant woman at church being advised, and so I held it like it was sacred.

Red thought it was gross. "Are you sure about that not washing your hair for forty days business? Sounds nasty."

"I remember them saying it was a way to remind the world that you're not ready to return, and to remind yourself that your body's still healing."

"Well, I guess smelling so bad nobody wants you around is one way of keeping people away. But your baby smells too good for words, don't you, little one?" This she said as she snuggled Artemis, inhaling her in gulps.

Artemis was covered in the magic smell of baby, and breast milk on her breath. Her exhale felt like kisses long before she could pucker up to give one. I returned as many as I could. I kissed every inch of her from her tiny toes to the soft spot on the crown of her still crusty head of hair. I had been patting it down with baby oil to remove the blood and dry skin, but I'd been too scared to wash it. She smelled like hope and love and everything Grace and I had ever tried to scrounge up in our own way. The whole miracle was so powerful every baby reeked of the divine like a perfume.

The first two weeks felt like a walk through a cold, dark tunnel with only a single beam of light burning my eyes with love to keep me from dying. It was essential not to look to the sides because everywhere was dark and wet and covered in blood and milk. I was constipated. I was bleeding. I was exhausted. My breasts were hard, hot, and violent with milk. La Leche League had to be called to come to the rescue, a number my midwife had given me in case I ran into trouble.

Red popped open a forty when the nursing consultant told me it would help the milk let down if I had half a cup of beer and took a hot shower while pressing on my tits, which felt like rocks from a volcano. Red held Artemis and the forty, looked down at her, and said, "Look at you, taking your moms out for a drink already. You are one badass baby." Then she kissed her on the forehead.

One day Red came in with a bassinet and set it by my bed. "That fancy room Grace made is for pictures and toys and bath time and stories, but you need to keep this little one right up next to you. Save you some trouble at night and make her feel safe."

Red being everything I needed was the big surprise in it all. Sugar had hugged me hard at the baby shower. "You need help, you come to my crib, and I will take care of you right."

I knew any one of them would have taken me in, but none of them could put their lives down and wrap themselves around mine. Red was the one always making fun of me getting fat, but she also drove me to the birthing classes and waited in the car to take me home, went out day or night to buy the shit I was craving, and convinced Grace to chill the fuck out from afar. She was protecting me from all of it. I would never understand why. I was too grateful to ask questions.

I cried every time I heard a phone ring. Red turned the ringers off and said, "Let the fuckers call back, or better yet, they can just go away."

Grace was nowhere and everywhere. I wasn't surprised, but I was angry. I knew she was laying low to let the attention die down. Toro and Doña Durka were gone. If she played it right, those who had been looking to replace them would never even give her a second thought. She had made it clear she thought having a baby in this life was a mistake, even as she had my back by letting me stay in the safe house. She also bought Artemis every little thing imaginable, but she wasn't there when she was born.

Grace had forbidden me from telling Pete the location of the safe house. She was right about that. He was too much of a risk. He called crying every day, saying I was keeping him from something he would never have again.

At night when Artemis slept, I roamed around in the dark trying to get my feet under me. Sometimes Red would follow me around and tell me stories about her father and her sisters, how they were all better off without her and her mother. I started to feel like we were both filling the void Grace had left for the other.

One day she said to me or to the ocean that surrounded us, "Some people need to be cut away so a family can survive. Nature does that shit all the time."

I wanted to argue. I couldn't though. I was too tired and too raw, and completely dependent on her. All I could do was let her talk. Sometimes I wished it was Grace, but even that was fading fast. When I was really tired, I wished for Pete. I started to notice how often Red mentioned going to meet Chad. I tucked it in my pocket for things to think about when I could think again.

I was almost ready to give up breastfeeding when I woke up one night wrapped in sheets wet with milk. Some of this shit was crazy and gross. After that first full feeding, Artemis fell out drunk on milk. Red sat by the bassinet while I was fast asleep, playing "Love Alive" like a lullaby on her guitar.

She sat there all night. She'd bring the baby to my breast when she cried and let me fall back asleep as she burped her or changed her and rocked her.

After I'd gotten about ten hours of rest a night like that for a few days, she stood me up and said, "Pete is really freaking out. Calling everyone, leaving messages on Chad's phone, saying he'll call the cops. His parents are freaking out. This isn't good. It's time to go to Brooklyn."

I stared at her as if she were speaking some foreign language. "I feel like shit. I'm bleeding balls and buckets. I can't just go to Brooklyn."

"You act like I'm trying to put you on the subway. I'm not gonna give you any shit, it's too soon for that, but it's time you started really thinking about the situation you have put all of us in with your baby. That baby is one of us and we will die for her like we would die for each other, but she is also the daughter of your legal husband, and you don't get to just run away with her. That brings heat on us. Plus, why would you want to keep her from what none of us have ever had, a father who actually wanted us?"

Red walked me to the nursery where she'd take the baby while I slept. It was down the hall from the bedroom where I was staying on the second floor, on the side of the house that overlooked the ocean. I had seen it in stages, but the baby and I had stayed in the bedroom together since coming home. Only Red had taken her in there to give me breaks. I was seeing it for the first time with the baby in it, and it felt like Grace was holding us both. She had it done up in red silk curtains, an orange and red wall painted like a sunset facing, on the opposite side, a yellow and orange sunrise wall. The shelves were stacked with books. It was a room fit for the daughter of the Goddess. It could not have been further from the way Grace and I had lived as babies. It also reminded me of the little ocean theme Pete had been creating. Grace was giving her the real ocean, but I was cheating him and Artemis from something he probably wanted more than he wanted me. I started crying again.

Red put her arm around me and sat me down on the red velvet rocking recliner in the corner. She wiped my tears before placing the baby in my arms. "It's okay, it's the hormones. Just keep holding her."

I had never seen Red cry. Not drunk. Not at the many funerals we had attended. Not when Artemis was born. Red was fierce and holy in the dark hallways of the safe house. If anything, she was the only one really keeping me safe, but she never cried where anybody could see her. There were things Red carried for others she had not been able to give herself.

In preparation for our trip to Brooklyn, Red announced, "Okay, baby, drink up and get ready for a big treat. Your first bubble bath." She turned on some lullabies, pulled out the plastic tub, a little rubber ducky, and the baby duck towel she had bought for Artemis herself. She set it all up on the changing table. She brought a pot of cool water, a teapot of hot water, and some lavender oil Sugar had given me to add to the bath. One drop, Sugar had said. All it needs is one. Red used the dropper to let fall one drop, which filled the room with gentle lavender steam. She mixed the water till she felt the temperature was perfect. She checked with her elbow and then had me do the same thing. She looked at me as she said, "Let's help her love the water."

Red cleaned her belly button—the end of the cord, which still hadn't fallen off, though it showed signs of drying—gently rubbing it with alcohol till it came off in her hand. I looked away. Red laughed and said, "You best not be turning your head when shit you don't like turns up. That is a sure way to get your kid in big trouble."

She dipped Artemis in the water toes first while she cooed to her, "See, little baby, you put your toe in first and then you go in nice and slow. No rush."

At first Artemis blinked and shook as if a small shock had crossed her tiny body, then she relaxed and tried to open her eyes. One eye was kind of stuck shut. Red whispered, "Are you winking at me or are you giving me the stink eye already?" She wiped the eye with a tiny corner of the washcloth and it opened.

I had no idea how teenage girls, even grown women, did this alone. I was terrified.

Red slipped my hands under the baby's tiny body and gave me the washcloth. "You get it by doing it. Just get in there."

Artemis had Pete's beautiful thick black curls. Her hair had been matted down by blood and baby oil, but it sprung to life soft as dandelions once it was washed and dried. She was reminding me already that she wasn't, and couldn't ever be, only mine.

Once she was dressed and asleep, I took a shower. I covered my hair with a shower cap, prayed to my grandmother for protection, and stepped under the hot water to cry where no one could see me. If I had been a crybaby before, postpartum had turned me into a weeping willow. I came out in a towel I could barely wrap around what still felt like a pregnancy body, and found Red pumping her girl power hip-hop mix that went from Queen Latifah to Lauryn Hill, picking out outfits for Artemis and laying them on the bed.

She saved the edge in her attitude for me as she called out orders. "Time to get back to being, my dear, even with your stinky, dirty hair. A little quick, but that is the way of the world we have chosen."

I reached for a pair of my favorite jeans from the bottom of the closet, and she pulled them from my hands.

"Don't bother. It ain't that time yet. Just wear the maternity ones."

I rolled my eyes and called her out, "How do you know so fucking much about babies and bellies and all this shit? You look like a damn midwife in here."

"I mean, I was a kid when my mother had my sisters back-to-back. I had to help. Plus, when you're little, you dig that shit. It's like playing with dolls. Had they been born when I had my guitar or basketball, I would not have been about it. But I was only ten when the last one was born, and my mother's mother was dead by then. I had always helped, but that little one, Colleen, I did all the things for her my mother didn't feel like doing anymore."

Red told Grace these stories on demand, but rarely talked about herself to any of us unless Grace was there. She sat by the window on a built-in blue velvet bench, folding and unfolding her long pale fingers on top of a pillow with gold edges like she was itching to throw it.

"Make sure you look good. Not sexy or anything stupid, but like you're good. Pete is not the one who walked away. You can't go there looking like a scrub. If you're badass enough to walk away with your belly, then you best show up looking like you got this. You gotta keep him calm and off your back."

"How the fuck do you know who walked away? I told you I went there that night, and he was gone. That showed me exactly who he was going to be." I slipped my breast pads into my bra.

Red called across the room, "Too bad those shits ain't bulletproof, that would be cool as hell." She went on, "And yeah, he was pissed, but he didn't pack his shit and drive away to an undisclosed location. That was all you."

I laughed at her stupid breast pad joke, even though she was getting on my nerves. "Whose side are you on anyway?"

She shrugged. "Mostly yours, but Artemis needs an advocate here too."

"Yeah, okay, who knew you were a mother earth type and the Children's Defense Fund all rolled into one."

"I'm a lot of things, girlie girl. I be knowing my shit somehow someway. Don't put me in no box like you like to do."

She switched it up after playing "I Used to Love Him" and started pumping Hill's track about having a baby everyone told her not to have. Red was sending her usual cryptic signals. She had my back even if it never really felt like that. She danced around the room while I put on my makeup like war paint. I was not prepared to face Pete. Artemis was a miracle in my arms that he had helped create, no matter how much it felt like she had sprung from my ovaries fully formed. I did not want to face that at all.

22

A RETURN TO BROOKLYN

Red pulled over and put us in a cab several blocks from Pete's building. She strapped in the car seat. Her final words of advice: "Let's not give Pete any ammunition. You live alone and you never see any of us. For now, it is better for everyone that he not know where that is. He may not believe it, but you need to believe it and sell it. Also, don't be an ass-hole. Negotiate with him. Agree to stick around a few days, so he can hang with his baby. Cool the whole thing down. We need that." Then she kissed Artemis and said, "See you later, brave one. We gonna be all good. Go have fun."

When we pulled up, Pete and his parents were waiting in front of the building. It tore me up when they greeted us crying, hugging me and Artemis. Pete kissed me on the cheek and pulled me in hard as he whispered, "How are you? I've been worried about you."

All I could think as I climbed the stairs behind them was that Grace was right. I had made a huge fucking mess.

The apartment was cleaner and brighter. He had moved all his art supplies into his studio across the hall. There were white curtains in-stead of different-colored sheets covering the windows. I looked over at the corner that used to be our bedroom. He had set up a freestanding room divider that was folded back to reveal a beautiful bassinet and changing table near the unfinished mural on the wall. Pete saw me looking. His mother was holding Artemis. He took my bag and walked me into the bedroom.

"It's a lot for all of us right now. I know you are as trapped as I am. I wish it could be different. We have a lot to work out, but for today I just want you and Artemis to be comfortable and feel at home. I'm sure you're tired. We can take care of her while you get some rest. Are you still breastfeeding? Shit, I can't believe I even have to ask that question." He broke down in tears.

Getting through became suddenly very clear to me. Getting through meant going through a dark spot in the middle where everything felt fucked. Right then, watching Pete cry, I knew I was in the dark middle; I was as far from the entrance as I was from the exit, but definitely not where I'd started.

I reached out and held his hand. "I am, but I am pumping enough milk for you and your mother to feed her maybe twice in a day. We can figure this out."

I took the two bottles I'd brought from the bag and gave them to him. "I'll take a nap and pump another when I get up. That should give you the rest of the day with her on your own. If she gets too fussy, just bring her in. She doesn't spend too much time away from me yet. So don't take it personal if she cries."

He laughed a little. The gentle lines around his eyes creased deeper. "I'll try."

He shook his head as if still in shock that it was like this, but also gratitude that it wasn't worse. He took the bottles and walked away. I knew Pete. I knew he had a thousand things he wanted to say right then, and he knew enough not to say it. We had both grown. I heard Artemis crying beyond the room dividers. Already my body ached to go to her. When he looked back, I waved him off to see to her first. We were already separate—she and I—and there was nothing I could do to make it stop.

. . .

After my nap, I pumped another bottle and went out for some air. I walked around Williamsburg, taking in the vestiges of the Puerto Rican presence at the core, a flag in a window, the community center El Puente. The edges that had been blooming slowly around it were quickly taking root, like all invasive species do, replacing bodegas with cafés, community rooms with art galleries. We were a part of that, so I couldn't really feel one way or the other. It was not my hood, but it landed hard to see so much impact that we had not planned. I was eating a slice of pizza as I walked. Vinnie's was still on Bedford and looked like maybe it would adapt and survive. Some always do.

It was my first time alone without Artemis. I felt empty, off-balance, but also free. It was a strange feeling that I assumed would be how I would always feel now, like walking around with one sneaker and one boot, never quite even, always a little off. My boobs were on fire, so I knew it was time to get back and pump again, but it was good to breathe and be without Grace, Red, Pete, or Artemis. My body was a country with a new border. I was starting to learn the map.

I stopped at a real estate office housed in a beautiful brownstone on a quiet tree-lined street. I had been looking at listings, peeking around Realtor windows as I walked. Despite everything I had, this would be my first time trying to get an apartment on my own. It was intimidating as hell. I had the money to buy cash, but they'd still want application forms and job references.

I knew if I went through Chad, or even China at this point, all of it would be handled. That was the whole point. It wasn't for someone else to handle, it was for me. I went into the last real estate office I passed because a broker I saw through the windows reminded me of Remy.

She waved me in as soon as I opened the door. "Hi, can I help you?" Like Remy, Carol was fast talking and with little prodding. She told me all about how she'd lived in the neighborhood her whole life and hoped to never leave. She added, "It is changing fast, so it's important that we hang on to what we can. What do you have in mind?"

I decided to try to stay as close to the truth as I could manage. I told her I had been a stripper for years, invested my money wisely, owned a club and a pawnshop, and needed to finesse a cash sale. She looked me up and down.

I laughed and said, "Don't judge me on today. I just had a baby."

She laughed. Her sister just had one too, and that opened the path between us. Baby talk was safe and universal. She set up a few meetings for me to see some places. Carol didn't know it, but she was my very first step out of the darkest spot in the middle.

· · ·

After that, Pete and I set up a system of weekends where I still lived at the safe house and spent time at his place with the baby. He slept in the studio. I slept with her in our old room. His parents came every weekend we were there. He also took her out for walks on his own. They were making plans for Thanksgiving. There was a lot to be grateful for, so I kept my distance as I tried not to catch feelings about what this might look like.

To prepare for whatever came next, I'd go off with Carol while Pete and his family had their time with Artemis. Carol was showing me the best of what she had. After we got to know each other a little better, I told her I didn't really have a price range.

She smiled and said, "Girl, that moneymaker must have been something fierce in your prime."

I wasn't even near thirty yet, but it was true that I both felt and looked past my prime. Not because I looked bad. I was just tired. It was funny to find myself still counting my life in weeks after the pregnancy, like discovering a new way to be in time. Week to week with goals and expectations, instead of minute to minute or day to day. Artemis was almost four weeks old. I dreamt about decorating, moving, and house-warming parties in every space I saw.

I liked everything Carol showed me. It was like leaving home for the first time, so even a shitty little run-down studio would have felt like a palace. I had done so much weird shit in my life. Still, I had never picked a pair of curtains or my own bookshelves or a couch. It was the most basic shit. It was exciting me like nothing I had ever done.

. . .

Before closing on anything, I wanted to let Pete know that I was thinking of moving to Brooklyn so he could see Artemis more and we could try to give her a normal life. I was thinking like that. Normal. Stable. What he'd wanted to force, I was coming to on my own, and that was how it had to be. This was my journey past the point of being told what to do and following orders for lack of a better plan of my own. Even my mistakes would be my own. I wasn't out, out, but I was finding my way. I approached him in the kitchen as he was making coffee.

"I'm glad to hear that. I'm staying away from lawyers because I don't want our daughter to go through any more chaos. Lawyers are only going to bring you trouble you don't need. But I am ready to fight you if it gets there. I'm glad to hear you talking like it won't."

He said it shaking his head, as if to let me know I had disappointed him. As if I didn't know that. He'd never admit that he knew Grace and her lawyers and her records of his money would eat him alive if he even tried it.

"I appreciate that. What's going on with your painting?"

"Not too much these days. Kind of uninspired, but it comes back. It always does. I was offered a job in an art school in California. I turned it down. Artemis is the best thing that ever happened to me, and there is no way I want to leave her." He was looking at Artemis, who was looking at the mural as if she could really see it and kicking her tiny feet in the air.

He looked cynical and old right then. Maybe he had always been that way. The shining Pete of my memory was probably an invention. He was still the best person I had ever known. Pete was a man who wanted the good and believed in it hard, even if he didn't always know how to make it happen. Who did? Artemis was lucky to have him. I gave her a good dad. I could always be proud of that. Her mother, to quote Santa, was a work in progress.

"So give me an idea of where you think I should buy, a place that'll have good schools for her and that will work for you. This is a list of my choices right now. I really don't care. You know I'm not that attached to Brooklyn."

"You planning on doing anything else to keep her safe?" He looked at me with that mix of fear and passion I remembered. Those big brown eyes stared through me with no regard for what I wanted to keep private. He still had that.

"Let's not go there today, Pete. But yes, I am. I'm already doing it."

· · ·

But what was I doing exactly? Listening. Watching. Waiting. For a sign? Did I need more? For strength? Would there ever be enough? I was still trying to feel my way out. I left for the safe house with Artemis in the middle of the night to make sure Pete didn't try to follow.

Red helped me settle in. After asking about Pete and his parents, she announced, "I have to go."

"At this time? Where are you going?"

She looked at me hard. "Unlike you, I don't have a curfew or babies to feed."

"Okay, but seriously. Where are you going? I feel like everyone is always on tiptoes around me. I have no clue what the fuck is going on."

The girls had been calling and reaching out. Destiny and Remy had met me in Brooklyn to hang out with Artemis. I had gone to Sugar's house with the baby twice. Santa had been cooking meals for me and sending them with Red to the safe house. She put a little note in each bag. The first was my favorite: *I can only imagine what Red is feeding you, and the greasy bag it comes in. Start eating right.* They were surrounding me and letting me go all at once. I was, more than ever, floating in and out of the life, but still too firmly attached.

"Isn't that how you like it? Acting like you don't know anything is your way, no?"

"No. No, it's not. I'm not going to keep letting you or Grace or Pete tell me who the fuck I am."

"Whoa, hold on. I don't belong in that group. I'm not even close to being that important. I'm just saying, chill the fuck out. If out is what you want, then keep figuring that out for yourself. Don't keep asking questions that get you buried deeper in. Anyway, it's not a secret. I'm meeting Chad. We're working on things and sometimes we meet up at night in Brooklyn to keep a low profile."

The waves outside the safe house were invisible in the dark, the sound a constant reminder of how close to the edge we were.

"Isn't Grace meeting with him and China now? Wasn't that the new setup?"

Red's eyes were always full of shadow and smoke, or anger. Her gaze turned sharp when I mentioned Grace's name. "In case you haven't noticed, our queen has gone MIA."

"But I know you talk to her every day, so if she can talk to you, she can talk to whoever she wants. No?"

"I guess, but she doesn't seem to want to talk to the people she needs to be talking to, so I'm going to go ahead and keep doing that till she gets back on the saddle."

We both shifted on the couch. I turned to face her more squarely, and she turned away from me just a little.

Red added, "Anyway, I don't trust China. Do you? Especially now. She came out of nowhere, and she has the keys to the money kingdom? Nah. Letter or no letter from Doña Durka, may she rest in peace, this is not . . ."

I tried to see past my need and newfound love for all Red was doing for me. I tried to see the Red who was sitting here questioning Grace's judgment in ways I had never heard her do before. Artemis let out a tiny whimper that I would have ignored till she went hard on the crying.

Red sprang up like she had willed that cry into being. "It's okay. You rest, I'll get her."

Red came back with Artemis. She put her in my arms and left without another word. There was no rest in the dark middle. It was time to go back in, one last time, to clean up and clear up. The only way I would find out where Grace was or how to reach her directly was to get back to work. Every day another lie that I'd told myself about myself fell to the ground. I was done. I was out. Then I was in, and there was just one more thing, always the one more thing.

23

UNDER A SHARED FULL MOON

The end of my cuarentena became a rallying cry for celebration. Artemis was six weeks old. She could sleep for more than two hours at a time, and I'd stopped bleeding and crying when the doorbell or phone rang. The forty days did matter.

Red joked, "Hell, yeah, we gotta celebrate, this smelly bitch is going to finally wash up."

I actually smelled better than I ever had. I was combing my hair with lavender and lemon oil. I felt the power of containment every time I wrapped it in a headscarf. I was reminded of Durka in her final days. There was something to a ritual that forced people to acknowledge that you'd given birth and were not quite back from the place you had gone to do so. I had used those forty days to heal the wound of giving birth, and to examine all the old wounds the giant new one had opened for me. I also had to get back to work. I had a plan that involved going in for one last round. I needed to know that when I left, it would really be over.

. . .

We had recently moved from the two-bedroom apartment on Valentine to three more apartments in the same building. They had sliding doors connecting them behind bookcases, and specially built drop floors in the closet to send stuff from the floor we worked on to the apartment below in case the cops ever showed up. It made me wonder if we owned the building outright.

I was still living at the safe house until I closed on my new place in Brooklyn, and all the girls had their own too. But some portion of us went there every day as if it was corporate headquarters. We kept odd hours, but we blended in, and we were good neighbors. No dirt. No noise. Those who dared to talk to us were given favors. It was the way of that world to look out for those who could make a phone call on you, though no one ever did. Cops were more complicated than we were, and we were infinitely more helpful and generous.

The mystery around Toro and Nene had simply been absorbed, more out of a need to stick together than any real clarity on what it might mean. I missed most of the small shifts in loyalties and the shit-talk while I was off with Artemis, but I could feel the tension between China and Grace in every breath. The life moved fast, so if you wanted to stay alive, you kept moving. I had been granted maternity leave, but it was not a paid leave. I only got paid when I worked, and though I had more than enough in a million corners, I didn't really know what enough was. We had never known.

. . .

In honor of my first trip to the hair salon, Red devised some outlandish hyperprotective plan for us to get dressed in one place, meet at another, and then finally get into some of the fancy cars we stored in various garages around the city. The plan was to just swag the fuck out. We still had moments that looked like something that made people think this was the life to live, though they were becoming scarce.

The desire to be that girl on the block had all but disappeared with Artemis's arrival. Her vulnerability made me hyperconscious of my own.

Coming back to my body was letting me feel how all the parts of me from the abandoned infant to the wounded teenager to the badass on the block were still present and always would be. Getting stronger meant fearing no part of myself. I was going slow but getting there.

Red had also convinced Grace, who'd recently reappeared as if she'd never left, that after the whole shit with Toro and Nene, and China feeling out of it, and the baby, and the nightmares we were all having, that we needed to do something unifying and fun. Nothing deep. Something that would make us feel it was all worth it. Pete had taken Artemis to his parents' house for her first sleepover. I had been pumping and freezing milk for a week. My tits were gigantic for our girls' night out on the town. We went to one of those secret clubs that move around and change their names to keep it exclusive. We took several cars and pulled in one after the other. We walked straight through the line and heard people whispering about whether we were rappers or actresses or somebody's NBA wife. We looked so official it was like we had never been poor or hungry or beat up. For that night the Cinderella dream was on, and we'd worry about the glass slipper later.

There were bottles upon bottles at the table, guys and girls trying to get our eye all night. The music was loud and filled with a bass I felt in my chest as I danced. I could see it in our eyes, even Red's, that this shit was both stupid and deeply meaningful. The worst part of being poor had always been the nagging sense that we were missing something big about what it meant to be alive. That night we spent money, we danced on tables, we laughed hard. We wore our crowns. Teca wasn't drinking. I knew she was pregnant even though she wasn't saying anything. I recognized it now, in ways I couldn't before I had watched my own body change.

Grace turned to me when Teca ordered tonic water. "See what you started?" She was shaking her head. She didn't look mad though, just annoyed. "I'm gonna stop hiring people with a uterus."

We all laughed, and Sugar said, "Well, you gonna have to lay off the whole damn operation and start fresh."

Grace made a face at her, and Sugar pulled her in for a kiss on the cheek.

Grace was miles away since her return. It was hard to get close. Everything was short spurts of attention, few words, and forward movement. I didn't have much left to say to her at that point, so the distance worked for me. I had questions, but none she would answer. I wasn't drinking since I was still breastfeeding. Remy, Red, and China appeared to be drinking for all of us though. Destiny was drinking and dancing, and Sugar was keeping her close. Remy and China had to be pulled out of the bathroom crying, telling each other how much they loved each other and how it was going to be all good. China broke down into sobs so hard it served as the last call for us to head home.

Looking back, the signs were everywhere, only none of us, except maybe Sugar, who went home early and took Destiny with her, could see anything other than exactly what we wanted to see. It was a special brand of communal blindness taking us all down at once. We left the club singing, "Ever since I was a baby girl, wanted one thing most in this world, it was to keep my love alive."

. . .

The next day Sugar cracked open the sky like she was just making another cup of tea. She made me a raspberry tea and said, "This is good for breastfeeding, and this is something I call a homemade 'mixed tape' for the cramps."

I had read about those, postpartum uterus cramps while breastfeeding, so I wasn't surprised when I started feeling them. The book had not told me to expect the kindness and love that was Sugar though. She patted the chair next to her as she drank what she called her farewell cup. It was one of those Celestial ones called Bengal Spice. It had a tiger on the box that reminded me of the one Durga rode in the statues where she wasn't on the lion. It smelled like cinnamon and cloves. Grace and all the other girls were out. I was manning phones and pickups, but I had a younger girl, a new one named Tanya, that I was training. She was covering the phones while I was in the kitchen with Sugar.

It was quiet for a long while before she said, "This place is some kind of lost and found for girls, but now a bunch of us are mothers, and all of us is grown. No girls left. I did so much shit up in here I feel like I went away to college twice. But I think it's time to go for real."

I looked up at her and smiled. "To college? That's awesome. Grace is gonna love that."

"Yeah, she always said I had to go back and try to be the nurse I said I wanted to be when we first met. But this ain't about Grace. I gotta go from here. My girls is getting too old to be hanging around. They ain't lost, you know. They starting to ask too many questions I can't answer right. I mean, I kept it low, super low. They still feel like the richest girls on the block, and they don't know the half of what we got. All that stupid bank money we put in like we was strippers and all the interest and investments. It's crazy. But I can't have my girls thinking this is an option. Never mind my little boy. That shit scares me to death. He's still little enough, but he'll be asking questions soon too."

I looked away so as not to let her see the tears. "I don't know what to say. I can't really imagine us . . ."

She patted my thigh. "Don't worry, girl, them hormones still got you going from zero to sixty with the waterworks. It gets better soon."

She went on rubbing my thigh as she continued, "Destiny is scared out of her skin every damn day of her life. This is killing her. She has ulcers and anxiety. She just wants pretty things, you know. She's not strong yet, or maybe she's young in long years like Granma likes to say. We got more than enough to keep her in the good till she done growing up. She's talking about working with little kids. Kindergarten, child psychology. She's not sure yet. That would be good for her. She got a lot of growing up to do first, but I got her back till she gets there."

She gave me a paper towel and I wiped my face. "Why now? I mean today."

"Nah. I been working on this for a while. Probably since Miami, to tell you the truth. Only reason I put my own kids on the front line was cuz I didn't trust none of y'all to be able to keep it cool under pressure. I got feelings that I just need to walk today. You know. It's just time to go. Finish your tea. It's good for your nerves." She looked at me seriously before finishing her own.

"You ain't Grace, you know. You got a plan? You need to start thinking about leaving too. I'm sure your dreams are talking to you. You spend a lot of time writing down everyone else's. Are you keeping track of your own?"

"Yeah, I mean, of course. That's always been the idea. I'll be out soon. Bought a place and everything"

"Yeah, I ain't never seen nothing work out how it's planned. Just look out for your own. Grace got her own back."

I cleared my throat. "Yeah, but we go back long before this."

"I know and you can bet she will still be there for you somewhere down the road, just don't keep following her lead. Follow your own. We all born with a direct link to the divine. We mothers of our own souls. Listen to your own little voice and maybe you'll lead Grace where she needs to go. You don't need to stand behind her all the time. Maybe it's time for you to go up front."

She got up and held me. Sugar knew when time was up and made her choices accordingly. Not because she was psychic, but because she was smart as hell and not to be fucked with. She would leave knowing in her heart she owed no one anything more than what she'd given, and she'd given more than any of us had even known to ask for. She called us what we had been: lost and found girls. No room in that for the grown women we all were.

• • •

Chad rarely came to the Bronx and had never been to the apartment. No man I knew of had ever been in that apartment or even knew where it was. It infuriated Pete that I'd never even tell him what it was near. So, when Chad called saying he was in the Bronx looking for Red, it made me nervous.

"What are you doing in the Bronx? Does Grace know you're here?"

"What? I don't have to ask Grace for permission to come to the Bronx. I'm not you. Anyway, do you know where Red is?"

The sound of Chad's voice saying he was in the Bronx should have been the thing that sent me right out the door following the clear path Sugar had laid an hour ago. Instead, I went fishing for information.

"Where the hell are you anyway?"

"I'm like a block or two away from Doña Durka's old house. I'm over by that Armory under the train. I have business here because Grace wants me to buy the house. Evidently, the brother is selling. I'm supposed to buy it under someone else's name. Grace doesn't want him to know she is the one buying it."

"So, you do have permission to be in the Bronx?" I couldn't help it, and enjoyed hearing him grind his teeth over the phone.

"Why am I telling you all this shit you probably know? Just tell me where I can find Red."

"I can't do that."

"Why not?"

"Did you call her?"

"I did, but I can't sit in my car waiting for her to call me back all day. Why can't you just tell me where to go and find her?"

"Hold on a second."

Red was in the other apartment getting a shipment ready. I went across the inner hallway and called out to her.

"Chad is looking for you. He's in the Bronx and wants to see you. We can't tell him to come here. What do you want me to tell him to do?"

"Go fuck himself."

"Seriously?"

"Seriously!"

"Shit, can you at least come and tell him yourself. I really don't want to be in this."

"Fine."

She left the apartment shortly after that call. As she left, she called out to me, "Tell Grace I'm going to Chad's and that she should meet me there. My mother always said either you pay now or you pay later, but pay you will. That should be the title of my first album, or maybe it should be *Pay What You Owe*."

Of all of us, Red, Santa, and Sugar were the ones to really cling to what good some mothers and grandmothers and even foster fathers had given them, and Red threw her random quotes around like a reminder that mothering can be shared. It was as much an attitude, a way of being, as it was a biological act.

I was trying to learn how to be a mother to Artemis from the inside out. I caught on quick to the feeding and bathing and dressing. I loved the shit out of her, that was for sure, but I was still here. I knew enough to understand that wasn't a good choice for either of us. Even my plan of leaving felt flimsy after watching Sugar just walk out the door. I thought having a baby was going to make me different. In some ways, it showed me to myself, and I was seeing a bunch of shit I didn't like. I called Grace with our secret code so she'd know it was me. She called back immediately.

"I just wanted to put you on that Red went to meet Chad and said I should tell you to meet her at his place. Something feels weird, you know, off somehow."

"Yeah, a lot of shit is off right about now. Chad wants Red to do something I don't want her to do. I told him that already."

"Red is never gonna go against you for that dick."

"I know, but he is a sneaky and convincing bastard. He's gonna sell it to her like I want her to do it. I'll figure it out. It's good that you called because that guy is not as solid as he used to be. Ever since Toro and Nene went down, the whole street feeling that has brought to our shit has him edgy. I don't trust him the same."

We stayed quiet for a second. It was hard to hear her so easily mention Toro and Nene as if it had been a long time ago. As if it had just been a thing. As if she hadn't loved them at some level, even I had loved Nene for his way of being real, like a brother who told it straight no matter how much you didn't like it. As if he wasn't the father of China's kids. I wanted to push her hard, but not so hard she would cut me out.

"What about Toro and Nene's crew? Are they looking for who did this? Do any of them think maybe it was us?" Part of me needed to know if she was back and ready for more of the same. If yes, then she was no longer Grace as I'd known her. It would be a sign that she had crossed a line and had no intention of coming back.

"Let's just say they were never their own crew, and shit started falling apart as soon as Doña Durka was killed. A lot of people think that was an inside job. Lots of confusion and breaking off right now. No one has their eye on us because we don't compete for the same customers. Since when, anyway, do you care so much about the details?"

I thought about telling her that Sugar had left, but it seemed like too much at once, so I just played along.

"Well, you know, dead bodies, new baby. A lot of shit is changing, right? Best to keep informed."

"Sure, yeah, right. But I got this. No stress."

I waited to see if she would ask about Artemis. She rarely did, and when she did, she was always careful to say that Red kept her up-to-date. Artemis was just one more "thing," one more plate spinning in the air of Grace. It was making it easy to imagine walking away.

"Okay, but you sound stressed. I think Red knows better. She knows she takes her orders from you, not him."

"Yeah, but Red is not feeling me or my orders right now, and that's his in. Let me go and deal with this. I'll call you later."

I paused before pushing for more. "What do you mean Red is not feeling you?"

She had already hung up. I had the sensation all through my body that something was happening, but I couldn't separate it from what was going on in the apartment or Artemis. Mostly I was exhausted and overwhelmed by Artemis, who had arrived and changed everything and nothing at the same time. Artemis was making me choose, and I was still making bad choices, trying to turn the corner into a good one. I sat there in the orange room feeling off-balance, but also kind of glued in place.

**Exiting the Spiral
According to
Carmen and Grace**

2002

24

Grace

PAY WHAT YOU OWE

Our last night at the clubs we looked like we'd given ourselves gold medals, since no one else ever would, for having survived a life that felt like a marathon through hell. We ended the night in Washington Heights. The Dominicans were killing the game and the private clubs felt like little Miami with tables and ropes and everybody looking to see what you had and who you were with. We danced hard and went from merengue to salsa to bachata and back. It was a beautiful circle within which we mostly danced with each other. We were grabbing tight. Carmen and I hadn't danced like that in a long time. We closed the club with several bottles of champagne. It was all the glitter we'd ever wanted. Only Remy and China drunk crying all over the place made the cracks visible. I rubbed the chain around my neck, trying to feel protected by Ma Durga, with her nose ring and many chains and bracelets, reminding us we were allowed to wear our power if that is what we chose to do.

I was loose and open when I asked Red, "Can you stay at the apartment with me tonight?

She was drunk and unmoved. "Nope. I'm busy." She didn't say

another word after that and took a cab home by herself. Carmen went back to Brooklyn to be closer to the baby.

I spent a restless night at the apartment alone. I slept on the couch with all the lights on, my gun on the table next to me. Security was there 24/7, but it still felt like the most unsafe I had ever been. Chad had come through the last club and left quietly. His only comment was to Red in a corner, and he'd walked away mad.

I found Carmen's book of dreams in the meditation room and flipped through the pages. The nightmares had been piling up. Everyone had been having them. Carmen had been writing them all down, underlining words and images, scribbling notes on the side to add details when she caught them. She'd note the name of the dreamer, the date, and give each one a title. The last two, "Lucky Sevens" and "Snakes and Blood," belonged to her and Teca. They were violent and filled with warnings. I had seen enough. I closed the book. Carmen worried me more every day. A slowpoke since we were kids, she was almost at a standstill since the birth of Artemis. I fell asleep with her book of dreams tucked under my head, and the decision to tell her to stop working in my heart. It was dangerous for all of us for her to be here and out of focus. There was plenty of work elsewhere. This wasn't for her anymore, if it had ever been, and the new girls were sharp and ready. I'd tell her in the morning and figure out how to transition a new team.

· · ·

I woke up the next morning from my own nightmare. It featured one of Carmen's dream tigers with a bloody paw about to attack me. I sprung up and couldn't get back to sleep. I canceled a meeting I'd scheduled with the congresswoman who was helping me build the community center in honor of Doña Durka, and went to the park where me and Carmen used to hang back when we had nowhere else to go. I hadn't been there in years. It was close to where I wanted to break ground for the center. When I got there, it was still dark turning light and the park was mostly empty. I went straight for the monkey bars, took off my shirt, and started doing pull-ups in my sports bra. It was cold out, but that was the point. I was breaking past the rules.

A big muscular guy came just as I was finishing. He had a little radio with him and removed his shirt. He looked at me and said, "What you went in for?"

It took me a minute to realize he thought I had been in jail. He had seen the tattoo of Durga on my back and my arms, and it occurred to me how I must have looked doing pull-ups in a sports bra in a playground at dawn. "For trying to survive."

"Ain't that the shit for all of us, man. Keep it real and play it cool out here. Nothin' waiting for us on the inside. We need to, got to, find new ways to survive."

"Absolutely."

"Peace."

"Peace."

I sat for hours on the bench by the open field where me and Carmen used to sit. I had the strongest urge to just break into a run, but she wasn't there to race me. It was the same bench I'd found her sitting on with that fool in high school whose name I can't even remember except that it was biblical. We had come so far and stayed in exactly the same place in so many ways.

Red. Chad. Red's father. They kept passing through my thoughts in weird combinations that did not feel right. Everybody kept giving me different reports. I had been gone too long and my ears on the ground had started listening to other voices.

Right as I was getting up to leave, Carmen called me to say Red was on her way to Brooklyn and said I should meet her at Chad's place. Carmen had raised concerns about Red that I already had. I didn't have time to explain to her that Chad had been working with Red on going places I was not interested in going. He had a whole frat house network expansion planned. I knew those guys were dangerous and protected in ways we did not understand. They had rules of their own. Who else got away with more dead bodies in plain sight year after year? We would never be safe there. Red hadn't wanted to listen to me. She'd used my time away to move it all forward. Whether Red thought she was doing me a favor or branching out on her own or just being reckless was hard to tell.

. . .

I called both Red and Chad and neither called me back. I made a few more stops, each one taking longer than I wanted, then drove to Brooklyn. The traffic was brutal and the guy on 1010 WINS made me laugh when he said, "All the exits and entrances to New York City feel like some version of awful that will make you wonder why you still live in New York." I liked 1010 WINS on days when I needed order for the chaos in my mind. The repetition of the same information with a New York edge. It made you feel like everything could be the same and still be okay.

The new security guy we hired to watch the building was just returning from a break. He still had his coffee cup in his hand and smiled at me. He buzzed me in, looking at his watch to check if he was late. I had the slightest feeling of nerves in my stomach on the way up, but I wrote it off. I felt for my gun instinctively.

The new building was still empty and under renovation, so there was plastic, paint, and dust everywhere. I walked the long hallway and turned down the back stairs to the office Chad was building with a view of the courtyard. I knocked and no one answered. I knocked again, and this time pushed at the door and turned the knob.

The smell struck me first. It was like the floor where I'd left Toro and Nene, a hot flesh and metal scent that turned the air humid. I shook my head to get clear. The fucking nightmares in that stupid book were clouding me. I pulled back for a second and tried to smell deep, to sniff out my trouble like a dog. I looked up and down the hallway in both directions. A dim light came off the plastic covers laid out on the floor to protect them from the paint.

All of this is the minutiae I held on to when trying to reconstruct what I could not really see no matter what I tried to make visible. I found it strange that I had to push so hard to open the door of a newly renovated space. Dense. Thick. Heavy. The air was warning me to leave. I pushed harder against something blocking the door on the other side. When it opened, there was a table wedged against it. It wasn't till I entered the room that I saw four dead bodies chained around an exposed beam and handcuffed to each other. There was a river of blood across the room. Blinking. My eyes darted back and forth looking for Red? Chad? Blinking. Squinting, my eyes kept trying to adjust, to see what was impossible to believe. I shut the door behind me, drew my gun, and started calling for Red. There was a soft cry from the bedroom, and I walked, awake and sharp like an animal being hunted. I gave myself instructions. Move away from the blood. I looked hard at the bodies and saw that they looked young and similar, of a type. None of them looked like anyone I knew. My heart beating filled every inch of my body. It felt like my head was swelling. Sweat was burning my eyes. Sensory memories are the easiest to retain. I squinted, then wiped my eyes as if I could maybe focus harder and somehow change what I was seeing. Emotional memories are a vacuum. Adrenaline erases memory. I was erased.

· · ·

I found Red in a corner on the floor with Chad's head in her lap. She was covered in blood. I couldn't tell if any of it was hers.

She went limp when she saw me like she had been holding on and could let go because I'd come. "He fucked us. He fucked us hard, and he tried to get me to fuck you, but I would never do that. You know I would never do that."

"Shit. Of course you wouldn't. Fuck, Red, are you hurt? We gotta get out of here. What the fuck happened?"

I went to her and tried to pull her up. It was all dead weight. My hand almost slipped inside a hole in her side I hadn't seen. "Jesus, Red. What the fuck?"

"My father. Chad was working with my father. Giving the cops information. My father was following us and knows everything. I think he set Chad up like an informant and offered to keep him out of trouble.

Shit. I was trying to fix it for you and this guy was trying to trade me back to my father like some sort of offering. He was going to give him me, get you guys caught, and keep everything. I tried to fix it . . . but they kept coming on top of me, you know, so I had to take them all out. They started pulling guns, but I guess they were protecting me cuz of my dad, so they didn't shoot at first. It was weird, but kind of easy once I decided it would have to be them and not me. Not you. I wasn't going to let them have you."

She was breathing fast and shallow and pushing to tell me what happened, to tell me she'd failed, but not the way it might look when she was gone. She was trying so hard to let me know she had gone down trying. I could feel her leaving and I was frozen. I started doing stupid shit like pushing her hair away from her face and just fucking crying on top of her like I could heal her. "Fuck! Come on, Red, let me call the ambulance."

". . . I thought they were fraternity guys, you know, that was the story. I figured weak and easy to scare off. But they were cops. We were all talking, then one guy stood up and I was like nah, wait, and then I saw it. It clicked. Fucking cops, young, fresh out the academy, so passing for college boys. I had to go hard, Grace. It was us or them. I just started snapping necks and pulled out my knife and went hard, you know. I had them all. But fucking Chad. He had been hiding in the room. He scared so hard when he saw all that blood that he shit his pants and then he fucking shot me. Like trying to prove he was on their side or something, even though they were already fucking dead. Get out, Grace. Get out. My father's coming. Chad called him. The whole fraternity thing was a setup. It was all bullshit. I'm so sorry . . ."

"I can't leave you." I thought, for a second, of just lying there with her and letting it all go, like I could fall asleep in her arms and wake up from one of my nightmares screaming. But the blood was hot and sticky, and the room smelled like dying. Real was all it could be.

"You can't leave me, you never will, but you have to get out of here now. Chad was talking crazy about everything he told my father before I took his stupid ass out. You won't be able to keep much, but I know you can figure out how to go. The apartment is marked. Be careful."

"Jesus, Red, I can't leave you."

"Go. Have some fucking balls. If I'm supposed to live, let my fucking father save me. I'll meet you on the other side. Get Carmen out. We can't let Artemis go down with us."

She put her hand on my face and left a bloody thumbprint on my forehead. Only the thought of Artemis and Carmen moved me. It was all I had left.

What did it take for me to leave Red lying there in a pool of blood?

Everything.

I left quietly through the back. I kept my eye out for backup, but it was like no one had found the way to call or they were late, or they were focusing on the Bronx. I could not think.

The descent is not something you ever plan for—you can try, and you can practice, but you can never know who you'll become when you fall through the gates of hell even as you walk the streets you have always walked and sleep in the same bed. I understood my mother in ways I had never understood her as I fell apart.

25

Carmen

LEARNING TO DIE

Pete called and left a message that Artemis was hungrier and fussier than usual, and I should probably head back early. I was going away for good. I was sure of it, so I took extra time to move through the apartment. There would be no turning back. Leave nothing behind. I hadn't heard from Grace again since we spoke earlier in the day. I'd call her once I was gone. There was no point in having her tell me to wait till she got back. Seeing her would make everything harder.

The light coming through the small kitchen window was early sunset orange across the counters I'd just scrubbed clean. Every plate and fork put away. Teca made sure our expansion included hired help to clean the kitchen, but I was doing dishes at the sink, a way to say goodbye. The first apartment had been a kind of home base. It was empty now, even though I could hear noise in the apartments next door that were also ours. The hum of business as usual.

China came in through one of the connecting doors. I jumped a little.

She smiled and turned as if to leave. "I can try that again more quiet-like, but you probably shouldn't be here if you scare like that at the sight of me."

I folded the rooster dishrag and hung it carefully on the stove's handle. "Nah, I'm good. Just getting ready to leave. What's up?"

"Listen, we need to talk. That piece of shit Chad is trying to pull some shit and I can't keep it to myself anymore. I can't seem to get Grace to focus, you know what I mean. She is not the same since she came back." She stopped there. I could feel her holding in tears and rage. She had said what she felt, and we'd all been talking in our separate corners about what felt obvious but impossible. Why had Grace gone underground right as Toro and Nene were killed? Why the big ceremony at the beach before it all went down? Why? We all felt like Grace had done it, but we had no proof. China had been the only one to go so far as to say it out loud.

Red kept repeating in one way or another, "If she did it, and isn't telling us, you can best bet she did it to protect us. We need to respect that we are alive, and she might be the reason."

All of this sat between me and China as she took a deep breath and went on. "I know I'm nobody's favorite around here, but my ass is out there just like the rest of you."

"I'm listening."

China opened two laptops and started moving through screens, talking faster than she usually did. "Chad has been asking to see my laptop lately, you know with some bullshit about making all our numbers match. I decided I would keep my files on two and give him one of them and then compare to see what the fuck he was doing. I'm not sure why Grace ever trusted that prick, but then again, I'm one to talk. I trusted and loved a prick of my own, and I miss his stupid ass still."

The lemon candle I was burning in the kitchen gave off a soft light as it grew darker outside. I could see the conflict etched in lines across the once-smooth surface of her face. We had not known her long enough to really take her in. China was solid in ways most of us didn't know how to be yet. She brought balance. It made sense that we didn't trust that either. I stood up to turn on the lights. We went to the little meditation/period room and sat on the cushions as she showed me the accounts and exposed what Chad was changing, and even what she thought he was just copying.

"I don't know who he's planning to give this shit to, but he was very selective, you know. Like there was information he would give away, but bigger shit he wanted to keep for himself. We all have fake names and social security numbers in one file, but the one we keep with our real names and incomes he didn't touch. There are multiple versions of the same accounts. Shit that is hard to follow."

"Look, you know that I was kept mostly out of the numbers game. Why are you showing it to me?"

"Because Grace listens to you. I can't talk to Red because she doesn't trust or like me, and frankly the feeling is mutual. To me, her and Chad seem too tight. I'm not saying she's in on it, but she goes off to see his ass all the time. Red thinks she can manage Chad, control him, but that shit is a lie. You have Grace's ear, and she needs to know that this guy is trying to fuck her and it's not just about money anymore. It's like a power thing. Like he is trying to shake her off. I don't know, but I don't like it. He's been trying to slide me over to him, but I know from experience when someone is selling me a dream. That asshole won't take two breaths after he gets what he wants before he throws me under the bus."

"Okay, I'll talk to Grace. Leave these with me and I'll show her what you showed me."

"No, I want to drop them off in the safe deposit box. I want her to see them on neutral ground and away from everybody. I want her to see for herself. You know. She is smart and she will figure it out, but you need to get her to look and to go alone. I don't want her reviewing these with Red or anybody else who might try to tell her what to see."

"Then I'll let her know she should really count on you to help her figure it out."

"Whatever, I don't need her to use me. She doesn't trust me either. I just need her to know she can't trust him. She can decide if she wants to talk to me or not, but if she doesn't deal with it, I'm out. That guy is dangerous. I got more than enough for what I wanna do. I'm not going to hang around risking my ass knowing he is stealing what is mine and wanting more than he deserves. Me and my kids have already lost too much."

We both fell into silence for a minute. We were barely done processing Doña Durka being gone, and hadn't even started with Toro and Nene, and here we were running at full speed like we knew where we were going and what we were doing.

There was a whole young crew waiting in the wings, under Grace's watchful eye, to replace us all, but it felt like the death of the singular body we had been to hear so many of us talking about leaving. Everything had to go the way of disintegration. I wasn't ready to let go of Grace ever, so she was being yanked from my hands.

We stood and China leaned her gorgeous muscular body in several directions. I stretched my newly plush body sideways and joked, "I think I might be needing to hire you as my trainer."

She looked at me kind of surprised. "Who told you that shit? Only my brother and Remy know my plans to open a gym. Fuck, people got leaky mouth syndrome up in here." She laughed and hugged me, squeezed my hands. She shoved the computers in her bag. Then she put a single earring on the small altar.

"I'm leaving this here so that all that has ever protected us protects us still and helps us figure our way out of this shit alive."

China opening up like that felt good, but it gave me no sense of security. I wasn't even sure I totally believed her. It didn't work like that. You didn't go from not trusting somebody to hopping on their shit from one minute to the next. Her honesty, though, about knowing she was down with us but never really accepted hit home. Whether she chose me because I had Grace's ear or thought I was the weak link was something I had to consider. It could have been a call to arms or a cover-up for whatever she was doing with Chad. That was a major downside to this world. The deeper in you got, the more you found yourself with no one to trust.

I stayed too long in the little orange room and thought about the crew and decided that in fact this would be my last day. Nobody had told me about China and her gym, though it was obvious she had dreams. It got me thinking about how she had gotten here and how we might all fall apart at once if we didn't get out. It felt like we were rotting from the outside in. This kind of shit happened all the time, and big cartels rode violence like waves. Thirty bodies could show up in a day and it would bring more dead, but nobody would be packing their bags to go. It was the cost of business. In smaller groups like ours, one thing too many toppled everything, and your best hope was not to be under it when it fell. China wanted to open a gym. Grace and I had wanted to be teachers. Sugar wanted to be a nurse, Red wanted to be a rock star, Santa wanted to own a restaurant, and Remy wanted to be a lawyer so she could get paid to argue all day. Destiny and Teca were full of dreams like people their age were supposed to be. They were confused and searching, not written in inevitability and carved in stone. Grace, always happy to help, offered that Teca would make a great medical examiner. She had the brains for medical school with the steady hands of a surgeon.

Teca loved how seriously Grace took her, we all did, how often she asked us questions just because she wanted to hear the answers. We'd all wanted something other than what we had, and Grace cared about those things. She believed we actually deserved them. It frustrated her that we didn't have them. It was coming clear to me that we had a whole new generation of girls we were wrapping into this, and that was the worst of what we did. To succumb to hopelessness was one thing, but to seduce others into it made no sense at all.

I went to the bathroom, and I was surprised to find blood. Artemis wasn't nursing as much now that she stayed with Pete and his parents more regularly. The pumping didn't have the same effect. I guessed it was the return of my period. I had a new love and appreciation for my body, even the fat, even the blood, maybe most especially the blood. It was a mystery and a gift, not the curse we had been taught to fear and loathe. I opened the medicine cabinet and saw our neatly stocked goods: ibuprofen, tampons, pads. I was already missing Sugar hard and gripped by the power of how much stronger we had been because we had found each other.

My boobs started hurting and I remembered Pete's call. Artemis was getting hungry, and I was far. They had enough bottles, but she would only take so many before she wanted me and the endless supply.

I was lost in the routine and ritual, blowing out candles, puffing pillows, folding blankets, and pulling curtains. The things I always did when I was the last to leave. Locking closets, drawers, and storing boxes was now the work of skeleton crews that held it together and kept it safe. The apartments were never really empty, though we went quiet at night to stay off the radar. Nothing had ever been said to me about those open safes. I closed my mind to whatever questions were left. There was no time. I was ready to go. I thought about leaving my gun, but it was safer to keep it till I was really out. No use leaving myself totally open like that.

The apartment phone rang and snapped me out of it. We had a landline for clean business, and it was rarely used after hours. I saw my beeper vibrating on the table. I walked over, picked it up, and saw Grace had sent code blue. I ran to the phone.

All I could hear was Grace screaming, "Get out of that apartment. Red is dead, Carmelita. Red is fucking dead and so is Chad. Her father . . . he knows where the apartment is and he's sending people. Get out. Get everybody out, Carmelita, get out. Push the closet buttons and get out."

Red is dead. It couldn't be true. She was so fucking alive that morning. So beautiful and alive. Red holding Artemis and kissing her forehead. That was the new way I saw her in my mind. My stomach flipped in fear before I could even go near the grief. I grabbed my bag and ran for the door. I forgot to press the buttons that would release the stash in the closet into the apartment below us, but there was no time to turn back. I could hear the heavy feet of cops running up the stairs. I saw lights flashing outside the window in the hallway. There were no sirens, a tactic they used so we didn't hear them, but innocent people knew to get out of the way. I ran up to the roof. The sky was deep blue with a streak of orange peeking from behind the clouds. More cops were already on the roof of the building next to ours and they jumped over in my direction as the one from the stairs behind me burst through the door.

Héctor Lavoe was singing, "Todo tiene su final, nada dura para siempre." It was playing like a soundtrack, as Héctor often did, straight from the window of the guy across the way. Was he watching, had he been watching the whole time? Had he chosen that song just for me? I could see him moving back and forth from his kitchen to his living room in his white tank top. He never looked over. I realized then why Grace was always pulling curtains and shades. I watched him pour himself a cup of coffee. I started fixating on details to help me even out my breath. We had trained for this. I needed to calm down. Focus on one single point and breathe deep and slow. Hear the panic but don't believe in it. The panic is a lie. As long as you're breathing you are still alive. I am alive. I will leave this place alive. When I put my hands in the air, I took one last deep breath and exhaled all my fear about how I would tell Pete what had happened . . . and what he would tell Artemis about me. By the time I hit the ground with guns pointed at me, and hands all over me, I was leaving my body through my breath unsure of when, or if, I would ever come back.

Start Where You Are

2003 - 2014

26

Carmen

LEARNING TO LIVE

I got to jail full of breast milk. My clearest memory of that first night was milk leaking all over my pillow and bed. I could smell Artemis everywhere. I cried the hardest I ever had knowing she was crying too, looking for me in the middle of the night. I woke up drenched and empty.

Breakfast came and the whole thing reminded me of school. Muscle memory helped me stand in line, hold out my tray, and take what was given. Thinking about Artemis would have killed me slowly, so I turned it into something soft, cool, a kind of thinking from a distance. A waking dream I could step in and out of. All my instructions for how to be in unsafe spaces as if they were mine to control continued to guide me. Pull yourself together quick or drown. Molt like a bird and drop the feathers that no longer serve you. I decided Artemis was better off without me. It was December. She was spending her first Christmas without her mother. There would be no more crying about that, at least none that could drown out the voices that ran on a loop in my head: *Survive, bitch, and keep that love alive.*

In my earliest days and months, the D.O.D. came to me in my dreams to wake me up or help me fall asleep; those were the two transitions that felt the hardest. Sometimes it was Sugar offering me tea, or

Red giving me a hard time, Santa cooking dinner while Remy told me a story, Teca and Destiny stood weeping for me in ways I could no longer allow myself to do. They appeared like a mosaic of stained glass, scenes of miracles and cures projected on concrete walls and across steel bars. Their names became a prayer. They took turns sitting by my bed and reminding me of all the ways we had learned to tuck ourselves away and become something else just to survive. I had to put myself away. Crybaby was not going to do the trick. I could feel China standing behind me during my first few fights. I didn't have to prove myself too much after that. All except for Grace. She never came, no matter how hard I tried to call her with my mind. It might have been the rage. When I learned to stop crying, I became the angriest I had ever been and that feeling had Grace's name all over it.

• • •

It had been almost nine months and I still hadn't seen or heard a peep from Grace in my dreams or otherwise. I started writing her letters, though I had nowhere to send them. About when we were kids. About our mothers.

Then I started writing my dreams down again, and Grace appeared. I had so many violent ones, I was afraid for her life. By the time the lawyers reached out to tell me she had been killed in a car accident, I had already dreamt of her dying by fire, and walking away with her body in flames.

It was too much to take in; it was not anything I could believe. I could not lose Artemis and Grace in one breath. It was also true that I had already lost Grace, and jail with its limited possibilities for reaction made for a perfect place to grieve. It fit in with all the other grief like one more shade of gray.

I cried that night, and then stopped. I started cursing her out in my mind and telling her to cut the shit and send me a sign she was alive. My final words to Grace, in my last letter never sent: *How dare you fucking die and leave me behind to deal with all this shit? If I can't cry over Artemis in here, I'm sure as hell not going to cry over your stupid ass.* Of course I would, and did, but I had to let her go.

. . .

I received my first letter from Sugar three months later. It had been a year on the inside and I was still alive, but barely. I had taken to shallow breathing, so as not to go beyond the surface of things. Sugar reached out like she knew I needed some reinforcements. After updates on Granma Helen, Destiny, and the lemon tree outside, she wrote about Grace: *Our fearless leader has gone the way of the underworld journey. All good fairy tales demand getting lost in the dark, dark woods. Sometimes for a long time, but the whole point is to come out on the other side, alive. Remember that.* I took it as a sign of needing to accept that it didn't matter if Grace was dead or alive or asleep in a glass box somewhere. I was on my own dark journey in the woods. I would have plenty of time to figure out how to feel about it. I had more pressing needs. Grace was not the one at the center anymore.

I wasn't surprised when Pete didn't send me letters. I was hurt though. What could he have written? I told you so? I was grateful he reminded Artemis about me and let her write and even draw pictures before she could write. I was surprised he never filed for divorce. I just figured he thought that would've been too much too soon. Pete never did try to hurt me.

The decision not to have Artemis visit had been Pete's, and at first it was hard to accept. When I asked him over the phone what he'd told her, he said, "We talk about you, and I show her pictures and I say, 'Something very hard happened to your mom and one day she will tell you all about it. She loves you very much.' As she gets older, she asks more questions and I try to give simple answers."

Sometimes I wrote to Artemis and gave her pieces of my soul. Snippets from a dream of who I had planned to be when I still felt possible. These were all letters I would never send. My real ones to Artemis were careful and scripted and written with Pete in mind. I knew he would be the one reading them to her. The fantasy that would not die: the idea that Artemis could still be mine and know my world. That I could have both and she'd be spared. How would something like that even work? I could feel Pete asking, but fantasies don't require logical explanations.

. . .

After six years of learning how to survive, I decided to go back to school. Where else could I go to hang out with Grace? It no longer hurt to think about her, but I still missed her. There were no cathedrals with stained-glass windows in here, only a small library with a classroom behind it. It was close enough.

The first writing assignment they gave us in the GED prep class was to "write about a person you admire." When I saw the assignment written on the board, it was as if Grace had just walked into the room. Who else in my life had I ever admired? I started: *The person I most admire in the world is my cousin Altagracia De los Santos. We called her Grace.*

"Carmen, can I see what you have so far? You seem to have written quite a lot? Wow, you have beautiful handwriting."

The teacher had snuck up behind me and caught me by surprise. I knew she was greasing me up, trying to make me feel good about myself by mentioning my handwriting. I knew her well-meaning kind very well indeed, but she wasn't lying. I did have beautiful handwriting. Grace and I learned how to write like Catholic school girls from Ms. Sunshine. I don't know how Grace did so much school. She took the good with the bad and kept taking from each whatever she could. Back then I didn't have the patience or the will for all that. It made me tired with its nonsense. I loved the books as much as Grace did, but I could not do the work it took to stay inside those buildings.

I responded, "I'm not ready yet. I'm just getting some ideas on paper. You know, brainstorming."

I could tell she was surprised that I knew her language. I looked up at her and smiled like writing that essay was the most fun I'd had in years, and really it was. Here in the dark middle of my long-term confinement, school had once again become my only beacon of hope. I went back to get my GED because Grace had made me swear I'd go back when Artemis was born, and swearing to Grace felt like swearing to God sometimes. Now it also felt like maybe she might be watching me from out there in the great beyond way. I had been furious when she hadn't come back for the baby's birth and avoided the safe house when we were there. I also knew that she had gone down the dark path with Toro and Nene, and stayed away to protect herself and us. Betrayal has layers. She had, by the end, gone through all of them short of killing me. And I had let her. We were partners in crime till the end. I wanted to write about that, but I had no idea how.

The well-meaning ones encourage you to tell it like it is, but they can't really handle it. What they mean is tell it in a way that will help me understand you, like you, care about you. As if that were my fucking job in this life. Like I don't have enough shit to deal with. Still, I had to write something, so I focused on how I wanted to remember us.

We had class three days a week, and I wrote and rewrote it back in my room till I couldn't look at it anymore. I told the story I had not intended to reveal, but probably could not be free without telling. It took me almost two weeks to finish. It wasn't an essay, but it didn't matter. I felt like I had lost ten pounds when I was done. I was so proud I even gave it a title: *Possible Girls*.

· · ·

The well-meaning one at the front of our little classroom made amazed faces and gave lots of praise to those of us who actually knew how to write. I was not the only one. There were thousands of stories like mine in there, and some of us really did know how to tell them; we had just never bothered to write them down because no one had asked and no one cared. It always made me laugh to think how the well-meaning ones were surprised to find skill and even genius among us. Did they really think there were no smart people born in the ghetto? Did they really believe that people ran entire drug empires like small countries or operated small businesses on shoestring budgets or raised six kids on minimum wage and some food stamps, on broken English and ignorance? Most of the people I knew who dropped out did so out of frustration or financial need, not a lack of skill or intelligence. It didn't make sense to sit in school when there was so much shit to do in order to survive, and so much of what you knew was neither valued nor recognized, and so much of what you were that was powerful and beautiful was ignored and kept out of sight. Grace was a genius, went to school, kept going and going, long after the rest of us had given up, and even then, she hadn't been able to pull up and walk away from what she knew would kill her in the end. If her last name had been Capone or Gambino, there would already be books and movies and long articles celebrating her brilliant criminal mind and her loyalty to family. But Grace only had me, and my GED practice essay would have to do.

. . .

During the last class before the official test, we were working on introductions. Of course, the teacher again picked on me to read aloud. It made me think of Santa, who'd once told a story over one of her beautiful dinners: "Every time a teacher asked me to read out loud, I knew kids were gonna get bored, hiss, and call me stupid. By the third or fourth time the teachers knew too. That shit made me want to punch them in the face. Like, I had a learning disability, and they knew that shit and just decided to humiliate me anyway."

I cleared my throat and read from my favorite part, out loud for Santa.

Hope matters, even though, no one really knows how or why. Why we got lost is hard to say, and it definitely didn't feel like it mattered to people who could have maybe helped us find our way back.

Once, when we both still lived with our mothers, we were on an elevator in one of those buildings that had welfare offices and a mix of people moving in circles looking for help. Some woman, with clean, neatly dressed quiet kids on either side of her, was riding the elevator with us and watching our mothers nod in and out of their perpetual high. She hissed under her breath, as if we weren't even there, "I don't know why people have kids they can't take care of. All they do is make all of us look bad because those are the only ones anybody can see." Grace didn't skip a beat, and talking to everyone and no one in particular, said it loud enough for the woman and her friend to hear, "Everybody so worried about how bad we make them look should focus all that energy on fucking helping us." Grace was a twelve-year-old with the body of a fifteen-year-old. The woman acted like she hadn't heard anything. Then Grace added, "All I know is you won't be fucking seeing me trying to act better than nobody if we both get the same shitty welfare check we on this elevator for right now." Grace was only a kid, and already she was defending our honor.

What it took me my whole grown life to figure out, Grace knew from the start, that in fact we were perfectly invisible. Useless, unwanted, and unprotected. It was only our mothers they could see and even they were invisible except for how poorly they treated us. No one paid any mind to how poorly they treated themselves. Had been treated by others. Didn't that matter? Who could see them for who they had hoped they might someday be? Not even us and we had come from inside of them.

The class went quiet, then erupted in applause and "Preach it."

Even Willow, the girl with crooked teeth I had beaten up during my first week just to prove a point, said, "Wow. That is some real-ass shit."

I don't know what I was expecting, but I was relieved to discover that I still cared about feeling good about myself.

• • •

I laughed when I saw the essay question on my official GED practice exam: *Write about something you have learned how to do well and explain how you would teach it to someone else. Give a detailed explanation on how to do the thing you have learned how to do.* It was too good to be true. Too easy. I had too many things to choose from. It was all I had spent the ten most important years of my life doing: learning shit. I used so much of what we got from Grace's little school for lost girls—positive thinking, transcendental meditation, yoga, my random bits of everything from world religions to interior design and even conflict resolution. All of them real skills and perspectives that truly came in handy in jail.

I chose to write about swimming. Swimming in deep waters was the most important lesson any of us had learned by her side. I passed the reading and writing exam on the first try, though I did have to work hard to learn the damn math. It took years. Luckily, there were women on the inside who were both good at math and very patient. They helped me get through.

* * *

Prison had a very strict calendar that marked time with harsh and unforgiving boundaries. Your time was your time, and some years were an eternity. But there was also plenty to read, more than enough time to think, and women who, once they traveled far back enough in time, had similar stories that allowed us to see the patterns emerge, even if only a few of us used that information to move forward. I read a lot of weird books that I wouldn't have read were it not for the limited choices and the unlimited time to read. The more I read, the more I thought about Grace.

The last one I read before getting out was about Howard Hughes, and it caused a stir in my little GED book club. We took turns being Oprah and did a free-for-all thing since we couldn't all read the same book at once. Mostly we met at meals or out in the yard to talk about what we had read and why someone else should read it. Since I would be leaving soon, they moved my turn up. As I started talking about Hughes's life, Olivia, the oldest woman in our group, who was serving twenty-five to life for murder, said, "I read that one. That man made almost no sense in his personal life, but he could see the bigger picture way ahead of his time in many other ways."

I added, "He sort of reminded me of my cousin Grace. She never became unhinged like he did, or maybe she did. I didn't know her after her world fell apart, so maybe."

Olivia answered, "Unhinged to some can feel like finally getting your mind right to others. It ain't never what it looks like on the outside, though."

Willow agreed. "You know tha's right."

I nodded before closing with what had struck me the most. "In the book, Hughes said this thing about how men are constantly policing themselves in an attempt to make a woman happy until they don't even know what makes themselves happy anymore, confusing a woman's happiness for their own."

We broke into a good laugh over that and started talking over each other in circles about the thousand and one ways we knew this not to be true.

An inmate named Jeanie, who wasn't part of our circle and who had Betty Boop tattoos all along her pale white arms the size of my thighs, overheard us as she walked by. She quietly added, "See right here how we all talking 'bout men like they don't never do nothing right, that there is exactly what he means. Theys spend theys life doing doggie tricks for mommies and girlfriends and wives who think they garbage just straight out the can no matter what they do. They don't know no better how to be happy than we do. They just know how to act out better is all. How to be angry. How to take it out on somebody other than theyselves, but they ain't no better off, they just got more money and more freedom to destroy. We ain't no damn picnic either."

She walked away after that, and everybody got quiet. It was a deep, dark thought in a place that wasn't safe for that kind of thinking. It stank of personal accountability in situations where many of us felt we were paying a price for someone else's mistakes and abuses. Most of us in prison had a fantasy about a defining moment that should have been the turning point for out, and just became deeper in: the beating that pushed them over the edge, the final act of molestation or sexual assault that simply meant it had been enough, the person who wore them down and made them do shit they knew they shouldn't do till they didn't know any better. Deeper in, we all knew the final moment was random. It was all the shit that led up to it, the lifetime of feeling lost and abused, that made us vulnerable to the impact. On the inside it was hard to meet a woman who hadn't been sexually abused or raped or both. We used to go there sometimes, to the topic of personal choice and what we might have done different if we knew then what we knew now, etc. . . . but it was easier to get by when we were angry at someone other than ourselves. It was not one or the other. It was both. But one was easier to carry, especially as I got ready to leave.

As the countdown to exit began, I started rereading all my letters from Sugar. I was looking for advice coded in her wisdom and kindness. How I might make it stick and do right, be right with what I had waiting for me out there. I didn't have the courage Sugar had found. She left for Georgia the same day she said goodbye to me. She bought a nice house for her and the kids, in the same town as her grandmother. Destiny had decided that she didn't like kids enough to work with them, but that she maybe liked old people, so Sugar said she'd try it out by living with their grandmother first. I loved her letters and packed them as I got ready to get out. She sent them with a library as the return address, and faked it like she was a librarian pen pal talking to me about good books and the weather in Georgia. She sent me code that all the other "princesses in the fairy tale we had talked about" had gotten a version of happily ever after. There were restaurants and gyms, poetry readings and biology classes. There were futures and dreams. They were not in touch regularly, but at least she knew the other girls had gotten out and were good, or good enough, which was all any of us were ever going to be. This had to mean there was hope for me.

• • •

Leaving jail involved passing through many gates. I counted seven. Every time one opened and closed behind me, I felt my crew gathering around me to give me strength, but I also had that old familiar fear of wanting to look over my shoulder to see if someone was waiting to stop me. Finally, at the second to last one, they gave me my personal belongings. I was shocked to see they still had my chain with the Durga and Virgen de Guadalupe medallion that Grace had given us all on the beach. I could not wear it, but I could accept the protection. I kissed it and slipped it into my pocket. I was careful not to open the wallet because I knew I had a picture of Artemis only six weeks old, from right before I last saw her, tucked into the front plastic.

The only person waiting for me on the side of the last gate was a stranger Grace had left behind to become my friend.

Mareeka stood under a giant yellow umbrella that trembled in the wind. She hugged me hard with one arm and slipped a beautiful wine-red raincoat over my shoulders. Mareeka had written me a letter a few months after I was arrested, saying she knew what I meant to Grace, and that Grace had changed the lives of so many people through the Community Center she had helped her build. Mareeka hoped to offer even a small return by being a support system for me. She visited me at least four times a year before or after big holidays, and on my birthday. She also came to tell me in person that Grace had been killed in a car crash months after I'd received the letter with the newspaper clipping. Neither one of us seemed to believe it, though we'd cried together anyway. I knew Mareeka now, I liked her, but she was not home.

In the car she handed me a folder with some papers from my lawyer. I kept them in my lap. I didn't want to read anything about Artemis in the car. I needed to be alone for that.

Mareeka seemed to sense how lonely I was and tried to fill the space with talk of Grace. "You know I liked Grace from when we met in school, but I really came to respect her when I watched her work with some of the girls at the center before she died."

"I didn't even know Grace got involved like that. I thought she was behind the scenes."

That Grace had lived out here, that everyone had gotten away, while I was inside, was the work of lawyers and street code, and the fact that China and Chad had built miles of discretion around what we had. I was the only one linked to the apartment. When they caught me, I had my real wallet, my ID. I had been planning to leave, so it was my wallet and my gun in my bag. None of our guns were legal; in New York City carrying them was the biggest risk we ever took. I had been too scared to leave the gun after Grace said Red was dead. I wasn't thinking. The gun had been enough to take me down. I was offered deals to serve up everyone and everything. I had no drugs on me, but they had surveillance linking me to the apartment. Hard as it was to give up Artemis, I knew it wouldn't go well for me if I gave up my girls. Beyond the love we had, and that was enough, there was the fact that if they were all in and I was out, there would be no one to protect me or Artemis from dangers I couldn't even remember anymore. I didn't know enough to do real damage anyway, but I knew enough to know I'd be better off taking a deep breath and serving whatever time came my way. It made me happy to imagine Grace trying to do something different before she left the world. It gave me hope to hear that Mareeka had loved her, that new girls had known her, and that she'd not died feeling alone.

Mareeka went on, "Oh, she did it all right. The girls can be tough, but I don't need to tell you Grace pushed them and really had an impact. One exchange she had with a young girl stands out to me because the girl was honest and brave enough to go up against her. That alone was a sign of growth. She went up to Grace and said something like, 'I just don't get why you so hard on girls who's already pregnant.' And Grace answered without hesitation, 'Being pregnant don't make you special, it just makes you pregnant. You are that precious something real, not just your baby. I want you to know that.'"

Mareeka smiled at the memory before adding, "Grace would say those kinds of things all the time and the girls felt it. I could see something registered in their eyes. I loved Grace for telling that girl she was the precious thing who was already here."

"Picking on pregnant girls. Sounds like Grace, all right."

Mareeka laughed with me as we drove away.

• • •

The halfway house we pulled up to looked nothing like the safe house, but the concept was the same. Chill out. Lay low. Get yourself together. It was an old house divided into single rooms, with twin beds and creaky dresser drawers. It was clean. The rooms were shared and monitored. Not jail, because I could come and go, but like jail in that I was being watched. It was set up to give me credibility. Now that Grace was dead I had very little and would be building my life from scratch. As long as I was finished in six months, I could slowly take back what was still mine. I dropped my one bag by the dresser, hugged Mareeka goodbye, and signed up for kitchen duty in my new home. My hands in warm water felt like a good place to start bringing my body back to the world at my feet.

. . .

I've been out six months, three weeks, and two days. I have a job cleaning offices in Manhattan. When I am not working, I take long walks and call Artemis on the phone. I'm exhausted and in no mood for school, work, or my probation officer, all of which are on the agenda for today. The lawyer's office calls as I am leaving for work. I let the phone take the message, so I'm not late.

Nights can be hard. Last night was one of them. I dreamt about Grace all night long. Dreams took turns with nightmares. In one, we were little girls playing with puppets we made in the library, and in the next, Grace was going down in a storm of bullets during a rainstorm. I haven't even been to her grave. I've made plans to visit with Mareeka and then the center after that, but I keep canceling. I still don't really believe she's in there. To me she feels completely alive. I don't think her name engraved on concrete is going to do the trick for me.

27

Grace

LEARNING TO DIE

Haunting is a word with a lot of meanings, none of them true. Like the words we have for colors, they approximate but can't really say what the thing is: Red. Blue. Yellow. Can we say we know what they are for sure? I am haunted. I am also a ghost. Yet I am very much alive.

I kept touching my phone to call Carmen, long after that was no longer an option. Was that yesterday or last week? I kept remembering what I'd forgotten in pieces about that day. I'd kept moving, not wanting to stop. I had planned to do it, thought to do it, reached for my phone to do it, but I kept moving to get out. Get out became drive, and drive became drive faster until I got to the safe house. How the fuck could I have been so selfish and stupid as to wait that long to call? Did I wait that long? Was I driving when I called her? Was I getting in the car? My memory had gone blank on that one detail as if to protect me from the fact that it was my fault she'd been arrested. Since I couldn't remember, I decided that in fact it was my fault. One more thing to add to the list of shit I'd never meant to do, but somehow did with ease.

. . .

So many of us killed in a row, but it was Red's scene of carnage that received a ton of press. Four dead cops, the daughter of a cop, and a child of the trust fund set had been difficult for the city to let pass. It went on for months, and would, I was sure, come around again for new leaks and leads for years.

My favorite opening line to one of the stories: "Not since the mob killed at will have the streets of New York City run with this much blood." Not true. It ran with our blood all the time, but that wasn't news. They barely mentioned Chad's actual criminal record and past and instead fixated on the lost daughter of the cop he had fought so hard to release from the "savages" who clearly had done this thing. I could have taken offense at that, but it actually made it easier for me to disappear and stay alive, because no one really gave a shit about the savages. It was assumed we would destroy ourselves.

• • •

During those first few months, lots of new groups quietly waiting in the wings took over our connections, but none that really understood who we were or what we did or how we did it all over the world. Lots of smaller crews connected to us had instructions to splinter off in foreign countries. We had always known that we were part of a very long death-eating worm that could lose a chunk, regrow a tail, and keep slithering in the dark. Durka had seen the writing on the wall, and Red had helped her know it on paper. Governments were over letting cartels become their own little governments with better weapons and no rules. They would be legalizing shit so they could tax it, make a profit, and let the kids who had done the same rot in jail. Big pharmacy companies were more than happy to join the "get high" party, and though they themselves didn't pay much in the way of taxes, they hired workers who did, and so they paid governments more than we ever would. It wasn't big news yet, but if the shipments of pills that were already flooding the market gave us any hints, the writing on the wall was in a language the street did not yet speak but would quickly learn. Durka had given women across the globe a chance to organize and get ready for the transition. Instead of just cleaning the rooms for the rich who traveled, they could supply them with safe, risk-free stashes tucked under pillows and paid in advance. Maybe it would work, but most likely not. Either way, I would never know.

. . .

I waited nine months to the day that Carmen was taken into custody to give birth to my own death. Nine months felt like a tribute to her own fucked-up journey. I had all the feelings about that shit and how I'd acted, but also, I had not been wrong. The timing was about letting the fanfare in the newspapers and the heat in our old neighborhood cool down too. I had gotten out. I was alive, but it was not sustainable.

I called Octavio at the funeral home. He had become my first and only fully legitimate business partner. It was a good fit. I had decided, in a very Hollywood move, to stage my own death. It would be a burial rite for all of us and we needed it. You have to bury the dead somehow. You have to show respect. You don't want to help the haunting by leaving things hanging around that hungry ghosts can rattle and drop and use to scare you. It was time to clean house and close the shop.

Red's father was still my big concern. He would be very interested in verifying my death. It would have to be public and somehow beyond a doubt. Many people had to be paid so that a dead body no one else wanted to bury, that was just the right height, could make its way out of the morgue and appear burned in a fire in my car on the West Side Highway. Face melted clear away, fingers charred to the point of no fingerprints, tons of ID and some of my best jewelry sacrificed in the fire, even some getaway cash to make it look real.

None of us had been able to go near Red's funeral. It was a sea of blue, and they were all looking for us. Her father had made it public that he was certain his daughter was incapable of killing four police officers, and so an escaped cop killer, presumably me, was on the loose. My favorite was the doorman we had hired. He was asked to ID everyone who came in the building that day, and he said, "I saw a cute Puerto Rican chick, real cute, but nobody else, she probably came through to apply for the receptionist job. She was in and out. Only the white guy who hired me, and his friends, had been there all day."

We hadn't installed cameras yet, so there was nothing more to see. He told the reporter to call him Puerto Rican Ed from Brooklyn. Good looking out, Puerto Rican Ed, well done. No charges, no evidence, no legal need to hide, but a hunger for revenge was the hardest thing to escape from on these streets. Red's dad had never known how powerful his daughter really was, and that had been his biggest mistake. They found those cops all cuffed to each other, and like she said, when things got crazy, she just got focused. Fuckin' Red. She took a bunch of egos out with her for sure, starting with Chad's.

● ● ●

Mareeka and Octavio were the ones who had to identify me, since there was no one else on record that I had any ties to that could be easily found. According to Octavio, the congresswoman came after dark, when he was preparing what was left of the body and actually cried when she saw the melted remains of Doña Durka's chain. Octavio had melted the chain separately to make sure it was recognizable. La Virgen de Guadalupe and Durga melted into each other, just like that dream I'd shared with Carmen in church. My burnt corpse had dental records we were able to switch with mine for the right price at the dentist office. Anyone who had ever seen my smile would know those jacked-up teeth weren't mine, but it would have to do. They may have been crooked, but I still had teeth, even in the grave. I could, if pressed, still bite back.

I smiled, then cried as I thought of Carmen. Mine was a gruesome death. I deserved it. I really deserved so much worse.

Octavio and I discussed all the details carefully. He ran it like any other funeral meeting as he went down the list. "Obviamente it will be closed casket. Go over the announcements, the prayer card, the obituary, the gravestone, and the paperwork."

I signed the whole funeral arm of our business, which he had helped me expand, over to him. I also gave him a massive infusion of cash I took in a duffel bag. He deserved it. He had never judged a body for how it had lived. He treated all of us with respect.

There were people at every level that could be paid off, but the death certificate would be a high-quality phony because coroners were not yet on the payroll. Somebody told me about a blond chick in Brooklyn who could get me one in the Philippines, but I was done trying to make shit more complicated. I was also done with Brooklyn.

The planning of my funeral felt more like the planning of a wedding. I splurged on the flowers: marigolds and cockscombs and extravagant wildflowers in every combination. The requisite messages in glitter on each satin sash, quotes from some of my favorite books. I sent each one as if they were from people all over the world. I wrote them as love notes to every version of myself that I did not become. I was no one's beloved wife, mother, daughter, or even friend, but I could pretend.

The flowers on the casket were a wild spray of orange, red, yellow, and gold with sangre de cristo flowers down the middle. The sash simply said, "LOVE ALIVE" FROM YOUR HEART—THE LITTLE MOTHERS AKA THE D.O.D. I paid in cash and sent arrangements to myself from my favorite writers dead or alive. It had to look real and be untraceable. It was also fun, since so many people don't read and would have no clue what I'd done.

I had always held back on the "look at me" part of our lifestyle, but I craved a funeral that had that flavor. Look at me one last time and see what the fuck I did. That was my mood. "I found God in myself and I loved her fiercely." A line by the beautiful writer Ntozake Shange. I saw it as a tattoo on a badass poet's back and knew I wanted it engraved on my tomb. It was all anyone needed to know about me in the end.

. . .

The center had been open a few months by the time Carmen went in, and I spent time there when I could. I was waiting till the ribbon cutting to take Carmen to see it. I waited too long. I called it the Center for Growth and Change. I have probably grown and changed the most of anyone who has passed through its doors. There is a picture of Doña Durka and a little story about her life in Puerto Rico near the mural at the entrance. It's a painting of the mountains of Puerto Rico she came from, and all the spiritual iconography from all over the world she introduced me to. At the bottom it reads: "All paths are one."

Mareeka is in charge of it all—from the pain management workshops to the period circles, to the one I loved most, the one that reminded me of Carmen. Mareeka had titled it, "How to Give Birth to Yourself as a Mother."

I snuck in and out, from time to time, over those nine months of learning how to die, but all that was over now. My last visit was a week before my fake death. I knew I'd be leaving soon, and I was itching for a fight, which is to say I was wanting to make an impact. I wanted them to remember me. We had a long argument about abortion, the kind Carmen would have loved.

That night five or six girls were talking shit until one stood up and said, "Well, if my mother had an abortion I wouldn't even be here and I'm glad to be alive, so fuck that, babies deserve to be born."

I answered her: "For all that I have, I can't say that my mother should not have aborted me. Maybe if she had, her own life wouldn't have gone down the toilet. What makes me so fucking special that I deserve more than her? Nothing. It's all bullshit. Hungry mouths. That's all any of us are, a bunch of hungry mouths to feed, and my position is if you can't feed yourself, you have no business bringing more hungry mouths into the world. Period." I gave it to them bitter every once in a while, just to see what they would make of it, but sometimes because that was all I felt. They went quiet then. They always do. One jumped up; one always does.

"Miss, that right there is genocide against poor people. Like my uncle is Muslim and he talks to us about that all the time. Like poor people are not allowed to have babies, and most of us poor people just so happen to be Black and brown."

"Preach it, sister," came from the back of the room.

We went on like that for the full hour. I almost cried from how much I loved how hard they stood up for themselves, for each other, for their babies. I pushed all their buttons. They pushed right back. Leaving this bunch forced me to reckon with all that I had given up. I brought it to a close, though I didn't want it to end.

"This discussion continues next week with Mareeka, but I want to leave you with a question to think about until then: What might you do for yourself, your community, your family and, for some of you, even the children you already have by not having any more right now. I'm not talking about the ones you have. We are here helping you figure that out. Don't come back with your sappy 'every life counts' nonsense. We all know some lives count more than others to a lot of people out there. Go to jail or war and talk to me about how every life counts. To who? I don't want to hear that. I want to hear about you. Ask yourself, now that you weren't aborted, and you are here: What are you doing with your place upon this earth? Don't get it twisted, this ain't just about money. What are you contributing? What problems are you trying to solve? How are you easing someone else's journey? Let's make some moves to take down the idea that having a baby is the only power you have, which by the way doesn't mean you can't have one. For the record I really don't care how old you are either, I mean the human body be doing things, right? This isn't just about abortion. You all deserve to be mothers in your time and way, if that is the choice you make and a gift that nature offers you. It's about having a vision for your own life before you bring another into the mix, and if not before, then at least once you bring that life here. We just started in the most controversial place. The hot seat. If you never get pregnant unintentionally in the first place, you won't need to be making choices like that. But I hold my stand that it is a choice that you should have. Always."

The most spiritual of this particular bunch, Xiomara, called the circle at the end. She lit the incense and pulled the newest girl in to light the candle of intention at the center. We all held hands and most avoided mine till there was none left to grab. Xiomara began, "Jesus God Mary Buddha

Yemaya Allah Oya and Durga, and the many names we do not know, to all that we believe in, and all the mystery we don't understand . . ."

We teach the girls to take seriously the idea that we are made in the image of the divine; we have a right to imagine that divine in the way that feels truest. Religion is another thing entirely, one we mostly don't touch.

After our two minutes of meditation, we all clapped. I walked up to the girl who had become the spokeswoman during our argument.

"Hi, Annie. Welcome."

She looked at me confused and kind of annoyed as she said, "You go hard in there, miss. I'm not sure I feel that welcome."

I answered, "That's okay, ma. We don't have to agree on everything to have each other's backs. I just need you to know that you matter as much as any baby you might have. You both matter, and you matter all by yourself."

These would be my last words in the Bronx. It was all I had ever wanted to say or know anyway. Maybe what my mother had lost herself trying to feel.

. . .

I'd wanted to ask if my mother came to the funeral but had no way of doing that without revealing that I didn't know where she was. That was better left untouched. A few girls from the center went with Mareeka to pay respect. Some even cried, or so Octavio told me. The D.O.D. obviously couldn't attend and had scattered as instructed. Chad had managed not to leak our real names to Red's father or the location of the safe house and the international connections. China, in a super clutch move, had locked her laptops in the safe deposit box and sent me the code to pick them up. I would never know if she was involved, but it made me think that if she had been, she changed her mind and hid the most important things that maybe she had promised to deliver. It could be that Chad hadn't planned to go through with the whole thing either, only to sacrifice Red to get to me. I had a million theories. None of them made me despise him any less, which was easier than hating myself. I

took turns doing both. None of it mattered anymore though. Those details would sink into a sea full of the many-headed monsters waiting to
replace them with details of their own. That part of our story was just
one among so many.

. . .

The next morning, I read in the newspaper that my funeral was a small
affair. Lots of urban legends, but very few facts appeared. I had told Octavio to make sure they mentioned one true thing in my obituary: that
I had graduated from college and been accepted into business school
at NYU. One reporter picked it up and did a short investigative piece
on me. She didn't find much but wrote that my education made me an
enigma. The 4.0 on my transcript impressed her far more than the many
zeros in my bank accounts. I enjoyed that one. I also knew it wasn't true.
It was no mystery to be both educated and criminal. From all I had seen,
the world looked to be run and organized by that combination. Schooling
just gave you more choices about how to navigate the particular world
you occupied; it offered perspectives, skills, and validation. A degree
might vouch for your capacity, but in the end, what you wound up doing
with it was based on who you thought you could be in the world and
what you deserved at whose expense.

I had used mine to hang myself out to dry, but also to survive in ways
that were still serving me. You needed home training, as Sugar called it,
to make sense of what school was really for. That was where so many fell
far from the good intentions of every devoted third-grade teacher. People
forget that the world is our home, not a classroom or even a family, and
if it teaches us early to hate ourselves or others, no amount of reading
or math can undo that damage. It has to be healed, but most of us are
too busy trying to survive to have any time for that shit. I loved school,
but school could not save me. I love Carmen and Red, and that did not
go well either.

. . .

In the deep dark middle of life after death, hiding out was not that hard. Fading away just took money and patience. Every year I thought might be my last, but as they kept passing, I started dreaming that maybe I'd wait for Carmen to get out. My lawyer kept tabs on the girls and gave me updates. When I heard that Remy had moved upstate and gotten into performing at the Nuyorican Poets Café as a storyteller slam poet under the name "La Última," I couldn't resist. I didn't really get out that much. I was between worlds. I decided to go to one of her readings. I was pretty sure no one would recognize me there.

Poetry was a good language for this hiding place that was nowhere and everywhere at once. I was careful. I still looked for Red's dad everywhere I went. But having gone unfound so long also felt like an invisibility cloak.

As soon as I walked into the dark, cool space, I could hear Remy's voice playing like a steady conga beat. I sat in the back. Easy in or out if need be. There she was, dressed in tight black as usual, shining like the moon. She built a universe out of thin air every time she lifted her hand or opened her mouth.

"HOPE"

I been thinking about hope.
Dique, Esperanza
Some people talk about hope like it's a good thing.
Keep hope alive and all that bullshit.

Those of us who have the least be needing hope most of all;
which should suffice until we get to heaven.
Or hell,
which is never mentioned as a possible outcome for all that hoping,
but a likely one,
especially when you don't get
what you been hoping for
and start taking shit into your own hands.

¿Y tú? ¿Qué has hecho? Mejor dicho, ¿qué no has hecho?
Hope is a lot of bullshit to keep people from taking any action on
their own behalf,
and most people are glad to have it,
Hope is cheap and easy. Fuck hope.

Everybody started snapping, letting her know she was giving them life with her words. Remy's fuck hope spirit was giving me all the hope I had ever known. She paused in her performance, looked out at the audience in my direction. I knew she couldn't see me, though I hoped she could. She grabbed the mic and said, "When I write about my sorrow, people say, 'Cheer up.' When I write about my rage, people say, 'Why you so angry?' When I write about my battle scars, people say, 'Prove it,' like I need to show them bruises and cuts and scars that never healed." The crowd was snapping and hissing, and humming along, low and rhythmic, like they knew her better than I did, and what was coming next. "You know what I say to people?" The audience called out in unison, "Tell us what you say!"

"I SAY"

I am not a lesson

If you want to know me, and chances are you don't,
long stretches of my life are inked along my body.

My tattoo of San Lázaro on his crutches stands guard
over the many times I have had to rise from the dead.
Durga Maa across my back protects me and reminds me
how many weapons are needed to fight my enemies.

Alongside my tattoos and my gray streak
run invisible scars that mark all that is broken
and cannot be fixed or told,

at least not in this life,
though maybe in the next.
¿Quién sabe?

She was majestic on that stage. I slipped out while people were still showering her with love. There was a little book for messages at the door. I wrote, *Keep that love alive.* I also bought the book a young girl was selling: *Las hijas de tu maldita madre* by La Última. On the table was a little card with a description. Remy still had her sharp tongue and her in-your-face sense of humor. "This book was written and published by me, una de las tantas que le dicen, 'esa hija de su maldita madre.' Sí, lo soy. ¿Y qué te importa a ti? Printed on soft paper are some hard words. Read them if you dare."

Remy made us all one body again. She killed it on that stage. Swagger like that does not come light. The crowd loved her. She must have been writing for years, maybe even performing without telling us. She self-published that book with a red cover. Money was good in that way. It let you do what you wanted. All our voices now resided in her.

I drove back to the safe house through the Midtown Tunnel thinking about Doña Durka. She had given me more than hope. Good or bad, she taught me to make things happen and not just to let things happen to me. It doesn't mean we got it right, it only means we fucking tried.

I was watching a sedan three cars back that felt like it had been with me too long. It was past midnight and traffic was light. I clicked into my instincts. I knew the little sticks dividing the lanes were plastic made to look metal. I knew I could cross over if I needed to, but I would be patient and wait to see if it was paranoia. I picked up speed as we got closer to the exit. It sure would be something to die in a car accident now. Después de tanto show.

28

Carmen

ARTEMIS

I have a custody/visiting rights hearing coming up soon. Artemis has been with Pete since I went in. They've been living in California for most of that time. I buy her something every day. Some days, it's only a pack of barrettes for her hair or a toothbrush. Other days I buy her clothes, coloring books, dolls, the feathery pens Grace used to love so much. None of it fits her current life, which is foreign to me. We talk all the time, but in my heart, I'm still trying to let go of the baby I never got to know. At the end of each week, I donate all the stuff to a church, then I start over and get a little closer to her actual age now. She is twelve years old. I keep wondering if she has her period yet. I got mine when I was twelve. I don't dare ask. We don't know each other like that yet. I buy her a book about girls and their bodies and a box of pads anyway, to pretend that maybe we will.

I have all the pictures and letters Pete sent over the years. He has been living with a gorgeous Chicana, Gloria, who teaches literature at the same college where he teaches art. Although it is hard to hear Artemis's affection for her, it feels better than the other possibilities that might have awaited her. I am grateful. Artemis used to write to me like a pen pal, but she recently read a book about a girl whose mom is in jail and wrote me a long letter about how it made her feel because she never tells anyone in school that her stepmother isn't her real mother, and now she is starting to change her mind. She wrote: *Maybe in high school, once I know you for real, then I can tell the truth. Maybe.*

Over the phone last week she said, "I'm older now, you know. You can start telling me the truth." I cried all night and went to work the next day with puffy eyes and no sleep. The truth. I clean offices for a living now. That is a truth. What would it even look like to tell the real truth? I could start by writing a letter, a place that had become home for all my truth.

Dear Artemis,

If I have stayed close to Ma Durga it has been by praying for you, my beautiful girl, to know a mother's love though I was not able to give it to you myself. My prayers have been that you know the love of the Divine Mother, and her many names, and find in her the strength to not feel slighted or abandoned by the choices I made. What I know of all that I became, and all that I didn't, is that I made you pay for what I had already paid in full. I will never understand why I did that. I also can't exactly apologize, although I'm sorry to have made you suffer. I love you and ache for you is all I know how to say out loud. But if it is the truth you are asking for, then I must also tell you that we are all born alone in this world. We make choices for ourselves every step of the way, and sometimes the wrong people pay, but we can't apologize for being who we are. That is the deepest truth I know.

How could I ever say any of this to her? Writing it in a letter felt safe, but also like wasting the freedom I now had to talk to her on the phone. That was the new truth. She was asking for me by name, and I could answer, and neither one of us really cared, not yet at least, what I revealed. So, I tucked it away. The truth could wait.

• • •

I've started calling California every night before going into work. I can feel her mother hunger. It's different from mine, but familiar; it is an awkward, eager desire for more of me wrapped in a shroud of fear. Artemis knows the sound of my voice as soon as she overhears it. Pete won't talk to me much and seems annoyed by the increase in contact, but he has promised to bring her to New York as soon as they have a vacation. Artemis hardly lets him finish a sentence before she grabs the phone. She has a sense of humor and changes how she greets me every time. It goes from the obvious to the super silly, "Hi, Carmen . . . Hello, woman who gave birth to me . . . Hi, stranger in New York . . . Hi, person who kind of looks like me . . . Hi, car honk because that is all I hear in the background. Do people in New York even know how to drive without honking their horns?" She laughs loud and free and it is a relief not to hear her sadness, which I heard for a long time when she was younger on her birthday and holiday calls. I'm always looking for signs of me in her. Maybe I'm also searching for damage.

She has not yet called me mom or ma, but the countless names she does use make me feel like she is maybe working up to it. She can call me by a thousand names, and I am always here, so long as she is looking to find me, and even when she isn't, I will wait.

. . .

My lawyer's receptionist called and asked me to come to his office in Brooklyn. My heart sank. Maybe Pete was finally filing for divorce. That would be fair. I also worried Pete was going to fight the custody/visiting rights issue harder than he'd admitted to me. He'd said he was willing to give me a few weeks over the summers and some long weekends and maybe one holiday. I really wanted her birthday. I didn't dare ask for it, but that day feels like it belongs to me and her. It was the last time we had ever been alone together without words or skin to separate us. I'd added it in last minute, maybe Pete was done playing nice.

. . .

I walked from my job in lower Manhattan to the lawyer's office. It was cold and the walk felt good. Walking had become a way to make my freedom seem real and possible, long distances to put things together for myself. One of the hardest things about being locked up for all those years was the feeling of pacing around in circles in the same small space: your cell, the hall, the cafeteria, the yard. Over and over again. To think we'd also done it while free, walking the same blocks and bullshit year after year. Physical mobility is a gift we take for granted. I thought of the spiral the good Dr. Fuck That had talked about. I was walking the same streets, but now I knew there was an exit. My favorite these days was crossing bridges. I crossed the Brooklyn Bridge on foot, praying to the river that all will be well and flow with ease at this meeting. My whole body tingled with the sensation of crossing over water. Artemis will walk these bridges with me and know them well. So much of the simple shit I do these days would have made Grace happy. We certainly did not need all that we went after, but famine has a way of making hunger twisted, disconnecting it from what you really need to feel full.

. . .

By the time I got to the lawyer's office I was sweaty and sort of twisted up with memories and fear. I stopped in the bathroom to clean up when I saw her in the mirror.

At first I was sure I was hallucinating. "Grace?"

She jumped back and we both screamed.

"Jesus, you scared me. I thought it was a fucking ghost or something."

I threw myself on her, sobbing. She held me and wiped my tears and whispered in my ear. I could feel her crying into my neck.

"It wasn't my plan to meet up in the damn bathroom. Shhh, we don't have a lot of time. Pull yourself together. You can't let Pete and Artemis see you like this."

"What are you talking about? Oh my God, I knew you weren't dead. I knew it. I refused to go to that damn cemetery."

Her face was soft with tenderness and age as she whispered, "Of course you knew. I was calling you with my mind."

There we were at the exit, together. It was more than I had dared to believe when I was in jail, but had never given up entirely. We held hands and let the tears flow. Then she reached up and said, "Stop for real. You look a mess. Artemis is in that office. Pete will have to explain everything. I'm risking a lot by being here and I'm leaving for good. I'm dead, right, so I'm not even here right now."

I felt my Grace in every bone in my body. I grabbed her harder to make sure.

"Why do you keep talking about seeing Pete and Artemis? They're in California."

She looked down at her feet as she spoke, "I fucked up, you know. Big. I'm so sorry you and Red and Artemis had to pay. I will never forgive myself for that."

"Stop it. Stop. We're old already. We're grown. You were never supposed to take care of me in the first place. We're the same damn age. Just stop. I did everything I did. I might have done worse on my own. We can't know. Stop talking like that. You gave me everything I used to survive. The rest is on me."

"We don't have time to argue, though I know you love that shit. I love you, Carmelita, and I really wanted to tell you one last time in person. I won't be coming back for you this time, but it's good. You and Artemis will have everything you ever need, so no worries there. All of you will. Those are going to be some rich old bitches someday."

We hugged again. I wanted so badly to convince her that she could stay, that we could fix it, that I could go with her, but I knew none of it was true and we were done selling each other false dreams. It was a miracle she was alive and that would have to be enough. She pulled something out of her bag and handed it to me. Our old copy of *Ludell*.

"Remember your little red wagon, girl, 'pull it or stand still, it's up to you.' Here, you keep it. You were the one who carried it in your bag and took the big risk."

We laughed, still wiping tears.

"How did you get that? I thought I had it last."

"Actually, it was Artemis who had it last. I mailed it to Pete a while back. She brought it with her today and said it was one of her favorite books."

Grace looked both beautiful and gone. Like she had left her body. I was so caught up in the joy of having her again that it took me a minute to actually look at her and notice we were both nearing our forties now. She had a tight buzz cut, no makeup, and gray hairs where you could see it. Her eyes were sort of caving in, and she looked tired. Her face fell when she spoke again. "I never meant for Artemis to live what we did. I never meant to take you away from her. She was supposed to have two mothers, nine mothers, not none. I'm so sorry."

Grace leaned into me, crying, her body heavy with remorse. I weighed at least fifty pounds more than she did, and for the first time in our lives, she felt like a little girl in my arms. Her pain closed down the possibility of any more words. There were no words for so much anguish. There had been too many words and they had never been enough. I hugged her hard, wiped her face, and kissed her. Durga would help her fight her way back, and Yemaya would carry her when she needed to float. It was hard letting her go, but as soon as she felt me pulling away, she stepped back and waved me off.

I turned to wash my face, and realized it was pointless. I was only going to cry as soon as I saw Artemis. Pete. Grace walked out of the bathroom without looking back. I held the sink for a long time just to keep from falling.

I was so unprepared, but I have never known joy so big as the moment when I opened the door to that office and that beautiful girl ran into my arms. She was already as tall as I was, so I couldn't pick her up, but I squeezed her with all my joy. She laid her head on my shoulder and let me hold her. Pete waved us into the office. We stayed glued in place. I was too scared to let her go. Finally, she took me by the hand and we walked in together.

. . .

It is the orange, red, and yellow season of witches, pumpkins, and leaves again. Since our first meeting, Artemis calls every day when she gets home from school and we're planning her upcoming birthday and Christmas week in New York. I signed the divorce papers, and the final agreement on the custody. It's fair and even generous. Pete agreed to bring her to me for her birthdays and Christmas. As long as she has dinner with his parents, I get to have her the rest of the time. She is already talking about going to college in New York. I love that at twelve she is thinking about college as if it were her natural right, which of course it is.

I finally moved into my brownstone in Brooklyn. Carol had looked out for me. When I sent her a note about where I was, she quietly rented the brownstone I'd closed on, and had my lawyer open an escrow account for the rent. I'd done it in Artemis's name, so no one knew about it. It was clean. On paper, I'm renting the bottom apartment with the garden and two bedrooms from Carol's management firm. Artemis will always have her own room in my house no matter how often she gets to use it. I let the family that was renting stay upstairs. I didn't need the money, but I could use the company. It feels good to help the mom out every once in a while and take care of a baby and a toddler. I missed all that.

When I'd turned over the signed documents, the lawyer smiled at me as he pushed a final folder on his desk in my direction. It had an address, some keys, and a letter postmarked from India in a soft translucent envelope with Grace's loopy script across the front. "I take it you recognize the handwriting. I worked with this girl since she was about eighteen, and honestly, you work with a lot of people you don't like in this business, but she was different. She made some bad choices, but she also made some very good ones. She was smart as hell. She would have made a great lawyer."

I loved how he was talking about her in past tense. She was dead and, as her lawyer, he kept all his tenses in check, even as he passed me a letter postdated in the current month of the current year. Grace would have been a great lawyer and many other things, but she was also great at simply being who she was. The lawyer went on: "You need to keep working and living a simple observable life while on parole. Keep going to school, that looks good. Besides that, you still have time to do something you love. You should work on finding that. These days, they call it your second act."

I wanted to tell him I hadn't even had my first act, but that was a lie. I had lived a life. It just wasn't one that could stand the test of time.

He continued, "They can't see any sudden movements or changes. You look like you're renting the brownstone apartment from Carol's company, so that works. You have more than enough to live well for the rest of your life. Your daughter's schooling will be paid for from that escrow account, which Pete by the way agreed to allow. Since even Grace didn't know about your brownstone in Brooklyn, I guess she meant for this to be some sort of parting gift. You have a beautiful townhouse across the Hudson in New Jersey. It is one of the best views of the New York City skyline you will ever see. Everything is in there, but like I said, don't do anything without calling me and checking when it's okay. You can go by and check it out, but you can't stay out of state till your parole is up, so we will rent it."

I touched the envelope, turned it over in my hands a hundred times. I wanted to open it, but I also wanted to savor the possibility of hearing her voice one last time.

• • •

I drove to West New York and marveled at the promenade and the view of the Statue of Liberty and the skyline. I parked in front of the address on the paper the lawyer had given me. It was a beautiful townhouse with a small garden in front, a terrace, and a garage. I opened the door and disarmed the security code. I knew it would be the same one we had used in the safe house. There were three floors. I didn't know whether to go up or down first, so I followed the light up the stairs. The top floor was empty and shimmered with sunlight. The terrace had double doors and the view from inside was as breathtaking as the view outside. There was a little alcove off to the right, with a floor-to-ceiling bay window, and a little chair and table. In the center there was the small murti of Durga. The one the doctor had given to Doña Durka so long ago. I touched her feet and bowed my head. We had been protected, even if we would never fully understand how. I opened the letter. It had another envelope inside like the trick of a box in a box. The next one read: *Don't read me till the sun sets and you watch the skyline burn bright in the dark. That is you. That is me. That is Artemis. We burn bright no matter the dark that surrounds us.* I waited. I was still following her instructions. Maybe, finally, she would start making some sense. I laughed and lay across the wooden floors. I had two houses, and knew I would live in the one I had bought for myself, but this was like a temple in honor of all that was lost and all that survived.

I called Artemis while I was waiting for the sun to go down. The room burned with orange, the fast-shifting light of late fall. Chatting about nothing had become our everything. We were making plans for her thirteenth birthday. Right as we were getting ready to hang up, it occurred to me to ask, "This might be too personal or something, but have you gotten your period?"

Her answer gave me what I had been waiting for. "Of course not. I would totally tell you if I did. Duh. I gotta go. Dad is giving me the 'do your homework' evil eye. You know how he is. Talk tomorrow."

I toyed with not reading Grace's letter after that. For one second a giant breath of rebellion filled me from end to end. It said, "Fuck that, why give Grace the last word." I stepped out onto the terrace with the letter in hand as if to toss it and saw that it would land in my own garden. This was no penthouse. It was a low-to-the-ground structure with unobstructed views of the absurd beauty of a city built both from imagination and abuse of every kind, the whole spectrum of what human beings were capable of—the worst of us and the best etched into the sky.

The world was ours and we still didn't know what to do with it, but we had to try. The letter smelled like Samsara. I didn't know they even made that perfume anymore.

Hey you,

Check it. If you are standing on that little terrace, you are standing where I once stood amazed at all those fools paying rent to live in Manhattan when the best view could be had much cheaper from the other side. I know, but it's Jersey. This was supposed to be my exit house when I still thought making myself live in New Jersey was punishment enough. Imagine that.

The game we played comes with rules everyone understands. ¿Quién no lo sabe? Surviving the ones who made me possible and trying to figure out why it wasn't me that went down is its own form of punishment. Not as bad, but just as real. Even during the last days before I left, I had a scare coming out of the Midtown Tunnel, it was pure paranoia, but it made it all so real. How we had lived could so easily have been how we died.

No one on the outside of a circle that tight ever understands people who take the fall for others. People want that kind of loyalty, but they don't know what it means to give it. You understand. You gave everything. I'm out here pretending to be dead, but I am very much alive. A real one died for us. That is how this shit goes.

Tonight, the streets here are full of people dancing and worshipping. There are huge handmade papier-mâché versions of Durga, and elaborate altars in her honor everywhere. It's the last night of Navratri, the nine-night celebration of Durga and her many aspects in India. We dance around altars of Durga as if our dance might destroy the world and make it new. The older girls from our school wear their best clothes and some have huge fake tattoos of Durga on their backs. The girls did my hands and feet in henna and were surprised and impressed when they saw the real tattoo on my back. These girls only know me as the bald lady far from home. They have no idea what or who I have been or how the same Durga Maa they worship brought me here from the Bronx, a place they only know because they have seen the videos of Jenny from the Block on YouTube. Sometimes they sing the song in a circle around me, and we laugh and laugh. I twerk a little and they go wild. How could I have known that on the other side of the world

I could also feel at home? I would never have known if I hadn't been forced to kill who I thought I was all along. Qué mierda.

It is hot as hell out here, for real, and all the food stands remind me of "Un verano en Nueva Yol." You know, like the Puerto Rican Day Parade, La Fiesta de la Calle 116, and Orchard Beach all rolled into one. When I first arrived the cilantro, garlic, and cumin in the air made me feel at home; only the curry reminded me I was not in the Bronx ordering arroz con gandules y pernil. During these nine days and nights there is fasting, praying, chanting. The mornings are for cleansing, pujas, and prayer. At night the colors, the music, and everyone dancing make it feel like a giant block party. We dance all night, and tomorrow morning, with great sadness and reverence, we submerge the images of Durga Maa, an image of the holy that entirely resembles us, into the river. She then flows out to the sea, where I picture her in the good company of Oshun in rushing waters to meet Yemaya, until she returns next year, and the fiesta starts again. We are all connected.

At night, when I can't sleep, I think about how our lives might have been different, how our mothers' lives might have been different, if someone had told us that we did not need to look or be like something other than what we were to be saved. To be Divine. But then I fall asleep and the nightmares come, and I wake up with no one to share them with who will ever write them down.

Don't get me wrong, this is not paradise any more than home was. India is filled with brutal violence against women, and women fighting for what they need and want. Violence against dark skin, like everywhere, rampant. Nothing is easy here. Beautiful colors fill the streets and garbage runs in the rivers. Sound familiar? It should. Far from home and right back where I started. It is the only way. Also, it is not like the movies where everyone is in a robe praying or dancing. Nope. They live in every complicated way we live.

I am surrounded by skinny brown girls with big, beautiful, brown eyes and giant smiles. I like to pretend one of them could be Artemis and I will know her through them. Mostly I pretend they are versions of

me and you. They make me so happy as they laugh and huddle around
the books I give them as presents, which they share and exchange as they
build their own library by instinct.

I tutor English. I help with homework. I do some fundraising on
the phone. I sweep floors and clean bathrooms. Sometimes I cook,
especially when I can get my hands on fresh cilantro. I think Santa
would be proud. I do what is needed and what is asked. Only the
founder knows who I am and how much money I have given. She is a
no-nonsense kind of woman. Very serious. She has agreed that for my
purpose of seeking a new life it's best to leave all of that behind. Even
my name.

She gave me the name of Akhilandesvari, not so far from Altagracia
De los Santos if you write them next to each other. Akhilandesvari
was the gift I had not been expecting. I knew Durga well and needed
Akhilanda badly. Akhilanda is the never not broken Goddess who rides
a crocodile and wears her brokenness like a shield. I thought I was a
badass, but no, she is the real deal. All the cracks along her body are
what allow the light to pass through. Deep shit. No lie. The woman
who runs the place said to me, "It is your very brokenness that will
allow you to give light to others." I cried like a baby. You would have
been proud.

The girls here now call me Ms. Akhi. I live in a small room above
the school with almost no furniture, only a bed and a chair and table.
It looks a lot like the last room I shared with my mother. It teaches
me every day that you can be standing right where you started and be
someone completely different.

There is no forgiveness in this tradition, no confessors. I've been
craving confession. Just drop that shit off on someone else's door and
go sit with my rosary beads. Here, there is only self-forgiveness and
compassion for others that you pray for, and practice, knowing it will
take many lives to come even close. I have not forgiven myself for what
I did to you and Red. I'm not sure I will in this lifetime or even the
next.

Sometimes in meditation, I am so filled with rage and sorrow I

collapse. I don't know if I faint or have a fit or what the fuck. All I
know is that I pass out. Imagine doing that shit back home? Sometimes
I feel like I can hear Red's whistle and I wake up smiling. Sometimes
it is the sound of your voice saying, "Cut the shit," and I cry. Or my
mother's voice saying, "Wake up, don't you have school today," and
I come to furious and sad. I understand our mothers so differently
now, but I am still working on forgiveness. The woman who is
helping me practice says I need to work on controlling my attention
and my emotions. She says that I'm giving everything I feel too much
importance. Wepa, she has no idea, does she?

You know I've always been a sucker for a good teacher, and she is that
for sure. The nuns called us supplicants and here they call us devotees.
In the end it just means bowing in reverence to that which you don't
understand and asking for help from within when you feel you have
nowhere to turn. That part I do well. It has always been my way.

She's trying to teach me to allow for space. She laughs and waves as
she says, "Guilty guilty bad bad is very American or Catholic, right?
Here just try to practice no big deal. Only my head. No big deal." I
tried to tell her once that I was Puerto Rican. She laughed at me and
said, "Okay feeling guilty guilty bad bad is very Puerto Rican. Same
instructions. Practice no big deal." I wanted to tell her what I had done,
so she could see that it was a big fucking deal. That I had caused great
harm. She stopped me and said, "Big story. Very interesting, I'm sure.
But confession is you looking for me to make you feel better. Relief.
Forget confessing. Practice to sit in the pain and not hold on to it so
tight. Ask Kali Maa to cut away your ego. Slice your head off, so full
of so much thinking. Just slice. Get rid of it. If you belong in jail, turn
yourself in. If not, go sit in meditation." I guess I finally found exactly
the teacher I needed. The one who will get me to sit my ass down
for real and cut off my own head?! "Aquí no hay pa' nadie," as Doña
Durka liked to say when I went soft from time to time. Qué jodienda.
Of course, to some I belong in jail. There is a lot worse than me loose
out there, and a lot better than me locked up. Instead, I keep going to
meditation.

I am a very big fan of the chanting. It reminds me of when we would sing "Love Alive" together or our version of "99 Problems" (but a dick ain't one, ha, remember that?). Chanting creates a wave of sound I can rest in and sometimes it calms me. When you miss me, and I know you do, so don't front, listen to some chanting. It will be like you are right here with me.

This is a damn long letter because I keep walking around the fire in the middle that is what I really wanted to say. I never had kids. I never will. I always wanted you to know why. I made Red go with me because I knew for sure you'd never have allowed it. You would have thrown a fit, screamed and cried and acted out like you always do when you think you are gonna save me from myself. But I paid hard cash for getting my tubes tied when I was only eighteen. It was not hard to do, but hard to get anybody to agree to do until I finally found a doctor I convinced.

All the men refused. A woman I found finally asked, "Why so permanent?" She was the first one who didn't tell me I would regret it or that I was too young to know any better. She just asked and I told her that I could barely take care of myself, and I had no business trying to take care of anyone else. I also said, "I just don't want no kids." She said, "That could change." I think she saw it in me. The bone-dry exhaustion. She said something about not agreeing with this at my age, but as long as I knew I was worthy of my own life, there was no need for me to feel I owed the world anything more. She rubbed my back, explained the procedure, said there were ways to undo it, but they were not guaranteed to work, and in her experience mostly didn't. She went over the long-term birth control options available instead. I started telling her about being abused and not feeling like I could protect a child. She stopped me and ended on the final note, "You are of consenting age, and you have the right to do with your body what you choose so long as you are willing to live with the consequences."

I was. I still am. I knew what I could not say was that a baby felt like a wound I couldn't protect. A vulnerability walking the world with my name and heart in it. I was not willing to get down with that kind of suffering and fear anymore. Enough already. That it turns out to have been a good decision is not a big surprise. I'm just grateful it was a choice at all.

Keep in mind that Artemis will be a stranger to you all her life. Don't be afraid of that. She will know love in ways we only dreamt of. It will make her different too. Tell her everything, in little parts, across her life. Take her, at least once, to Orchard Beach and remind her we are the Daughters of Durga, a wild and fierce mother who will never let us go.

The path I took, and the one I take next, is one and the same; they are only different turns on the road. That is the message we are trying to get across at the center. No matter how far from good you think you have gone, you are still on the same road you were on when you started; you just need to take a different turn. To hell with a fresh start, just start where you are. That is what I want to say to you, Carmelita, and that I love you with all my heart and miss the shit out of your ugly grill.

Jai Maa!

This is a beautiful thing they say here to each other during this time. It means victory to the mother. Victory to you, my Carmelita, victory to all of our little mothers.

Look at me still trying to tell your ass what to do. No matter, you never listened to me anyway.

With all my heart, your never not broken cousin,
Akhi

As I stood there on the terrace, the sunset felt like golden orange nectar being poured into me through Grace. A few scattered birds, seeking refuge for the night, flew past. I had come to understand birds a whole other way on the inside, not for their beautiful songs or colorful cloaks, but for their courage to release feathers that no longer served. New feathers were falling off me with every breath I took. Some that I'd loved and made me beautiful. I went back inside and locked the terrace doors behind me. I folded the letter and put it in a small cabinet with the murti of Durga on top. It would be for Artemis someday, as this house would be hers.

I am here. I am alive. Grace is alive. That part of the mantra still rang true. The last part, I will leave this place alive, was for a danger so intense it could never really be shared, only lived, and hopefully survived. Also, it was obviously untrue, since none of us leave this place alive. It was my prayer that Artemis would never need it, but I will teach it to her just the same, and with the same instructions. When terror grips you, breathe anyway and repeat to yourself: *I am here. I am alive. I will leave this place alive.* Until you don't.

ACKNOWLEDGMENTS, SHOUT-OUTS, AND PIROPOS

A quiet wave turned tsunami of support and tiny miracles made this book possible, carried it through decades, continues even now.

Gratitude is that which all who know me have already felt and received. I will say it here universally to cover everyone: To all who read and listened: Thank You. To all who simply loved, supported, or followed their own light and served as example (especially all of my students over the years from GED to ESL to Bronx Community College): Thank You!

Abuelas are a special breed, not all just sugar and spice, but frequently fierce and intense. I am because they were. I was blessed with a multitude that included three great-grandmothers who inspired me and took care of me: Abuela Lola (Gloria Cardona), the queen of my heart and the kitchen; Abuela Eppie (Esperanza Coss), the poet and doll maker; Abuela Quintina (Quintina Guerrero), the warrior; Abuela Tuta (Asuncion Rivera), the spiritual advisor; Abuela Carmela (Carmela Arocho), the one who taught me how to play dominoes and watched over me like a crow from her sixth-floor window.

To my husband, Fernando Aquino, and my two sons, Antonio and

Gabriel Aquino, I owe a depth of gratitude for never doubting the value of the time I spent writing, both at home and away, and for all the love and joy that made my ongoing creative life possible. Cue the family theme song.

The publishing industry is built on stories and I am grateful to be part of one that includes these immensely intelligent, talented, and generous women: my fierce and fabulous literary agent Soumeya Roberts Bendimerad, Hannah Popal and the team at HG Literary, and my brilliant editor Jessica Williams, Julia Elliott and the incredible team at William Morrow and HarperCollins.

Sun Cherme, and her work at Sun Literary, deserves her own essay for that summer of 2020 journey she took with me through grief and this book. Everyone should be gifted such a writing doula to guide the way under a shared moon.

I want to give a special thank-you to those who read early drafts and engaged with giving feedback, questions, and encouragement that kept the work moving forward, especially Tiye Geraud, Amy Veach, and my brother, William Coss.

Organizations, mentors, teachers, and guides along the way were many. From Ms. Cheryl Jones in high school all the way through to my first writing mentors Jaime Manrique, Jane Lazarre, and Suzanne Oboler in college; my thesis advisor at City College, Emily Raboteau; and finally to the organizations for writers like IWWG, VONA, AROHO, and Hedgebrook who supported the work through space and workshops (with too many incredible writers to name) for thinking about craft and how to care for a writing life over the long haul.

I am blessed with an army of siblings, cousins, nieces and nephews, and friends who are also my sisters. Too many to name, but you know who you are! I will aim for the heart with my sisters Jennifer Coss and Cheryl Coss; my cousins Lissette Cardona and Tracy Tirado Jimenez; my sister friends Mary Dillon, Lorin Gold, Arnetta Nash; and my aunts Mercedes Tirado and Lourdes Kemper.

At the heart of this book was a spiritual journey (that began when I was a child) along which I encountered spiritual guides, practices, ancestors, and retrievals of images of the Feminine Divine across cultures that realigned my understanding of what it means to see a woman as part of a much longer history than patriarchy. A special thank-you to Dr. Clarissa Pinkola Estés, Paula Scardamalia, Gloria Rodriguez of DeAlmas Institute, Laura Amazzone, and Leslie Jones of Afro Flow Yoga, for direct transmission and practices (and in many cases friendship) that helped sturdy the ship for the work ahead.

ABOUT THE AUTHOR

MELISSA COSS AQUINO is a Puerto Rican writer from the Bronx. She received her MFA from the City College of New York, CUNY, and her PhD in English from the CUNY Graduate Center. She currently works as an associate professor in the English Department at Bronx Community College, CUNY. She is a proud alumna of the International Women's Writing Guild, Voices of Our Nations Arts Foundation, A Room of Her Own, and Hedgebrook.